THE ZERO BLESSING

THE ZERO
BLESSING

Christopher G. Nuttall

Text copyright © 2017 Christopher G. Nuttall

ISBN: 1544770839
ISBN 13: 9781544770833

http://www.chrishanger.net
http://chrishanger.wordpress.com/
http://www.facebook.com/ChristopherGNuttall

All Comments Welcome!

DEDICATION

To the memory of Enid Blyton, who introduced me to boarding school stories, and to Thomas Hughes, who was truly - dismally - accurate about boarding schools.

PROLOGUE

I suppose I should start at the beginning. It is, after all, a very good place to start.

My sisters and I are triplets, fraternal triplets. We don't really look *that* much alike, although we all have dad's black skin and dark eyes, as well as our mum's silky smooth hair. Alana is so pretty you'd think she'd been glamoured; Belladonna would be pretty if she took more exercise and bothered to put some work into her appearance; I, always in the middle, look more like a tomboy than anything else. You probably wouldn't think we *were* related if you passed us on the street, let alone that we were born on the same day. But we were.

Our parents - Joaquin and Sofia Aguirre - are two of the most powerful magicians in Shallot City, if not the kingdom. Dad's a skilled enchanter with a whole string of apprentices working under him; mum's the best potions' brewer in the world. Having three children - and *triplets*, too - is a big thing for them. The magic grows stronger, we are told, when children are born and raised together. My sisters and I should have safeguarded the family's inheritance for the next generation. Instead...

We were seven years old when it happened.

We'd had a birthday party, of course. Lots of presents, lots of sweet foods and a big cake dedicated to the three of us. Our friends came round and we had a great time, but our excitement was dulled by the knowledge of what would come afterwards. Dad had been talking about teaching us magic for some time - we'd already learnt some of the background knowledge taught to every magical child in the kingdom - and today we were going to start. I was excited. We all were. We'd seen Dad work wonders, ever since we were old enough to understand. We couldn't wait to work wonders ourselves.

And so, when the party was over and the guests had gone, we walked into Dad's study and sat down at the table. The tools were already waiting for us.

Anyone can do magic. It's a rare person indeed who cannot master a basic firestarter, a water-cleaner or the other housekeeping spells listed in *1001 Spells for Practical Work*. Fishwives use them to clean the air; broadsheet writers use them to send messages right across the kingdom. But magic, like music, requires talent. Anyone can learn to tap out a tune on the piano, but playing properly is hard. So it is with magic. The sooner you start learning, the better you'll be.

I was so excited that I could barely contain myself as I picked up the tool. It didn't *look* like very much - it was really nothing more than a silver pen - but it was the key to a whole new world. If I could learn how to use it, I could cast spells. And then I could use magic. Our parents had forbidden us from using magic in the past, when we were too young to know the dangers, but they would have to change their minds once we actually had some proper training and knew what we were doing. I couldn't wait.

Alana went first, as always. She waved the tool in the air, as Dad ordered, and produced a stream of silver light. She giggled, then twisted the tool, changing the colour from silver to red and then gold. Her dark face crinkled into a genuine smile. I don't think I've ever seen her so utterly *delighted* than the moment she used magic for the first time. And I couldn't wait to try it myself.

"It *tickles*," Alana said.

"That's your gift responding to the magic in the tool," Dad said.

Belladonna went next, waving the tool casually in the air. Her eyes crinkled as nothing happened, just for a moment. Dad spoke to her gently, then told her to try again. This time, the light appeared, flickering in and out of existence as the magic weakened. Bella grimaced, then waved the tool a *third* time. The light grew stronger, floating in the air. Alana picked up her tool and wrote a word in the air, giggling. Dad shot her a quelling look before she could write something that would upset our mother.

"Your turn, Caitlyn," Dad said.

I picked up the tool, feeling nothing but cool metal. A cold shiver ran down my spine. Alana had said the tool *tickled*, hadn't she? Maybe she'd meant *after* she cast the spell. I held the tool in the air, silently promising myself that I was going to devote the rest of my life to magic studies, then waved it around.

Nothing happened.

Dad's eyes narrowed. "Let the magic flow," he ordered. In hindsight, it was clear that he'd realised that something was wrong. "Your instincts should guide you."

"It's easy," Alana put in. "You can *feel* the magic."

I couldn't. I couldn't feel anything. The tool still felt cold.

I took a deep breath, then tried again. Perhaps I'd been too excited to work the spell. We'd been taught basic breathing exercises, so I ran through them before lifting the tool and waving it in the air again. There *should* have been a line of light, hanging in the air. But there was nothing. I couldn't even *feel* the magic.

"Hah," Alana said. "She can't *do* it."

"Be *silent*," Dad said.

Alana's mouth closed with a snap. Our father is very even-tempered, most of the time, but when he gets mad...watch out. Normally, I would have enjoyed Alana's discomfort; now, panic was bubbling at the back of my mind. What if I couldn't work magic? Bella – lazy, pudgy Bella - was drawing line after line in the air, giggling to herself as she sketched out faces. She couldn't be doing better than me...

But she was.

I tried, again and again. Dad talked me through it, bit by bit. He even held my hand as I waved the tool, despite the risk of using his magic to power the spell. Mum came in and marched my sisters off, leaving us alone...nothing worked. I just couldn't cast even a basic spell.

"I don't know," Dad said, finally. I could hear the disappointment in his voice, clawing at my heart. I loved my father and I had failed him. "We'll keep trying..."

We did. We tried every day for a year, then once every week...nothing happened. I had no sensitivity to magic at all. My sisters learned to cast hundreds of spells; I sat in the back, reading books and trying to figure out what had gone wrong. Why was I different?

But I never found an answer until it was almost too late.

CHAPTER
ONE

When our father wishes to punish us, he sends us to school.

Or so my sisters say, after spending four years of their lives in the classroom. They complain all the time, whining and moaning about having to walk to the school and learn about everything but magic. Most magical children are homeschooled, but we had to go to school and *learn*. Alana hates it because she's not learning about magic; Bella hates it because she's not allowed to get away with not doing her work.

And me? I rather like it.

Not that I would have admitted it to them, of course. Alana blames me for us having to go, even though Dad was the one who sent us there. *She* thinks that my lack of magic is why we go to mundane school. Dad can't teach us everything, can he? Mum taught us how to read and write, but they don't have the time to teach us maths, history and all the other things *normal* children learn as they grow up. And while I could never work a single spell, I enjoyed studying magic and magical history. I wanted to be a historian before I grew up.

The school itself was a relatively small building, playing host to the children rich enough to afford an education, but lacking the magic or family connections they need to get an apprenticeship with a magician. Half of our classmates would leave at the end of the year, instead of going on to the upper school. My sisters would leave too, now we'd celebrated our twelfth birthday. This was their last day. *They* would be going to Jude's Sorcerous Academy, where they'd learn how to turn their already-impressive magic into *real* sorcery. Dad had already booked their places. I envied them, even as I looked forward to being without them. Having two powerful sisters is a nightmare when you can't even sense magic. I kept blundering into traps because I couldn't *see* them.

The teacher, Madam Rosebud, was a middle-aged woman who eyed my sisters and me with dire suspicion, mingled with envy. I think she probably wanted to be a sorceress in her youth, but she lacked the talent to get some real education. She envied us for our easy magic - I don't think she realised I didn't *have* magic - and didn't hesitate to point out our failings in front of the class. Dad had told us, in no uncertain terms, that we weren't to use magic at school, but my sisters were good at intimidating their classmates. Hardly anyone dared laugh.

"The difference between an Object of Power and a Device of Power is that Objects of Power last forever," Oz droned on. He was thirteen years old, kept back a year for failing the last set of exams. He was handsome enough, I suppose, but his voice was so boring that it put the class to yawning. "They simply do not fail."

I resisted the temptation to roll my eyes as Madam Rosebud's baleful eyes moved from face to face. Oz was right, but really...I'd learnt about Objects of Power from Dad, and Dad's lessons were far more interesting. Dad's apprentices are *very* skilled at making Devices of Power. And yet, nothing they make lasts longer than a year. I'd heard of swords, charmed to cut through anything in their path, that needed to be charmed again within months. Dad's clients found it a constant frustration. Some of them even think Dad does it deliberately, even though everyone else has the same problem.

My sisters snorted rudely as Oz took a bow and returned to his seat. He flushed angrily, but he didn't say anything. Strong as he was - he was the biggest boy in class - he was still helpless against magic. My sisters could have hexed him before he could even take a step towards them, if they wanted. There were some desultory claps from the front row - the sneaks and swots who were working desperately for a scholarship - but nothing else. Half the class was trying hard not to fall asleep.

"Caitlyn," Madam Rosebud said. "If you will come to the front, please?"

I picked up my essay and headed to the front row, ignoring the quiet snickering from behind me. For once, I was actually looking forward to reading my work to the rest of the class. I'd been told to write about the history of the Thousand-Year Empire and the Sorcerous Wars, a subject I found fascinating. Hundreds of secrets were lost in the wars, including the technique used to make Objects of Power. My father had so many books on the period, including some that couldn't be found anywhere else, that I'd been spoilt for choice. Boiling it down to a couple of pages had been a headache.

My sisters were smiling as I turned to face the class. In hindsight, that should have been a warning. My sisters spent as little time with me as they could. I rustled the paper for attention, then opened my mouth. Words came tumbling out...

They weren't the right words. "Madam Rosebud is fat, fat, fat," I said. My hands, moving against my will, started to clap. "Madam Rosebud is fat..."

The class stared at me in stark disbelief, their faces torn between an insane urge to giggle and an overpowering urge to flee. No one, absolutely no one, mocked Madam Rosebud. Fat she might be, ugly and smelly she might be, but no one dared mock her. I tried to clamp my lips shut as word after word spewed forth...the spell collapsed, far too late. Alana was covering her mouth to keep from laughing out loud, her eyes sparkling with malice. She must have hexed me on the way up, I realised...

A hand caught my arm and swung me around. "I have *never* experienced such disrespect," Madam Rosebud thundered. Her face was so close to mine that I could smell the onions she'd had for lunch. I cowered back, despite myself. "You..."

She marched me into the naughty corner, muttered a cantrip and then left me there, staring at the wall. My feet were firmly fixed to the ground, held in place by magic. I struggled, but I couldn't lift my shoe. Madam Rosebud's voice boomed in my ear as she silenced the class, ordering my sisters to take a note to my father. I hated Alana in that moment, Alana and Bella too. Not content with going to Jude's, not content with being able to escape their hated *zero* of a sister, they'd ruined my prospects of entering the upper school. Madam Rosebud wouldn't let me stay in her class, not after everything I'd called her.

And dad wouldn't let me tell her the truth, I thought, numbly.

I'd never been able to cast a single spell, not one. Even the basic cantrips are beyond me. It isn't uncommon for children to be unable to cast spells until they reach a certain age, but most authorities agree that magical talent shows itself by eleven. If it doesn't show itself by then, it isn't there. And I was twelve...a *zero*. No magic, no sensitivity to magic... my father had forbidden me to tell anyone, but rumours were already getting out. Alana and Bella, showing off their spells whenever they wanted, didn't help. People were asking why *I* wasn't such a show-off.

I stood there, helplessly, as the class filed out for the day. Madam Rosebud was making me wait, then. I crossed my arms and waited, hoping that Dad would be in a good mood. But I knew he was probably going to be unhappy. Sir Griffons was visiting, and that always annoyed my father. I don't know why he didn't simply tell the knight to go to another enchanter. It wasn't as if Sir Griffons was more important than my father. Knight or not, he was no sorcerer.

It felt like hours before the door opened and I heard my father's measured tread crossing the room. I could feel his gaze on my back as he spoke briefly to Madam Rosebud, cutting off a bleat from the harpy before she could work herself into a frenzy. I tensed, despite myself. I was going to pay for that, next term. Very few people would pick a fight with my father - and no one would do it twice - but Madam Rosebud could mark me down for anything...

"Caitlyn," Dad said. He heard him walking up behind me. "Free yourself. We have to go."

I twisted my head to scowl at him. The cantrip was simple. My sisters wouldn't have had any trouble escaping when Madam Rosebud's back was turned. But for me...it was utterly unbreakable. My feet were firmly fixed to the ground. No power at my disposal could budge them.

My father scowled back at me. "Now."

He was a tall dark man, dressed in black and gold robes that denoted his status as the High Magus of Magus Court. His dark eyes normally sparkled with light, particularly when his daughters were around, but now they were grim. I knew I was in trouble, even though it was Alana's fault. Dad...had told her off, more than once, for casting spells on me, but he also expected me to learn to counter the spells. And yet, without magic, it was pointless. I could say the words and make the gestures, yet I always ended up looking stupid. Sure, I know the *words* to turn you into a frog, but without magic the spell is useless.

I knelt down and undid my shoes, then stepped out of them. The shoes themselves remained firmly stuck to the floor. Dad eyed me for a long moment before sighing and cancelling the cantrip. I picked up my shoes, pulled them back on and followed him towards the door, not daring to look at Madam Rosebud. My sisters wouldn't be back, next term, but they'd ruined my life anyway. Any hopes I might have had of a life without them were gone.

"You have to work harder," Dad said, as soon as we were outside. The summer air was warm, but I felt cold. "Your magic needs to be developed."

I didn't look at him. "Dad...I don't *have* magic," I said. "I'm a zero."

"No daughter of mine is a zero," Dad said, sternly. "You have magic. You just have to learn how to access it."

I felt a wave of despair, mingled with bitter guilt. My father had expended more money than I cared to think about, just trying to undo the lock on my magic. I'd used tools designed to bring out even a tiny spark of magic, brewed endless potions in the hopes of instinctively using magic to trigger them, undergone rituals designed to put me in touch with my magic...the only thing we hadn't tried was left-hand magic. Dad had been so furious, the moment it had been suggested by one of his relatives, that no one had dared mention it again. And nothing had worked. I was as powerless now as I'd been on the day I first picked up a focusing tool and tried to use it.

"I can't," I moaned. If I hadn't found magic by now, I didn't have it. "I don't *have* any power."

Dad gave me a sardonic look. "And what about Great Aunt Stregheria? You broke her spell."

I shuddered. Great Aunt Stregheria was a witch with a capital B, an ugly old crone somehow related to my father. She dressed like an evil witch from a fairy tale and talked like everyone else, including my parents, existed to do her bidding. And she hated kids. My sisters and I had done something to offend her - I forget what, now - and she turned all three of us into frogs. We'd been ten at the time. It was the first time any of us had been transfigured against our wills.

Dad was utterly furious. He literally picked Great Aunt Stregheria up and threw her out of the grounds, then reset the wards to deny her admittance ever again. But, for all of his power, he couldn't unravel the spell she'd placed on us. Neither he nor mum could undo it. We'd feared - even Alana, who'd got on best with the witch - that we would be stuck as frogs until the end of time, or at least until my father swallowed his pride and asked her to remove the spell.

But the spell on *me* had worn off in an hour, leaving me human again. My sisters had been stuck that way for a *week* when *they* returned to normal.

My father said, afterwards, that I must have used magic instinctively. He insisted that I had somehow broken her spell and freed myself. He even cast spells on me himself to encourage me to develop my talent. None of his spells lasted as long as he had intended either. But it was never something I could do consciously. If I had a talent - and he seemed to think I had something - it wasn't one I could develop. My sisters sneered that magic was allergic to me.

"Dad, I don't have magic," I said, finally. It had taken me long enough to come to terms with it. "I'm just a zero."

Dad sighed as he walked on. I trotted beside him, looking around. Normally, I would have enjoyed the chance to spend some time alone with him, but now...now I just felt tired and bitter. I'd never backed down in front of my sisters, I'd worked hard to find ways to extract revenge for their humiliations, yet there were limits. They would get better and better at magic, while I...the best I could hope for, I suspected, was theoretical magician. And even *they* tended to have magic. They needed it to prove their theories.

There were other options. I wasn't a bad forger, even though I lacked magic; I was smart, capable...I could have found work easily, if I hadn't been born to House Aguirre. The family name is a blessing, but it is also a curse. I was expected to be a powerful magician and I couldn't even light a spark! There was no way I could work for anyone without magic, even the king. They'd all expect great things from me.

I sighed as we walked down the street, other pedestrians giving us plenty of room. It was just growing busy as more and more people finished their work and came out onto the streets to shop or merely to chat with their friends. A shopgirl was using magic to sweep dust out onto the streets, a blacksmith was chanting spells as he hammered metal into its shape...a street magician was showing off, but hardly anyone was paying attention. Shallot has a larger population of magicians than anywhere else in Tintagel, as well as Jude's and a couple of magical universities. You had to do more than swallow fire and breathe water to impress *this* city.

But that clown has more magic than I do, I thought, feeling another flicker of bitter resentment. Illusionist or not, he was still a magician. *And he can do something else with his life.*

We crossed the bridge from Water Shallot to North Shallot, the guards on the gates saluting my father as we walked past. North Shallot is the richest part of the city, home to merchants and traders as well as sorcerers, alchemists and enchanters. I'd often wondered why Madam Rosebud and her superiors hadn't opened their school in North Shallot, although the costs of buying land in the north are much higher. No doubt someone in Magus Court had objected, loudly. Magicians rule North Shallot. Everyone else lives on their sufferance.

"Things are changing, Cat," my father said. I shivered. He only called me Cat when he was worried. "House Rubén has been making advances in Magus Court. My position may be under threat."

I looked up at his dark face. He was worried. House Rubén was our family's great rival, our only real equal in Shallot. I'd grown up listening to horror stories about how they treated their friends and so-called allies. It would be hard for them to unseat my father, I thought, but they could undermine him. Stepping down from his post was one thing; being unseated was quite another. The other Houses would back away from us.

"He can't do that," I said. "Surely..."

"He's trying," Dad told me. "House Rubén has wanted to win power for generations. Now...they might have a chance."

"Because of me," I said. "Because I don't have any powers."

Magic is stronger, I have been told time and time again, if children are twins or triplets...there's even a legend of a witch who gave birth to five magical children. My parents, with three daughters, should have been powerful indeed, their bloodline secure for generations to come. But I had no powers...

...And the trinity my sisters and I should have formed had never come into existence.

House Rubén had only two children, as far as I knew. Twins, rather than triplets. But both of them were powerful. There was no weak link.

"You have power," my father said, sharply. He sounded as though he was trying to convince himself. "The spells I have cast on you...they should have stayed in place until I took them off. But you broke them."

I looked down at the pavestones. *But I don't know how!*

"Figure it out," my father said, sternly. He squeezed my shoulder, gently. "Time is not on our side."

I shook my head, helplessly. Maybe I did have a gift. But it was more likely that I was just a freak, a child born without any magic at all.

A *zero*.

CHAPTER
TWO

Aguirre Hall is more than just my family's residence. It's the centre of our power.

I followed my father through the gates - warded extensively to keep out hawkers, traders and pedestrians, even though I couldn't sense the spells - and up towards the hall. It is an immense building, a mansion composed of stone and practically coated in protective enchantments and spells. The magical community is fond of testing our protections from time to time, sending probes over the walls and into our wards. So far, none of them have actually managed to break through the defences.

Travis, the butler, opened the door as we approached. He's lesser family - he has a blood tie to us - and it gives him an ability to sense the more senior members as they walk into the mansion. I rather liked him, despite a snooty attitude that grated on my nerves from time to time. My sisters joked he had his nose so high in the air that he kept walking into walls, but I didn't think so. Besides, he had always been kind to me.

"Sir," he said, addressing my father. "Your family is gathered in the lower dining room."

"Very good," Dad said. "We shall attend on them at once."

I sighed - I'd hoped for a chance to sit down and plot revenge - but Dad clearly had other ideas. It was too much to hope that he would punish Alana, of course. He wanted me to develop my powers...and if that meant allowing my sister to jinx and hex me whenever my back was turned, he'd allow it as long as she didn't do anything life-threatening. Social death, of course, didn't register. It never seemed to occur to my father that while *he* had the power to be rude to all and sundry, *I* didn't have the same luxury. No one made allowances for *zeroes*.

The hallway opened up in front of us as my father headed for the stairs, his calm measured tread echoing in the air. I followed him, pausing just long enough to glance at the Family Sword, buried in the Family Hearthstone. The sword is a genuine Object of Power, crafted over a thousand years ago and handed down from generation to generation. According to legend, only a true member of the family can draw the sword from the stone. I've seen a couple of apprentices, strong young men, try and fail to pull it free. The sword had been utterly unmovable.

I'd tried to pull it out myself, one day when Alana's taunts had become unbearable. The sword had come out easily, even though I'd only been nine years old. It was proof, I suppose, that my parents *didn't* take in a foundling they'd found on the steps...but I still couldn't do magic. Half the sword's true powers seemed beyond my reach. My father, wielding the sword, could work wonders. But then, he could work wonders without the sword too.

"Come on," Dad said, crossly. "Don't dawdle."

I gave the sword one last look, then hurried up the stairs after him. The lower two floors of the mansion are devoted to my family's work, ranging from living rooms for the apprentices and servants to forges, spell-crafting chambers and the lower library, one of the finest libraries in the world. The *really* interesting - and unique - texts are kept in the upper library, but most magicians would be pleased merely to have a look at the lower library. It's the greatest store of magical knowledge in the kingdom, outside Jude's, and it's all *ours*.

The upper two levels, protected by a set of inner wards, are reserved for the family. No one, not even Dad's most trusted apprentices, can pass through the doors without permission, unless they're recognised as being of family blood. The doors open easily at my touch, but won't move an inch for someone who isn't keyed into the wards. And there are more powerful defences lurking in reserve, just waiting for someone foolish enough to break through the outer layer. A magician who tries to break into our private quarters will spend the rest of his life wishing he hadn't.

I wanted to go to my bedroom, if only long enough to splash water on my face, but Dad led me down the corridor and into the dining room before I could say a word. The smaller dining room is still larger than the classroom, easily big enough to sit thirty or forty guests...I've often wondered why Dad insists on having family dinners, when we could easily eat in our rooms. There are only five of us, after all. My parents, my sisters and myself.

Alana shot me a smug look as I entered the room. She looked...*regal*. My mother had been teaching Bella and her all the tricks she needed to get herself crowned queen bee, once she entered Jude's. I'd sat in on a couple of lessons, when Bella had insisted on not suffering alone, but I'd found them immensely boring. Popularity was meaningless compared to power and I had none. As long as my sisters were around, I'd always be an outcast. Who would be my friend when it would expose them to my sisters' malice?

I rolled my eyes at Alana, trying not to show how much it hurt to see her. Alana held herself like an adult, her long dark hair hanging down to brush against her shoulders. The dark blue dress she wore drew attention to her face, which was carefully made up to hide all traces of imperfections. Even at twelve, Alana was tall. She'd be taller than my mother by the time she graduated and went on to run the family. And the simple necklace she wore, glittering with eldritch light, was a sign of power.

"Dad," Bella said. "You're back!"

Dad smiled at her. I tried to keep my expression under control as I sat down. Bella had always been Dad's favourite, although I'd never understood why. She was short and pudgy, barely putting in the minimum effort to succeed at anything. I could imagine her graduating from school and then coming home to spend the rest of her life vegetating, despite having more magic in her fingertips than most people have in their entire bodies. She was clever enough, when she could be bothered, but she rarely cared enough to put in the effort. *I* would have done far more if *I'd* had her powers.

But then, she didn't need to work, not if she didn't *want* to. The family would take care of her for the rest of her life.

Dad clapped his hands, the sound echoing outside the room. I groaned inwardly - even *that* simple spell was denied me - and watched as Lucy wheeled the food into the room. The last day of school, it seemed, was special. Cook had produced his finest roast beef, then used magic to keep it hot until we were ready to eat. Lucy might be a maid, but even *she* could cast the spells to release the food. She'd always been nice to me, at least when she knew I was listening, yet I'd seen her cast a few disdainful glances at me when she'd thought I wasn't looking. I don't know why. Alana had targeted Lucy with a few nasty spells before Mum had put a stop to it. Whatever Mum had said to my sister had clearly been effective.

"Let us eat," Dad said, after casting a spell to make sure the food was safe to eat. I don't know why he bothered - the cook had been with the family longer than I had been alive - but he insisted on checking, every time. He'd taught us all the spells too, although I couldn't make them work. Someone who wanted to poison me would have an easy time of it. "Lucy, carve the meat."

Henry, the cook, had exceeded himself - as usual. I would have enjoyed the meal, I thought, if I hadn't been brooding. Alana had probably ensured I wouldn't get to enter upper school, even if my father shovelled money in their direction. Madam Rosebud was probably already complaining to the headmaster about my cheeky attitude. And if I didn't get to go on, what then? There were no apprenticeships for students without powers, at least in Shallot. I couldn't even get hired as a sailor until I was older!

And I'd still need some spells if I wanted to sail, I thought, numbly. *What can I do with no magic at all?*

"I worked out the last stages of the potion," Mum said. "The idiot who wrote the book left out two steps *and* altered five of the quantities."

"Well done, Mum," Bella said. "Can *anyone* brew it now?"

"Caitlyn can't," Alana said. She snickered. "*Zeros* can't brew potions."

I felt my cheeks heat with helpless rage. Mum had taught me how to brew, but - of course - I lacked the magic to trigger the cascade that turned the potion from a mixture of odd ingredients to something *useful*. It didn't matter how carefully I followed the instructions, or what changes I made if I felt like experimenting...nothing worked. Alana or Bella could take a potion I'd brewed and trigger it, but I couldn't trigger theirs. Maybe I was doomed to work in an apothecary. Someone who had enough magic to start the cascade, but lacked the patience to brew the mixture properly...

"That's very good, dear," Dad said. "Are you going to write it up?"

"I think so," Mum said. "It isn't anything worth trying to reserve for the family."

"Don't let Stregheria hear you say that," Alana said. She was trying to be grown-up, acting as though she was an adult already. "She'd *expect* you to reserve it."

Mum looked annoyed, her lips thinning until they were almost invisible. Great Aunt Stregheria certainly *would* expect the recipe to be held in reserve. She was a selfish old biddy, utterly devoted to herself. Mum had never liked her, even before she'd turned us into frogs. I'd heard, afterwards, that Mum had been on the verge of calling Stregheria out for a duel. Stregheria was old and powerful, but I wouldn't have bet against my mother. She was powerful too.

"There is little to be gained by keeping it back," Mum said, stiffly. "It's a basic healing potion, not something *radical*."

I listened, absently, as we finished our dinner. I'd hoped, as soon as Lucy had removed the plates, to be allowed to leave, but no such luck. Dad told all three of us to follow him to his study. I sighed, even as Alana exchanged excited looks with Bella. Dad's study, to them, was a hall of wonders. To me, it was just another dangerous room in a dangerous house.

It was, in many ways, the sort of study *I'd* like to have. The walls were lined with bookshelves, including many volumes I knew were unique or forbidden; the chairs were charmed to be comfortable, all the better to allow my father to work. But I also knew the room was strongly warded, so strongly warded that even Mum couldn't enter without permission. Alana had tried to sneak in a few times, but she'd always been caught. Dad had not been amused.

"Your mother and I have made some decisions about your futures," Dad said, once we were sitting on comfortable armchairs. They were so large that I half-wondered if someone had cast a shrinking spell on me when I wasn't looking. Even *Dad* looked small, sitting on his chair. "The three of you will be going to Jude's."

It was so unexpected that I didn't quite grasp what he'd said, not for a long chilling moment. It had to be a joke, a cruel joke. Even my sisters looked shocked. Alana actually *paled*. And why not? I'd long since given up hope of going to Jude's. Entering a school for magicians without magic...it would have been safer to cover myself in fish sauce, then go for a swim in the shark tank.

"Dad," Alana managed, finally. "Caitlyn *can't* go to Jude's!"

Dad fixed her with his stern look. "And why not?"

Bella spluttered. "Because she's a *zero!*"

"Caitlyn defeated a spell that bested *me*," Dad pointed out, icily. "Can either of you say the same?"

"...I," Bella said. "Dad..."

Alana took over. "Dad, she hasn't been able to cast a single spell," she said, talking about me as if I wasn't there. "She can't even do *this!*"

She waved a hand in the air. Sparkling light appeared out of nowhere, surrounding her like a halo. It was a very basic spell, perhaps one of the *most* basic. Light could be bright, perhaps even blinding, but it couldn't cause any real harm. Most parents preferred to use light spells to teach their kids because the risk of accidentally starting a fire or injuring themselves was minimal.

And she was right. I couldn't even do *that*.

"Your sister has magic," Dad said, firmly. It was a tone that promised punishment to anyone who dared to disagree with him. "She just cannot *access* it. Being at Jude's will help her to develop her magic."

I swallowed, hard. "Dad...I can't go."

"You will," Dad said. "The family *needs* the trinity."

"We have a weak link," Alana muttered.

Dad gave her a long considering look. "Do you still want to go to the party tomorrow evening?"

Alana winced. "Yes, Dad."

"Then be quiet," Dad ordered.

He looked back at me. "Caitlyn, I understand your concerns," he said. "Be that as it may, you do have magic. You have to be trained to use it."

"I don't," I said, miserably.

Alana had told me that I'd be disowned when I turned twelve, if I didn't show any signs of magic. I didn't want to believe her, but I'd always worried. *She'd* certainly made it clear that *she* would disown me, when she became head of the family. Her great and terrible future would be blighted by a powerless sister...

"You can and you will," Dad said. "Your mother and I are in agreement. You and your sisters will enter Jude's after the summer holidays."

Bella looked...nervous. "We could learn from you instead..."

"You're growing older," Dad said. "And there are limits to what we can teach you."

"And we have to make friends and contacts," Alana added.

"Quite right," Dad agreed.

He launched into an explanation of the problems facing our house, the same explanation he'd given me earlier. I barely heard a word. My sisters had spent the last four years tormenting me with magic, but now...now I was going to school. Jude was a good school, according to my parents, yet I'd heard horror stories from some of the apprentices. If you had strong magic, the school was great; if you were weak, you were picked on by everyone else. And the teachers did nothing to stop it. Alana and Bella wouldn't have any trouble - the family name would make up for any problems - but me...? I'd be lucky if I wasn't permanently trapped as a frog by the end of the first week.

Alana poked my arm. "Pay attention."

I looked up. Dad was looking back at me, annoyed.

"Now, there will be some specific accommodations made," he said. "Alana, Bella...you will *not* discuss your sister's problems with *anyone*. You will both be under a binding spell to make sure of it."

"But Dad," Alana protested. "I..."

"The matter is settled," Dad said, firmly.

Alana shot me a nasty look that promised trouble. A binding spell wasn't particularly *dangerous*, not if cast by a skilled mage, but it was a very blunt way of saying that my father didn't trust her to keep her mouth shut. It was an insult, in many ways. And I wouldn't put it past my sister to figure out a way around the binding. Dad wouldn't risk putting a strong spell on his daughter. If nothing else, Mum wouldn't let him.

I tried, anyway. "Dad, I can't work magic," I said.

Dad cocked his head. "Do you *want* to work magic?"

I nodded. I'd wanted it ever since I'd understood that my parents were magicians. And I still wanted it. The power Bella wasted so casually...what could I do, if that were mine instead of hers?

"Then this is your best chance," Dad said, seriously. He clapped his hand on my shoulder, reassuringly. I knew he meant well, but..."The tutors are the best in the world. *They* can teach you."

"Your *last* chance," Alana said.

I shook my head. I'd never been able to get a spell to work, not one. There were people with no talent who could do better than that. But me? I couldn't cast a single spell.

Perhaps I should run away, I thought. It was a tempting thought. *But where would I go?*

Dad clapped his hands together. "Caitlyn, you can go," he said. "Alana, Bella; I have some other matters to discuss with you."

I nodded, then turned and left the study. My sisters were going to *hate* me after today. The binding wouldn't hurt them - Dad would see to that - but it would be humiliating. I'd find it humiliating too, if someone had cast such a spell on me. And they had...

Revenge, I promised myself. Alana might have magic, but I wasn't going to bow the knee to her. I wasn't doing anything else until bedtime, so I might as well plan revenge. *And then see if I can give her a fright.*

Smiling, I hurried back to my room. I had some thinking to do.

CHAPTER

THREE

M y mother has a fool proof way of getting us out of bed in the morn-
ings. The bell sounds at eight o'clock, followed by the bed shaking -
and eventually pitching us out of bed, if we haven't managed to scramble
out before it's too late. It was a surprise, therefore, when I awoke the following morning and discovered that it was nearly ten. My mother had
clearly decided to let us sleep in for once. I knew it wouldn't last.

I sat upright, muttering words I wasn't supposed to say under my
breath. It hadn't been a nightmare, then. I was going to Jude's, like it or
not. My sisters might not be able to tell anyone about my problem, but it
would become impossible to hide my lack of magic the moment I tried
to cast my first spell. And then...I looked around the bare walls, feeling
despondent. A simple spell would be enough to decorate the room any
way I wanted, but I couldn't cast it. And my parents had flatly refused to
let anyone else cast it for me.

I glanced up as there was a sharp knock on the door. The wards surrounding the room would have alerted the maid as soon as I awoke.

"Come in," I called.

The door opened. Lucy stood there, beaming. She had always been
a morning person, while my sisters and I hated being woken to go to
school. I blinked in surprise as she held out a tray of cereal, pancakes
and juice. Breakfast in bed was very rare, in our household. We were
normally expected to stagger down to the dining room before we were
allowed to eat.

"Your mother said you could have breakfast in bed," Lucy said, answering my unspoken question. "She thought you might like it."

"Thank you," I said. Mum had always said I had to be nice to the servants. "Where...where are my sisters?"

"Miss Bella is still abed," Lucy informed me. She put the tray on the bedside table and smiled, rather dryly. "Miss Alana has already left the hall."

"Off to buy yet another dress," I muttered. Alana bought a new dress for every party, even though she already had enough to outfit every girl in the class. "Do you know when she'll be back?"

"I believe Sonja will be doing her hair this afternoon," Lucy said. She bowed. "Will that be all, Miss?"

"Yes, thank you," I said.

I watched her go, then opened my drawer and removed the magic sensor. It wasn't much of a Device, to be honest, but I'd designed and built it myself. All it *really* did was vibrate in the presence of magic, alerting me to any traps someone might have left in my vicinity. I wouldn't have put it past Alana to hex my food, if she was still mad at me...I shook my head, ruefully. Of *course* she was still mad at me. I'd ruined her plans to be a social butterfly just by existing.

The device didn't move as I waved it over the food. I put it aside, took a long swig of juice and then tucked into the pancakes. Cook had done an excellent job, as always. I was a little more reluctant to finish my cereal, but I knew better than to leave it. Mum would have noticed and told me off, then banned me from eating pancakes for a month. My mother is very keen on healthy eating.

I put the tray to one side as soon as I had finished, then showered and dressed before hurrying out of the room and heading down towards the forge. Alana could be relied upon to spend hours shopping for clothes - I'd once seen her try on everything in the store - but I needed to get my trap in place before it was too late. If she came back too soon, all was ruined. I passed through the secure door and headed on downwards, passing through two more sets of warded doors. Dad would know where I was going, I was sure. He just wouldn't know why.

The forge itself is really more of a large workshop, with everything needed to make Devices of Power. My father and Sir Griffons were in a sideroom, talking about something; one of my father's apprentices was standing in front of his desk, carefully hammering out a piece of metal. Apprentice Brian was kind, I had always thought. He wasn't a particularly strong magician - certainly not compared to my father - but he was good with his hands. He'd made quite a few Devices of Power that had lasted for several weeks before starting to show signs of decay.

"Hi, Caitlyn," he called. "You alright?"

"I'm going to Jude's," I said. I opened one of the drawers and dug through it to find my stash of makeshift Devices. "Do you have an etching knife?"

"Ouch," Brian said. He reached for the knife and passed it over to me. "You'd better be careful there."

I looked up and saw very real concern in his eyes. Brian hadn't been told anything about my power, or lack of it, but he wasn't blind. He would have noticed, I was sure, that I'd never cast a spell. Maybe the forging would make up for it...or maybe not. No Device is unbeatable, whatever you may hear from the forger. Only Objects of Power are unbeatable - and even they have their weaknesses. A smart man can outwit someone wielding one and beat him easily.

"I will," I said. Maybe I *should* run away. I did have some brewing skills...I just couldn't make the potions work. But my father would track me down, easily. "Do you have any advice?"

"Try not to annoy the upperclassmen," Brian said, after a moment. "And don't annoy your Dorm Head."

"Thanks," I said, rather sourly. "Anything else?"

Brian shrugged. I shrugged back, then turned to work on my little project. Forgery had always been an interest of mine, ever since Dad thought it might just serve as a key to unlocking my powers. Alana and Bella had never shown any interest in learning the skill, but I had. It was the closest I had come to real magic. I carved runes into the metal, then shaped it carefully. Brian kept a wary eye on me as I worked. It was annoying, but I didn't blame him. Dad would never forgive him if something happened to me in the forge.

"That's a complex piece of work," Brian said, when I had finished. "Do you want me to check it?"

"No, thanks," I said. I gave him a smile. "It should be fine."

I took the Device - and a couple of others I had made earlier - and stuck them in my knapsack before hurrying out onto the lawn. My mother's herb garden lay on the other side, a vast collection of plants and suchlike she used to brew potions. She'd taught me how to harvest them, years ago, but the knowledge had never really been useful. Any fool could harvest herbs, with a little care. Getting the more exotic ingredients had always been a pain. I pitied the men who hunted basilisks and manticores for their skins. One or two dead beasts were enough to make a poor man rich, if he survived the meeting. Manticores were *nasty*.

The pond sat on the far side of the garden, teeming with life. Small fish, frogs...even water snakes...my sisters and I had refused to visit for a long time, after hearing that they were being bred for potions ingredients. A single small frog can supply enough material for a dozen potions, if prepared properly...I pushed the thought aside and knelt down by the pond, watching for my chance. The frogs were bred and trained not to run when a big hand reached down and grabbed hold. Suppressing my revulsion, I scooped up the frog, dumped him into my knapsack and hurried back to the hall. Time was not on my side.

There was still no sign of Bella as I reached the fourth floor, but I wasn't surprised. I knew from past experience that Bella would stay in her bed as long as possible, unless Mum decided she'd slept long enough and ordered the bed to tip her out. There was no sign of Alana either. I hoped that meant she was still out shopping. Getting caught sneaking into her room would be disastrous. I tapped the door, making sure she wasn't in, then pulled the first Device out of the knapsack and held it against the doorknob. It revealed nothing. I was careful, anyway. Alana had been told not to hex her door - the maids cleaned the room every week - but I didn't trust her to listen to our mother. She knew I was probably planning revenge.

I pushed the door open, very carefully. The room was brightly lit - warm sunlight streaming through the windows - but quiet, very quiet. I glanced around as I inched forward, holding the Device in front of me like a wand. Alana had decorated her room in a manner fit for a queen, red and gold everywhere. I couldn't help feeling a stab of envy as I studied her bed and wardrobes - and the piles of clothing that lay everywhere. My parents had rewarded her for every spell she'd learnt to cast, while I...

Not now, I told myself, sharply.

Alana's trunk - a deceptively simple wooden design - was sitting by the side of the room, seemingly out of place against the gilt decor. The maids wouldn't dare touch it, even to dust the lid. I held the Device close and tensed as it vibrated. Alana could have used almost any spell to protect her most treasured possessions, but I had a feeling I knew which one she'd used. She had a habit of messing around with transfiguration spells.

I removed the second Device from my knapsack, braced myself and held it against the golden clasp. If I'd gotten something wrong, I was about to find out the hard way. There was a brilliant flash of light - just for a second, I saw the image of a surprised-looking frog hanging in the air - which faded rapidly. I smirked and removed the frog from my bag, dropping him on the floor. Alana would know, of course, that someone had been in her room. But would she realise that that frog wasn't *me*?

I slipped back out of the room and closed the door, very quietly. There was no other way out. The frog wouldn't be able to escape. I put the two Devices back in my knapsack - the spell-drainer was already burned out, judging by the smell - then settled down in a nearby cupboard to wait. It wouldn't be long, I hoped, before Alana returned home.

It was nearly an hour, according to my watch, before I heard her shrill voice echoing down the corridor. I couldn't help feeling a stab of sympathy for whichever maid had been asked - ordered, more like - to accompany her. Taking Alana shopping was a thankless task. And then I heard Alana giggle. She thought she *had* caught me.

"Leave the bags here," she ordered. I didn't have to strain to hear her voice. "I'll take them inside later. Go tell Travis you're back."

"Yes, Miss," Sonja said.

I felt another stab of sympathy as Sonja hurried away. She was a nice girl, I thought, but she was clumsy. Travis had probably ordered her to escort Alana as punishment for something, although I found it hard to imagine a crime that merited *that* level of punishment. It was definitely cruel and unusual. I smiled at the thought, then listened carefully as Alana opened her door.

"Well, little zero," Alana said. I had a mental image of her rubbing her hands together in glee. She'd done that years ago, when she'd turned me into a frog for the first time. "You *do* look a sight, don't you?"

My sister loves to gloat. And, if I had been turned into a frog, I would have had no choice, but to listen. She went on and on, mocking my lack of magic and threatening all sorts of hexes...and then cast the counterspell, dramatically. I forced myself not to giggle as I heard the sound. Nothing happened, of course. There's no point in trying to counter a spell that didn't exist.

Alana screamed. I covered my mouth to keep from laughing out loud. The spell she'd used was very basic. She certainly hadn't learnt anything *too* complex, yet. It should have been easy to remove the spell. Instead...I heard her sputtering, repeating the spell time and time again. It was useless, of course. And yet...she was clearly having problems trying to understand what had happened. Her protection spell had triggered, of course. She *knew* someone had been turned into a frog.

Except I forced it to discharge instead, I thought. The trick had been simple enough, with a little preparation. And my sister would never even consider the possibility. The spell had snapped, but it had snapped at nothing. *She can't tell the difference.*

The door opened. Alana hurried out of her room and down towards the sitting room, where my parents would be having lunch. I slipped out of the cupboard and followed her, glancing into her open door to make sure the frog hadn't been left behind. Her voice echoed up the corridor as she spoke to Dad, begging him to undo the spell. The panic in her voice caused me a pang of guilt, even though she'd done worse to me. My parents might be disappointed in my lack of magic, but they wouldn't be pleased if I'd been seriously hurt.

"There is no magic on this frog," Dad said, sternly. He didn't sound pleased. "Alana..."

"It's *Caitlyn*," Alana insisted. She went on and on about it, her voice rising higher and higher. Her words rattled out so fast that I had trouble making them out. "She sneaked into my room and triggered the trap and I can't turn her back! I..."

Dad's voice darkened. "This is a *real* frog," he said. "I don't know where your sister has gone, but there's no magic on *this* frog. Which spell did you use to protect your trunk?"

"The one from *Hawker's Index*," Alana managed. She sounded as though she was trying not to cry. The joke had probably gone far enough. "I should be able to break it..."

I chose that moment to step into the room. "Dad," I said, as casually as possible, "can we talk about...?"

Alana let out a furious scream and pitched the frog at me. "You..."

"*That will do*," Dad snapped. Alana's hand lowered, a moment before she could throw a change spell at me. "Alana, I do not have *time* to deal with your practical jokes!"

"Particularly one that could have ended very badly," Mum added. "Go to your room. We will discuss your conduct later."

"And you are grounded for a week," Dad said. His voice was icy cold. "Go."

"But I have a party," Alana protested. "Dad, I promised I would attend. Cythera..."

"Go," Dad snapped.

Alana shot me a look that promised murder - or at least a humiliating hex - as she stamped past me and down the corridor. I turned to watch her go, trying to school my face into something resembling calm. I'd confess later, perhaps. Alana being grounded would be very satisfactory - the sound of her slamming the door was loud enough to be heard outside - but it meant she'd be in the hall instead of wandering the grounds or visiting friends.

I turned back to Dad. He was giving me a very sharp look. I half-expected him to demand answers, if he hadn't worked out what had happened already. But he chose not to ask any questions. I decided it would be better not to ask why.

"I assume you don't want to go to the party," he said. "We'll have a family meeting tonight, then."

I shrugged. I'd grown to loathe birthday parties as I'd grown older. Most of the guests were from magical families and knew enough spells to be dangerous. It wasn't uncommon for two-thirds of the guests to be turned into animals or objects as the rest showed off their powers, trying to establish a pecking order. I was always the first to be turned into something - or worse - before I'd stopped going to parties. That hadn't helped the rumours about me.

"You can help me brew potions this afternoon," Mum said. She sounded cross, although I wasn't sure if she was angry at me, or Alana, or Dad. "And you can do a little research in the library for me."

"Yes, Mum," I said. There was something in her voice that told me that Mum knew everything. Maybe she thought Alana needed a shock, but she wasn't going to let me get away with it. "What would you like me to do?"

"Research Fingal's Tonic," Mum ordered. "I have to brew it this afternoon."

Dad smiled. "Good luck."

I sighed. The tonic was complex, *very* complex. And utterly beyond most magicians, even the ones with formal training. And me, of course. It said a great deal about my mother that she could brew it so easily. She didn't really need my help - or anyone's, for that matter. But then, my mother had always been *very* capable. How else could she have proven a match for Dad?

"And we will discuss other matters over the brew," Mum added. "And I want you to listen."

"Yes, Mother," I said.

CHAPTER

FOUR

The book open in front of me was technically illegal, but my parents had never seen fit to ban me from reading it. They *had* banned Alana and Bella from entering the darker sections of the upper library, much to Alana's irritation...I really didn't know what it meant that they'd allowed *me* to look. Was it an attempt to trick my magic into emerging or a quiet admission that much of the knowledge within the library would be useless to me? I wasn't sure I wanted to know.

Merely touching the pages made my skin crawl, but I worked my way through them one by one, parsing out the Old Script word by word. It wasn't good news. As long as I shared blood with my family, I would always be part of them. Anyone with a blood connection to me - my sisters, my parents, my grandparents - would be able to track me down, merely through the blood. There *were* ways to cut the link, apparently, but they *all* required sophisticated knowledge and powerful magic. I couldn't begin to craft the spell I'd need, let alone cast it. I was doomed to be Caitlyn Aguirre until the day I died.

Or I get disowned, I thought, sourly.

I sat back in the chair and sighed, heavily. The last month had been spent preparing for school and trying to find a way to get out of going, but I had failed. My parents had proven grimly resolute. No amount of begging and pleading had convinced them to change their minds. And while I *had* considered ways of running away, I hadn't found a way to escape without being dragged back in disgrace. I couldn't break the blood tie...

and the only people who could help, apart from my family, were my family's enemies. There was no way I could go to them and ask for help. I'd be lucky if they only laughed at me.

Closing the book, I looked up at the towering shelves. They were lined with books, hundreds of forbidden and semi-forbidden volumes... half of them written in Old Script or a couple of languages that dated back to the mythical days before the Thousand-Year Empire. I could read them, barely - my parents had taught me four different languages as I grew older - but half of the knowledge within their pages was either outdated or warped in some way. My mother had often complained that many of the great brewers had changed their recipes, concealing key details from their readers. I'd helped her experiment - trying to fill in the gaps - enough to know she had a point.

Although it might not have been deliberate, I thought. *They took so much for granted that they never realised we might not know what they knew.*

"A good read, isn't it?"

I jumped. I'd been more twitchy than usual over the past month - Alana had been on the warpath - but Apprentice Vassilios had still managed to sneak up on me. I hadn't even known Dad had granted him access to the upper library, although he must have. No one could enter without Dad's permission. I certainly couldn't have broken into the library without taking my life in both hands.

"It's a creepy read," I said. "The author was a right nutcase."

I turned to look at him. Vassilios was tall and thin, only marginally shorter than Dad. His hair, already greying because of an accident back in school, was cropped close to his scalp, giving him a severe look. There was something about him that worried me, an odd disdain that was clearly evident in every word he spoke. He looked down on everyone, except my father. And he never spoke to me unless he had no choice.

"Most of the old magicians were of dubious sanity," Vassilios informed me. "But they pushed the limits of the possible."

I shrugged. I'd heard the debate before and I hadn't cared much then, either. There was no point in worrying, as long as I couldn't work magic. I couldn't cast basic spells, let alone push the limits of the possible. And I really didn't want to be anywhere near Vassilios. I got quite enough sneering from my sisters.

"It doesn't matter," I said. I picked up the book and returned it to the shelf. "I'll see you later."

He looked faintly disgusted - as if he had smelt something unpleasant - as I turned and walked out the door. I ignored him as best as I could. Dad had chosen him as an apprentice and that meant we were stuck with him, at least until he gained his mastery. No doubt Vassilios would go on to be a valued member of Dad's patronage network, one of many working to advance the family's interests in Magus Court. And I...

I fought down a wave of bitter despair as I reached my room and threw myself down on the bed. There was no escaping it. I was going to Jude's...and I wasn't likely to leave again, whatever happened. Some of the horror stories were actually *true*. The trunk sitting in the middle of my room mocked me, a grim reminder of all the supplies we'd purchased and packed over the last week. I might have enjoyed it, perhaps, if I hadn't known it spelt my doom. There were some classes, perhaps, I could take without magic...but I didn't have a hope of passing the practicals.

There was a sharp tap at the door. "Mum says you have to come to dinner," Bella called, through the wood. "Now!"

I groaned. The cook had prepared a feast to celebrate our last day at home - as if we weren't going to come back - but I knew it would taste like ashes in my mouth. I was going to be humiliated, if I was lucky. At worst...I might not survive the first month. There were plenty of horror stories about students who'd been seriously injured or killed and there was a grain of truth in most of them. Careless students, stupid students... at least they'd had magic. I had none.

But there was no point in trying to defy Mum. She'd just use magic to haul me down to the dining room. I stood, checked my appearance in the mirror and hurried down the stairs. The smell of roast turkey and all the trimmings wafted up to greet me. Mum was standing by the table, looking impatient. I bowed my head in apology and took my seat. A second later, I heard a loud raspberry. I jumped up in shock.

Alana giggled. I glared at her. "Oh, *very* mature."

"This is your last day before school," Mum said, gently. For once, she sounded almost relaxed. "You'll meet a better class of practical joker there."

I snorted as I sat down, more gingerly this time. Alana was good enough to put a second spell on the chair, hidden under the first. But nothing happened as my father started to cut up the turkey and load up the plates.

"White meat only, please," Bella said. "Dad..."

Dad shot her a sharp look. "You'll eat what you're given."

"I'm looking forward to going to school," Alana said, just a *little* too loudly. "I want to try out for team captain and..."

"You don't get to be captain until you're an upperclassman," Mum said. Alana looked downcast. "And you normally have to hex all your rivals before you get the post."

Dad smiled. "Was that how *you* became team captain?"

"No one dared oppose me," Mum said. She smiled back at him. "*And* I had been playing netball since second year. The team wanted to keep some continuity after the last captain and three of the players graduated."

I kept my face expressionless. Alana had been talking about netball all month, but only as a way to network with other schools and students. She didn't want to play merely for the fun of it. I couldn't help finding that somewhat pitiable. I would have liked to play, if I'd been able to cast the spells. As it was...

"It should be great," Alana said. "We'll sleep in a dorm, we'll have midnight feasts, we'll..."

"Great," I said, sourly. I'd never be able to get away from my fellow students. Jude's was in Shallot - we could see the towers from our bedrooms - but students weren't allowed to leave the school during term. Alana would love it. I'd find it a nightmare. "What will you do if the Dorm Head refuses to turn a blind eye?"

"Bribe her, of course," Alana said. She smiled, confidently. "The family name..."

"...Will not get you out of trouble, young lady," Dad said, sternly. "And if you want to waste your inheritance bribing upperclassmen, you're being silly."

Alana batted her eyelashes at him. It looked profoundly unnatural. "But Dad..."

"But nothing," Dad said. He tapped the table, sharply. "The family name is *not* to be taken lightly. You are *not* to expect that people will bow the knee to you, merely because you carry my name. You are to *earn* the right to have people bow to you."

He leaned forward. "I would be *most* displeased if I heard you were using our name as a weapon," he added. "And you would regret it."

Alana looked down. "Dad..."

"You need to be *worthy* of the name," Dad said. "You have to *earn* it."

Bella and I exchanged glances. Triplets or not, only one of us could inherit Dad's position...and I wouldn't have cared to bet against Alana. Bella was lazy, too lazy to put in the work necessary to maintain the family; I couldn't cast a basic cantrip, let alone modify the wards protecting the hall. Dad would have to pick Alana as his successor by default, unless he chose to seek a successor from our cousins. And Mum would be furious if he chose to look outside the immediate family.

"This will be a challenge," Mum added. She sliced her turkey slowly. "But we have faith in you."

"You're sending Caitlyn into a school she cannot handle," Alana pointed out. Her voice dripped sweet reason. "She will..."

"She will have all the time and encouragement she needs to develop her powers," Dad said, firmly. "You will help her, of course."

Alana shot me a bitter look. She'd *hate* trying to help me, particularly as she believed it would be futile. Bella wouldn't be much better. Sure, she wasn't often malicious - although she'd hexed me badly a few weeks ago - but she was lazy. I had the feeling she'd do as little work as she could get away with, once she was in school. Perhaps I could work with her...

"Of course, Dad," Alana said, sweetly.

Dad's eyes narrowed. Only a complete idiot would have believed her - and Dad was one of the smartest men I knew. Perhaps *the* smartest. Running the family alone was a full-time job.

"Remember the binding," Dad said, finally. His voice hardened. "And remember - the weakest link isn't always the obvious."

Alana lowered her eyes. "Yes, father."

"You have an advantage because your parents are both magicians," Dad added. "And that gave you an education many other students lack. But it has also made you dependent. Now...you have to prove that you can stand on your own two feet. You have to learn to be strong and resourceful. What will happen after I die?"

I shuddered. I knew *precisely* what Alana would do, after our parents died. Her very first step would be to kick me out, if she was feeling generous. If not...I didn't want to think about it.

The turkey was perfect, the potatoes crisp and yet soft...even the vegetables tasted nice, after Mum glared me into eating them. And the pudding was utterly wonderful. But it still felt like my last meal before death. Tomorrow, I'd put on the uniform and walk with my family to Jude's and then...would I come home again? The family name wouldn't protect me, not if Dad was right. There would be too many students keen to test the latest generation.

"The family depends on you," Dad said, when we had finally finished the meal. He rose and beckoned us into the sitting room. We followed him, surprised. "And we have faith that you will rise to the challenge."

Thanks, I thought, sourly.

Alana looked pleased as Lucy poured us all small glasses of fruit juice. My parents had never allowed us to join them in the sitting room after dinner, not until now. It was for grown-ups, we'd been told. The children - us and any guests - went elsewhere. But now...I sipped my juice, feeling very young indeed. Dad was right. All three of us - even me - had lived a protected life. Now...we were going out into the big wide world, where our family name was as much a curse as it was a blessing.

And I'm completely defenceless, I thought, morbidly. *All someone has to do is shoot a spell at me if they want to test the rumours.*

I'd made a small collection of Devices, but Dad had confiscated them the moment he'd checked my trunk. They were forbidden, he'd explained. I'd argued, to no avail. Students weren't allowed Devices of Power unless they were forged in the school itself. There was a risk of someone producing a genuinely dangerous Device...

"But I know what I'm doing," I'd protested.

"They don't know that," Dad had countered. "And they won't make exceptions for you."

"You have seven years of schooling to enjoy," Dad said. The way he said it suggested that *endure* would probably be a better word. "After that, you will be adults. You can enter apprenticeship contracts or live apart from us or even get married. And then, you will speak to us as equals."

As if, I thought.

"And the whole world will open up before you," Mum added. She smiled, clearly remembering something from her life before becoming a mother. "You may travel, if you wish."

I would have liked that, once upon a time. I'd never left Shallot, not even when Dad had travelled to Tintagel to consult with the king's sorcerers. The maps had fascinated me - I'd read all the stories of great explorers prowling the oceans or probing the Desolation where the Thousand-Year Empire's capital had once been. I'd never been put off by stories of wild magic and strange transformations. But as I'd grown older, I'd come to realise that my complete lack of a gift hampered me in more ways than one. I might never be allowed to leave the hall and explore.

Maybe I could, as an adult, I told myself. It wasn't as if the family *wanted* an overgrown child - or a cripple. *Alana would be glad to see the back of me.*

"Or visit the capital," Dad said. "The king might grant you audience."

"I could be presented to the queen," Alana said. She smiled, suddenly. "Would you take me there?"

"When you're eighteen, if you wish," Mum said. Her eyes narrowed. "But I would advise against it."

Dad spoke before any of us could ask questions. "None of this will be easy," he admitted, warningly. "But your mother and I survived it. And you three will survive too. Alana, Belladonna, Caitlyn...you will learn what you need to know. Make us proud."

Alana beamed. "Of course, father."

Dad checked his watch. "You should be in bed soon," he added. We groaned. It was only seven in the evening. "You'll be waking up at six tomorrow, ready to start your first day at school. The first day is always the worst. Just remember...you were born and raised in Shallot, with magic all around you. Some of your fellows will not have had that honour."

"They might be commoners," Alana said, shocked. "Dad..."

"They're commoners with *magic*," Dad said, sharply. "Not just little spells, but *real* talent. I advise you to remember that, young lady. Or it won't be pretty."

"Particularly as your maternal grandparents were both common-born," Mum added, crossing her arms. "At Jude's, talent is all that matters. Your birth isn't *that* great an advantage if you keep being outdone by commoners. Trust me - when the time comes to decide which of you will join the upperclassmen, you will be judged on your magic, not on your family name."

Great, I thought, sarcastically. *They'll kick me out then for sure.*

Alana looked embarrassed. "But...but they won't know how to comport themselves in society."

"They can learn," Dad said. He gave her a sharp look, then glanced at Bella and I. "And you can teach them."

I wondered, suddenly, if Dad had ever faced any problems with his side of the family for marrying Mum. Great Aunt Stregheria had never liked us. Some of his other relatives hadn't been that kind either, although none of them had been more than impolite. But then, Mum *had* given birth to a zero. My existence suggested there was something tainted about Mum's magic. I could easily imagine some of my paternal relatives sneering at her behind her back, maybe just out of earshot. They wouldn't have cared to admit that the problem might have come from the other side of the family.

"Go to bed," Mum said, gently. She kissed each of us, one by one. I wondered, suddenly, if she thought she wasn't going to see us tomorrow. "And tomorrow...tomorrow you start your adventure."

I swallowed. Tomorrow was going to be the worst day of my life.

CHAPTER

FIVE

"You look nice, Miss Caitlyn," Sonja said. "Do you want me to brush your hair?"

I shook my head as I examined my appearance in the mirror. Jude's uniform looked...odd, at least to me. A black skirt, reaching all the way down to my ankles; black shoes, shining under the light; a black shirt, a black blazer...I looked like a professional mourner going to a funeral. I couldn't help thinking that I should be practicing my wailing. A single white band wrapped around my right arm, marking me out as a first-year student. Other than that, everything was black.

"It could be worse," Sonja said. "Do you know what the boys at Evesham have to wear?"

"No," I said. Evesham was a university for older boys intent on entering the civil service. It probably had an even *more* absurd uniform. "And I don't care."

Sonja's face went blank, a clear sign she was annoyed. I felt a pang of guilt, which I swiftly suppressed. There was a good chance I would never see home again, unless I did something so appalling that Jude's kicked me out within the first week or two. And yet, going by all the horror stories, what *was* expulsion-worthy? Jude's seemed to be *very* tolerant of misbehaviour, bullying and magical accidents. I was dead.

I hadn't wanted to eat, when I was dragged out of bed. Mum had forced some toast and orange juice down my throat, while lecturing Alana and Bella for chatting too loudly. Mum doesn't like getting up early either, even for us. Dad put in an appearance at breakfast, then vanished again while we were getting dressed. I knew he would be taking us to the school gates, but it still felt as if we were being abandoned. The butterflies in my stomach were breeding. And yet...

"I'm sorry," I said. I meant it. "I just..."

"You'll be fine," Sonja said. "You're not as clumsy as me."

I sighed. Sonja *was* clumsy. But she could cast spells, which made up for a lot. She'd never be a great sorceress - she didn't have the time or inclination to train - but still...she could work magic. She had plenty of opportunities in her life, if she left our service. I had none.

She checked my uniform one final time, then hurried me down to the lobby. Alana stood there, somehow managing to look regal even in the absurd black outfit. We looked at each other and started giggling, just as Mum pushed Bella into the room. Judging from her sour expression, Bella had tried to go back to sleep instead of getting dressed. I understood precisely how she felt.

"You remind me of me," Mum said, briskly. "I'm sure you'll do fine."

I rolled my eyes as she turned away, ordering the servants to have our trunks shipped to the school. Alana looked good in the uniform, but Bella looked sloppy and I felt like a fraud. I *was* a fraud. I couldn't even sense the protective magic fizzing around the hallway. How many traps had I walked into because I couldn't sense the magic waiting for me? I'd lost count. And here, I was one of the family. I wouldn't have that advantage at Jude's.

Mum turned back and launched into another lecture about how she expected us to behave ourselves while living up to the family name. I did my best to pretend to listen, although I'm sure she didn't buy it for a second. My heart was beating so fast I rather suspected my sisters could hear it. By the time Dad emerged from the shadows, decked out in his black robes of office, I was almost relieved to see him. It was time to go.

Travis and the servants waved goodbye to us as we walked through the main door and headed for the gates. They swung open at Dad's touch, allowing us to stride onto the streets. The sun was barely in the sky, yet the streets were already crammed with magicians and their families, walking or riding to school. I saw a number of familiar faces - girls and boys I had hoped would be my friends, once upon a time - but none of us spoke. Magic or not, we were all nervous. Jude's would be the making or breaking of us.

The breaking, I thought numbly.

I glanced back at the hall as it vanished into the distance. Would I ever see it again? Dad didn't understand, not really. He didn't want to think that he might have sired a daughter without magic. And yet...what value was there in having triplets when one of them didn't have magic? Did we really bring him good luck? Could he call upon the promised protections?

But in the end, it didn't matter. I couldn't cast the simplest spell.

The streets remained silent, despite the crowds, as we crossed the river into Water Shallot. I glanced down into the river, watching the fishing boats as they headed out to hunt, then looking past them at the giant sailing vessels. Traders went everywhere from Shallot, I'd been told; they visited distant lands, then came back with rare goods to sell. I felt a wistful pang of longing, mingled with the grim realisation that I would probably never be allowed to leave the city. Even if Dad had let me go, I wouldn't be able to get a job on a sailing ship.

"There," Alana said. "I see it!"

I looked forward. The gates of Jude's Sorcerous Academy loomed up in front of us, guarded by stone statues that moved when no one was looking. I should have been able to sense the complex spells keeping them alive, but I couldn't. The gates were already swinging open, a line of men and women in fancy clothes standing on the far side. They were the tutors, I guessed, some of the greatest magicians in the world. Jude's reputation has spread so far and wide that people have been known to come for thousands of miles, just to find a place within its walls.

They can have mine, I thought.

Dad hugged all three of us. "You'll be fine," he said. Parents weren't allowed to enter the gates, unless something had gone very wrong. "Don't forget to write to us."

"We could just pop over to see you," Bella pointed out. "Dad..."

"You can't leave during term," Dad reminded her. "And you *are* going to write to us."

Alana caught Bella's hand. "Come on," she said. "Let's go!"

I shot Dad one final look, then turned and slowly made my way through the gates. The other students - my classmates - wore the same attire, save for the boys wearing trousers instead of skirts. Their parents, however, wore hundreds of different styles, ranging from the understated elegance of the aristocracy to the blatant display of the *nouveau riche* or makeshift garments of the peasantry. I wondered why the latter had bothered to come to the city, even though their children had won a scholarship to Jude's. Merely staying a night in Shallot would cost a month's wages. And their children would have nothing in common with them when they graduated.

Alana was already chatting to a couple of friends as they walked down the lane towards the school, Bella clinging to her side like a limpet. I felt a flicker of bitter envy, which I rapidly suppressed. There was no *point* in moaning any longer. Instead, I looked past her, trying to take in the school. It looked like a giant palace, but with so many different styles blurring together that it was obvious that Jude's was constantly growing. Merely *looking* at it made my head hurt. Parts of the building simply didn't look *right*.

A tall girl strode past me, her long blonde hair shining in the sun. An equally tall boy followed her, glancing from face to face as he passed. He caught my eye for a long moment, just long enough for me to recognise him. Akin Rubén, son of Lord Carioca Rubén. The girl had to be his sister, Isabella Rubén. I groaned inwardly as Akin nudged his sister, drawing her attention to me. Lord Rubén might have twins, instead of triplets, but there was no doubt that both of his children had magic. I'd heard stories about Isabella Rubén.

But those stories came from Alana, I reminded myself, sharply. Alana and Isabella Rubén would be rivals, if they weren't already. *They might not be true.*

I looked back at them as evenly as I could. Unlike my sisters and myself, Akin and Isabella Rubén were almost identical. If Akin had grown his blond hair out, it would have been hard to tell the difference between them. Their blue eyes seemed to glitter coldly at me before they turned away, seeking out new faces. I felt cold, despite the warmth, as I followed the others into the building. The last thing I needed was a feud on the first *day!*

"Girls over here," a voice called. I saw a friendly-looking woman standing inside the door, holding a sack. An older man stood on the other side of the room, calling to the boys. "Take a token, then pocket it!"

Alana reached into the sack. I saw something gold in her hand, but I didn't get a good look before she pocketed it. Shrugging, I reached into the hat myself and touched a number of small objects. I picked one at random and glanced down at it. The badge was a tiny golden raven. It seemed to sparkle in my hand.

"Move on, into the hall," the woman ordered. "Don't delay!"

I stopped, dead, as I saw the Great Hall for the first time. It was immense, large enough to hold well over a thousand students. The hundred or so first-years rattled around like peas in a pod, forming small clusters based on power and popularity. I did my best to ignore the crowd gathering around Alana and Bella as I looked around the hall. The walls were lined with giant portraits of famous witches and wizards. There were no names, but I recognised half of them from my father's lessons. They'd all done wonders in their time, from a man who'd saved the kingdom to a woman who'd codified the essentials of alchemy. I'd wanted to be like them, once.

The doors banged shut. A loud clap echoed through the air. We turned to see a middle-aged man standing on a podium, peering down at us. I recognised him instantly. I'd actually *met* him when he'd visited the hall, back when I'd been eight or nine. Castellan Wealden had been kind enough, I supposed, but he hadn't had much to say to a little girl. Even now, I couldn't help thinking that he looked too young to run a school.

"Welcome to Jude's," Castellan Wealden said.

His voice hung in the air, just loud enough for me to hear. It had to be projection magic, of course. I wondered if there were spells included to keep us calm. It wouldn't be difficult, not for the Castellan. And he might see advantage in keeping us attentive while he spoke. Some of us had the attention span of gnats.

"Jude's is the finest magical academy in the world," he continued, after a brief pause. "Kings and princes, sorcerers and alchemists...many of the most famous men and women in the world have passed through our doors, studied with us and then left to make their mark. I expect each and every one of you to live up to our reputation."

He droned on and on for several minutes, listing all the famous sorcerers who'd made an impression on the world. I would have been more impressed if the details hadn't been included in the booklet Mum had forced us to read from cover to cover, then quizzed us mercilessly until we knew it backwards. Jude's was famous...big deal. It wasn't as if anyone was going to remember me as anything other than an utter disgrace.

"There are rules in our school," he told us. I perked up. This sounded as though it might be a little more interesting. "Most of them you'll learn over the next week from your teachers and supervisors. But there are some we need to go over right now.

"First, as long as term is in session, you are forbidden to leave the school grounds without permission. That permission will not be granted unless there is an urgent need - your parents being ill, for example. You are here to learn, not to be distracted. Anyone caught trying to sneak off the grounds will regret it."

I kept my face impassive, somehow. Dad had talked about upper-classmen sneaking in and out of the school, trying to smuggle sweets and cakes to their fellows, but he'd admitted that fooling the wards was far from easy. The walls were so heavily charmed that they were almost alive, just waiting for someone foolish enough to try to climb over. Getting caught would be embarrassing. Even now, he'd warned, he wouldn't care to try to break into the school. What hope did *I* have of circumventing the wards?

"Second," the Castellan continued, "you are expected to attend classes as scheduled on your timetable. If you are repeatedly late for class, steps will be taken; if you purposely delay your fellows so they miss class, you will regret it. We will not be amused by your games if they interfere with someone's education. Do *not* test us on this.

"Third, and perhaps most important, left-hand magic is utterly *banned* at this school. If you - if any of you - are caught experimenting with left-hand magic, you will be expelled and handed over to Magus Court for judgement. There is a very good chance, if you are proven to have used such magic, that you will be executed. There will be no further warnings."

I swallowed. I'd heard of left-hand magic, but I knew very little about it. None of the books I'd read, even the forbidden tomes, had talked about it. Dad had flatly refused to talk about it, when I'd asked him. Clearly, there was *something* sinister about left-hand magic. But what? If I didn't know what to avoid, how could I avoid it?

But I probably couldn't work left-hand magic either, I thought, bitterly. *The warning is pointless.*

The Castellan's words hung on the air for a long moment. I saw several students exchanging nervous glances, trying to determine if their fellows knew more than themselves. Alana looked nervous - I guessed she'd asked Dad too, only to walk away with a flea in her ear. I looked at Isabella and saw she was just as puzzled as everyone else, although she was trying to hide it. Her father hadn't told her anything about it either, I guessed. And wasn't *that* interesting?

"You'll pick up the rest over the next week," the Castellan said, finally. "Now...does anyone *not* have a badge?"

He paused, just long enough to give someone a chance to speak up, then went on. "Every year, students are sorted at random into the dorms. For the next year, each of you will be sharing a dormitory with nine other students and an upperclassman who has been volunteered to serve as your Dorm Head. These dorms are your homes for the next year - keep them clean and tidy or you'll be living in squalor."

His face twisted into a smile. I didn't get the joke.

"You will *not* be allowed to transfer without a *very* good reason," he added. "I suggest you learn to get on with your fellows, because you don't have a choice. Next year, you will be sorted into a different dorm with new faces. By the time you join the upperclassmen in fifth year, you will know every young magician of your generation. You'll have made friends and contacts that will last you a lifetime."

And enemies, I thought, morbidly.

"You will spend the rest of the day unpacking, learning about your dorm and exploring the school," the Castellan concluded. "Lunch is served at one o'clock, dinner is served at six; classes will start tomorrow, at nine. Your timetables are already waiting for you in your dorms. I suggest you spend some time locating the different classrooms so you aren't late."

He gave us a toothy smile. "And *listen* to your Dorm Head," he added. He waved a hand towards the rear of the hall, where a dozen older students stood. Each of them had an illusionary animal hovering over their heads. "Good luck!"

I looked down at the badge in my hand. A raven, a golden raven. I shook my head, then followed the other students to the upperclassmen. Neither Alana nor Bella seemed to be in Raven Dorm, thankfully. Alana had picked out a golden cat, while Bella had chosen a nasty-looking shark. I hoped that wasn't a bad omen. The upperclassman - a girl four years older than me - peered down her nose at us, then shrugged. She didn't seem very interested in us.

And then Isabella strode up and stood next to me. I glanced at her in surprise, then looked away as she waved goodbye to her brother. She was a raven? I looked back at her, just in time to see her pin the badge to her blazer. She *was* a raven.

I felt my heart sink, even as the upperclassman counted the ten of us before turning and leading us through the door. Sharing a dorm with my sisters would have been bad, but sharing one with my family's rival? The *daughter* of my family's rival? It was going to be *very* bad.

"Make sure you have your badges on," the upperclassman said. "You'll need them to get into the dorm."

I pinned mine on, feeling cold. I was doomed.

CHAPTER

SIX

Raven Dorm was nicer than I had expected, to be fair. Two large windows, charmed to keep people from peering in, allowed sunlight to stream into the room. Eleven beds and bedside cabinets, surrounded by drapes for privacy; four showers and a bath...the walls were bare, of course, but Mum had told us that we were expected to decorate the walls ourselves, using magic. I just hoped no one paid close attention when I decided not to decorate my part of the dorm. Our trunks were stacked neatly against the far wall, our names clearly visible in the light. It would have been nice, I thought, if I'd been able to relax. I'd expected to be hexed in the back all the way to the dorm.

The upperclassman clapped her hands together. "All right, you lot," she said. She sat on the front bed. It was larger than the others, clearly intended to show her importance. "Gather around me, please. There isn't much time."

I did as I was told, taking the opportunity to study her more carefully. She was pale, her skin so white that it was almost translucent. Her eyes were a faint pink - I wasn't sure if that was normal or if she'd had a magical accident over the last few years - and her nose was so small that I would have believed it belonged to a toddler. She was slight, yet she carried herself with an assurance I envied. *Alana* would have envied it. There wasn't the slightest doubt in her mind, I thought, that she was in charge.

Isabella recoiled, just for a second. The girl next to her recoiled too. I blinked in surprise, then looked at the upperclassman. She was looking back at me, her eyes narrowing speculatively. I realised my mistake a moment later. She'd flared her magic, just enough to make it clear that she was more powerful than the ten of us put together, but I hadn't reacted to the surge. Of course not. I couldn't sense it. And now she thought I was challenging her.

I groaned, inwardly. Of all the things to happen...

"For those of you who don't know me," the upperclassman said, "my name is Sandy Macpherson. You've probably heard of my family, but I suggest you put everything you know out of your heads. The only thing you need to remember is that I'm a fifth-year student who has been... *selected*...to serve as your Dorm Head for the next year. That means you do what I say."

Ouch, I thought.

House Macpherson was neutral, if I recalled correctly. Dad had certainly drilled all the major families into my head, along with our allies, enemies and rivals. Too small to pose a significant threat to the balance of power, House Macpherson tended to stay out of Magus Court as much as possible. Sandy...was probably caught between two fires, with Isabella and me sharing a dorm. Any hint of favouritism could reflect badly on her.

"Now, I have to start preparing for the upper-level exams," Sandy continued. "And that means I have less time to tend to you babies than I might have wished. If you need help, you can seek me out...but if the problem is one you could have solved by yourselves, I will make you wish you *had*. I'm here to keep order, not to hold your hand, help you with your homework or give you the answers on a silver plate. Do I make myself clear?"

"Yes," I muttered.

Sandy's eyes swept the room. "Basic rules first, then," she said. "Each of you has a bed, which you can choose after I finish speaking. You are expected to make the bed every morning before class and change the sheets every weekend - that's pillows, duvet and mattress cover. Each of you will also spend at least one day each term cleaning the toilets and dorm floor. If you can't do your duty, I'll show you how; if you won't do your duty, I'll stand over you until you do.

"I imagine most of you have brought cake or chocolate from home. If you want to eat it in the dorm, clean up the mess afterwards. The same goes for anything you buy from the tuck shop or sneak out of the kitchens for a midnight feast. I will be *most* displeased if you make a mess and refuse to clean it up."

Isabella coughed. "No servants?"

Sandy sneered at her. "No," she said. "You are expected to pick up after yourselves for the first time in your lives."

I flushed, suddenly understanding why Mum had insisted we make our own beds over the last month. She'd known what was coming and had worked to prepare us for it. But I'd never mastered the cleaning spells I'd need to do the bathrooms. How could I?

"Lights Out is at nine o'clock, every evening," Sandy continued, snapping out point after point. Her voice was growing sharper. "You will *not* be able to get an excuse note from your teachers, so don't bother to try. You should all be in the dorm by then, tucked up in bed. Do not try to read under the covers, because you need your sleep. If you are caught outside the dorm after that, expect to suffer for making me look bad. Rest assured that I will take any black mark I get on my record out on you.

"If you have any disputes or disagreements, I expect you to handle them carefully - and without getting the staff involved. Don't go sneaking to the staff unless you want to become Miss Unpopular. Talk, argue...if you want to fight, you can clear a space and have at each other. I will be *most* displeased if you cause any damage to the school or any innocent bystanders."

She paused. "Not that there *are* any innocent bystanders in this school."

It was a joke, I thought. But I didn't find it very funny.

Sandy didn't smile. "You are not to damage each other's property," she rattled off. "If you do, the cost of replacing it will be taken from your pocket money or billed to your parents, if you don't have enough money in your account. You are *not* allowed to invite any boys into the dorm. I don't care who they are or what they want - they're not allowed to enter. You *can* invite other girls into the dorm, provided they are quiet and don't disturb anyone. If they do, I will ban them from entering and key the wards to reject them. Do you have any questions?"

There were none. Somehow, I wasn't surprised.

"Very good," Sandy said. She pointed to the nearest bed. "You'll each find a large packet on your beds. They're all the same, so don't waste time trying to choose. Inside, you'll find two notebooks and your timetables. You--" she jabbed a finger at a girl I didn't know "--take one of those packets and open it."

The girl hesitated, then did as she was told. Two black notebooks fell out.

"Keep the timetable, for the moment," Sandy ordered. She held up the first notebook. "This is your spellbook. Make sure you write your name on the cover. Every time you master a spell - not learn it, master it - you write it down in the book. They'll be inspected at the end of each month, so be careful. Improper spell notation will get you detention. Do *not* play games with this because the charms magisters will not be amused."

I nodded. Dad had drilled that into me too, although he'd grown more and more reluctant to continue as my lack of magic became apparent. A mistake could cause the spell to fail - or go spectacularly wrong. There were horror stories about that too.

"The second book," Sandy added, "is your punishment book. Carry it with you at all times - you'll be given detention if you're caught without it. Every time you get a punishment or a detention, it will be written into these pages. Should I give you lines to write, you will write them in the book; should you be given detention by a teacher, the time and place will also be written here. Most detentions are served on Saturday or Sunday, but there are exceptions. Try not to be one."

She smiled, rather unpleasantly. "Yes, I *can* make you write lines until your fingers start to cramp," she warned. "And so can any other upper-classman. So *behave*."

There was a long, awkward pause. "You'll pick up the rest as you go along," Sandy finished, snidely. "Until then...any questions?"

A redheaded girl held up a hand. "When do we write to our parents?"

"Whenever we want," Sandy said. She gave the girl an oddly reassuring smile. I wondered if she was trying to be nice. "*Official* letter-writing day is Sunday and you are all expected to write a letter, but you can write additional letters whenever you want. Bear in mind the postal service outside the city isn't good. It may be weeks before your letter reaches home."

Another girl leaned forward. "Where do we collect our pocket money?"

"From the office, after lunch," Sandy said. She snorted. "And I suggest, if you brought more money in your trunk, that you don't show it off."

She glanced from face to face. "Pick a bed, get unpacked, then I suggest you spend the rest of the day exploring the school and meeting new friends," she said. She rose. "Don't be late for lunch or dinner - you'll regret it. And *don't* bother me unless it's urgent."

I watched her go, then tried to choose a bed. Most of the girls hurried towards the rear of the room, trying to stay as far from Sandy's bed as possible. I didn't blame them. Part of me was tempted to stay *close* to Sandy, but I doubted she'd be any help if I got into a fight. The school didn't encourage the upperclassmen to police the lowerclassmen that thoroughly. I picked a bed, then sat down on it and opened the packet. Two notebooks and a timetable fell into my hand. I took a pen from my pocket and scribbled my name on the cover - both covers - and then unfolded the timetable. It was surprisingly detailed, accounting for every hour of the day between nine in the morning and four in the afternoon. There would be barely any time to myself.

Not that it matters, I thought. *I never had much time to myself anyway.*

"I think they should allow us to bring our pets," Isabella said, loudly. She was talking to two twin girls I vaguely recognised. "My cat wouldn't have caused any trouble.

"Nor would my snake," one of the girls said. "But not *everyone* has a pet."

"They could all have pets," Isabella insisted. "They could *give* us all pets!"

I sighed, inwardly, as I placed the girls. Ayesha and Zeya McDonald. House McDonald was another neutral family, but they were considerably more powerful than House Macpherson. I didn't blame Isabella for trying to make friends with their daughters. Even if their family remained neutral, friendship might tip them towards aiding Isabella and *her* family. Behind them, Amber Alidade and Clarian Bolingbroke were having an argument over some long-standing dispute that dated back to their grandparents' grandparents. I silently rooted for Amber as I readied myself to duck, if the hexes started flying. Clarian was a distant relative on my mother's side, but she'd turned me into a pig three years ago and laughed when I complained.

Shaking my head, I hurried to the wall to pick up my trunk and drag it back to the bed. Mum had packed some cake, wrapping it in protective spells...I think she meant to give me incentive to learn how to *cancel* the spells. Henry's finest chocolate cake would remain perfectly preserved, until I brought it out of stasis. But I couldn't even begin to crack the spells. I put the cake aside, then silently unpacked my clothes and books, using a crayon to draw out a handful of protective runes of questionable value. They might buy me some time, but I doubted they'd slow down a magician for very long. They just didn't have enough time to charge. The only advantage to going to Jude's, as far as I could tell, was that Mum wouldn't be making remarks about unsuitable choices of reading material.

There was a flash of light. I ducked, instinctively, as I glanced towards Amber. Clarian was gone...it took me a moment to notice the snail on her bed. Amber giggled, then turned away. Clarian would be alright, of course. The spell wouldn't last very long. No one, not even Great Aunt Stregheria, could make such a spell last indefinitely without careful preparation. But she would be embarrassed and humiliated and...

The redheaded girl - I didn't recognise her - looked nervous. I resisted the urge to roll my eyes at her. What did *she* have to worry about? She probably knew a dozen defensive spells...Alana, for all of her faults, had mastered over thirty by the time she turned nine. There were adults who hadn't learned so many. She flushed when she saw me looking at her and turned away. I wasn't sure what *that* meant. Maybe she'd heard my name mentioned somewhere and thought I was just as good as my sister. Or maybe...

I felt a prickling and looked up. Isabella was staring at me, her blue eyes boring into my brown ones. I lifted my head and stared back at her, refusing to back down. It was stupid, perhaps, but I knew from bitter experience that showing weakness to a bully was a dreadful mistake. She was more powerful than me - that could not be disputed - but that didn't mean I was powerless.

She stared at me for a long moment. I could see her lips twitching, as if she was readying herself to cast a spell. I readied myself too...if I jumped down, I should be able to get out of the line of fire. And then...a loud croaking from Amber caught our attention, breaking the trance. Clarian had recovered from Amber's spell and hexed her in the back, while she wasn't looking. I allowed myself a moment of relief as I picked up the timetable and both notebooks and stuffed them into my pocket, before heading out the door. Isabella was a problem I couldn't solve, yet. My time would be better spent exploring the school.

I was glad I had, by the end of the day. The building might have looked odd from the outside, but it was a positive nightmare on the *inside*. Corridors seemed to run in all directions, classrooms were scattered about madly with little rhyme or reason...it took me hours to get a rough impression of how the school was actually organised. I was nearly late for dinner because I got lost twice. Walking through Jude's was like walking through the Family Labyrinth, only with the added risk of magical traps or being hexed in the back - or getting lost completely. By the time we were gently reminded to head back to the dorm, I was tired and worn.

At least Alana and Bella seem to be enjoying themselves, I thought, sourly. They'd both been sitting at different tables during dinner, chatting to small crowds of adoring fans. Neither of them had bothered to pay any attention to me. *They'll have a happy time here.*

"Lights Out in fifty minutes," Sandy said, warningly. Her voice was quiet, but it caught our attention. I thought she was definitely using a spell. "If you haven't showered, go shower now."

I wasn't the only one to look unhappy as we hurried to wash, get into our nightclothes and then get into bed. But there was no choice. Sandy moved up and down the dorm, barking orders and encouragement to anyone who wasn't moving fast enough to suit her. I pulled the drapes closed, hoping I'd be left in peace, then climbed into bed. My bed felt surprisingly comfortable, but I couldn't help feeling vulnerable. The other students would have cast protective spells - and traps - on their possessions...I couldn't, of course. None of the protective amulets I could have forged would have been *that* effective, not against real sorcerers. Or even sorcerers in training.

The lights went out five minutes later. There was a faint light surrounding the bathroom door, but otherwise the dorm fell into utter darkness. Silence fell too, broken only by a stifled sob. It was quiet, but it sounded very loud in the quiet room.

Sandy spoke a second later. "What was *that*?"

"I miss my mother," a plaintive voice said. I couldn't place it, but whatever she said next was lost in giggles. *Everyone* was laughing at her, everyone but me. I missed my mother too. "I..."

"Be quiet," Sandy snapped. I heard her mutter an incantation, just loudly enough for me to hear. A silencing spell, I thought. Whoever was sobbing could no longer be heard. I hoped that meant she'd merely been silenced, instead of being frozen in place or thrown into an uncomfortable sleep. "You'll all be kicked out of bed at eight thirty, if you're not up by then so...*get some sleep.*"

I closed my eyes, but it was hard to relax. People were breathing, someone was going to the bathroom...I had never shared a room with anyone, not since I was weaned. The near-complete darkness only made it worse. *Anything* - or anyone - could be lurking out there, coming towards me. It was easy to imagine Isabella sneaking towards me, warily watching for traps that weren't there...

Somehow, I slept. I still don't know how.

CHAPTER
SEVEN

W hen I awoke, I was still human.

I'd half-expected to wake up a frog or a toad - or worse. Turning someone into a slug or a snail was technically frowned upon - Alana had been grounded for a month after she'd done that to Bella - but Sandy hadn't punished Amber for doing it to Clarian. I *really* didn't like the implications of that, not at all. But no one had bothered to push back the drapes and hex me in my sleep. I was torn between relief and suspicion. What else did they have in mind?

"Wake up," Sandy called. She'd woken me, I realised dully. "Anyone not down for breakfast will regret it."

There was a loud bang as she walked through the door, leaving us alone. I sighed, thinking words I had never dared say out loud. Sandy had made it clear that she resented having to take care of us - and really, I didn't blame her. Isabella and I alone were a political nightmare, even without counting some of the other girls. I pushed the thought aside as I swung my legs off the bed and stood up. A glance at the clock told me that it was half past seven. We had an hour and a half until classes were due to begin.

I knew I should go to breakfast, that I would get in trouble for missing breakfast, but I didn't *feel* like eating. What would be the point? But Sandy would make me write lines if I didn't go...I sighed out loud, then bent down to open the drawer under my bed. The moment I touched the wood, there was a brilliant flare of light. I tried to jump back, too late. My limbs locked up. I couldn't move a muscle. I was trapped in this embarrassing and helpless position.

Someone opened the drape, but I still couldn't move. "You were right," Isabella's voice said. I could hear her, right behind me. "She *did* fall for it."

I would have cringed, if I could have moved. The trap spell she'd used, I was sure, was one of the easiest to cast...and avoid, if one had the slightest sensitivity to magic. Alana or Bella would have sensed the spell a long time before they touched it. They certainly wouldn't have had any trouble removing it - or escaping, if they accidentally triggered the spell. Me? I was stuck until the spell wore off. And if Isabella had overpowered the cantrip, which was possible, I might wind up being late for class.

"She could free herself, in a second, if she wanted," Isabella added, snidely. She was right. A simple cantrip, one every magician learned in her first lessons, would free me. But I couldn't cast it. "She's trapped."

"You can't leave her there forever," another voice said. I thought it was Ayesha McDonald, but I wasn't certain. Ayesha and her twin sounded very alike. "You'll get the blame, even if she doesn't tattle."

"The banshee will free her," Isabella said, dispassionately. It took me a moment to realise she meant Sandy. I felt someone poking my back, sharply. I could do nothing, but burn with helpless rage. "She'll have time to get dressed and snatch some toast before class."

I heard her footsteps as she walked away, pulling the drapes closed behind her. Someone giggled...were they laughing at me? I felt a surge of pure hatred, mixed with bitter helplessness as I heard the dorm emptying. If my rage had powered my magic, the entire school would have been reduced to rubble. But nothing happened. I just stood there, utterly unable to move.

Centre, I told myself. It was the most basic exercise, one taught to every child born to a magical family. *Reach out and touch the magic.*

I tried. I really tried. But nothing happened. The spell remained firmly in place, holding me utterly frozen. I couldn't help wondering if she'd turned me into stone, although my body still *felt* human. An odd calm fell over me as I waited. Dad had been wrong. Exposure to so much magic would not free power I didn't have. And it was only a matter of time until I was killed...

The spell broke. I fell forward, barely managing to throw out an arm before I cracked my skull into the bedside. My entire body twitched violently...I forced myself to stand, running through a series of exercises to get the blood flowing. Cramping up on my first day would be a miserable experience. My body ached as I opened the drawer and removed my clothes, then dressed hastily. It was eight-twenty and I *really* didn't want to be caught missing breakfast. I'd been frozen for far too long.

I heard the croaking as soon as I pushed the drapes aside. It was a plaintive sound, coming from the redhead's bed. Her drapes lay open, just wide enough for someone to peer inside. I would have known something was wrong, even without the noise. All the other drapes were closed and probably booby-trapped. I slipped forward, wondering if I was about to be hexed again and peered through the drapes. A frog was sitting on the bed, croaking noisily. It's big eyes - *her* big eyes, I realised dully - looked rather more hopeful when they saw me.

And yet, there was something *wrong*. She wasn't making any of the signs Dad had drilled into us when we'd started our lessons, the signs *everyone* knew to indicate that they were transformed humans, rather than *real* animals. I'd learned them religiously, just like everyone else in Shallot. The city has more magicians than anywhere else in Tintagel and a good third of them think that zapping passers-by into small animals is the height of humour. No one wants to be mistaken for a *real* animal and wind up in the stew pot. And yet, she wasn't making any of those signs.

I tried to remember her name, but I drew a blank.

"Sit still," I said, knowing it wouldn't be easy. I'd been a frog often enough to know their bodies *liked* to jump around. "You're...you're *her*, aren't you?"

The frog nodded. It was more of a bow, really, but I got the idea. And yet, I wasn't sure what I could do. I couldn't free her from the spell, any more than I could free myself. Why hadn't *she* freed herself? Surely, any magical family worthy of the name would have taught its daughters basic cantrips. They *certainly* should have taught her how to draw attention to herself. One of the reasons turning someone into a snail is frowned upon is because it's much harder to signal if you can barely move.

I sat down next to her, chancing the hexes she *should* have used to defend her bed. "I want you to focus," I said. "Close your eyes and clear your mind."

The frog closed her eyes. I hoped that she *had* managed to clear her mind, although being trapped in an animal body isn't conductive to meditation. But there wasn't any alternative, unless we waited for Sandy. Isabella was right about one thing, at least. I was no tattletale.

"Remember what it felt like to be human," I said. The frog quivered. That too was odd. Had she never been transfigured before? "Concentrate on that feeling. *Focus* on it. Grip that feeling in your mind, then focus on it."

Dad had said the same, back when we'd been trying to duplicate my escape from Great Aunt Stregheria's spell. His words had mocked me. No matter how hard I tried, I had never managed to repeat it. But *she* should be able to escape, surely. She wouldn't be here if she didn't have magic...

Why not? My thoughts mocked. *You don't have magic.*

I told that part of me to shut up. "Focus," I said. "Remember what it's like to breathe, to walk, to reach out..."

There was a brilliant flash of light. I leaned backwards as the redheaded girl appeared in front of me, her face pale and wan. She was sweating so badly that I couldn't help wondering if something had been wrong with the spell. Being caught by surprise and transfigured was embarrassing, sure, but hardly life-threatening. It wasn't as if she couldn't have broken the spell...

...Except she *hadn't* broken the spell until I'd helped her.

"Thank you," she gasped. "I...I thought I was stuck that way forever."

"It wouldn't have lasted," I assured her. I had no idea who'd cast the spell, but it really *wouldn't* have remained in place indefinitely. "Spells like that tend to wear off very quickly."

The girl looked at me. "I didn't know...it was my first time..."

I blinked. "Really?"

"Yes," the girl said.

I didn't believe her. Alana had turned Bella and me into dolls when all three of us had been eight. Dad had been both proud and furious. Since then, I'd been all sorts of objects and animals, both so I could learn how to cope with a transfigured body *and* to try to unlock my magic.

I didn't know a single magical child from the Great Houses who *hadn't* been transfigured, repeatedly. It was part of our training.

And then it struck me. "You're common-born?"

"Yes," the girl said. "I'm Rose of Erehwon."

Her eyes looked fearful. "Is that a problem?"

I stared back at her. Rose of Erehwon...she didn't have a family name, of course. She wasn't just a commoner, she was a peasant. Her family would have been peasants ever since the empire vanished and the kingdom rose in its place. They'd know a few spells, of course, but a real talent for magic...? Rose had been incredibly lucky that someone had noticed she *did* have a talent, that she *could* work magic on a far greater level than the rest of her family...

...With the proper training, of course.

My hands clenched into fists. I felt my nails digging into my bare skin. Rose was a commoner, from a low-magic background...and yet the fates had seen fit to give her the gift they'd denied me. No one would have noticed if she'd lacked magic, no one would have cared...she would have grown up in the countryside, married someone from the next village and had children, her life utterly unremarkable...while I, child of magic, was doomed to be a cripple. The entire city would laugh when the rumours finally grew too powerful to be ignored. My father would lose his post, my mother's papers would be ignored, Alana and Bella would have trouble finding husbands...

...And Rose, sitting next to me, could just reach out and claim *my* birthright.

I felt a surge of sheer jealously, so powerful that it almost consumed me. I wanted to hit her, I wanted to hurt her...how dare she? And yet, I knew it wasn't her fault. She hadn't stolen my power, had she? My thoughts were a bitter muddle. I wanted to throw back my head and scream, cursing the fates with every last word I knew, but wasn't allowed to say. Rose, a girl so ignorant she didn't even know how to signal for help, was my superior. She had power she didn't even know how to use.

Rose reached out. I flinched back automatically, half-expecting a hex. She'd take it out on me, of course. She had the power, while I had none. Of *course* she would. Magicians, trained magicians, have always believed themselves to be superior, even though it's more a matter of raw determination and training rather than innate ability. She could relieve her feelings by turning me into a toad or freezing me or compelling me or...

I stood, turned my back and stalked away. She called out to me, but I didn't hear a word. I was just too angry to care what she said or what she did. My dad would be delighted to meet her, I was sure. Common-born mages made the best apprentices because they had no other ties to the Great Families or Magus Court. Rose, born in a pigsty, had a brighter future than me. The surge of bitter jealously was almost overpowering. Mum had told us, more than once, that anger and hatred led to dark magic and utter madness. Alana had asked her if we weren't *already* black magicians and wound up cleaning the kitchens by herself, with a toothbrush...

"Well," a quiet voice said. "*Whatever* is the matter?"

I looked up. A pair of older girls, both sixth-years, were standing in front of me. One of them was eying me with barely-restrained contempt, while the other seemed more amused at my plight. I forced myself to calm down, despite the powerful urge to shout and scream at them.

"I asked you a question," the first girl snapped. She held out a hand. "Punishment book!"

I stared mutinously at her. My first day was shaping into an utter disaster...and I hadn't even had my first class! Sandy had said she - and the other upperclassmen - could sentence us to write lines...would they expel me if I refused to do them? Or if I tried to run...I dismissed the thought a second later. They'd just freeze me in place, then hand me over to one of the teachers. Or Sandy. I wasn't sure who I feared more.

The second girl placed a hand on her arm. "She's a firstie," she said, gently. "And it's the first day of school."

"Hah," the first girl said.

But she stalked past me without saying another word. The second girl shot me a wink, then hurried past me too. I scowled as I hurried down to the dining hall, feeling my stomach finally start to rumble. If I was lucky, I'd be able to eat something before I had to go to my first class. I really wasn't looking forward to it.

Isabella shot me a nasty look, mixed with surprise, as I stepped into the dining room and made a beeline towards the food. The cooks had piled up plates with everything from fruit and toast to egg, bacon, sausage and tomato. I winked at her - Sandy was still sitting with the other upper-classmen, so it was clear *she* hadn't freed me - and filled my plate. Mum would probably not have approved of *just* how much egg and bacon I'd loaded onto my plate, but I was hungry. And I needed the food to think.

Rose entered a moment later, looking downcast. I tried to ignore her - and the guilt gnawing at my heart. It wasn't her fault she had power and talent and I had none. But I didn't want to sit with her or anyone. I just wanted to be alone.

As I ate, I unfolded my timetable and read it again, more carefully. Charms - practical and theoretical. I might be able to do well on the-ory, but I didn't have a hope of actually making a charm work. And then Protective and Defensive Magic, after lunch. I doubted I'd do well at that either. The only prospect for some relief was Magical Growth, a course that *hadn't* been covered by my parents. I rather suspected it was intended to help bring out my magic.

A hand fell on my shoulder. I jumped.

"I hear you had some trouble this morning," Alana whispered, as I turned. She looked far too bright and cheerful for someone who'd woken up at a truly uncivilised hour. "Who helped you to get out of it?"

"No one," I said.

Alana beamed. Someone who didn't know her very well would have missed the malice behind the smile. "I *told* everyone you were a great magician," she said. "Thank you for proving me right."

I stared at her in stark disbelief. She'd found a way to circumvent the binding, all right - and in a manner I'd never expected. She hadn't told her dorm mates that I couldn't do magic, she'd told them I was *great* at magic! Of *course* someone had told Isabella. Chances were there was someone friendly to House Rubén in Cat Dorm. And then Isabella - of course - had decided to test me. Maybe she'd been surprised when I'd freed myself, but it hardly proved great magic. Anyone with a tiny spark could escape that spell.

"You utter..."

I ran out of words. There was literally nothing in my vocabulary that suited Alana, not at that moment. Even the words I'd learnt from apprentices who'd splashed molten liquid on themselves didn't seem to fit.

Alana...had set me up for utter disaster. It wouldn't take long for Isabella to realise that I wasn't a great magician at all.

Alana winked at me. "Well put," she said. She held up a timetable. I barely had a chance to glance at it before she yanked it away and refolded it. "And it seems we're sharing two classes today. Embarrass me and you'll regret it."

She skipped away, whistling. I gave her the finger, then turned back to my breakfast. It was cold, but I found it hard to care. All of a sudden, I didn't feel like eating. I cursed her under my breath as I tossed the remainder into the bin, then headed to the door. There were just over ten minutes before I had to be in class.

Rose waved to me as I passed, but I pretended not to see. I just couldn't bear the thought of talking to her, not any longer.

It wasn't her. It was me.

CHAPTER

EIGHT

The doors to the classroom were locked and warded when we arrived, so we formed an orderly queue and waited. I was glad to lean against the wall as Isabella and Alana glared at each other, neither one seemingly willing to cast the first spell. Given how both of them had formed a posse of other students, getting into a fight and *losing* would be disastrous. It was far too early for their reputations to survive taking a beating. The boys seemed to be organising themselves too, although it seemed a little more physical. There was much pushing and shoving, which quieted remarkably quickly as the magisters walked up and opened the door.

"Take a seat," one ordered. "And be quiet."

The other strode past him into the classroom. I followed the rest of the students, looking around with interest. The walls were lined with geometric charts and equation tables, each one referring to a different branch of magic. I knew some of them from Dad's lessons, but others were new. Deciphering the easier ones would take weeks, I suspected. I took a seat near the front of the class and waited. Rose sat next to me a moment later, her face pale. I did my best to ignore her.

She's trying to be your friend, a voice whispered at the back of my mind. *Why not talk to her?*

I shook my head. People had tried to be my friend before, until they'd discovered I had little or no magical ability. They *certainly* hadn't tried to befriend me after they'd realised I wasn't going to inherit. Alana would be popular for the rest of her life, simply because she could bestow largesse at will. What did *I* have to offer? Rose would try to be my friend until she learned the truth, then she'd reject me. And how could I blame her? Befriending me would simply paint a target on her back.

Stop feeling sorry for yourself, I told myself, sternly. *And sit up.*

The two professors stood at the front of the class, studying us. I studied them back, trying to place them. One was tall, his yellowish skin and dark almond eyes suggesting that he had travelled from far-off Cathay, although it was rather more likely that he was the son or grandson of a trading family who'd settled in Shallot. His companion was short, with pale skin and a bald dome lined with curly black hair. He wore three pairs of spectacles, one balanced on his nose and two more placed on his oversized head. I couldn't tell if his skull was an illusion, a trick of the light or the result of a magical accident. Someone *might* have tried to enhance his brainpower by making his skull larger, but it didn't strike me as very safe. Only a complete idiot would try to cast such spells on *himself*.

The tall professor stepped forward. "Greetings," he said. He waved a hand at the door, which closed with a loud bang. "The door will be locked five minutes into the lesson and will remain locked until the end. Anyone who gets here after the door is locked will be marked absent and will have detention, a very unpleasant detention. There will be no further warnings."

He gave us a tight smile, then produced a sheet of paper. "Alana Aguirre...?"

I forced myself to relax as he ran through the register, making a couple of sharp notes on the paper when two boys were found to be absent. Several glanced at me - including Akin - when they heard my name, clearly wondering if I too was a power. I rather doubted they were impressed with what they saw. I sat alone, save for Rose. And it wouldn't take them long to work out that she was common-born. None of them would have seen her before now.

"Right," the professor said, when he'd finished the register. "I am Magister Grayson, Practical Charms. This" - he nodded to his colleague - "is Magister Von Rupert, Theoretical Charms. You may have heard of us."

I felt my eyebrows rise. The Grayson-Von Rupert partnership was *famous*. They'd unlocked nearly a hundred spells from the old spellbooks, rewriting the equations until just about anyone could use them without some of the more exotic incantations. Their books were on the reading list of *everyone* who aspired to sorcery. And they were going to teach us? I sat upright, sensing the rest of the class doing the same. This was going to be a *great* class...

...Or it would be, if I didn't need magic.

Von Rupert stepped forward. "Welcome," he said. His voice was soft, almost impossible to hear. "How many of you have cast Anna's Amphibian?"

I glanced around the classroom. Nearly every arm was raised. Mine wasn't, of course. Nor was Rose's. A pale-faced boy in the rear looked torn between claiming to have cast it or not, his hand hovering in the air. I couldn't place the face, suggesting he was another common-born student. Chances were he hadn't been having an easy time of it in the dorms either.

"Of course you...ah...have," Von Rupert said. "It is one of the simplest spells, used to turn someone into a frog. Ah...it is practically *traditional* to turn people into frogs. But...ah...all it is good for is turning people into frogs. Why is that the case?"

Rose nudged me. "Why *frogs*?"

I opened my mouth to answer, then thought better of it. The common or garden frog is the most *useful* animal, as far as potions are concerned. There isn't a part of it that *can't* be used for something. Mum bred frogs in the garden because she needed a new one for her potions every week or so. But I didn't think that Rose would find that very reassuring, not after Isabella had turned *her* into a frog. It would be kinder not to tell her.

Grayson eyed her, sharply. "Why is that the case?"

Rose coloured. "I..."

I felt the back of my neck heat as I heard titters from behind me. The answer was obvious, of course, but *Rose* wouldn't know it. She hadn't had time to go through all the basic spellbooks, let alone the more advanced - or forbidden - tomes in the family library. I didn't think she was stupid, but she lacked knowledge. And I felt a stab of sudden, intense pity.

"The spell is tightly focused on the frog transformation," I said, quickly. Dad had drilled that into me, along with plenty of other useless pieces of knowledge. Useless to me, if not anyone else. "It cannot be modified, for example, to turn someone into a cat instead."

"Correct," Von Rupert said. His voice sounded a little steadier. "Ah... the spell is so tightly woven that it cannot be modified. A magician who wants to do something different would be better off writing their own spell or adapting a pre-existing one. Those of you who want to truly... ah...*master* magic must learn how to adapt spells, then write your own. A finely-tuned spell you crafted yourself will be far more flexible than any you might find in a spellbook."

Rose shot me a grateful look. I shrugged back at her. She'd need to read her textbooks from cover to cover, as quickly as possible. Could she even *read*? Everyone in Shallot could read, I thought, but what about commoners from outside the city? If she couldn't read, how was she expected to study the textbooks? Of *course* she could read.

"The first half of this class will concentrate on working out theoretical spells," Grayson informed us, as he dumped a pile of papers on the first desk. The boy sitting there took one and passed the others on. "The second half will attempt to put theory into practice. We will be most displeased if any of you attempt to cast a basic spell, instead of your own work. And we *will* notice."

I glanced down at my paper. It was a complex set of equations, only comprehensible because Mum and Dad had spent years training me - and my sisters - to read them. Beside me, Rose let out a tiny gasp. The notation had to be completely incomprehensible to her. I didn't think she could tell the difference between hand-waving directions, finger-motions and chants, let alone runes and sigils carved into metal or stone. Not that it mattered, I suspected. She probably had enough raw power to compensate for any early problems.

"There is a mistake somewhere within these equations," Grayson said. "Find it."

There was a groan, somewhere from behind me. I liked to think that Isabella found the exercise daunting, although I doubted it. *She* would have been drilled as intensely as any of us, with the added advantage of having a brother who was equally schooled in magic. Maybe it was one of the other girls. It had definitely sounded feminine.

I pushed the thought aside as I worked my way through the equations. It looked crude to my eyes, yet it should have been effective. And yet...Dad would have laughed at us, if we'd tried to present him with such a spell. It was utterly inefficient, wasting magic on a terrifying scale. Beside me, Rose looked utterly stumped. She didn't even know where to begin.

Think, I told myself. *What is the spell intended to do?*

It took me nearly twenty minutes to parse out the equations and realise what - precisely - was wrong. The professors had overdone it, working three or four spells into one. If someone managed to cast it - and I didn't think Alana could have cast it - the result would have been hugely amplified. A simple cantrip designed to lift a stone into the air would have sent it cracking into the ceiling instead. I looked up, wondering just how many times the ceiling had been damaged. But then, there would be protections in place...

...Wouldn't there?

Von Rupert cleared his throat. "Ah...are you all finished?"

There was a rumble of agreement. Rose looked terrified.

"Very good," Grayson said. He pointed a finger at Akin. "What was wrong with the spell?"

Isabella's brother *sounded* confident, at least. "There are actually five spells," he said, calmly. I blinked. *Five* spells? "Only one of them is strictly necessary. The remainder should be removed to save magic."

"Ah...interesting," Von Rupert said. "Ah...would anyone like to disagree?"

There was a long pause. I looked down at my paper. I couldn't *see* a fifth spell. Had I missed something or...had he separated one of the spells I'd found into two? I ran through it quickly, silently testing the concept in my head. If I was right, Akin had made a serious mistake. But did I dare comment on it? I already had far too many enemies...

I held up my hand. "Ah, you," Von Rupert said, pointing at me. "You disagree?"

"Yes," I said. All of a sudden, this seemed a very bad idea. I could feel my sister's gaze boring into my back. "There are two spells designed to lift something, one of which is too big to be efficient, and two spells designed to impart speed. You only really need one of each - and with a little effort, you can meld them together."

Von Rupert gave me an approving smile. "Very good," he said. I couldn't help feeling a flicker of pride. Praise from Von Rupert was worth more, far more, than praise from my parents. "Ah...more *advanced* spells are melds of incants, woven together into a whole. Separating them too far can weaken the combined effect."

Grayson took a step forward. "Many of you will think that we are going back to the basics here," he said. "And you will be right. You have to master the early steps before you can start writing your own spells. If you don't understand what you're doing, you can cause all sorts of problems. A simple misstep can lead to disaster."

He smiled, rather thinly. "And now, rewrite the spell we gave you," he added. "But do *not* try to cast it until we have checked it."

I bent my head over the paper as my mood soured. I could rewrite the spell until I was blue in the face, but it wouldn't matter. I couldn't even *begin* to cast it. They might give me high marks for theoretical work, yet I couldn't graduate without proving I could actually cast my own spells. Von Rupert's praise was meaningless. I couldn't even study magic without magic of my own.

Rose nudged me. "I don't know what to do," she whispered. "Help!"

"You're going to have to spend months studying the equations," I muttered back. Rose hadn't even touched *her* paper. "I can show you books, if you want."

"Please," Rose said. "Where do I even start?"

I shrugged as I started to work on my paper. "You don't need half of this," I said. I was fairly sure the spell was intended to lift something up into the air. There certainly didn't seem to be any other purpose, as far as I could tell. "Cut it out, then meld this section into that section..."

Rose shook her head. "I'm never going to get this right."

"You will," I muttered, sourly. "The more you use magic, the easier it will be to understand."

It felt like *years* before Grayson started to make his way around the room, reading papers and offering everything from approval to caustic comments. I couldn't help feeling a flicker of dark amusement as he berated Gayle Fitzwilliam for creating a spell that would send *her* flying into the ceiling, then despondency as he praised Isabella and Akin for their work. One by one, chairs and desks started floating into the air as the approved spells were cast. Gayle looked utterly thunderous when I glanced at her, her cheeks burning with shame. She was an only child, if I recalled correctly. Her family expected great things from her.

"Use mine, when the time comes to cast a spell," I muttered to Rose. She gave me a surprised look. "Yours is a mess."

She opened her mouth, either to argue or to thank me, but my chair shook before she could say a word. I drifted up into the air, held by an invisible force...I glanced back to see Alana smirking at me, her finger pointed at the chair. She could drop me from a great height...I gritted my teeth, refusing to let fear or panic overcome me. The chair wobbled a second later, threatening to tip over...

"Not bad, but your sister is a little *too* heavy for the spell," Grayson said. I found myself lowered back to the ground. "You need extra power if you want to levitate her safely."

"Thank you, sir," Alana said.

Grayson picked up my paper and studied it, then nodded curtly. "Cast the spell."

I lifted my hand and went through the motions, chanting the words one by one. Nothing happened, of course. Grayson lifted his eyebrows, then rechecked the paper. It should have worked. He wouldn't have let me try it if it shouldn't have worked. And yet...

"Try again," he ordered.

Nothing happened, again. Grayson frowned, then moved onto Rose. I wanted to cover my ears as he told her off for doing *nothing*, although it wasn't remotely fair. She didn't even know where to *begin*. And then there was a crash behind me.

"Detention," Grayson said. He strode past me, his robes billowing angrily around him. "Go to the kitchens on Saturday and do whatever the cooks tell you to do."

I resisted the urge to turn and look as I heard someone - a boy, I thought - spluttering behind me. It was an awful punishment for someone who had probably never cooked or cleaned in his entire life. But I found it hard to feel sorry for him when I'd just revealed my lack of magic to the entire class. Some of them might believe there had been a flaw in the spell, some overriding reason why I hadn't been able to cast it, but others would suspect the truth.

Rose glanced at me. "Do you want me to...?"

Von Rupert cut her off. "Ah, homework is an essay on the twenty-nine letters of the basic runic alphabet," he said. "I expect you to list all of the basics, then outline their uses in geometric diagrams."

"Do *not* attempt to use any of the runes or modified letters outside class," Grayson added, firmly. "We *will* know if you try and you *will* be punished. Dismissed."

I rose with the others. Three hours...it was lunchtime now. And after lunch...another chance to humiliate myself in front of my dorm mates. No doubt Isabella was already planning revenge for how I'd embarrassed her brother. The sooner I got my hands on some Devices, the better. I might just be able to surprise her if I had a Device or two up my sleeve.

"Come on," Rose said. She seemed to have attached herself to me. "We have to get to the hall before the food runs out."

I shrugged. "You need to do more reading," I said. "Go to the library after class."

Rose gave me a hopeful look. "Will you come with me?"

It was on the tip of my tongue to say no, but I reconsidered. I'd been cruel to Rose earlier, even as I'd helped her. Maybe I should...

And yet she will leave, when she finds out the truth, my thoughts mocked. *And you'll be alone again.*

I told my thoughts to shut up. I'd take whatever I could get.

CHAPTER

NINE

The Protective and Defensive Magic classroom was smaller than I had expected, but otherwise largely identical to the Charms classroom. Twenty-one desks and chairs, a single heavy chair at the front and a large fire, burning merrily in the fireplace. The walls were decorated with images of people being jinxed, hexed, or cursed. I felt my stomach heave at some of the latter, remembering my Dad's strict instructions never to even *think* of using curses unless we were in real danger. The average magician, he'd said, never needed anything more dangerous than hexes to defend himself.

A single old lady sat in the heavy chair, so frail and weak that I half-thought she was an illusion. She looked to be in her nineties, with bushy white hair, pale skin and bright blue eyes, which flickered over us as we sat down. She couldn't be the teacher, could she? I'd expected Protective and Defensive Magic to be taught by a man. But that proved nothing. I glanced at Rose - she'd stuck with me all though lunch - and then forced myself to try to calm down and relax. It didn't work. I knew this class was going to be another disaster.

The seats behind us rapidly filled. I heard my name and, turning, saw Bella sitting at the very back. She gave me an uncertain smile, then turned her attention back to her new friends. I supposed I should be glad to be ignored. Akin and Isabella followed, just as the clock started to chime. There was no sign of Alana.

I turned back, just in time to see the old woman rise from her chair. She looked even more frail as she stood, her mouth shaping into a smile that revealed a number of missing or rotting teeth. And yet, there was a strength about her that reminded me of my mother and her grandmother. She stood without a cane, without leaning on anything...her will was strong, even if her body was weak. And it was willpower that drove magic.

The door banged closed. We jumped.

"Greetings," the old lady said. I flinched. Her aristocratic voice sounded a little like Great Aunt Stregheria. "Welcome to Protective and Defensive Magic. I am Magistra Solana. You will have two years with me, learning the basics. Should you survive--" she gave us a toothy grin "--you will go on to take the *next* two years with a different teacher. I..."

A bell rang loudly as the door opened. I glanced back, just in time to see Alana and Zeya McDonald trying to sneak into the classroom. They both looked as if they'd run for miles, which wasn't too unlikely. The classroom was right at the far side of the school, well away from anywhere else. I couldn't help thinking that was a little ominous.

"And why," Solana demanded, "are you two young ladies late for class?"

Alana opened her mouth. She looked shaken. Solana probably reminded her of Great Aunt Stregheria too. "I..."

"I see the dictation of firsties hasn't improved," Solana said. She sneered. Alana cowered back. "Take a seat at the front of the class, then shut up. Your classmates can tell you what little you missed later."

She cleared her voice as the door banged closed, again. "I won't be merciful a second time," she added, as she produced the register. "Anyone stupid enough to be late will receive a detention."

I resisted the urge to smirk at Alana. Sitting so close to the teacher, there was no hope of getting away with anything. But she'd been looking forward to this class ever since she'd read the brochure. She knew hundreds of spells already, of course, but here...she would have a chance to learn more.

"This is the most dangerous class in school," Solana informed us, when she'd confirmed that everyone was present. "And yes, this is *more* dangerous than forgery, potions and charms put together. I will not stand for any tomfoolery in my classroom, unless I specifically authorise it. If you treat this subject with anything less than the utmost seriousness, I will give you detention and then ban you from my classroom. Those of you with a magical background may think you know everything, but that merely means you have a great deal to unlearn."

I frowned. Dad wouldn't have lied to us, would he?

"The *purpose* of this class is to teach you how to defend yourselves and others against hostile or dark magic," Solana continued, after a long chilling moment. "By the time you take your exams at the end of the year, you will know how to use defensive magic *and* have a reasonably good grounding in the law regarding defensive magic. Or, in simpler terms, you will learn what you can and cannot do."

She paused. "Not that such considerations matter," she added. "When you are at risk, you do everything in your power to escape and worry about the rest later."

"Escape?" Alana muttered. "Not fight."

Solana whirled around to face her, moving with surprising speed for such an old lady. "What was that?"

Alana looked downcast. "I...I...I thought we would be fighting, not escaping."

"Well, at least that's a marginally more coherent statement than your last one," Solana said, sardonically. She raised her voice. "Can anyone tell me why I'm more interested in teaching you to escape rather than to fight?"

There was a long pause. No one answered.

"You are *twelve*," Solana said. She stepped away from Alana, her cold eyes sweeping the room. I shivered when she looked at me. "No one, not even I, expects you to fight. And while you may *think* you can cast Anna's Amphibian in an eyeblink, I assure you that any half-way decent sorcerer could shrug the spell off even quicker. Casting the spell on your siblings or servants does *not* teach you how to fight sorcerers. Trying to turn a sorcerer like me into a frog will just waste magic.

"If you are cornered, then fight. But if there's a chance to escape, take it. You do not live in a storybook world where adults are useless and kids regularly win fights against enemies twice their age. The older the enemy, the more power they have at their disposal. Escape, not fight. Leave the fighting to the adults."

I wished, suddenly, that I dared look behind me. I wanted to know how the rest of the class felt. Rose seemed unsure; Alana looked cowed, as long as Solana was looking in her direction. The ancient crone had a point, I felt. But I didn't think anyone wanted to believe her.

Solana clapped her hands together. "And now we've got that out of the way," she said nastily, "what *is* dark magic?"

She pointed a finger over my head. "Yes, you. Boy who has his hand in the air."

"Dark magic is magic used to hurt someone," Akin said. He didn't sound too annoyed at his earlier failure. "To choose to cause harm is dark magic."

"Almost correct," Solana said. "Dark magic is magic used with bad intentions. You'll find there is no real legal definition of the dark arts because almost any spell can be used to hurt an innocent victim. Even a simple lifting spell can become dark if you float someone into the air and then let them fall."

I shuddered. I couldn't help myself.

"Your intentions shape the magic," Solana continued. "If you didn't want to hurt or kill someone, it doesn't count as dark magic. If you acted in self-defence or defence of another, it doesn't count as dark magic. You'll find, when you come to do your homework, that there are plenty of legal arguments surrounding even the simplest of curses. You'll be required to argue the question time and time again over the next few years."

She paused. "Yes? You have a question?"

I turned. A boy I didn't recognise had his hand in the air. "If I turn someone into a frog and they get squashed by a passing cart," he said, "would I have used dark magic?"

"Not if you didn't *mean* for them to get killed," Solana said, simply. She paused. "Do not imagine this would save you from consequences. You would be innocent of using dark magic, not of reckless endangerment."

She cleared her throat. "A further danger is that the use of dark magic tends to encourage the use of *more* dark magic," she added. "Once you cross that line, once you deliberately decide to embrace the darkness, it's very hard to save yourself. It becomes harder and harder to think clearly - eventually, you go insane. Even the simplest spells can send you falling into the darkness."

Rose nudged me. "Then why don't they ban dark magic?"

Solana proved to have very sharp ears. "Because they cannot forbid the use of nearly every known spell," she said, dryly. "A handful of spells *are* on the banned list, but I assure you that dark wizards don't need to use them to start their decline."

She smiled, rather coldly. "I want you all to *think* about what you're doing," she warned. "Rest assured, you will *not* pass this class without careful thought."

And magic, I thought.

Solana's smile grew wider. "Alana," she said. Her voice dripped honey - and ice. "Why don't you come forward?"

I felt a stab of unexpected sympathy as my sister rose and walked to the front of the class, her hands clasped behind her back. She hid it well, but Alana was clearly nervous, if not terrified. She looked as though she was going to her own execution. Solana pointed to a space in front of her desk, then stepped backwards. Alana held herself upright by force of will. I was, reluctantly, impressed.

"I am *sure* you know how to cast Anna's Amphibian," Solana said. "Cast it now."

Alana blinked. "On...on you?"

"No, on the floor," Solana said, sarcastically. "On me."

I tensed as Alana waved her hand. She was an expert at casting the spell, as I knew all too well, but she messed it up the first time. The spell splintered out of existence before it even left her hand, the light breaking up and fading back into nothingness. Solana snorted nastily and ordered Alana to try again. This time, there was a ball of light that flashed towards Solana...and stopped, dead, in the air. I stared in disbelief as the light hovered, just waiting. I'd never seen anything like that before, not even from Dad!

"You'll draw two lessons from this instead of one," Solana said. She spoke to all of us, but she never took her eyes off Alana. "The first one is that fear - an adverse fear response - is not conductive to casting spells. In the time it took Alana to get the spell *right*, I could have hexed or cursed her a dozen times over. If you should happen to get yourselves into real trouble, as you probably will if you walk around convinced you know everything, you'll be terrified. Learning to work magic even *when* terrified is important."

She eyed Alana unpleasantly. "And the second lesson is this," she added, jabbing a finger at the hovering spell. "When used on a defenceless victim, the spell is invincible; when used on a person who knows how to counter it, the spell is pathetic."

Not that it matters when you can't use magic, I thought. I'd ducked such spells more than once, but that only worked when I saw them coming. *She could toss another spell at me if she wanted while I dodged the first one.*

Solana put a hand forward, touching the spell. The eldritch light flickered, then darted back to Alana. My sister threw up her hands, too late. The spell crashed into her and she morphed into a wooden chair. My mouth fell open in shock. I heard gasps from behind me. Alana hadn't cast that spell, had she?

"Fates," Rose muttered.

"I rewrote that spell," Solana said. She jabbed a finger at the chair - at *Alana*. "Her magic, her power...rewritten by me. And now she is trapped by her own spell."

She gave us all a tight smile. "Any questions? You, girl who looks like a ghost?"

Isabella sounded annoyed. "Von Rupert..."

"*Magister* Von Rupert," Solana corrected. Her voice hardened. "Unless you *want* Magister Grayson to be supervising your detentions from now till winter."

There was a pause. "*Magister* Von Rupert said that the spell couldn't be altered," Isabella said, tartly. "Was he wrong?"

Solana smiled. "It would be more *accurate* to say that it would be easier to use a very different transfiguration spell than adapt Anna's Amphibian to serve another purpose," she said. "But as you're meant to be learning to build spells up from the bare basics, what he said serves the purpose."

She waved a hand at the chair. "I want you all to think about something," she said. "That girl is now a chair. She is trapped in a very different form, unable to move...she may not even be able to perceive the world around her. And yet she is still aware. She can hear us, somehow. But she cannot answer. She cannot tell us what's happened to her."

Her voice hardened. "Some of you may think that this is a great joke," she warned. "You're laughing, deep inside. I'm sure that most of you have *been* inanimate objects, just for a short while. But think about it for a moment. What happens to *her* if I break a wooden leg? Or toss her into the fire? The spell might be a joke, but the consequences could prove lethal."

I swallowed. Beside me, Rose looked sick. Solana was right. Alana was awake in there, she was aware in there...but she had no way to communicate with the outside world. I didn't pretend to know how she could hear - there were no ears on the chair - yet it wouldn't be enough to keep her from panicking. She might be on the verge of a breakdown...

Solana snapped her fingers. There was a flash of light. Alana appeared, kneeling on the floor where the chair had been. She looked...

I couldn't put it into words. It was fear and terror and something truly awful. But it shocked me more than I cared to admit.

"I hope you understand the dangers now," Solana said, very quietly. "A simple prank can become dark magic very quickly, if one does not think."

She waited for Alana to sit down, then launched into a long lecture. Most of it I already knew, but I took careful notes anyway. I didn't want to draw Solana's attention in my direction. Besides, there was always the prospect of learning something new...

"This is a very basic defence spell," Solana finished. She held up a hand and chanted a couple of harsh words. There was a flicker of light in front of her which snapped out of existence a second later. "You can use it to deflect basic jinxes and hexes - although most curses, alas, are rarely bothered by it. Unfortunately, without proper protection, the spell has a very short lifespan. Don't try to use it as a permanent shield because it won't last."

She made us practice, again and again. Alana already knew it, but her hand was so unsteady that it took her four tries to get it right. Rose managed it on her second try and smiled so brightly that I couldn't help a surge of pure hatred. The others seemed to get it just as quickly, save for me. I made the gestures and said the words, but nothing happened.

"Get the timing right," Solana ordered, as she started to move down the line of desks, casting small jinxes on each of us. Alana deflected her spell, easily. I thought I saw her smile, just for a second, as her confidence returned. "Cast it too early and it will fail, cast it too late and it will be worse than useless."

I shuddered as she stopped in front of Rose, then cast the jinx. Rose cast her spell a second later, sending the jinx rattling off into the ceiling. Solana nodded in cold approval - I could practically *feel* Rose vibrating in excitement - and then moved to face me. Her expression suggested I was in deep trouble. And I was right.

She cast the jinx slowly, giving me plenty of time to see it coming. It didn't matter. I said the words and made the gestures, but her jinx still struck me. My skin started to itch a moment later. It took all of my determination not to start scratching as she gave me a disappointed look, then cast a second hex. Once again, nothing happened. The itch only got worse.

"Work on it," she ordered, curtly.

Alana was muttering to Bella about writing to Dad, as we left the classroom. He could write an official complaint, perhaps even get Solana sacked. Alana's voice rose as she argued her case, but I found it hard to care. A simple spell, one so easy that a complete novice like Rose had managed it on her second try...and I had failed, once again. Everyone had seen me fail.

And the more they saw me fail, the more they would believe I was nothing more than a zero.

"You'll get it," Rose said, trying to be encouraging. "I'm sure you will."

"Hah," I grumbled. I peeked at my timetable. Had it really been over two hours since lunchtime? "One more class before dinner and sleep."

"And the library," Rose reminded me. "You said you'd come with me."

I sighed. The library...at least it would be better than being trapped in the dorm.

"All right," I said. "We'll go after dinner."

CHAPTER
TEN

"I must say you're quite an interesting case, Caitlyn," Magistra Haydon said. Her green eyes studied me as though she wanted to dissect me. "I've seen students with low magic before, of course, but you're lower than any of them."

I chose to look around her office rather than answer her. It was a simple room, lined with bookshelves and a large painting of a sour-faced woman in purple robes. There was something about it I would have found comforting, if Magistra Haydon hadn't reminded me so much of my mother. Mum could see through any number of excuses, half-truths and blatant lies. And Magistra Haydon gave me the same impression. She was a woman who was good at talking, but not so good at listening.

Reluctantly, I dragged my attention back to her. Her hair was blue, contrasting oddly with her dark skin, green eyes and white robe. I would have put her age at forty, although with magic a magician could look any age she chose. She wouldn't have gone into healing - and magical growth - if she hadn't been a very skilled magician. But that didn't stop her from looking at me as though I was nothing more than a particularly interesting specimen.

"I've had quite a bit of experience with low-magic students," she offered, after a moment. "I think they mostly came from commoner backgrounds, although a few" - her lips pursed -"had repressed their magic for various reasons. There was a girl who..."

She shook her head. "Can you think of any reason you shouldn't have magic?"

I shrugged. There was none. I'd been born to two magicians, I'd grown up in a magical environment, my two sisters were both strongly magical... there was no reason to assume I shouldn't have magic. And really, I'd had a comfortable life. My parents had given us tools to develop magic almost as soon as we could use them. They'd known precisely how to fan the spark into a flame.

"Your parents have given me permission to try a few experiments," Magistra Haydon said, softly. "Do I have *your* permission?"

I shrugged, again. This was a waste of time. "Do you *need* it?"

"You're not an adult, yet," Magistra Haydon said. "You won't come of age for another four years - and even then, you will be guided by your parents for another three. But it is better to work with you than against you. It *is* for your own good."

"And that means you're going to go ahead anyway," I said, tartly. There were horror stories about what happened to children who were deemed insufficiently magical. "Is that right?"

Magistra Haydon's smile grew wider. "I have no intention of doing anything to hurt you," she said. She *sounded* sincere. "Now, tell me. Have your parents done anything to you that you resent?"

"They made me go to school and talk to you," I said, before I could stop myself. The words just came tumbling out. She'd put a spell on me... no, in the air. Maybe not a full-blooded truth spell, but enough to encourage me to talk. "You..."

I stopped myself. Her smile grew a little strained. I felt a flicker of vindictive pleasure. Dad had talked about the downside of truth spells more than once - he worked with them at Magus Court - and about how the caster might hear more than they wished.

Served her right, I thought nastily. *She'd wanted me to talk, and she'd got exactly what she wanted.*

"Many other students have felt the same way," Magistra Haydon said. She recovered magnificently, I admitted. "But my help has often made the difference between success and failure."

She paused. "Why *do* you resent your parents for sending you to school?"

I clamped my mouth firmly closed until I had put an answer together. "I don't have magic," I said. Admitting that *hurt*, but it wasn't as though Magistra Haydon didn't know the problem already. "I can't cast a single spell."

Magistra Haydon looked back at me, evenly. "Do you realise how unprecedented that is?"

I nodded. Dad had gone through *stacks* of old books as he'd come to realise, slowly, that I would never match my sisters. Low magic was one thing, but *no* magic? And no *sensitivity* to magic? There were more stories of children being *born* with magic, using it in their cradles, than adults without magic. I'd even heard a story about a boy who'd been born with magic so powerful that none of the other magicians could match him. He'd been so strong that he could make spells work just by willing it...

But I didn't have any magic at all.

"It's much more likely that you repressed your magic, somehow," Magistra Haydon said, gently. "And whatever caused it would have had to be so far in the past that you've forgotten it."

I frowned. "Is that likely?"

"There was a boy I helped who was utterly terrified of water," Magistra Haydon informed me. "It turned out that he had almost drowned as a toddler. He'd forgotten the incident itself, but not the fear. I brought it out and helped him to come to terms with it."

"And he's a champion swimmer now?" I guessed. It was hard to keep the sarcasm out of my voice. If the solution was that simple, Mum or Dad would have thought of it. "And you think you can do that to me?"

"You're quite a defensive girl," Magistra Haydon said. "You wrap yourself up in sarcasm to keep from being hurt. And yet you also push back as hard as you can."

"That's not an answer," I said. I *had* to push back. My sisters would walk all over me if I didn't. "Do you think you can do that to me?"

"It's worth exploring," Magistra Haydon said. She shrugged. "I can give you tools and let you play with them for the next hour, but I think that would be pointless. Whatever is blocking your magic won't let them work. Think about it."

She rang the bell for a maid. "Do you prefer hot milk or chocolate?"

"Chocolate," I said, quickly. "Why?"

Magistra Haydon ordered tea for herself and hot chocolate for me, then smiled. "It helps you to relax," she said, simply. "And I need an answer. Do you want me to reach into your past?"

I tensed. "How?"

"I'd use a spell to put you in a hypnotic state, then walk you backwards until we reached the incident," Magistra Haydon said, simply. "Don't worry. I'm not allowed to share anything I learn with anyone."

"Apart from my parents," I grumbled.

The maid returned, carrying a mug of hot chocolate and a pot of tea. I sipped mine gingerly, wondering if she'd slipped a potion into the brew. It wouldn't be hard - the hot chocolate was flavourful enough to hide a mild sedative. But I thought not...I didn't feel tired, not after what she'd said. I felt alarmed. And yet, part of me wanted to believe she might be right.

"Very well," I said, finally. "Do it."

"Finish your chocolate first," Magistra Haydon said, wryly. "And then lean back in your chair and relax."

The hot chocolate tasted great, I thought, as an unaccustomed warmth spread through my body. I felt...I felt tired, yet safe. I was vaguely aware of her speaking to me, but it seemed unimportant. The entire world just seemed to fade away until I was floating in a warm haze of peace. Her voice was gone, I thought. There was just peace and quiet and tranquillity...

I jerked awake, almost dropping the mug. "What happened?"

Magistra Haydon was sitting behind her desk. "I'm not sure," she admitted. She *had* to be rattled. She would never have admitted that to me if she hadn't been. "The spell worked, at first. You fell into a trance. But afterwards...I'm not sure what happened after that. I should have been able to walk you back without trouble."

I sat upright. My body felt...odd, as if it couldn't decide if I was tired or not. "What *did* happen?"

"You just stayed in the trance," Magistra Haydon said. "I didn't dare try to bring you out, not when the spell was behaving oddly. I had to wait until you surfaced on your own."

She peered at me, narrowly. "What did *you* feel?"

"Peace," I said, finally. "Just...peace."

"I see," Magistra Haydon said. She reached into a desk drawer and produced a pen-like tool, holding it out to me. "Try this, will you?"

I took the pen and waved it in the air. Nothing happened. Why was I not surprised?

"I'll be in touch," Magistra Haydon said, after a moment. "I need to consult with your parents."

"You could tell them to pull me out," I said. The peace was gone. "I don't belong here."

Magistra Haydon lifted her eyebrows. "Do you know how many students are rejected each year?"

I looked back at her. "Do *you* know how many students are admitted because of family connections?"

"No, and neither do you," Magistra Haydon said. "All I know is that you have an opportunity to study that you would not get anywhere else."

"Or to get permanently turned into a frog," I snapped. The anger and bitterness threatened to bubble over. "I can't work magic. I can't *sense* magic. I'm blind and deaf in a world ruled by the seeing and the hearing. How long will it be before I get killed because I can't use magic to defend myself?"

Magistra Haydon looked back at me, evenly. It suddenly dawned on me that I had never dared speak to my mother like that, not once.

"You may also learn how to use magic," she said, finally. "Or how to... compensate for your problems. You would hardly be the first low-magic student to pass through the gates."

"I'm the first *no*-magic student," I snapped.

I rose and stormed towards the door. She could have called me back - or yanked me back - at any second, but instead she just let me go. I wasn't sure if that was a good thing or not, really. Magistra Haydon talked a good game, but everyone she'd helped in the past had *some* spark of magic. I had nothing.

"Caitlyn," a voice called. I turned to see an upperclassman, a fifth-year. He looked oddly familiar, with a lanky body and pale face, but I didn't recognise him. "How are you?"

"Fine," I lied. I wanted to sit down and think. Who *was* this stranger? He was an upperclassman. Would he be offended if I admitted I'd forgotten him? "It's been a long day."

"The first day is always the longest," he said. He stuck out a calloused hand. "Robin, Robin Brandon. I think we only met once."

I smiled as it clicked. "Brian's brother," I said. He'd been at the ceremony when Dad had taken Brian as an apprentice, but that had been two years ago. I vaguely recalled a pudgy boy who hadn't grown up yet...he'd changed, over the last two years. He'd lost weight and shot upwards like a rocket. "He always spoke well of you."

Robin smiled. "I'm glad to hear it," he said. "Are you enjoying your first day at school?"

I shook my head. "No," I said. A thought struck me and I leaned forward. "Can you...find some things for me?"

"Maybe," Robin said. "It would depend on what you wanted. I might have to get them smuggled through the walls..."

"Some tools," I said. "Casting Chalk, potions ingredients...maybe a few other pieces."

Robin's smile grew wider. "Planning to have some fun, are you?"

I smiled back. "Something like that..."

"I'll see what I can find," Robin said. "And how are you going to pay?"

We haggled all the way to the library. It was a new experience for me, although Mum *had* insisted that I learn to barter even as a child. Robin might be well-disposed towards me, but he wasn't going to give anything away for free. I finally beat him down to five golden crowns for the whole set, if he got it to me by the end of the week. As soon as we shook hands, he reached into his pocket and produced a piece of Casting Chalk.

"Bigger than that," I said, crossly.

"It'll do for starters," Robin assured me. "Just don't get caught with it or you'll be in trouble."

I nodded, then waved goodbye as we approached the library. Robin wouldn't want to be seen with a mere firstie, even if *I* was connected to him through a tangled web of apprenticeship and obligation. He had his reputation to consider. I pushed open the library door and instantly fell in love. The immense room was utterly *lined* with bookshelves, crammed with so many books that it looked impossible to pull even a single one from the shelves without bringing down the rest. And yet...

A dozen students were floating in the air, pulling books from the shelves and checking their pages before either floating the tomes down to the ground or replacing them on the shelves. I looked up...the stacks towered above me, reaching high into the air. A giant couldn't have reached the topmost shelf without magic. I groaned out loud as I realised I would never be able to reach more than the lowermost shelves. There were no ladders, no steps...just magic.

Rose was seated at a small table, looking despondent. I sighed and walked over to join her as she struggled through a textbook. Someone had lied to her, I noted, or they simply hadn't realised that a common-born wouldn't have read even the basic books. The textbook she'd been given was incomprehensible without some of the background details.

"That's not a good choice of book," I said, as I surveyed the nearby shelves. The library was nearly empty, thankfully. According to my mother, it was also neutral ground. The librarians wouldn't hesitate to evict anyone who caused trouble. "You really need to start with the basics."

I paused as a thought struck me. "Can you read?"

"Not much," Rose admitted. "I didn't even take any lessons until last year."

"Ouch," I said. I'd been reading since I was three. Mum and Dad had made sure I knew how to read and write before moving on to older languages. It struck me, suddenly, that Rose and I had something in common. I couldn't reach more than a third of the books in the library, if that, but she couldn't *read* them. "You'll get better at it, won't you?"

"I hope so," Rose said.

I pulled a book off the shelf and held it out to her. "This is the very basic textbook," I said. I decided not to mention that most magical children outgrew it very quickly. "It's the fundamentals you need to master before you can pass classes."

"You make it look easy," Rose said.

I gave her a sharp look, but she was sincere. It was all I could do to keep from bursting out into hysterical laughter. I could write out a dozen spells - a *hundred* spells - a day, but I wouldn't be able to cast them. And without that, I wouldn't be able to pass the exams at the end of the year. I was doomed.

"I worked hard," I said, in the end. I opened the textbook, pointing to the first set of detailed explanations and examples. "Now, if you want to start here...I'll look at the next book, then check your work."

In the end, I enjoyed spending time in the library more than I'd expected. Rose wasn't *stupid*, merely ignorant. And she hung on my every word. I knew I shouldn't get used to it - she would leave me as soon as she realised the truth - but it felt good. I watched her work, while flipping through several textbooks for the upcoming classes. Despite myself, I was actually looking forward to Forging. It didn't rely *quite* so much on magic.

"It's nearly dinnertime," the librarian said, finally. She was a sour-faced woman who looked to be permanently sucking on a lemon. Mum had told me that the same woman had been librarian in her day. Some of her classmates had wondered if the librarian was actually a golem under a very strong glamour. "And we'll be closing afterwards."

We checked out a dozen books each - the basics for Rose, a handful of more advanced textbooks for me - and headed down to dinner. Alana, Bella and Isabella were all there, looking flushed. I suspected that all three of them had been practicing their defensive magics - and taking advantage of the opportunity to hex their groupies. At least they hadn't been hexing me...

"The food here is great," Rose said. She was halfway through her second plate of roast pork and potatoes. "Is it like this all the time?"

I shrugged. I didn't have the heart to tell her that I ate better at home. Instead, we ate quickly and headed back to the dorm. Sandy was sitting on her bed, reading a textbook and looking very grim. It didn't seem safe to speak to her, so we showered, got into our nightclothes and pulled the drapes shut as Isabella and the McDonalds entered. Isabella was talking loudly and boastfully of the spell she'd cast after class. I did my best to ignore her as I pulled the Casting Chalk from my pocket and drew a set of protective runes around the bed. They weren't much, but they'd have to do. Isabella certainly wouldn't be expecting them.

And when I get the rest of the tools, I thought, *we'll have to see what happens then.*

CHAPTER
ELEVEN

The interesting thing about Casting Chalk is that it responds oddly to magic.

It was yet another detail Mum and Dad had drummed into me, ever since they started trying to school me in magic. Casting Chalk - the base for a number of spells and runic rituals - has little magic of its own, but it tends to flare when exposed to outside magic. Ritualists use it to check the edges of their diagrams, knowing that when the chalk starts to flare it's time to duck for cover. And the runes I'd drawn on the floor, of little worth in themselves, would ensure that almost *any* contact with the chalk would cause a flare.

I jerked awake as I heard a crackling noise. Someone had slipped through my drapes and was trying to sneak up on my bed. And they'd stepped on the runes. I forced myself up, throwing the duvet forward. I had a brief glimpse of Isabella, light flickering around her fingertips, before the duvet crashed down on her. There was a brilliant flash of light and she shrank rapidly. She'd meant to turn me into a frog - or something equally small - but the spell had exploded against her instead. A moment later, I picked up the duvet and saw a small frog staring up at me. The remains of the chalk were already fading away.

"Hah," I said. "Got you!"

It was amazing just how much anger and hatred Isabella could communicate, even when trapped in the shape of a frog. Her bulging eyes blazed with naked rage. I didn't really blame her. She'd been trapped by her own spell! It would wear off, of course, but she would then have to admit she'd ensorcelled herself or give up trying to convince her cronies I didn't have any magic. I couldn't help wondering what choice she'd make, when the time came.

Sandy pulled back the drapes. Behind her, I could hear a number of other drapes being opened. A glance at my watch told me it was seven in the morning, just about time to get up for breakfast. Thankfully, Isabella hadn't tried her little stunt in the middle of the night, when we both would have been blamed for any noise. I was sure Sandy didn't like me.

She glared, proving me right. "What are you doing?"

"Isabella tripped one of my traps," I said, as innocently as I could. It wasn't *really* a lie, was it? "And she got turned into a frog."

"I can see that," Sandy said, crossly. She jabbed a finger at me. "Just remember; if she's late for class, you'll be blamed."

She turned and stamped off, snapping at a couple of other girls for making noise. I looked down at Isabella for a long moment, then nudged her through the drapes and back out into the open air with my foot. She could probably undo the spell easily, if she wanted. Isabella wouldn't take the risk of getting into trouble if *I* was late for class. But if she decided to skip lessons...

I told myself it wasn't worth worrying about it as I dressed, then checked my appearance in the mirror. We had forging in the morning and I was actually looking forward to it. Forging was an art that didn't require magic, not really. I'd learnt a great deal from my father and his apprentices, while Alana and Bella had concentrated on other lessons. I had even dared to hope, once upon a time, that I could become a Master Forger. But even *that* required magic.

Rose joined me as I walked down to breakfast, grinning from ear to ear. She'd seen Isabella humiliated too, although *she* had no idea what had actually happened. I wasn't about to tell her, either. Isabella would hate her all the more if she knew Rose knew the truth. The dining hall was nearly empty when we entered, save for a handful of upperclassmen who looked as though they hadn't gone to bed. They were drinking coffee like it was water.

I told myself it didn't matter, but it was still a relief when Isabella and her cronies entered the dining hall. She looked quietly furious, unsurprisingly.

There was no way she could tell *them* the truth. I resisted the urge to smirk at her and concentrated on finishing my breakfast before the hexes started flying. Rose followed me as we left, picking our way down towards the Foundry. A small line of students - all boys - was already forming outside the doors. We joined them and waited, none-too-patiently, until the doors were slammed open and we hurried into the giant room.

It looked heavenly, I thought. Twenty-one workbenches, each one covered in tools; dozens of books detailing everything from chemical compounds to designs for Objects and Devices of Power; a giant set of forges, anvils and kilns...I fell in love at first sight. I couldn't help grinning like a loon as I cast my eyes over the piles of supplies, even glancing into the dustbin. Some of the pieces of wood and metal students had thrown out over the last couple of days were still usable, if one knew what to do. I was surprised the teacher had allowed such waste.

"Choose a workbench," a voice boomed.

I stared. Magister Tallyman - I'd looked him up specially - was in his early thirties, a true *giant* of a man. His head was bald, his face was a patchwork of replaced or regenerated skin, his arms were muscular... unlike the other teachers, he wore a workman's outfit rather than fancy robes. A large belt dangled at his waist, crammed with tools: knives, spanners, a giant hammer...He should have been intimidating, but there was something about him that made me relax. His bright eyes darted from face to face, quietly assessing us. I listened attentively as he called the register and issued the standard warning about not coming late. About the only difference between him and the other tutors was that he didn't bother to threaten us with a detention for non-attendance.

"Right," Magister Tallyman said, once he'd finished the register. "Some of you will have earned badges in forging. Who has a one-star?"

I held up my hand. So did two-thirds of the class, including Alana and Akin. I knew that Bella had failed her test - and Rose would never have had the opportunity to take it - but I was surprised that *Isabella* didn't have the badge. Maybe her father had declined to teach her how to forge. Too many older magicians believed that forging was man's work.

"Very good," Magister Tallyman said. "And a two-star?"

I held up my hand again. So did Akin.

"Only two of you?" Magister Tallyman asked. "Not to worry, eh? You'll be well ahead of a two-star by the time you finish this year and you can take the test over the summer, if you want to. It won't mean anything compared to your exam paper."

He smiled. "You," he said, pointing a finger at Rose. "What is the difference between an Object of Power and a Device of Power?"

Rose flushed. "Ah...an Object of Power *lasts*, sir," she said. She wouldn't have known that if I hadn't made her read a few books last night. "A Device of Power doesn't."

"True enough," Magister Tallyman said. He jabbed a finger at one of the rickety bookshelves. I couldn't help feeling that it was on the verge of collapse. "I have books copied from the old empire - I have *originals*, passed down through the generations. I have the *instructions* for making Objects of Power. And yet, I cannot *make* them."

He waved a hand around the room. "I have the finest collection of tools in the world, gathered here," he added. "I have raw materials from all over the world. And yet, I cannot make a *single* Object of Power! Nothing I do *lasts*!"

"You must be doing something wrong," Isabella muttered.

"Well, *quite*," Magister Tallyman said. Behind me, I heard Isabella squeak. She must not have meant to say *that* out loud. "But what?"

He picked a book off the workbench and held it out. "The materials are right. The process is right. Everything is as detailed in books that survived the holocaust that destroyed the empire. And yet, the Objects of Power do not work."

Rose glanced at me, clearly asking a question. I nodded. Dad - and his apprentices - had said the same thing. In theory, we knew how to make Objects of Power; in practice, something was missing. There had to have been something left out of the ancient tomes, *all* of the ancient tomes. But what? I had gone through some of the textbooks myself, even the ones that Dad had never shared outside the family. As far as I could tell, *nothing* was missing. And yet, we couldn't duplicate the secrets of the ancients. It was frustrating.

"One day, this problem will be solved," Magister Tallyman said. I suspected *he* wanted to solve it. "But until then, we are stuck with Devices of

Power. And while Devices of Power are laughably inferior, they *are* more flexible."

He studied us for a long moment. "Partner up," he ordered. "If you have an award, try and find a partner who doesn't. I'll expect the two-stars to be *very* helpful over the next few weeks as I work to get everyone up to speed."

Akin stuck up a hand. "Do we get to give detentions?"

"No, but you get to work on extra-credit projects after class," Magister Tallyman said. I looked up, attentively. "I also need assistants to help with *my* projects. If you're interested - if you have at least a one-star - talk to me after class."

I smiled. The chance to work with a Master Forger...it wasn't something I'd pass up, even if it was unpaid. And it wasn't unpaid. Brian had told me that *he'd* worked for his teacher, putting aside a nest-egg by the time he'd become an upperclassman. After that, he'd been too busy to continue. But I wasn't going to make it to the upper years anyway. I could earn something now to keep me going after I was disowned.

"Some of you already know this," Magister Tallyman said. "But just to make sure we're on the same page..."

He launched into a long and complicated safety lecture. Most of it I already knew - Dad had made sure I knew what I was doing before I started forging - but some aspects were new. No magic in the forgery without prior permission, no horseplay...his graphic warnings of precisely *what* would happen to anyone who fooled around in the forgery were welcome, as horrific as they sounded. The forgery would be a safer place for me than anywhere else, despite the risk of being struck by molten metal or worse.

"If you don't have a one-star, you are *not* to work unsupervised until you satisfy me that you can handle your tools," Magister Tallyman concluded, after a thunderous list of accidents that had taken place over the last decade. "If you don't have a two-star, you are not to *supervise* your fellow students - and even if you do, I expect you to be careful."

Rose nudged me. "You could make more money by supervising your fellows."

I shrugged, trying not to show how much that hurt. Isabella wouldn't listen to me. None of the others would listen either, particularly as it became clear that I lacked magic. Besides, her brother could supervise her.

Magister Tallyman continued. "Your homework will consist of essays on tools, materials and how the various different kinds of metals and gemstones interact," he told us. "I expect you to be *fully* conversant with this book" - he poked a finger at a large textbook - "by the end of term. Now... with your partners...I want you to design and build a magic-sensor."

"Boring," Akin muttered.

I would have agreed, if I hadn't *needed* the sensor. It was simple enough to produce, but it lacked flexibility. A magician could determine if the magic was a jinx, a hex or something *really* nasty, while all the Device could do was detect the presence of magic. But if you couldn't sense magic in the first place...

"You need a strand of gold and silver," I told Rose. "And you have to diagram it out."

Rose blinked. "Why?"

"So you know what you are doing," I said.

I opened the notebook and wrote our names at the top. Dad had insisted I write down everything, just so I'd know what I'd done. It was, he'd claimed, the easiest way to carry out experiments. A record of what *hadn't* happened could be just as useful as knowing what *had* happened. I opened the textbook, found the page detailing the different properties of metals and held it out to her. Rose would have a steep learning curve, but she'd make it. She wasn't stupid, after all.

"I don't see how it works," she muttered, picking up a spool of gold thread. "This...this is gold, right?"

"Yeah," I agreed. "Gold reacts to magic - linked with silver, you can *pinpoint* magic. Iron is magically neutral, so it serves as a base for Devices of Power."

Rose frowned. "If it's neutral...is *that* what causes Objects of Power to fail?"

"It's been tried," Magister Tallyman said. We both jumped. For such a large man, he moved with surprising stealth. Neither of us had realised he was coming up behind us. "Iron dampens the magic. When removed...the prototypes simply failed quicker, if they worked at all. They were nothing more than expensive Devices."

He patted Rose on the shoulder. "Good thinking, though," he added. "Do you have any more thoughts?"

I felt a flicker of jealously. Rose knew nothing, beyond what I'd shown her. And yet, she'd already had a good thought...I told myself I was being stupid, really. A person with more experience would have known it was actually a *bad* thought. Iron cancelled magic, among other things. It was why iron was rarely used outside the forge.

And why iron blades are so dangerous to magicians, I thought.

"This is gold," Rose said, instead. "It must be expensive."

Magister Tallyman shrugged. "Much of what you use can be recovered," he said. "The iron is the only component that *cannot* be recycled, but it can be sifted out and used for something else. And besides, it isn't *that* high a cost."

He turned and headed over to Isabella's table, where she was quarrelling with Gayle. I hoped they weren't going to start tossing spells around, even though it was nice to see Isabella angry at someone else. The giant room was full of dangerous materials. Who knew *what* would react badly to their magic?

I carefully cut three lengths of gold and three lengths of silver, then showed Rose how to twist them together. She picked it up very quickly. I found an iron rod and wrapped the combined threads around it, making sure to leave room at the end for my hand. There was nothing to be gained by accidentally channelling the magic into my body. I'd done that once, two years ago. My sisters had laughed themselves silly. Even Dad had been amused, although he'd done his level best to hide it.

"This isn't too hard," Rose said, as she copied me. "It can't be this easy..."

"This is a very basic exercise," I assured her. I made the third rod, then dropped it in my pocket. Magister Tallyman wouldn't notice if I took it. "It gets much more complicated later on."

Magister Tallyman whistled, loudly. I glanced up at the clock. Had it really been nearly two hours since we entered the forgery?

"I'll be testing your work now," he said. "While waiting, read chapters one and two of your textbooks, with specific reference to heat used to melt raw materials."

"Do it," I told Rose. "You need to know the melting point of all sorts of metals."

Rose did as she was told, while I skimmed the textbook to see if there was something I didn't already know before reading ahead. There was nothing, although someone had added a footnote about modifications to a standard magic-dampener. Someone else had scribbled a rude note about a fellow student's body odour. I hoped Magister Tallyman didn't blame *me* for writing it.

"You have a two-star," Magister Tallyman said, stopping in front of us. He placed three fist-sized gems on the workbench, all green. "I expect good things from you."

He took my Device and held it up to the first gemstone. The Device vibrated in his hand. He nodded, then moved to the second and then the third. The Device vibrated all three times.

"Very good," he said, approvingly. I couldn't help feeling proud. "*Very* good sensitivity."

He took Rose's and repeated the test. Her Device failed the third hurdle.

"You didn't wrap the two strands tightly enough," he informed her. "It should be capable of detecting most of the spells you will encounter, but some of the more subtle ones will be missed. That could be bad."

"It's my first," Rose said.

"You'll get better," Magister Tallyman said. "Keep it, if you want. It won't last, but the first Device is always special."

He checked the last two workbenches, then raised his voice. "For homework tonight, finish reading those chapters. After that, write me an essay on the uses of opals and iron pyrites in forging. I want you to pay special attention to the principle use of iron pyrites, including the dangers involved in using it without careful preparation. I'll see you again in two days. Dismissed."

"You go to lunch," I said to Rose. "I need to speak to him."

"I'll keep a seat for you," Rose promised. "Good luck."

CHAPTER
TWELVE

I wasn't the only student waiting to speak to Magister Tallyman. Akin, the only other two-star in the class, eyed me thoughtfully as the remainder of the students filed out of the forgery. Magister Tallyman ordered us to wait five minutes while he headed into his office, leaving us alone. I couldn't help feeling a shiver of fear as we stared at each other. I'd never met Akin before, but his sister was a menace.

He *did* look like her, I decided. Their faces were nearly identical: pale skin, blond hair, a faintly supercilious smile. It would be easy to mistake one for the other, at least until they grew up. But he didn't seem to have Isabella's easy malice...unless, of course, he hadn't realised I didn't have magic. Alana had done well in class. He might have assumed I could defend myself just as well.

Magister Tallyman returned, rubbing his chin. "I assume you both want to work as assistants?"

I nodded. Akin followed me, a second later.

"Very good," Magister Tallyman said. "You'll be working with your fellow firsties on Friday afternoon, if they require assistance, and working with me on Sunday...unless you have detention. I'm afraid I will *not* be paying you if you have detention and can't make it - and no, I will *not* cancel your detentions for you. The best I can do is arrange to have it rescheduled."

He paused, dramatically. "Your duties with me will involve going through the old books, preparing materials to my exacting standards and - perhaps - helping to put together a prototype Object of Power. I'll do my best to take care of you, but there *will* be dangers and you *may* be hurt. If you want to stop, just say so. I won't hold it against you."

"And you don't do the exam marking anyway," Akin said. "Sir."

Magister Tallyman smiled. "No, I don't," he said. He shrugged. "Not everyone stays with me for an entire term, let alone a year. If you want to leave, let me know. And you should see this..."

He tapped his face. "Forgers are rarely pretty people," he warned. "I was lucky to survive the string of accidents that damaged my face and nearly crippled me. I think nearly two-thirds of my body has been replaced, by now. Forging the more complex Devices--" he pointed towards a metal-lic...*thing*...at the rear of the room "--is a very difficult and dangerous task. Still want to work for me?"

"Yes, sir," I said.

"It should be fun," Akin said.

"Oh, it is," Magister Tallyman said. He made a show of thinking. "What else do you need to know? Let's see..."

"Payment," Akin said.

"I *knew* I'd forgotten something," Magister Tallyman said, mischie-vously. His eyes crinkled in amusement. "Payment is three gold crowns per Friday, five gold crowns per Saturday. I'll put the money in your account unless you want me to pay you directly. If so, clear it with your parents first. You'll have to get their permission for this anyway."

I nodded. Dad wouldn't object, I was sure. Mum might write me long letters, warning me to be careful, but she wouldn't insist I decline the chance to work for Magister Tallyman. Or so I hoped...

"I'll send out permission slips tonight," Magister Tallyman added. "If your parents agree, you can start a week from Friday. Can you both work together?"

I exchanged glances with Akin. Our families were enemies. I had already made an enemy of his sister. And yet, if we couldn't work together, one of us might be rejected. Or would get fewer hours...we stared at each other, then came to a joint decision.

"Yes," we said.

"Very good," Magister Tallyman said. "And one other thing...?"

He leaned forward, looking us right in the eye. "This isn't a class," he told us. "This isn't something I *have* to do. If either of you misbehave when working with me, you're out. I don't have the obligation to employ you. And I will not listen to protests from *either* of your parents. Do you understand me?"

I swallowed. "Yes, sir."

"Very good," Magister Tallyman said. "There are some of my unpublished research papers in the library. I suggest you ask the librarian to find them for you. They'll give you the background of what I have been trying to do for the last five years."

"Unlocking the secret behind the Objects of Power," Akin said.

"Quite," Magister Tallyman said. He sighed, heavily. "How did they do it? We don't know."

I glanced at Akin. If he figured out how it was done, his family would dominate Magus Court until the secret leaked out. And it would, eventually. Magister Tallyman and his fellows would spare no effort to duplicate it. My father would throw money around like water before the family was crushed by its rivals. But if *I* figured it out...

You don't need magic to forge, I told myself, firmly. It was something to hope for, wasn't it? *Anyone can do it.*

"I'll see you on Thursday," Magister Tallyman said, dismissing us. "If you have any questions about the research papers, see me then."

He turned and walked back into his office, leaving us alone. I felt Akin looking at me and raised my head, staring back at him. We were rivals, rivals for learning and experience we couldn't get anywhere else...I wondered if he'd throw a hex at me now, or wait until we were completely alone. Magister Tallyman's warning - no magic in his classroom without permission - rang in my ears. Surely Akin wouldn't be so foolish as break the rules with a teacher close by...

Akin turned and strode out of the room. I watched him go, feeling my legs weaken. If he'd hexed me...I would have been defenceless. I glanced into the nearest bin, trying to see what I could pick out for later use, then hurried out of the room myself. Magister Tallyman probably wouldn't care if I took waste and turned it into something more useful, but there was no point in tempting fate. My mind was buzzing as I walked through the maze of corridors, feeling genuinely optimistic for the first time since I'd been told I was going to Jude's. Give me a few weeks in the forgery and I'd have quite a few surprises up my sleeve. The tricks I'd mastered to give me a fighting chance against my sisters would be even more of a surprise to Isabella.

I heard a scream up ahead and froze. Someone was screaming, begging and pleading...it was Rose. I could hear the sound of magic, the *snap-crack* of stinging spells; I forced myself to listen, despite the urge to flee. Two more people were laughing, perhaps three. They were girls, I thought. And Rose...

My legs felt leaden. I could turn around and walk away. No one knew I was there. I could claim ignorance, when I saw Rose. And yet...I forced myself forward with more bravery than common sense. My legs were still unsteady when I walked around the corner and saw them.

Rose was leaning against the wall, her face streaked with tears. Isabella and the McDonalds were throwing stinging spells at her, each one striking with the force of a minor punch. I knew those spells, all too well. Alana had been fond of shooting them at me until she'd learned other, more interesting hexes. A strong man could shrug off the blows and keep coming - Dad's apprentices used them to practice their ducking and dodging - but Rose wasn't that strong. I felt a stab of pity for her, mingled with rage. Rose was a magician with very real promise. She shouldn't be treated like...

Like me, I thought.

"Stop that," I shouted. "Let her go."

Isabella turned, surprised. "Well, if it isn't the little *zero*," she said. Her nose twitched, as if she'd smelled something disgusting. "Go away."

She snapped a stinging spell at me. I dodged. Alana had given me plenty of practice.

"Let her go," I said, evenly.

Isabella stared back at me. "*Make* me."

"I turned you into a frog," I bluffed. *She* knew it was a lie, but her friends didn't. Would she want to reveal the truth in front of them? "I can do it again."

She shot a second spell at me. I grunted as it slammed into my chest. It stung, but I'd been hurt worse when I fell off a horse. I ran forward instead, hoping to strike her before she switched tactics. But it was too late. She waved a hand at me and I froze. I could neither move nor speak. I wasn't even sure I was still breathing, even though I could see and hear perfectly.

"Little *zero*," Isabella said, contemptuously.

I felt a wave of sheer hatred, strong enough to send me tumbling right into the darkness...if I'd had magic. I wanted to hurt her, I wanted to see her bleed, I wanted to tear her apart...nothing happened, of course. Isabella snorted, then turned back to Rose. The poor girl hadn't even taken advantage of the distraction to run. She was too scared to think of it, I realised slowly. Isabella hadn't even bothered to fix her feet to the floor.

And she didn't even bother to cast any other spells on me, I thought, numbly. *She doesn't have to...*

The spell broke. I stumbled forward, just as Isabella turned back, surprise written all over her face. She certainly hadn't *intended* to freeze me for just a few seconds. I forced myself forward and slammed a fist into her nose, sending her falling over backwards. Someone screamed, behind me, but I paid it no heed. Magicians are so used to tossing bloodless spells at each other that *real* violence always comes as a shock. Isabella hit the ground hard and I landed on top of her, drawing back my fist for another punch. Blood was leaking from her nose...

An invisible force grabbed me and yanked me up. "What is going on?"

I spun in the air. Two sixth-years, both girls, were standing there, staring at me in horror. I gazed back at them defiantly, unwilling to show any fear. Isabella gasped in pain, drawing my attention back to her as she struggled to stand. I didn't *think* her nose was broken, but it certainly *looked* bad.

The sixth-year lowered me to the floor. "What is going on?"

I had no answer. I didn't want to be the dorm sneak.

"You, take your friend to see the matron," the sixth year ordered. She nodded to Zeya. "And you" - she turned her attention back to me - "give me your punishment book."

I glared at her rebelliously, but there was no point in trying to fight. She took my book and checked the top cover, then opened it to the very first page. "One of Sandy's, I see," she said, darkly. "She didn't warn you about fighting in the corridors?"

I thought it was keenly encouraged, I thought. I wasn't fool enough to say it out loud. Sandy was going to kill me - or, worse, she was going to make me clean the washroom. *Isabella started it.*

"You will write *I will not fight with my fists like a common zero* one hundred times before Saturday," the sixth year said. She signed her name with a flourish - I couldn't read her signature - and gave it back to me. "Give the book to Sandy so she can countersign it or you'll have detention the following day. Understand?"

"Yes," I said, sullenly. A hundred lines...I think I would have preferred a grounding. Or being forced to help the cooks or maids. My wrist was going to be aching by the time I finished. "I understand."

"And no trying to find a spell to do them for you," the girl added, warningly. "Sandy *will* be able to tell."

I scowled at her retreating back as she walked away. Mum had told me that each year group pretended that the others didn't exist - they certainly wouldn't admit to knowing the names of anyone above or below them - but it looked like she was wrong. Or...I glanced down at my book, noting Sandy's name written just below mine. Maybe she - I tried to read the signature again, but failed - had picked it up from there. It didn't really matter.

"Caitlyn," Rose said. She sounded .. she sounded ashamed. I understood, more than I cared to admit. I'd felt helpless too, when my sisters had practiced their spells on me. "I...thank you."

I put the book back into my pocket and glanced around. Ayesha McDonald had fled, probably following her sister to the matron, and there was no one else in sight, but that meant nothing. The upper years could probably turn themselves invisible...Alana had tried, a year or so ago. I still giggled whenever I remembered just how badly it had gone. *She'd* been invisible, all right, but the spell had done nothing for her clothes.

"We need to find somewhere more private," I said. I had blood on my fist and Rose looked a terrible mess. "Come on."

"Thank you," Rose said. She bent down and scooped the remains of her Device off the floor, pocketing it. "I...they caught me...I..."

"It's all right," I lied. It probably wouldn't have gone any better if I'd been with her. Isabella would have frozen me from the start...and yet, her spell hadn't lasted. Had she failed to cast it properly? I *had* caught her by surprise. "Come in here."

I led her into a small washroom and motioned for her to clean herself. My hands were stained with Isabella's blood...I shuddered, helplessly, as I put my hand under the water and washed it clean. Dad had taught the three of us *never* to leave blood lying around without the proper rituals, although he hadn't gone into details. I'd read enough to know that blood magic was both very dangerous and highly illegal. Even *Alana* wouldn't mess with it.

Rose washed her face with cold water, then looked at me. Her eyes were shining. "You saved me."

"You're welcome," I said. I'd caught Isabella by surprise, once. She wouldn't make that mistake again. "What did she want?"

"I don't know," Rose said. "She hit me with the spell, again and again...I just couldn't fight back. I..."

"You have magic," I said, harshly. She reddened. "Why didn't you use it?"

But I already knew the answer. Rose hadn't been raised to think of magic as the solution to everything. And even if she had, the bombardment would have made it impossible to think...no doubt Isabella's aristocratic status had made it harder, too. If she fought back...Isabella might have done something worse. It was why I'd spent so long trying to fight my sisters, even though I lost more often than I won. I couldn't let them think I was nothing more than a punching bag...

"I hate this place," Rose said. She looked as if she wanted to cry. "I want to go home!"

She glared at her reflection in the mirror. "I want to go *home!*"

"I know how you feel," I said, stiffly. "I want to go home too."

I fought down a sudden surge of homesickness. Apart from forging - and the chance to work with Magister Tallyman - there was nothing else for me at Jude's. Perhaps Rose would have a better life if she partnered with Gayle or Yolanda or even Bella. Bella was too lazy to bully, yet too well-connected to be bullied. Or she could even partner with Akin. Isabella's brother had status too...

"You belong here," Rose said. "I don't."

She waved a hand at the stone walls. "I miss the fields," she said. "I miss the woods...I even miss the work, hard though it was. I had friends, I had family...and then they gave me the scholarship and told me to go. I miss...I want to go home."

I groaned, inwardly. Rose's family didn't have a *hope* of repaying her scholarship, not if she dropped out or somehow ran away. She only got to keep the money if she graduated. My father would consider it pocket change, but a commoner family would have a different idea. They'd be in debt for the next five generations, just paying off a loan they'd probably been bullied into taking. Rose had potential. Even *I* could see that. But she hadn't wanted to leave her village for Shallot.

"You can go home during half-term," I said, although I wasn't sure if it was true. Merely travelling to Erehwon - some tiny village in the middle of nowhere - would cost money, real money. "And you will get to go home during the summer holiday..."

Rose looked at me. "I won't fit in," she said. "Will I?"

She sighed. "There was a girl who went away to be educated," she said. "Not in magic, I think. She came back with fancy clothes and high ideals and looked down on all of us, grubbing in the mud. I'm going to be just like her, aren't I?"

Probably, I thought.

"Not if you don't want to," I said, instead. "You can help them, instead. There are spells you can use to help with farming, you know. And Devices of Power to help plough the fields."

"If I can afford to make them," Rose pointed out. "Do you know what that gold thread costs?"

"No," I said. I had never worried about it. "And if we don't get to lunch, we'll be hungry all through potions. And trust me...you don't want that."

THIRTEEN

I should have been good at potions.

Mum had drilled potions-brewing into me from the moment I was old enough to take an interest. She'd stepped up the lessons as my lack of magic became apparent, hoping that brewing time and time again would unlock my hidden potential. I knew all the tips and tricks, all the little shortcuts the best potion masters used to make their work easier...I could recite, on demand, everything that a underclassman might need to know about potions and their ingredients. But none of my potions worked.

I followed the instructions to the letter. I prepared the ingredients perfectly, getting everything ready before I set to work. I washed the caldrons and tools; I boiled the water and inserted the ingredients in the right order, stirring *precisely* as laid down in the recipe. And nothing happened, because I lacked magic. I should have been able to brew potions, just as I could create Devices of Power, but I couldn't. They never worked for me.

The classroom was larger than Mum's brewing chamber, but it followed the same basic pattern. I couldn't help feeling a little homesick as I walked through the door, Rose following me like a lost puppy. Large storage cupboards and storerooms at the rear, a dozen wooden desks, bare stone walls scarred and pitted by explosions within the classroom... even a skilled potioneer had explosions from time to time. A couple of my classmates were looking around uncomfortably, sensing the wards that provided a minimal level of safety for inexperienced brewers. Mum never used them. She said the wards interfered with her brewing. I took a seat near the front and motioned for Rose to join me. There were just too many ways someone could mess with our potion for me to be comfortable at the rear.

"Be seated," Magistra Loanda ordered. She marched to the front of the room and turned to look at us. "When I say your name, respond. Otherwise, stay quiet. We have a lot to get done over the next few hours."

I studied her, warily. Magistra Loanda reminded me of Mum, except she looked about a decade or two older. There was no kindness in her, no warmth...I thought she looked like a statue that had been brought to life by a passing magician. Her skin looked faintly unhealthy, as if she'd been breathing in her own fumes. Potioneers needed to regularly purge their bodies of toxins before they became dangerous - Mum did it every week - but Magistra Loanda might not have had the time. Mum normally locked herself in her room after breakfast and wasn't seen again until dinner.

She shot Alana, Bella and me sharp looks, then carried on call-ing out names. I thought she probably knew Mum - there weren't *that* many Master Potioneers in Shallot - although I had no way to know how Magistra Loanda felt about her. They might be friends or they might be rivals...I made a mental note to write to Mum and ask her, then sat up as Magistra Loanda finished the register. Her cold eyes swept the classroom, daring us to make trouble. I had a feeling that none of us would dare.

"Welcome to Potions," she said. Her voice was cold, but there was a hint of...*something*...beneath it. "How many of you have studied potions before?"

I held up my hand. So did two-thirds of the class.

"The first week will seem boring to most of you, I am sure," Magistra Loanda said. Her lips twitched, unpleasantly. "I expect you to pay atten-tion, regardless. There is a difference between brewing at home and brew-ing in a class, which you will come to understand over the next few days. I want you all to be *fully* conversant with the rules before the end of the week."

She paused. "Most of the classes you have already taken, I believe, cover ways to use the spark of magic within you, within everyone," she said. Her voice grew slightly warmer, although I suppose I could have been imagining it. "Those classes are designed to take that spark and fan it into a fire, teaching you both power and control. *This* class is not about developing your *own* powers, but unlocking the power within the natural world and using it to best advantage. Some of you will be tempted to compare this to left-hand magic. Rest assured that it is nothing of the sort."

Rose glanced at me. I shrugged.

"Everything has magic," Magistra Loanda continued. "Everything. A common potato has magic that can be unlocked and used, if done properly. So too can everything from garden herbs right up to dragon scales. Indeed, the latter have so much magic that using them in a potion without proper preparation is nothing more than signing your own death warrant."

Her lips twisted. "Rest assured, you will *not* be working with such materials.

"In class, you will be preparing and brewing potions," she informed us. "You will go through everything from cutting up the ingredients to actually brewing the potion and unlocking its magic. I will give you the recipes and you will follow them, slavishly. You are *not* to experiment with changing the recipe in any way. If you feel you can change a potion and improve on it, give me a written statement of what you intend to do and I may - I *may* - let you try it. And if I catch you trying to modify a recipe without permission, you will regret it.

"Outside class, you will study the different potions ingredients and their interactions. You will understand the *how* and the *why* as well as the what. Some of you may think you already know all this, but I expect you to do it anyway. I want *proof* you know. There is to be no brewing outside class without supervision, which will be offered on a twice-weekly basis to the first twelve who put their names on the rota. The older students will serve as supervisors and they have, at least in the classroom, the power to give detentions."

I groaned, inwardly. My punishment book already felt heavier. Was it charmed to remind me that I had work to do? Or was it merely my imagination?

Magistra Loanda leaned forward. "Should you *survive* the next four years," she added, "you will be upperclassmen, who have considerably more freedom to experiment. By then, you will be expected to know all the rules - and the *reasoning* behind the rules. And it is for *that* reason that your first homework assignment will be to determine that reasoning. I suggest you write the rules down instead of trusting to your memory."

We scrambled for our notebooks as she started to rattle off the rules, her voice echoing around the classroom. "Follow the recipe to the letter. Ask if you don't understand anything before trying it. Inform a member of staff if a bottle of supplies is running out. Do not interfere with another brewer's potion. Get under the table if the air above your potion turns red, as it is about to explode..."

My wrist ached by the time I had finished. Rose looked to be in agony.

"Very good," Magistra Loanda said. She clicked her fingers. A detailed recipe appeared on the blackboard. "The tools and ingredients are in the storerooms. I expect each of you to produce a perfect result, first time."

Rose muttered a word under her breath. It didn't sound pleasant.

"It's a simple recipe," I assured her. *She* would find it easy. "It just looks complicated."

"I never had to cook like this," Rose said.

"Potions and cooking are not the same thing," I said. Mum had told us that they were nothing alike. It was possible to recover from a mistake while cooking, she'd said, but a great deal harder to save a potion after making a misstep. "Don't say that to her or you'll regret it."

Rose nodded as we stood and hurried to the storeroom. It was huge, the walls lined with bottles and jars that towered up into the distance. Each one was clearly marked in three different languages, something that puzzled me until I realised that there could be no room for misunderstandings. Adding salamander skulls instead of gorgon eyes would be disastrous, even if one was experimenting with varying the recipe. The surge of magic would be powerful enough to cause a *big* explosion. I was surprised, coming to think of it, that the recipe hadn't been written in three languages too.

"Take a caldron," I told her. "And a bucket of water. I'll get the rest."

Alana nudged me. "Pointless, isn't it?"

I ignored her as best as I could. But she was right. She could splash a handful of herbs at random into boiling water and produce miracles, while I could follow the recipe perfectly and still wind up with expensive sludge. Mum had never seemed to care, but I knew some of the ingredients I'd wasted were costly. The only upside was that she could make the potions work herself, after I'd given up.

Back at the desk, we washed both caldrons thoroughly, along with the scale pan, the chopping block, the stirrers and the knives. Cold water wasn't a problem, not for firstie potions, but dust and the remnants of someone else's potion would be rather more disastrous. Magistra Loanda's eyes passed over us - just for a second, I thought I saw her nod in approval - before moving to Alana. Her eyes narrowed so sharply that I thought she was about to start shooting fire. She was *not* happy.

"How many of you," she asked coldly, "didn't think to wash the equipment before using it?"

Alana looked down, hastily. "Five of you washed your equipment," Magistra Loanda said, sternly. I noticed that both Isabella and Akin looked relieved. "Only five. These are not caldrons you can vouch for, are they? *Wash* them!"

Her eyes grew colder. So did the room.

"These caldrons have not been touched since last term, two months ago," Magistra Loanda reminded us. "You do not *know* they are clean. *Wash* them!"

I concealed my amusement with an effort. Alana had grown too used to having the servants wash her equipment, back home. But then, she'd never really had the patience for potions. I would have washed everything for a year, if I'd actually managed to produce more than sludge...

Rose frowned. "I would have missed that," she said. "Thank you."

"Assume someone's used the tools unless you know otherwise," I muttered back. I checked the recipe again, mentally listing the ingredients. "All you need is someone forgetting to wash up afterwards to have an explosion - or worse."

Magistra Loanda strode backwards and forwards as we found our ingredients, snapping out instructions and horror stories. One girl had labelled the wrong bottles and accidentally killed herself - Mum had told me something similar, although she hadn't been quite so gruesome when she'd detailed the results. Another had mixed up two different ingredients and managed to turn herself inside out; a third had somehow blinded the whole class; a fourth had somehow managed to create slime monsters that had crawled around the classroom for hours before finally being removed by the cleaning staff and dumped in the sewers. I made a mental note never even to *consider* going into the sewers as long as I lived, even though I thought she was joking. But then, my father *had* said there were all sorts of weird things below the ground.

"Get everything ready first," I said, as I sorted out the bowls. "It saves time when you're actually brewing."

Mum had done me a big favour, I realised. *She'd* taught me how to prepare the ingredients perfectly. Rose copied me, but just about everyone else was snapped at by Magistra Loanda as she walked around the room, pointing out mistakes in an increasingly nasty tone. I couldn't help wondering why she bothered to teach, if she hated children, although I did have to admit that an explosion in a crowded classroom could be very dangerous. Glancing at the door, I silently evaluated just how long it would take to run, if the air turned nasty. The wards should protect us from danger, but Magistra Loanda might just let us cough on smoke as an object lesson.

I wished, as I lit the flame under my caldron, that we'd been allowed to partner up. I might have been able to hide my failings for a little longer. But Magistra Loanda had forbidden it, unsurprisingly. She wanted - she needed - to have a good idea of where we each were, before moving us along. I had the feeling that I would wind up partnered with Rose permanently, although I didn't really mind that now. She needed help...

"When you were back home," I asked, "did you cook?"

Rose nodded. "I was helping my parents almost as soon as I could walk. My brothers would go work in the fields all day, while my sisters and I would clean the house and cook their dinner. We had a good crop last year, but the baron took half of it and..."

She broke off. "I..."

"Tax," I said. Taxmen didn't come to Aguirre Hall, of course, but Dad paid a certain amount each year to Magus Court. Very few taxmen were brave enough to approach a lone sorcerer, let alone a whole family. "Ouch."

"He'll want my earnings too," Rose predicted.

"Live in the city," I advised. "You don't get taxed so badly here."

Rose shrugged as the water started to boil, then poured in the first set of ingredients. I felt a sinking feeling in my chest as I followed suit, reminding myself that the first set needed to boil for ten minutes before adding the *next* set. I could get quite some distance without magic, I knew, but eventually...eventually I'd have to use magic. And I couldn't.

"Very good preparation," Magistra Loanda said. "Why did you wash the ginger root after cutting away the skin?"

"There might have been traces of dirt on the knife," I said. I'd cleaned the knife, of course, but there was no point in taking chances. A grain of dirt might pass unnoticed...or the potion might explode spectacularly. Water droplets wouldn't cause problems. "I wanted to be sure."

"Good," Magistra Loanda said. She narrowed her eyes at Rose. "And why have you kept *this*?"

I followed her gaze. It was a piece of root, but it was clearly old and decayed. I would have thrown it out without hesitation. Rose looked pale and started to stammer as the older woman glared down at her. She mumbled something, too quiet for me to hear.

"Speak up, girl," Magistra Loanda ordered. "Why didn't you throw it out?"

Rose paled further. "It's still usable," she said. "I..."

"It's useless," Magistra Loanda said, flatly. She picked up the root and threw it over her shoulder, without looking. It still landed neatly in the bin. "I don't know where you were brought up..."

"In the poorhouse," someone muttered.

"Detention," Magistra Loanda said, lifting her gaze to skewer the speaker. Gasps echoed around the room. It seemed a little harsh, I was sure. "Let me assure you, young lady, that we have ample supplies of everything you need. Find a new piece of root and chop it up. You won't be billed for it."

She stalked off to terrorise the other students. I shot Rose a reassuring look - it helped that she wasn't the only one to feel Magistra Loanda's sharp tongue - and then added the next set of ingredients. The potion started to bubble, smelling almost like soup. I would have thought it was soup too, if I hadn't known better. Drinking it would give me a tummy upset, at best.

"I'll take care of the potion," I told her. Magistra Loanda might complain, but Rose had already started. Someone had to keep an eye on the simmering liquid. "You go get the root."

We went through the rest of the process without incident, although I whispered a couple of pieces of advice to Rose. It helped that Magistra Loanda was distracted by a pair of explosions - somehow, Isabella and Zeya had managed to make a dreadful mistake. But, all too soon, the time came to make the final step. I picked up the stirrer and lowered it into the mixture, silently praying to the fates that something would happen. But nothing did...

I glanced at Rose. Her potion was now a lovely shimmering blue. My heart clenched, in rage or frustration or jealousy...It was perfect. Utterly perfect. I could practically *see* the magic rising from the liquid. Mum would have been thrilled if I'd presented her with such a brew...

She looked back at me. "What's wrong?"

I stirred my potion, savagely. Splashes of boiling liquid flew in all directions, but nothing happened. I thought I heard someone titter, behind me. Potions were simple, potions were easy...someone could make a potion without very much magic at all. I let go of the stirrer and slumped backwards. I was doomed. Magistra Loanda would see my failure and... and what? Feel sorry for Mum because of her useless daughter? Or take pride in her rival's failure? Or...

Rose reached out and stirred my potion. It turned blue. It was perfect. I'd brewed it perfectly. Everything was perfect, except me.

I saw red. I kicked the table so hard that the caldron flew off and crashed to the floor. Rose stared at me, her face shocked, as I stood and fled for the door. Someone called after me, but I didn't listen. I burst through the door and ran.

CHAPTER
FOURTEEN

I didn't know where I was going. Not really. I ran up the stairs and along corridors, ignoring all shouts and cries until I finally reached the roof. Cold air, blown off the sea, slapped against my face, bringing me back to reality. But reality was a nightmare...I sank down on the rooftop and cried. There was no escape from my curse, from...

I'd done everything right, I knew. I'd brewed the mixture perfectly. But it still wouldn't turn into a potion without magic, magic I couldn't infuse into the liquid. *Rose* had made it work, underlying my failure. The pride I'd felt in besting Isabella, in humiliating her in front of everyone, faded to nothingness. It wouldn't be long before the rumours started again, if they'd ever gone away. The entire class had seen my failure.

I rose and peered west. The port was clearly visible, a dozen sailing ships prepping for a trading mission to somewhere I'd never see. Birds wheeled in the sky overhead, their cries mocking me. They enjoyed a freedom I would never have, not ever...I wanted to walk to the edge and jump off, even though it was certain death. At least it would be an end. But something in me refused to just give up.

The air grew colder. I could see dark clouds sweeping in from the east. It was going to rain soon...I knew I should go inside, but why bother? There was nothing waiting for me, apart from humiliation. I sat back on the ground and closed my eyes, trying to focus, trying - one final time - to touch the magic inside me. But there was no response. I don't know why I even bothered to try. I'd long since grown used to failure.

My eyes snapped open. Rose stepped onto the roof.

I felt a surge of hatred, mingled with bitter frustration. "Go away."

Rose looked back at me, nothing but raw compassion in her eyes. Somehow, that made it worse. I would almost sooner be scorned than pitied. My father's attempts to teach me, my mother's patient lessons over the caldron...the pity and ill-hidden shame in their eyes when they realised I had no magic...I was used to that, now. Rose didn't understand, not yet. I knew she'd turn on me when she did.

"You shouldn't be alone," she said. She walked over to me and sat down, wrapping her arms around herself as it grew colder. "What happened?"

"None of your beeswax," I growled. "Go away."

Rose ignored me. I don't know why I was surprised. It wasn't as if anyone paid any attention to a lowly *zero*. Even Mum and Dad weren't quite as interested in listening to me as they were in listening to my sisters, although they would never admit it. They knew, even if they didn't want to think about it, that they'd have to disown me eventually, just to preserve something of the family's position.

"What happened?" she asked, again. "The potion was perfect."

I laughed, bitterly. "Of course the potion was perfect," I snapped. "Of *course* it was perfect."

She gave me an odd look, as if I'd started speaking in tongues. "And it worked," she said, puzzled. I thought she was needling me, but her face was open and honest. "What's the problem?"

I looked back at her, fighting down the urge to lash out. Rose...all my bitterness and resentment meant nothing, not in the long run. *She* would go on to a successful career, while I...she didn't understand. She honestly didn't understand. And the longer I kept it from her, the harder it would be to take it when she finally - inevitably - abandoned me. She was trying to be friendly, yet...she wouldn't want to be my friend once she knew the truth.

"I don't have any magic," I said, finally.

Rose blinked. "You made the potion work..."

"I *didn't* make the potion work," I snapped. Was she being dumb on purpose? "*You* did! I cut up the ingredients and brewed everything, but it was *you* who gave it the magic to turn a sloppy smelly mess into a potion. *You* made it work."

"That's not possible," Rose said. "Is it?"

"I've never had any magic," I said, softly. The anger and resentment was draining away, leaving me feeling numb. "None at all."

She looked doubtful, so I held up my hand and cast a spell. The words were perfect, the gestures utterly precise...Anna's Amphibian was a very forgiving spell, if one had the power to push through any little missteps, but my casting was perfect. Rose should have been turned into a frog. And...do I really need to say that nothing happened?

Rose flinched, but made no move to defend herself. "You messed up the spell..."

I shook my head. Dad had taught me carefully, ranging from pitch-perfect pronunciations to little hand and wrist movements that helped to focus the spell. For those with little talent, precision meant the difference between successfully casting a spell and complete failure. But for those with no talent, like me, it was nothing more than an exercise in futility. Dad had watched me like a hawk, ready to snap at the slightest misstep, but he'd found nothing to criticize. Everything was perfect, save me. I'd memorised fifty spells I'd never be able to use.

"The spell is perfect," I said. "It's the caster who failed."

Once I started, I couldn't stop. "My parents started to teach us magic when we were seven," I said. "My sisters took to it like ducks to water, but I couldn't cast a single spell. Dad looked for all sorts of ways to develop the magic he thought I had, Mum taught me how to brew potions, the apprentices taught me to forge...nothing worked."

I wondered, sourly, if Rose could possibly understand. She hadn't grown up in a magical household. Sure, her parents would know a few basic spells, but they'd hardly be the most important things in their lives. But for me...Bella was lazy, unwilling to apply herself, yet even *she* had more magic in her little finger than I had in my entire body. And there was nowhere I could go, either, to escape my family.

Rose cleared her throat. "Why did they send you here?"

"Dad thinks it will help unlock my magic," I said. "He's convinced I have talent."

"I see," Rose said. She reached out and wrapped an arm around my shoulder. "Why?"

I snorted. "He thinks I broke a spell cast by a very experienced magician," I said. "And so he thinks my talents are merely buried."

"He could be right," Rose said. "You *did* free me from Isabella's spell... didn't you?"

"You did it," I told her. Dad had taught *me* how to undo transfiguration spells, of course, but I'd never been able to break them at will. "I merely helped you to focus your mind. Your mind *wants* to return to a human body."

Rose shuddered. "I thought I was trapped forever..."

"It would have worn off," I assured her. "The old biddy's spell probably wore off too."

She shot me a questioning look, so I told her about Great Aunt Stregheria and the rest of the family. It was odd, I had to admit. I could easily believe that Great Aunt Stregheria hadn't thought it was worth wasting a complex spell on me, but Dad should have been able to unravel anything less complex easily. *He* wouldn't leave us trapped any longer than strictly necessary. Maybe he'd studied the spell and decided it would unravel on its own sooner rather than later...

But he was sure I'd broken it myself, I thought. *He wouldn't have lied to me about that, would he?*

Rose took a breath. "You forged something..."

"There's no magic in that," I pointed out. "No *inherent* magic, anyway. I can forge with the best of them."

It was hard to look at her, so I studied the stone beneath our feet. "I can forge, but I can't cast spells to test them. I can brew potions, but I can't actually make them *work*. I can prepare spell diagrams and notations, but I can't cast the spells myself. I know plenty of tips and tricks, but I can't ever use them for myself..."

I shook my head. "I don't have a hope of passing my exams," I added, reluctantly. "*If* I survive..."

"You will," Rose said.

"Accidents happen," I countered. "And if they don't *know* I don't have magic..."

I looked up at her. "You should go," I told her. "There's still time for you to make friends with *real* magicians. I can't help you."

Rose gaped at me, then jabbed me with her finger. It hurt. "Are you...?" She glared. "Do you really think I'd abandon you over *this*?"

"You should," I said. "You'll just make yourself a target."

"I'm *already* a target," Rose said. "And my family can't do magic!"

"They can cast spells though, can't they?" I asked. "And I bet they can sense magic..."

Rose leaned forward and slapped me, hard.

I recoiled in shock. I'd been jinxed and hexed and told off by my parents, but no one had ever struck me before. Neither of my sisters had ever thought to slap me...I wouldn't have punched Isabella, if I'd had magic at my command. The pain...I rubbed my cheek, utterly astonished. I'd never dreamt *Rose* would slap me.

"You are being *incredibly* selfish," she snapped. "I'm the only one in my family who can cast spells reliably, but that doesn't make my brothers and sisters useless! They'll be growing crops and raising animals for the slaughter while I'm stuck here, learning magic. There are *thousands* of people who get by without using magic!"

She went on without taking a breath. "There are plenty of things *you* can do, without magic," she added. "Even if you don't want to farm, you could become an accountant or a lawyer or even one of the King's Men! And even if you want to work with magic, you can forge or brew potions and get someone else to give them the magic! Stop feeling self-pitying and start *thinking*."

I found my voice. "I can't even *sense* magic!"

"Then make more Devices to *help* you," Rose snarled. She met my eyes, silently daring me to look away. "There's a girl I know back home who had a nasty accident and lost both of her legs. The doctors cut them off - her family couldn't afford the spells needed to regrow her legs or even give her a pair of wooden stumps! She's a cripple! She'll never get married or have children...she'll be completely dependent on her parents and siblings for the rest of her life. And you know what she does?"

Her eyes bored into mine. "She sits in her makeshift chair and makes clothes," she added, her voice quieting down. "I've watched her knit and sew - she used to give lessons to the little girls, back before I discovered a gift for magic. She can't get around without help, but she's still useful. She still has a place!"

I shuddered. Magic could heal almost anything, if it wasn't instantly fatal. I'd broken my leg a few times, only to have my parents repair it in a moment. But if someone couldn't afford the trained magicians needed to regrow a missing leg, then attach it...they'd be crippled for the rest of their lives. Rose had said that, hadn't she?

"You can walk and run," Rose snapped, breaking into my thoughts. "You can read and write better than me - better than most, I'd wager. And you have knowledge and family connections and good looks and plenty of other assets. You are not *useless*."

I felt a flicker of hope. I had shocked Isabella, hadn't I? She hadn't anticipated the Casting Chalk. Of course, she'd be more careful next time. And while I'd probably given her a nasty fright when I'd hit her, the healers would have fixed her up in moments. Her face had looked unscratched when she'd walked into the potions classroom. I had no doubt she'd already forgotten the pain.

And maybe there *were* options. I'd just been so fixated on magic that I couldn't think of life without it.

"There are non-magical classes," Rose offered. "And I can help you with the others..."

I looked at her, astonished. "You would do that for me?"

"Yes," Rose said. "Wouldn't you?"

I had no answer. If I'd been born with magic...would I have turned my nose up at Rose, merely because her family were commoners? Would I have missed her remarkable talent and skill? Or would I have become her friend anyway...friend? Were we friends? She should have rejected me... why *hadn't* she rejected me?

"I don't know," I admitted. "Rose...my sisters *know*. Everyone else suspects...at the very least. It's rare for a child from a magical family not to be using magic by the time they reach ten. People have been whispering about me for the last couple of years. I don't know how long I can keep up any pretence..."

Rose leaned forward. "Even with me helping?"

I shrugged. Rose *could* help me with potions. And maybe a couple of other classes. But there was no way she could help with Protective and Defensive Magic, let alone Practical Charms. Even if we worked together closely...a thought was flickering at the back of my mind, yet it refused to surface. I didn't think we could fool trained and experienced teachers for very long, if at all. They'd eventually realise I was cheating.

And yet...if I could get a couple of passes...

The thought was tempting. I couldn't get a degree in Charms or Defensive Magic, but I *could* get one in a non-magical subject. We would be covering law in the next couple of years, assuming I wasn't kicked out of the school at the end of the year. And with that degree, I could do something...something else. Lawyers had to protect themselves against magical interference, but I could design and build Devices for that...

...Or Rose and I could set up an apothecary. Or a forge.

Dad would front us the money, I thought, wryly. It wouldn't be *that* much of a come-down for me. Apothecaries were important people. *He'd be delighted.*

Rose cleared her throat. "Well...?"

"We can try," I said. I looked back at her. "I wasn't joking, you know. You *would* be better off without me."

"I don't think so," Rose said. "Cat...I need help too. All of this--" she waved a hand towards the distant towers "--is new to me. I don't understand half the equations I had to study...I don't even know the basic skills. My reading is...*poor* and my handwriting is terrible. You can help me as I help you."

I closed my eyes for a long moment, silently thanking the fates. Rose and I...in some ways, we were very much alike. I should have seen it sooner. I would have, if I hadn't been so consumed with self-pity. She was a stranger in a strange land, while I was the ultimate outcast. Part of me wanted to believe that she'd push me away, eventually...I didn't want to hope that I'd found a true friend. She knew my secret now...

...And she wasn't trying to take advantage of me.

"I'll help you," I promised. I held out a hand. "Friends?"

Rose smiled. "Friends."

We shook hands, firmly. There should have been a tingle, according to all the old storybooks - a flicker of magic that would bind us together permanently. But I felt nothing. Magical oaths and bindings are dangerous. Dad had taught us to be *very* wary of what promises we made, just in case magic - or the fates - decided to take them literally. Perhaps it was just a joke. Dad hadn't said anything about *how* to make an oath, but I was fairly sure it was more complex than just shaking hands.

"We'll go to the library," I said, standing. I didn't let go of her hand. "We can start looking at charm geometrics..."

Rose flushed, lightly. "We have to go back to the dorm," she said. "Sandy wants to see you."

I glanced at the darkening sky, then at my watch. How long had we been on the roof?

And Mum had warned me that upperclassmen could track lowerclassmen. "She told you where to find me?"

"Yeah," Rose said. "She didn't look pleased."

A low peal of thunder echoed through the sky. I saw lightning flickering in the distance, sparking oddly as it reacted with the magic protecting the city. Dad spent half of his time working on the protections, he'd told us. They were among some of the most complex pieces of magic in the world. And yet, there was something terrifyingly ephemeral about them...

I pushed the thought aside. "We'd better go," I said, as raindrops began to splash down around us. Sandy was going to be utterly *furious*. She was responsible for our behaviour, after all. Magistra Loanda had probably given her an earache about me. "We don't want to give her time to get madder."

Rose nodded, silently. Part of me wanted to tell her to go hide in the library, but the rest of me wanted her to come, even though I knew she couldn't help. Sandy could make the rest of the year miserable, if she wished...

And there's no way to avoid it, I thought, grimly. *It's time to face the music.*

CHAPTER

FIFTEEN

The dorm was very quiet when we walked through the door.
Sandy was sitting by the door, quietly furious. The remaining
eight girls were sitting on their beds, the drapes pulled back to deny them
any privacy. They were trying to read, I thought, but it was clear that most
of them weren't actually learning anything. Isabella had a faintly vindictive smile on her face, which brightened when she saw me. *She* knew I was
in trouble.

And that I don't have magic, I thought, as Sandy rose to her feet. *She
knows I couldn't brew a simple potion.*

"You," Sandy said. She jabbed a finger at Rose. "Go to your bed, sit
down and shut up."

Rose paled. "Yes..."

"I said *shut up*," Sandy said. She was moving her hands in an odd
pattern, interlocking her fingers and then releasing them time and time
again. "Go to your bed and keep your mouth closed."

I forced myself not to back off as Sandy turned the full force of her
glare on me. My mother could be terrifyingly intimidating when she
chose, but I'd never really believed she would actually hurt me. Sandy...
she looked as though she wanted to wrap her fingers around my neck and
squeeze. It struck me, suddenly, that Magistra Loanda would have done
more than merely given her an earache. Sandy, an upperclassman, might
have been given detention too.

"You ran out of class without being dismissed," Sandy said. Her tone was so harsh that I flinched, despite myself. There was so much anger in her words that they could burn through seven layers of wards. "What were you *thinking?*"

She went on before I could think of an answer. "Magistra Loanda has given me detention for the next month," she snarled. Her hands were flexing in a more complex pattern. "I won't be trying out for the netball team because of *you*."

I swallowed, hard. I'd never considered sports important - I'd never been able to play - but I knew that others did. Sandy hadn't just been embarrassed by me. She'd lost the chance to play netball. Perhaps, just perhaps, she'd be lucky enough to win a reserve slot...I groaned, inwardly. She was going to *kill* me.

"My weekends have been lost," Sandy said. She twisted her hands again. It dawned on me that she was casting a spell. If I'd been able to sense magic, I would have picked up on it sooner. "What were you thinking?"

"I'm sorry," I said. It wasn't really true. I might have embarrassed myself and landed Sandy in hot water, but I'd also found a friend. It was worth a year of detentions. "It was my fault and I will tell Magistra Loanda that, tomorrow."

Sandy leaned forward until our noses were almost touching. "Do you think your family connections will get you out of trouble?"

I shook my head, not daring to speak. Mum would be furious, when she found out. I had no doubt that Magistra Loanda had already written to my parents. I'd probably get a letter back tomorrow, telling me precisely what an idiot I'd been and threatening all kinds of punishment when I went home for the holidays. Mum was probably going to ground me forever, if she didn't put me to work weeding the entire garden by hand...

"I'm glad to hear it," Sandy snapped. She drew back, still working on her spell. I wondered, absently, just what she was doing. I didn't recognise the hand movements. "Let me get a few things straight..."

She pinned me in place with her gaze. It was more effective than any spell.

"I am responsible for your behaviour in this school, unless you get expelled," she said. "Do you understand what that means? Your bad behaviour reflects on *me*! You running out of a class without being dismissed means that *I* get in trouble. Do you understand me?"

I nodded, hastily. There was a *very* nasty glint in her eye.

"If you have a dispute with your dorm mates, you settle it honourably, using magic," Sandy added. "There are plenty of traditions passed down through the generations for settling disagreements. Use them, instead of punching someone like a common thug! And if you have problems with the teachers...suck it up! You are here to learn, not to have the entire school bend the knee to you."

She pushed her hands together one final time, then yanked them apart. I gasped. Invisible ropes were twisting around me, pushing against my body...choking me. I felt my feet floating off the ground as the spell tightened, Sandy pulling her hands further and further apart. It was suddenly very hard to breathe. I tried to move a hand, hoping she'd think I was casting a spell, but one of the ropes caught me before I could complete the motion.

"Let her go," Rose shouted. She started to climb off her bed. "You'll kill her..."

Sandy nodded in her direction. Rose froze, then tumbled off the side and hit the ground with a thud. I knew she'd be unhurt - one advantage of the freezing spell is that it prevents damage - but it would be embarrassing. Isabella and the others looked as if they wanted to laugh, yet didn't quite dare. Sandy was...*impressive*. Casting multiple spells at once, without proper preparation, was very difficult. It had saved me, once or twice, from my sisters.

The magic tightened around me. My struggles were futile. It felt as though she really *was* trying to kill me...I started to panic, trying to move, trying to call on the magic I didn't have...nothing happened. The grip lightened, just for a second, as she flipped me over, leaving me hovering upside down in front of her. I was utterly helpless.

Sandy glared at me. "Are you going to listen now?"

I nodded, hastily.

She flipped me over again, then dispelled the magic. I fell, landing on my backside. A faint titter ran around the dorm, only to vanish utterly as Sandy glared around the room. *No one* wanted to annoy her, after what she'd just done. She was so far beyond us that she was effectively untouchable.

I rubbed my neck, feeling phantom fingers pressing against my skin. A reaction to the magic, I knew, but they felt real. My entire body was drenched in sweat...I wanted to crawl away, yet I didn't have the energy. Had she drained me too...?

Sandy held out a hand. "Punishment Book."

My fingers refused to work properly. It took me two tries to pluck the book out of my blazer and hand it to her. She glanced at it, then turned it around so I could read it. Under the earlier set of instructions, there was a new set of words in bright red ink. DETENTION - POTIONS CLASSROOM - SATURDAY. Magistra Loanda had signed it, somehow. I wondered, just for a moment, how she'd done it, then dismissed the thought. A witch like her would have plenty of magic at her disposal. My punishment book was probably twinned with a central register some-where in the building.

"You will wash the bathroom every Sunday for the next month," Sandy informed me, as she wrote in the book. "*And* you will turn in two hundred lines for me by Lights Out - *I will not get my Dorm Head in trouble.*"

There was no point in arguing. "As you wish..."

Sandy eyed me, one hand clutching the pen. "Would you like to make it *three* hundred lines?"

I shook my head. "No."

"Good," Sandy said. She shoved the book back into my hand. "Go to your bed."

She glanced at the clock. "You have two hours before dinner, more or less," she added, nastily. "Why don't you get started on your lines?"

I groaned as I picked myself off the floor. Two hundred lines...any hopes of going to the library with Rose were now gone. But I could take the book *to* the library and do the lines there, couldn't I? I didn't think there was a rule against it, as long as I was quiet. I could help Rose *and* complete my lines. I wasn't sure what would happen if I didn't hand the lines into her, but I had the feeling I didn't want to find out.

Sandy raised her voice as I limped towards my bed. "And I suggest the rest of you remember this," she ordered. "Settle your problems in the hall."

Hah, I thought.

I was vaguely aware of her leaving the dorm as I sat on the bed. Rose was still lying on the floor, unable to move. At least she knew I couldn't come to her aid...I gritted my teeth in bitter frustration. She'd said she'd stay with me, but it was hard to believe she *would*. I couldn't help her... perhaps I should urge her to befriend Bella instead. Bella wouldn't be *that* unpleasant to her.

Sitting on the comfy bed, I placed the writing board on my lap and opened the Punishment Book. Someone had charmed the ink - or, more likely, the book itself. Sandy's words looked unnaturally large, a reminder that I was running out of time. I reached for a pen and forced myself to concentrate. It was a shame there was no way to cheat, but if Dad hadn't been able to find a way to beat the system *I* wasn't likely to succeed. Besides, I was in deep trouble already...

"Hey," Isabella said.

I looked up. She was standing by the edge of my bed. "What do you want?"

"Oh, *nothing*," Isabella said. She jabbed a finger at me. I froze. "I just wanted to know if you could break my spell. You did it earlier."

I wanted to scream, but I couldn't move a muscle. Isabella had messed up her spell earlier, hadn't she? I should have been helplessly trapped until someone cancelled it or it wore off on its own. But it had broken...

"Come on," Isabella said. "I don't have all day."

She smiled, unpleasantly. "And neither do you. I really wouldn't let Sandy down."

I thought a number of words I didn't dare say in front of my parents. I had four hours - no, less than four hours - to write the lines. Sandy would be utterly furious if I failed to hand them in on time...and I *knew* she wouldn't listen to any excuses. Being frozen wouldn't be enough to deter a *real* magician. I made a mental note to teach Rose the counterspell as soon as possible, then forced myself to calm down. Isabella would have her fun and then go away.

But she thinks I did break her spell, I told myself. *What if I did?*

It was a warm thought. I wanted to believe it. And that made me nervous. Dad had told us, more than once, to be careful what we believed. Older men and women had been tricked because they'd been told what they wanted to believe. But I *had* escaped her spell, hadn't I?

I tried to think about it. I'd been angry at Isabella, just as I'd been angry at Great Aunt Stregheria. But I'd been angry before, when Alana had practiced her hexes on me, and nothing had happened. I tried to recapture that feeling now, thinking bloodthirsty thoughts about crushing Isabella under my boot heel...nothing happened. No matter how angry I got, the spell remained firmly in place. I was trapped.

"I knew it," Isabella said, nastily. She walked around the bed and bent over to whisper in my ear. Her lips were so close I could feel her breath tickling me. "Zero."

Anger flared, again. I wanted to lash out at her. I wanted to slam my fist into her. But I couldn't move. My body was frozen, utterly helpless. Nothing worked. I even tried to think of the counterspell - all the best wizards could cast the counterspell without needed to move - but nothing happened.

Isabella patted my head, then drew the drapes around my bed. Sandy wouldn't think twice about it when she returned, I knew, as Isabella winked at me. She'd think I was asking for privacy while I did my lines. Instead...Isabella was powerful. Powerful enough to keep the spell in place until dinnertime?

I would have cried, if I could. There had been so many ups and downs that I just wanted to lie down and *think*. Instead...I was trapped, utterly helpless. And facing a worse punishment, when Sandy found out that I'd skipped dinner and not done my lines. I wanted to make Isabella pay - I was *going* to make Isabella pay. But how?

If nothing else, I thought, *I have time to think of something nasty.*

It felt like hours before the spell finally broke. I slumped forward, feeling aches and pains everywhere. Isabella hadn't just frozen me. She'd cast the cruellest freezing spell I knew, the one that locked up muscles. And now...I needed a bath, just to work the kinks out of my body. But I knew that wasn't an option. Bracing myself, I peeked out of the drapes. No one was in sight, apart from Rose. She was still lying on the floor, helplessly frozen. I was honestly surprised that Sandy's spell had lasted so long.

She must be powerful, I thought, as I hurried over to Rose. *And very well trained.*

But it made sense, I supposed. Students had *always* played practical jokes on one another, testing themselves against their rivals. It was a long tradition - each student would *always* have a rival. The staff wouldn't want the firsties to start playing pranks on their supervisors, would they? Sandy *had* to make it clear that she was a *long* way ahead of any of us. And that anyone stupid enough to try to hex her would regret it.

"I can't break the spell," I muttered. I knelt down next to Rose, resting my hand on her shoulder. I knew she could hear me. "You have to unfreeze yourself."

Nothing happened. I wasn't surprised. Casting the counterspell without using hand movements wasn't easy - and Rose didn't even *know* the counterspell. I forced myself to think, hard. The Device I'd...taken from Forgery wouldn't do more than report the presence of magic, while the Casting Chalk would merely give her a fright. I *might* be able to get something more useful from the Forgery classroom, but that would take time... even assuming I could get *in*. Magister Tallyman wouldn't have set the wards to allow me entry yet...

My blood ran cold. What if he'd changed his mind about allowing me to help him?

The door opened. I looked up as Henrietta Maria entered the dorm. I vaguely recalled her from one of Alana's birthday parties, but she hadn't made much of an impression. I'd spent most of that party hiding in my room, hoping to escape the inevitable game of 'last guest in human form.' Needless to say, the winner hadn't been me.

"Isabella was saying you'd be frozen until dinner," Henrietta commented. I tensed, but she sounded amused rather than malicious. "Did you break her spell?"

"Yes," I lied. I had no idea why the spell hadn't lasted, but I wasn't about to admit it. "I can't break Sandy's spell."

"Sandy was proper raging," Henrietta told me. Her voice was oddly accented. If I recalled correctly, she actually lived some distance outside the city. "We should probably count ourselves lucky she didn't turn us all into pigs."

"I suppose," I said. I'd have to teach Rose how to signal that she was a transformed human, preferably before someone tried to turn her into a frog again. "Can you try to break the spell?"

Henrietta frowned, stroking her chin. "What's it worth?"

I winced. "What would you like?"

"Help with my homework," Henrietta said, after a moment. "I don't want to turn in a bad potions essay."

"Me neither," I said, although I had a feeling it was too late to make a good impression. "If you can break the spell, I'll help you with your homework."

Henrietta cast the counterspell. Rose slumped forward. I caught her a moment before her head could hit the floor.

"Thanks," I said, seriously. "I think she must have keyed it to resist *my* magic."

I did my best to ignore Henrietta's doubtful look. Keying a spell to make it impossible for a specific person to unravel was *very* difficult. Sandy would have gone to a lot of trouble for no real gain. But it was better she believed that Sandy had put in the effort, instead of looking for other explanations. It wouldn't take her long to put two and two together and come up with four.

Or zero, I thought.

Rose sagged against me. "Are you all right?"

"Sure," I lied. "I'm fine."

I helped her to her feet, then glanced at the clock. We had another hour until dinner. It *should* be enough time to finish my lines, if I worked hard. My hand was going to be aching tonight...I sighed. It couldn't be helped.

And I could get a potion to soothe the ache, I thought. *But getting it from the healers might be tricky.*

"I'll meet you in the library tonight," Henrietta said. She touched my shoulder. I almost flinched. "Bring your books."

"There's copies of everything on the shelves," I assured her. Some of the rarer books were actually chained to the shelves, just to make sure that absent-minded students didn't walk off with them. "We'll see you there."

I met Rose's eyes. It was going to be a very long evening.

CHAPTER
SIXTEEN

The rest of the week went surprisingly quickly, much to my relief. Isabella gave me an odd look when she realised I'd somehow escaped her spell, but otherwise she left Rose and I alone while we studied in the library. Alana even *thanked* me for distracting Magistra Loanda from *her* potion. For once, she didn't even try to hex me.

But I couldn't help feeling nervous as I crawled out of bed on Saturday and headed down to breakfast.

Normally, according to Sandy, students were allowed to sleep in over the weekend. It made up for having to get out of bed at seven-thirty on weekdays. But I had strict orders to report to Magistra Loanda for detention and *that* meant I couldn't stay in bed. Sandy had practically tossed me out of bed almost as soon as the bell rang. Rose *had* offered to come with me, to breakfast if not to the classroom, but I'd told her to get some rest. We'd be working in the library as soon as Magistra Loanda let me go.

I braced myself as I reached her classroom and knocked on the door. I'd only managed to eat some toast and tea for breakfast, but it still sat heavily in my stomach. Sandy had entertained us by telling gruesome stores of dangerous detentions over the last few days and while I *thought* she was joking, it was hard to convince myself of that. Magistra Loanda's door felt more ominous than ever before...

It opened, revealing a darkened classroom. Magistra Loanda sat at her desk, looking incredibly prim as her eyes fixed on me. I resisted the urge to run - again - as I forced my legs to carry me into the room, coming to a halt in front of her desk. She looked me up and down without speaking, her dark eyes cold and utterly unforgiving. I was, I realised, in deep trouble. She looked as though she wanted to cut me up and use me in a number of highly-illegal - and *definitely* dark - potions.

"Miss Aguirre," Magistra Loanda said. "Do you know why you are here?"

I nodded, shortly.

"Speak up, girl," Magistra Loanda snapped. "I don't have all day."

"Yes," I said. "I know."

"I have five storerooms in this section, all reachable through that door," Magistra Loanda said, pointing a finger towards the rear of the room. There was indeed a door there, one I hadn't seen before. She must have charmed it to make it harder for people to see. "I want you to go through the store, piece by piece, and make a list of any bottles or jars that are less than half-full. As you are a mere *firstie*" - she spoke the word as though it was an insult - "you may use ladders to climb up and down. Do *not* use magic in my storerooms or it will be the last thing you ever do."

"Yes, Magistra," I said. Some potions ingredients were volatile, *very* volatile. A loose flare of magic could set them off, easily. It was why Mum had banned my sisters from the storeroom back home. "Do you have paper for me?"

Magistra Loanda nodded, producing a large sheet of paper and a pen. "Make sure everything is clear," she ordered, shortly. "I want to be able to read it without having to use deciphering spells."

I took the paper and headed towards the door. It opened easily, revealing a massive storeroom that dwarfed the one we'd used earlier. There were hundreds of shelves, each one lined with jars and bottles...a number were covered in dust or protected with nasty-looking runes. I recognised enough of them to know that touching the jars with my bare hands would be a dangerous mistake. The eerie green light floating down from somewhere high above didn't help. I knew enough about preserving ingredients to understand that it was part of the store's defensive system.

"Try not to upset some of the spices," Magistra Loanda called. I hoped I was imagining the dark amusement in her voice. "They're *very* unhappy souls."

I swallowed as I reached the end of the first storeroom and found the corridor to the next. It was massive, a section of the school that I had no idea existed. Four additional storerooms, a couple of hidden workrooms... Magistra Loanda had more potions ingredients in one place than anyone else, even Mum. Judging by the dust, a number of ingredients hadn't been touched for years. The charmed bottles would have preserved them, I thought, but most brewers would have preferred fresh ingredients. A little potency was lost if they were stored for the long-term.

And there are so many cobwebs around, I thought, *that she's probably breeding spiders.*

"I don't hear writing," Magistra Loanda called, loudly. "Do I have to take more stringent steps to enforce your obedience?"

"No, Magistra," I called back.

I hurried back into the first storeroom, found a ladder and leaned it against the uppermost shelf. If I was lucky, I could scramble up, check the bottles and then make a list of empty ones. I could hear Magistra Loanda talking to someone outside as I climbed the ladder, feeling nervous. I was only twelve, but the ladder creaked loudly enough to suggest I was a grown man. It didn't feel safe at all.

You can be healed, I told myself, as I reached the top. *Let's see what's missing.*

It was easy enough, thankfully, to read the names without sneaking closer. Most of the bottles and jars were nearly full, although there were some exceptions. I wrote their names down - and then added the location, as Mum had taught me. Magistra Loanda might have been waiting for me to make that mistake before she dropped a hammer on me. The next shelf was just the same, followed by the next...it was easy to tell which ingredients she used regularly. Shiny new jars sat next to bottles that were so old I didn't know if the contents were still safe to use. I made a note of some of the more odious ones, even though it wasn't part of my duties. Magistra Loanda might be glad to hear of it.

I fell into a routine as I worked my way down the shelves, picking out names and adding them to the list. It felt like the kind of work I'd done for Mum, back home...I wondered, despite myself, if there was a future after all. But that rather depended on getting at least one degree. Magistra

Loanda might not have realised that Rose had made the potion work, but I didn't expect our luck to hold forever. I made a mental note of some of the more interesting ingredients and their locations, then kept moving. And then the door opened...

"You look a mess," a familiar voice said. "Good thing the uniform is black, isn't it?"

I looked down. Robin Brandon was standing there, looking up.

"I heard you got into a spot of trouble," he said. I scowled as I realised I was blocking his path further into the storerooms. "She got you counting the empty bottles?"

"Yeah," I muttered. I scrambled down to the floor and pushed the ladder aside. "You in trouble too?"

"Nah, just thought I'd pop in to say hello," Robin said. He towered over me as soon as I was on the ground. "And to let you know I found the rest of your stuff."

I blinked. I'd almost forgotten. "Everything?"

"Yep," Robin assured me. "I've got it all stowed away in my locker. Come to the common room this evening and I'll let you have it."

"Thanks," I said. "The Casting Chalk came in handy."

"I'll bet it did," Robin said. He leaned forward and lowered his voice. "Word is that you stormed out of class, slamming the door behind you."

"I didn't slam the door," I said. Or had I? I honestly couldn't remember. "But I did storm out."

"Very impressive," Robin said. "No one else has dared to do that for years,"

He made a show of glancing around the storeroom. "I'm surprised she hasn't done something nastier to you."

I looked down at my shirt. It was stained with dirt and grime. I was going to need to shower afterwards, if I managed to make it back to the dorm. Some passing upperclassman would probably toss me into the swimming pool, just to make sure I didn't tread mud through the school. Or cast a cleaning charm so powerful my clothes would fray.

"This is nasty enough," I said, finally.

Robin clapped me on the back. "Just try and make it a little more spectacular next time," he told me. "You've made more of a splash than John Johnston did when *he* was a mere firstie."

I shrugged. I had no idea who John Johnston was, but I wasn't going to admit it. I'd look him up in the library, if I had time. Rose and I had been working on the basics, when we weren't working on homework. Thankfully, Henrietta's homework had been easy. I'd done more complex exercises for Mum. If I managed to get out of the potions storerooms before the end of the day, I might even have time to do some of my own homework.

"Keep up the good work," Robin added. "We'll be watching you."

I resisted the urge to stick my tongue out at his retreating back as I clambered back up the ladder and got back to work. There were hundreds of jars and only a handful of them needed to be replaced, but they all had to be checked. I lost track of time as I worked, only jerking back into awareness when I heard the door open again. This time, Magistra Loanda stood there, looking grim.

"It's lunchtime," she said. "How many bottles did you find?"

I glanced at the clock. Three hours? How had three hours managed to pass without me noticing? But the clock didn't lie.

"Fifteen bottles need to be replaced," I said. "Seventeen more are on the borderline."

She took my list and ran her eyes down it. "I'll make sure to replace them all," she said, drolly. "Running out of ingredients in class would be annoying."

"Yes, Magistra," I said.

Magistra Loanda nodded, then beckoned me into the classroom. "I do not expect to see such behaviour again, young lady," she said. "You acted disgracefully."

I nodded, trying to look submissive. "Yes, Magistra."

"Your mother is one of the greatest brewers in the world," Magistra Loanda added. "She will no doubt contact you to explain the error of your ways."

I swallowed, hard. I'd hoped Magistra Loanda wouldn't contact my parents. Some hope!

"However, you appear to have done a good job," Magistra Loanda said. "Next time, you will be scrubbing caldrons in warm water. I dare say you will find it an interesting experience."

And an explosive one, I thought.

I wasn't stupid enough to say that out loud. Mum had told me that allowing different potions to mix together was asking for trouble. The interaction between normal potions was carefully controlled, but random mixing tended to lead to explosions - or worse. She'd told me that the potions mould sometimes developed intelligence and set out to take over the world - or at least the Hall - but I thought she was joking. Regardless, only an idiot would allow the remnants of a dozen different potions to mix. There might be just enough magic left in the various brews to trigger an explosion.

"Thank you," I said, instead.

Magistra Loanda gave me a baleful stare. "Go back to your dorm and shower," she ordered, shortly. "And I don't want any more trouble from you."

I nodded and fled out of the room before she could change her mind. The corridors were almost deserted - two-thirds of the school were either in the gardens or still in bed - and made it back without incident. Thankfully, the charms on my boots kept them from treading dirt inside the school. Sandy was lying on her bed when I entered, her eyes going wide when she saw me. And then she smiled.

"You *do* remember you're going to be cleaning the washrooms, don't you?"

"You couldn't have planned it better," I said. Provoking her wasn't wise, but I was too tired to care. "Well done."

Sandy gave me a sharp look, but didn't bother to rise to the bait. "You have a couple of letters," she said, instead. "They're on your bed. Wash *before* you go to read them."

I nodded and grabbed my dressing gown before hurrying into the washroom to shower. My clothes would have to be dumped in the hamper for laundry. I just hoped the washerwomen could get the stains out or I'd have to buy a new set. Mum and Dad wouldn't notice the cost, but Mum - at least - would be very sarcastic about it. It wouldn't have been that hard to wear an apron.

As soon as I was showered, I headed back to my bed and pulled the drapes closed. The two letters lay on the duvet, both covered in my father's handwriting. I sat down and picked one at random to open. It contained the permission slip for Magister Tallyman and - surprisingly - a note of congratulations from my father. I felt a glow of warmth as I read it.

Caitlyn.

I am very proud that Magister Tallyman has seen fit to offer you the chance to work as one of his assistants. While I do not believe he will have any more success than any other Forger with his obsession, he is one of the leading men in his field and I am sure that you will learn a great deal from him. I will be happy, if necessary, to purchase materials and suchlike for you to use over the summer holidays.

My smile grew wider. He was proud of me!

My sole concern is that you will be partnered with Akin Rubén. I have heard little about the young man himself, but his father will not hesitate to insist that he shares anything he may discover about you with him. Their ambitions in Magus Court will not fade easily, Kitten. I advise you to be very careful around him. Naturally, anything you happen to discover that may be of interest to us should be forwarded to me at once.

I frowned. Akin Rubén hadn't given me any reason to think ill of him, apart from a really bad choice in sisters. But that hadn't been his fault, had it?

Do not waste this opportunity.
    Your Loving Father, Joaquin Aguirre, High Magus of Magus Court

I had to smile, again. Father didn't *need* to sign his letters with his full name and title. I knew who he was. But the letters started to fade, even as I reread it to fix the details in my mind. Dad had made sure no one else could read it. I suspected he'd probably charmed the envelope too.

Shaking my head, I opened the second letter. It was from my mother.

Caitlyn.

I was extremely displeased to hear about your decision to leave potions class on Tuesday. Magistra Loanda is an extremely experienced brewer who should be able to provide you with the training you require. (I notice that she gave your potion high marks, although she did have to recover traces from the floor.) I assume she will ensure that you receive sufficient punishment for this. Rest assured, I will take steps if you continue to act up in her class.

For the moment, I have ordered Henry not to send you any treats for the next two weeks.

I sighed. Mum *wasn't* pleased. She knew I *loved* Henry's treats.

I understand, dear heart, your feelings about the school. Please remember that your father and I have only your best interests in mind. It is vitally important that you develop your talent and learn to fit into our community. The friends and contacts you make at Jude's will follow you for the rest of your life. Making a good impression - and not just in front of your peers - is important.

Your father and I look forward to seeing you - all three of you - during half-term holidays. Until then, I remain.

Your Loving Mother, Lady Sorceress Sofia Aguirre, Potions Mistress.

I closed my eyes for a long moment. When I opened them, the letter was blank.

Of course, I thought. *Mum wouldn't want her words shared with anyone else either.*

I tore up the paper and dumped the remains in the bin, then rose and headed for the door. It was lunchtime. I could grab something to eat, then join Rose in the library. And then...I swallowed, hard. We were going to have to practice spells, while planning revenge on Isabella. And then...

"You appear alarmingly cheerful," Sandy commented. "Is Magistra Loanda losing her touch?"

"My parents wrote to me," I said. "Isn't that good?"

"You do need to write to them tomorrow," Sandy reminded me. "Can I trust you to do that?"

"Yes," I said, stiffly. "But it would be so much easier if I could just walk over and see them."

"They could also come crashing into the school at the slightest excuse," Sandy pointed out, dryly. "You'd miss out on some of the experience."

I scowled. "*What* experience?"

"Learning to stand on your own two feet," Sandy said.

She gave me a twisted smile. "And you're going to be doing the washrooms tomorrow," she added, darkly. "Make sure you bring your toothbrush."

"...No," I said.

Sandy laughed. "I must be losing my touch," she said. "That got Yolanda."

Her smile widened. "Brushes will be provided," she added. "But you're not allowed to use magic."

I shrugged. I couldn't use magic anyway.

CHAPTER
SEVENTEEN

S andy was as good as her word.

I had barely finished my breakfast, the following morning, when she dragged me into the washroom and taught me how to clean. The maids had taught me some tricks - Mum had been fond of making us help them whenever she wanted to punish us - but Sandy insisted on watching me like a hawk, telling me what to do every time I moved to a new section of the washroom. I think she wanted to make sure I didn't use magic. She, at least, didn't believe the rumours about me.

"Good enough," Sandy said, when I had finished. "You will be doing it for three more weeks, of course."

I sighed. My clothes were damp and my back was aching. I wanted a shower and a change, sooner rather than later. It had been a hard job, even if *I* had washed and cleaned before. No *wonder* Sandy considered it an effective punishment. Isabella and her cronies had probably never been forced to clean up after themselves until they came to school. The only amusement had come when Isabella had *accidentally* made a mess after I'd cleaned one of the basins, only to be given five hundred lines to be handed in by the end of the day. She'd probably blame me for her aching wrist, afterwards, but I found it hard to care. It wasn't *my* fault.

And I have some supplies now, I thought, darkly. *I can take revenge.*

Sandy led me back into the dorm and clapped her hands. "If I could have your attention, please," she said. "There's a small announcement I have to make."

She waited until the entire dorm was paying attention, then continued. "The netball team captains have decided to hold the first set of tryouts over the next few days. If you want to play, go to the sports office and sign up there. They'll give everyone a shot at playing before determining the teams for the rest of the year. But you'll have to be very good to get a slot on a team."

"That's not fair," Isabella said. "First years..."

"The *world* isn't fair," Sandy snapped at her. "And if you don't finish those lines, you won't be allowed to join the tryouts."

I smiled to myself. Mum had made it clear that very few firsties were ever invited to join a team, unless they had real talent or the team captain was desperate. We could - and most of us would - play to learn the game, but the odds were strongly against any of us joining a team and winning the cup. It didn't bother me that much. The spells one needed to play netball at Jude's were *well* beyond me.

But it might keep Isabella out of my way, I thought, as I joined Rose and listened to a handful of other minor announcements. *A couple of nights on the field would tire her out.*

Isabella and her cronies started to chat happily about the upcoming games, but I ignored them as best as I could. Instead, I showered and changed into weekend clothes, then joined Rose by the door. The others were so interested in their discussion that they didn't even notice us leaving. We hurried up to the library, passing a couple of fourth-year students having a loud argument. I hoped it wasn't anything that would spill down to the younger years.

"She could have told us about netball before breakfast," Rose said. "Why did she make us wait?"

"She's trying to remind us who's in charge," I answered. I didn't think anyone actually doubted it, but Sandy clearly felt a little insecure. "And besides, she has to make sure we get *all* the announcements."

I'd put our names down for a workroom yesterday, but I wasn't particularly surprised to discover that a trio of seventh-years had taken it. The librarian had warned me, after all, that they got priority. I chatted briefly with her, then found a number of books we could work through as we waited. Rose *was* learning quickly, but she was trying to cram four *years* of study into a single term.

"I don't understand how this works," she moaned, holding out a sheet of paper. "How *does* it work?"

"The iron focuses the spell on its target," I explained. "And the equations ensure the spell stays in place longer."

"So it doesn't weaken," Rose guessed. "Right?"

"Right," I confirmed. "As long as the runes are carved precisely, the spell should stay in place indefinitely."

It was nearly an hour before one of the workrooms was empty. We watched a small group of fifth-years heading out of the library, looking rather stunned by the work they had to do now that they were upperclassmen, then hurried to take the room for ourselves. The librarian had assured me we couldn't be kicked out once we were actually in possession, but I wasn't sure I believed it. Upperclassmen *did* have first call on the school's resources, after all. They were the ones trying to earn advanced degrees.

I closed the door, wishing I could lock it. But none of the spells I knew could have kept the door shut if an upperclassman wanted in, even if I'd been able to cast them. I pushed the thought aside and sat down on the floor, motioning for Rose to sit opposite me. She looked attentive, even though she knew there were limits to what I could teach her. There was certainly no way I could *demonstrate* the spells for her.

"Right," I said. I couldn't help feeling nervous. This could easily go very wrong. "Did you read the spells I wrote out for you?"

"Yeah," Rose said. She produced a sheaf of papers. "I haven't dared test them."

"I know," I said. My throat was suddenly very dry. "You're going to test them on me."

Rose's mouth dropped open. "Are you mad?"

"I'm used to it," I said, sourly. If I had someone - someone *else* - I could trust, it would be a great deal easier. "You *do* know how to cancel spells now, right?"

"I think so," Rose said, nervously. She paled. I wouldn't have thought it was possible for her to pale any further. "But what if I get it wrong? What if" - she glanced down at the sheaf of papers - "what if I turn you into something forever? I mean...what if...?"

"You won't," I said, more confidently than I felt. Sure, a transfiguration *wouldn't* last without careful preparation, but there was plenty of scope for things to go wrong. Alana - and Isabella, I assumed - had learnt in a warded chamber, under adult supervision. But there were no adults here. "The worst you can do is trap me for an hour or so. We reserved this room for three hours."

Rose looked at me. I saw a hint of affection, even *admiration*, in her eyes. "Cat...are you sure?"

"You need to learn," I said. "And there's no way we can ask anyone else."

I *had* given the matter some thought, to be honest. But I hadn't managed to come up with a better answer. Anyone I asked would wonder, quite rightly, why *I* hadn't taught Rose the basics. Combined with the rumours about me, they would have no trouble putting two and two together and coming up with *zero*. Allowing Rose to test her spells on me was the safest option, although there *were* risks. I just hoped I'd managed to counter all of them.

"Read the spell carefully," I said. "And when you're ready, let me know."

Rose nodded and started to read. I watched her lips move soundlessly as she parsed out some of the words. Alana was already beyond the stage where she needed to chant such a simple spell, but Rose had to learn to walk before she could run. I was suddenly very aware of my heartbeat pounding in my chest. If I was wrong about Rose...I was about to put my life in her hands.

But she could have told everyone, after I told her, I thought. Isabella would probably have forgiven Rose everything, if Rose had confirmed Isabella's suspicions. *She kept my secret.*

"I think I'm ready," Rose announced. She looked me in the eye. "Are you sure...?"

"Yes," I said. It was *almost* true. "Cast the spell."

Rose hesitated. I didn't really blame her. I had grown up in a city where sudden transformations - or worse - were just a part of life. I'd learned to cope with having my body changed. But Rose thought it was horrific. And really, how could I blame her?

I tensed as she muttered the words, moving her hands in a pattern. Nothing happened. I blinked, wondering if I'd messed up the spell somehow, then leaned forward as I realised the problem. Her gestures were precise, but her pronunciation was a little off. And she didn't have the experience to override the problem and make the spell *work*.

"Focus on the words," I said, firmly. Rose was starting to look as though she wanted to give up. "And try again."

Rose lifted her hand and tried again. This time, the world spun around me. I squeezed my eyes closed as I felt my body change, then opened them again to see Rose staring down at me. She was a giant...no, I'd shrunk. My head swam, just for a second. I might have been used to transformations, but there was something disconcerting about suddenly being a great deal smaller. My arms twitched and I looked down automatically. Rose had turned me into a frog.

I looked back up at her. She was staring, her face clearly caught between exultation and horror. She'd successfully cast a spell, but she'd also reduced her best friend - her only friend - to a frog. I wondered how long it would be until she started abusing the spell when she went home for the summer. Alana hadn't taken long to start turning everyone she could into small animals.

My new body wanted to jump. Its instincts insisted that it should be a long way away from Rose. I took control with an effort, then started to make signs on the floor. Rose's eyes went wide, then she nodded and started to cast the counterspell. I saw panic cross her face as the spell failed, the first time she tried to cast it. She needed three tries to get it to work.

"I'm sorry," she gasped, as I returned to normal. "I..."

"Don't worry about it," I said. I sat upright, torn between a quiet pride in her success and a flicker of bitter jealously. "I've spent much longer as a frog - or worse."

Rose gave me a sympathetic look. "Isabella?"

"My sisters," I said.

"My older brother was a bit of a bully," Rose said. "If he'd been able to turn people into frogs..."

Her voice trailed off. I knew what she was thinking. *She* could turn people - including her brother - into frogs. What would she do when she went home? Maybe she would teach her brother a lesson. Or maybe...

"You need to master the signs," I said. "If someone does that to you, again, you have to be able to ask for help."

Rose made a face. "That doesn't happen in my village," she said. "I never heard of anything like it..."

"There was a story I heard a few years ago," I said. "There was a man who had a very clever horse - a horse who could actually do sums. He used to take it from place to place to show off and earn money."

"Let me guess," Rose said. "The horse was actually a transformed man?"

"In a manner of speaking," I said. Dad had told us the story, years ago. I'd had nightmares afterwards. "People used to cast cancellation spells at the horse, because they suspected...well, you know. It didn't work. The horse seemed to be a normal horse. But one day the man took the beast to a blacksmith's...and when the blacksmith removed one of the horseshoes, the spell broke. The beast became a young woman."

Rose looked horrified. "What...*how*?"

"It depends on who you believe," I said. "Apparently, she was cursed by her husband and turned into a horse. He *then* crafted runes onto the horseshoes to *keep* her in that form permanently, as long as the horse-shoes remained on her hooves. And then he sold her to the trader, who thought she was just a remarkably clever beast. He never realised she was actually *human* because the horseshoes kept the counterspell from working."

I leaned forwards. "She never bothered to learn the signs," I added. "And that's why it took years for her to become human again."

That, according to dad, was the true moral of the story. He'd insisted that we learn, drilling us time and time again until we could make the signs in almost any form. We *could* be trapped permanently in another shape, he'd warned, if someone wanted to *really* hurt us - or simply render us harmless for a long period. And I'd taken his warnings to heart. Alana might tell herself, after doing something like it to me, that she hadn't actually committed murder.

"That's *sick*," Rose said. "Who would *do* that to their wife?"

I shrugged. "I don't know," I said. "Just make sure you know how to ask for help."

"Maybe it's not a true story," Rose said. "Just...just a horror story to focus the mind."

"Maybe," I said. Dad had told us *lots* of horror stories, each one a warning against misusing magic or trusting in the wrong person. "But trapping someone in another form permanently is possible, with the right preparations. You have to be able to signal for help."

Rose swallowed. "I don't think I wanted to know that."

I smiled at her. "You need to cast the spell again," I said. "I want you to be able to cast it in a heartbeat."

"I can't," Rose said. Her hands were shaking. "Cat..."

"You can do it," I said. "What would you do if you had a choice between hexing Isabella and being hexed yourself?"

Rose gave me a sharp look, then cast the spell. This time, she got it right first time. I wondered, as I signalled for her to turn me back, if she would leave me a frog for a few minutes, but she clearly didn't bear a grudge. She turned me back, then cast the spell again and again. It would be a while, I thought, until she could cast the spell in a second, but she was definitely on the way.

"Well done," I said. "You want to move on to the next spell?"

"Please," Rose said. She sounded relieved. It would be a long time before she grew used to transfiguring people, let alone being transfigured herself. "I'm not sure how I can break the spell if someone uses it on me."

"The way I taught you should work," I told her. "But you probably do need to practice that too."

I contemplated it for a moment, then shrugged. "I don't know how we could practice that," I admitted. "I can't turn you into anything."

Rose smiled. "We *could* dare Isabella to turn us into frogs."

"That would work, I suppose," I said. It wouldn't be long before Isabella did something nasty to us. She was probably still smarting over her wrists. "Or we could provoke her..."

I shook my head. "I think that would be dangerous," I added, after a moment. "She might not do as we wanted."

"True," Rose agreed.

I picked up the next sheet of paper. "This one is a little more complex," I said. "But it's easier to cast, once you master it."

Rose frowned. "How do you know that?"

"Alana picked it up with terrifying speed," I said. Mum had insisted we all learn some self-defence skills, if only to defend ourselves against footpads, but I'd never managed to get them to work. Alana had only mastered them so quickly because she'd learned by practicing on me. "Can you see how it works?"

"I think so," Rose said, after reading the instructions. "Are you ready?"

I nodded. She jabbed a finger at me, muttering words under her breath. Nothing happened.

"Try again," I ordered. I hardened my voice, pretending to be my mother. "Now."

Rose jabbed her finger at me again, saying the words out loud. This time, I froze solid.

I would have frowned, if I could have moved a muscle. The spell felt... odd. I couldn't put it into words, but there was something wrong with it. Rose reached out and prodded my forehead, pressing her finger into my skin. It should have felt immovable, but instead it just felt weird. Maybe she'd accidentally locked my muscles instead...no, that shouldn't have been possible. I'd written out the spell myself...

It broke. My entire body cramped.

"I'm sorry," Rose said. She sounded as though she was on the verge of panic. "What happened?"

"I don't know," I said. I'd had muscle cramps before, but this was different. The *spell* had felt different. Thanks to Alana, I was very familiar with the spell...but it was different. "I..."

The door opened. "Out," a sixth-year said. "We need the room."

I wanted to argue, but I knew it was pointless. The librarian would take their side and we would just end up with more lines to write. I didn't want to blot my copybook again.

"Fine," I said. Rose didn't look like she wanted to continue, anyway. I didn't really blame her. She'd been pushing herself to the limit. "We were just finishing here."

CHAPTER
EIGHTEEN

The week would have gone smoothly if it hadn't been for Isabella. Her grudge against me had mushroomed into a monster and she was forever shooting hexes, jinxes and dirty looks at me. The only good thing that could be said about it was that she was giving Rose a great deal of practice with the various counterspells, although it came at a high cost. By the time Friday rolled around, I had already decided that I was going to push back hard. But I still had to wait for an opportunity before I could strike.

Isabella had, somehow, convinced a team captain to let her take one of the reserve slots on the team. I suspected she'd either paid a bribe or made a promise of future favours, if only because I didn't want to believe she might have any real talent. Alana had done the same, I'd heard. I was torn between relief that my sister was out of my hair - although we didn't actually share a dorm - and irritation that she'd claimed such an important post so easily. I had no doubt *she* would have manipulated her family connections to convince the team captain to give her a chance.

But it did work in my favour, I thought. Isabella and her cronies - and the others - were out of the dorm and wouldn't be coming back until just before Lights Out. Rose and I had some privacy to carry out our revenge.

Rose caught my arm as I checked the washrooms. "Are you sure this is a good idea?"

I shrugged. "Isabella needs to be taught a lesson," I said. I'd learnt *that* from dealing with my sisters. "Bullies cannot be allowed to walk all over you or they just get worse."

"As long as she doesn't know who did it," Rose muttered.

"Go watch the door," I told her. "Come straight back in if you see anyone who might want to enter the dorm."

Rose nodded and hurried off. I waited until she was standing in the door, then turned to look at Isabella's bed. It was identical to mine, save for the stuffed teddy bear resting by the pillows. I felt a flicker of envy, mixed with concern. The teddy bear's eyes might be nothing more than marble, but Isabella could easily have charmed them to watch over her possessions while she was away. Alana had had something similar, a couple of years ago. Dad had charmed it to protect her, but Alana had taken the charms apart to see how they worked and the poor teddy had never been the same again.

I pulled the magic sensor out of my pocket and held it out, feeling it vibrating gently in my palm. There was enough magic in the room's protective wards to make the Device hum, although I'd checked earlier to figure out a baseline for the dorm. Sandy had forbidden us from placing traps anywhere outside our beds, pointing out that someone who needed to use the toilet in the middle of the night *didn't* need to suddenly find themselves stuck to the floor and trapped. The racket alone would wake the rest of us up.

The Device thrummed louder as I crept towards Isabella's bed, carefully feeling out the wards and trap lines. Isabella had done a very good job, I noted as I measured the emissions and compared them to past experience. She'd ensured that no one would be able to open her drapes without waking her, even if they *didn't* trigger a hidden hex. I was fairly sure she'd charmed the drapes too, probably to distract an intruder. If she hadn't had the idea before I'd humiliated her, she'd certainly had it now.

Drat, I thought, as it became clear that the bed and bedside cabinet were far too heavily protected for me to sneak closer. Alana might have been able to pick her way through the maze of incants, but *I* couldn't. Maybe I could discharge some of the spells, perhaps even repeat the fake frog stunt...I shook my head. There was too much chance of the frog getting lost before it was too late. *I'm not going to be able to touch her bed.*

I stepped backwards and glanced at Rose. She was still standing there, looking nervous. I didn't really blame her. The worst Isabella could do was turn us into frogs - if she didn't tattle on us to Sandy - but Rose didn't really believe it. She was far too used to thinking she could get into worse trouble. I winked, then carefully made a very slight mark on the floor with the Casting Chalk. If I was lucky, it would go completely undetected. I took one last look at the teddy bear - its sightless eyes seemed to look back at me - and then hurried back to my bed.

"Come here," I called. I held out the Device for her to inspect. "There's no point in keeping a look out now."

Rose still looked twitchy as she examined my work. I'd taken advantage of some private time and sketched out the runes and sigils onto a tiny sheet of iron. Robin had done a very good job. He'd found enough tools for me to create a more interesting Device, once I'd borrowed some materials from Forgery. I made a silent promise to do whatever I could to help him, later on, as I put the last sigil into place. It would take time for the runes to go active - they would have to draw on the magic field directly, rather than work through a magician - but Isabella would have real trouble figuring out what was going on. I put the tiny Device at the end of my bed, then winked again at Rose. Even if Isabella *did* realise what was going on, she would have to search *my* bed to find the Device.

And it will look like she's been hexed, I thought, as I opened a book and motioned for Rose to sit next to me. *No one will go looking for an alternate explanation.*

We were midway through a large potions tome when Isabella and her cronies returned, laughing and joking amongst themselves. I felt a flicker of jealously, which I ruthlessly suppressed. Isabella's friends weren't *real* friends. They were just hanging around her because of what she could do for them, in later life. Rose had stayed with me even though I couldn't do anything for her.

"Losers," Isabella jeered. "Guess what I've been doing?"

I made a show of inspecting her muddy clothes. "Mud-wrestling an alligator? Swimming in the sewer?"

Isabella's face reddened. "You're talking to the youngest netball player in fifteen years!"

"Oh," I said. "How much did *that* cost you?"

She clenched her fists. "You take that back!"

I smirked, even as Rose looked alarmed and hastily prepared a spell. There was *no* way Isabella would have been playing netball before Jude's. I was sure of it. Alana would have whined and moaned until Mum and Dad allowed her to play, if Isabella was actually playing with her friends. And unless she *was* a natural talent, the second or third-year students would have far more experience. I could believe she had managed to make the reserves, but a spot on the *actual* team? Not a chance.

"You must have shelled out a *lot* of money," I gibed. I knew it wasn't wise to provoke her, but I couldn't resist. "Or did you promise a place in your household or..."

"And why is *everyone* tracking mud through the dorm?" Sandy shouted. She'd come back into the dorm while everyone was watching Isabella and me. "What are you *thinking*?"

Isabella shot me a murderous look, but she wasn't stupid enough to do anything while Sandy was on the warpath. Instead, she muttered an apology in Sandy's direction and hurried into the washroom. Her cronies followed, looking tired and sweaty themselves. I pitied the washerwomen who'd have to deal with their clothes. Whoever had designed the sporting outfit was a sadist beyond compare.

Rose poked me. "Are you mad?"

"I can't back down," I muttered back.

Sandy stomped up and down the room, snapping at anyone moving too slowly to suit her. I guessed she had some reason to be up early, just like me. Even *Isabella* looked cowed when Sandy threatened her with a ghastly punishment if she didn't get into bed by Lights Out. It was almost a relief when everyone was in bed and the lights were out. But I was too excited - and nervous - to sleep. I lay back in my bed and waited, thinking about ways to escape yet another humiliating disaster in Charms. Rose simply didn't know enough to help me without being caught.

It was nearly thirty minutes, I think, before I heard the sound of someone scratching. It had to be Isabella. She was trying to be quiet, I thought, but there was no other noise in the dorm at all. Everyone could hear. The sound was growing louder and louder, as if the itching had grown too overpowering for Isabella to care about being heard. And I knew that the runes I'd carved - and the chalk I'd used to direct the spell - were steadily breaking through her protections.

I stifled my laughter with an effort. Most magicians don't pay too much attention to basic runes, even though they're used to direct magic. They tend to jump straight to the geometric designs used in Charms. I'd only studied them intensely because I'd hoped they would provide a key to magic - and, perhaps, a way to master forging. *Akin* would probably guess what was happening, but would Isabella? I rather doubted it. *Aluna* hadn't known, the few times I'd done something similar to her. She'd focused on her charms and ignored everything else.

The sound of scratching grew louder. I could hear muffled giggles coming from some of the beds. Isabella wasn't universally popular, even in the dorm. I heard her mutter a counterspell, then a more advanced counterspell. It didn't sound as though it had brought her any relief. I concealed my amusement with an effort. The runes wouldn't last very long, but they *were* effective.

"For heaven's sake," Sandy snapped. Her voice was so loud that I jumped. "You've been hexed, you silly girl. Cast the counterspell!"

"I've been trying," Isabella said. "It's not fading!"

"Then cast it again, stronger this time," Sandy ordered. There were more giggles, echoing round the dorm. "And the rest of you, get back to sleep!"

Isabella said a vile word, then cast a *third* counterspell. I caught enough of the words to be impressed, despite myself. Dad had told us that the spell should only be used if one was desperate. It was harder to target on a specific spell, which meant that a magician could accidentally knock down his own protections while trying to eradicate the pesky hex. I wondered, absently, if there was a way to convince Isabella to use the spell again, when we were waiting to ambush her.

I lay back in my bed, satisfied. Isabella's spell should have cleared the air - and the runes wouldn't last long enough to recharge. She would have an uncomfortable night and probably feel utterly wretched in the morning. I closed my eyes and tried to sleep...

...Only to be jerked back to wakefulness by *more* scratching.

"I said *cancel it*," Sandy thundered, from her bed. "Do it!"

"I can't," Isabella pleaded. "I just can't stop itching!"

"You did annoy one of the fifth-years," Clarian Bolingbroke offered. She sounded as though she was trying not to laugh. "I bet she hexed you..."

I frowned in disbelief. The runes...they should have faded by now. They'd channelled enough magic to give Isabella an itch...

"Shut up," Zeya ordered. "Isabella won fairly!"

"Sure," Clarian called. "If you define *fairly* to include bribing the team captain."

"Be quiet," Sandy snapped. I heard her climb out of bed and push back her drapes. "The next one of you to speak before dawn will be stunned."

Ouch, I thought.

I could hear Sandy walking down the dorm towards Isabella's bed. A couple of others were opening their drapes to peer into the semi-darkness...I took advantage of the noise to slip up and remove the rune-carved iron from its hiding place. It felt warm to the touch, but otherwise intact. The runes didn't seem to have faded at all. I stared at it in astonishment, ignoring the ear-blasting Isabella was getting from Sandy. The runes should not have lasted long once they gathered enough power to work the spell.

I calculated them perfectly, I thought, numbly. *It shouldn't have lasted.*

There was no time to figure it out. The Casting Chalk wouldn't prove anything, but Sandy would have me writing lines for the next seven years if she found proof I'd disturbed everyone's sleep. I hastily scratched out the runes, cancelling the spell, then hid the Device in my cabinet. Sandy would find it, if she bothered to look, but I didn't dare put it somewhere safer. She might hear me opening my trunk and realise I was still awake.

"The hex is gone," Sandy said, crossly. I wondered, precisely, what she'd found. There hadn't been a hex anywhere near Isabella's bed. "I suggest you all go to sleep."

I leant back into bed and pretended to be asleep as I heard Sandy walking back towards her bed. Isabella was still moaning faintly, a sound that cut off abruptly. I hoped that meant Sandy had cast a silencing charm, rather than freezing or stunning the younger girl. The former would probably drive Isabella mad. I'd itched before, when my sisters had frozen me, and it was horrible.

It felt like no time at all had passed before I jerked awake. Sunlight was streaming through the windows. I glanced at my watch - it was nearly eight - and hastily jumped out of bed, grabbing my clothes and dressing hastily. I didn't want to be late. Magister Tallyman would not forgive me. I opened the cabinet and blinked in surprise. The Device I'd made had crumbled into iron flakes, as if it had rusted away overnight. I stared at it for a long moment, then swept the remains into the bin. Sandy could look for the Device all she wanted, if she worked out what had happened. She wouldn't find anything.

I pulled open the drapes and headed to the washroom. Isabella's drapes were open, but I didn't think much of it until I walked into the washroom and saw her standing in front of the mirror. Her face was covered in tiny blotches, as if the spell I'd cast had been massively overpowered. I stared at her, torn between grim satisfaction and guilt. Even after everything she'd done, I felt guilty.

She turned and looked at me. I knew she knew who'd hexed her.

We stared at each other for a long moment. I could see anger - and confusion - written all over her face. She *knew* I was a weak magician... and she suspected I couldn't do magic at all. And yet, she *also* knew I'd hexed her. Or did she? She might wonder if Clarian might have been right after all. A fifth-year student, kicked off the netball team, might just retaliate, even though it would get her in trouble. There was no way Isabella could cancel a fifth-year spell without help...

I tensed, bracing myself to jump. If she decided to hex me...

She didn't. Instead, she stalked past me and out of the washroom. I breathed a sigh of relief, then hastily splashed water on my face before hurrying down to breakfast. Rose would be sleeping in today...I hoped, grimly, that Isabella would let her sleep. She might wonder if *Rose* was the one who'd hexed her. And yet, her instincts were clearly telling her that *I'd* done it.

And she's right, I thought.

I wrestled with my conscience as I walked down the stairs to breakfast. On one hand, Isabella had been awful to both Rose and me. She deserved to suffer. But on the other hand, the itching spell had been nasty - nastier than I'd realised. I still didn't know how it had lasted as long as it had. No matter how I worked the problem, I couldn't think of an answer.

She froze you in place on your very first day, I thought. *And she picked on Rose too. She won't stop until she gets slapped down.*

Akin was sitting at a table as I entered, munching his way through a plate of scrambled eggs and toast. I tensed, then reminded myself that Akin wasn't likely to start a fight. Magister Tallyman wouldn't hesitate to toss him out on his ear if he did something stupid. I'd just have to share forging with him, at least until he gave up. *He* didn't *have* to remain tied to forging for the rest of his life.

"Caitlyn," he said. He sounded as though he was *trying* to be friendly. "Did you sleep well?"

I eyed him suspiciously. Was that a trick question? Had Isabella spoken to him before I woke? I didn't see how, but they *were* twins. They might have mastered twin-speak before coming to Jude's.

"Well enough, after I got to sleep," I said. "There was a lot of noise in the dorm."

"Snoring," Akin said. He smiled, rather thinly. "If you get off to sleep quickly, you keep everyone else awake."

"Cast a silencing spell," I advised. I picked up a plate and filled it with eggs, sausages and fried tomatoes. Magister Tallyman had told us to eat well. There was a good chance we would miss lunch. "That would work, wouldn't it?"

"Too many wards around," Akin said. He smiled. "And too many idiots tossing pillows around, too."

CHAPTER
NINETEEN

"Caitlyn, Akin," Magister Tallyman said. "Come on in."

We glanced at each other, then stepped into Magister Tallyman's private workroom. It was immense, easily the size of a ten-person dorm. Workbenches were everywhere, half covered in Devices of Power that looked to be in the experimental stage. The walls were covered in bookshelves or giant tool cabinets, including a number of tools Dad had only permitted me to use under supervision. A couple of large textbooks lay on the nearest workbench, open to reveal a diagram of an Object of Power. Beside it, a smaller textbook contained notes for using the diagram as a base for a Device of Power.

"Close the door," Magister Tallyman ordered. "I've keyed you both into the wards. You may use this room for your private projects" - he pointed a finger towards a smaller workbench in the corner - "as long as you work for me. My budget will cover any *reasonable* use of materials."

I smiled. Unless we made a habit of using *very* rare materials, it was unlikely anyone would even notice our work. And I doubted we *would* be experimenting with something rare...I glanced at Akin, and saw that he was smiling too. I felt an odd moment of kinship, even though he was the enemy. He loved forging as much as I did.

Akin coughed. "Are we allowed to bring our friends?"

"No," Magister Tallyman said. His mouth turned down. "And *don't* defy me on this."

He pointed to the textbooks before Akin could come up with a response. "What do you make of *this*?"

It took me a moment to switch gears and decipher the text. The Object of Power drew on magic and used it to provide locomotive force, which could then be used to drive a ship - or even an airship. It all *looked* to make sense, as far as I could tell, but...something had to be missing. There were plenty of stories about the great flying machines of the Thousand Year Empire, yet no one had managed to duplicate them. Airships, thankfully, had balloons to keep them in the sky. Flying machines almost always crashed within minutes.

"It looks doable," Akin said, doubtfully.

"It does," Magister Tallyman agreed. He stabbed a finger towards one of the nearer workbenches. Two immense machines sat on it. "One of these is a *genuine* Object of Power, dragged from the wreckage of a flying machine that was discovered in mud, somewhere in the Black Mountains. The other is my work, put together from diagrams and examinations of two similar Objects of Power. And neither of them work!"

I stared at him. "Neither?"

"I should have been able to fix the recovered Object of Power," Magister Tallyman said. I watched as he walked over to the table and ran his scarred hands over the machine. "It looked so *simple*. A few components needed to be replaced...that was all there was to it. I made them myself - I didn't even let my *last* set of assistants *touch* the work. And do you know what happened?"

I nodded, mournfully. "It didn't work."

"Precisely," Magister Tallyman said. He tapped the machine in frustration. "The original Object of Power simply refused to work. My duplicate worked for a short period, then collapsed into rubble. I replaced half the components and tried again. Still no luck. There must be something missing from the instructions, something so simple the Ancients never bothered to write it down."

Akin shot me a mischievous look. "I seem to recall there was some hoo-hah about feminine vibrations being different from male vibrations," he said. "And how the presence of women altered the magic field..."

"That was discredited within a year," Magister Tallyman said, before I could give in to the impulse to land a punch on Akin's nose. "The Congress of Ruthven considered it as a possible theory, as they were dealing with an outbreak of forbidden magics at the time, but experimentation proved that there is very little difference between male and female magic and certainly nothing that should interfere with Objects and Devices of Power."

He tapped the machine, again. "We have experimented in many different ways," he said, rather crossly. "Yes, we *have* had machines built by all-male and all-female teams. And hundreds of other variations besides. None of them have worked. It is a major frustration."

I caught his eye. "Why *did* the Congress of Ruthven consider it as a possible theory?"

"They were running out of ideas," Magister Tallyman said. He shook his head as he led us towards another workbench. "By then, they were getting pretty desperate. One theory was that the laws of magic *themselves* changed after the Thousand-Year Empire; another that the Objects of Power were tied to a specific bloodline and no one who wasn't a blood relative could handle or produce them. But all our research suggests that neither theory is remotely accurate. We just don't know."

I heard his frustration growing stronger. "There are hundreds of Objects of Power, ranging from swords and spell-casters to movers and flyers," he added. "And all of them are completely irreplaceable."

He sighed, then pointed to the workbench. "You have used charmed knives, correct?"

"Yes, sir," I said. "They're used in potions and harvesting and..."

"Quite," Magister Tallyman said. He opened a box, revealing a handful of sharp knives and a couple of golden sickles. "There are five knives in this box and two sickles. I want them all charmed for potions work. Magistra Loanda made me promise to charm some personally."

I couldn't help feeling disappointed. Compared to some of the work we'd done in class - and I'd done back at the Hall - charming knives was boring. But I had a feeling we didn't really have a choice. I *wanted* access to the workroom, even if it meant doing boring work instead of working on Objects and Devices of Power.

And the blades are technically Devices of Power, I thought, as I took one from the box and held it up. *Or they will be, after I have finished.*

"I'll be checking your work in an hour," Magister Tallyman said. "If you're both finished before then, give me a shout. I'll be in my office."

He turned and strode off, leaving us alone. We exchanged glances, then opened the toolboxes and went to work. Charming a knife isn't actually that hard - Dad carries one he says can cut through any defensive spell in existence - but doing it so the magic doesn't interfere with potions is a great deal harder. Getting it wrong would make the blade worse than useless. It would have to be melted down and recycled.

"You could add a sharper rune at the top," Akin offered, as I finished the first knife. "It'll cut through bare skin."

"The runes can't be tuned to discriminate without using too much magic," I countered. Mum had charmed some of her blades to keep them from cutting our skin, but it had had the unfortunate side effect of rendering most of the potions ingredients useless. The practice blades had screamed loudly whenever they'd brushed against our skin, teaching us what to avoid. "We don't want to contaminate the ingredients."

"Some of the others *have* been cutting their skin," Akin pointed out. "We could make money selling practice knives."

That was a thought, I silently admitted. And it was one I should have had for myself. Rose had had plenty of experience harvesting and preparing crops, even if she hadn't brewed a genuine potion until she'd entered Jude's, but plenty of the other students had managed to cut themselves over the first two weeks. Magistra Loanda had been very sarcastic about it, even as she healed the wounds and told the victims to get back to work. It wouldn't be *that* hard to charm practice knives. There would certainly be no need to worry about contaminating ingredients.

"Something to try," I mused. I met his eyes. "If we make them...do you want to sell them?"

Akin flushed. It looked odd on his pale skin. "Isabella would be *great* at selling them."

"Isabella hates me," I said, dryly. "And hardly anyone listens to me."

"I'll think about it," Akin promised. "She doesn't listen to me either."

I gave him an odd look, then resumed work on the second knife. Akin copied me silently - I wondered if Magister Tallyman would accept his first piece of work, or insist that he charm yet another blade. The golden sickle was harder to charm - gold-cut herbs can be very useful in potions, but gold is softer than it looks. I'd heard of a few druids who made do with iron sickles - or gold-covered sickles - yet their potions were always inferior. I had a feeling Magister Tallyman was not going to be pleased when he saw my work. The knives might be fine, but the sickle was not.

"That's mine done," Akin said. I bit down a sharp response. He *had* done a better job than I with the sickle. "Should we call him?"

I glanced at the clock, then nodded. We'd used most of our hour.

Magister Tallyman looked pleased when he inspected my knives, but he frowned when he saw the sickle. "You'll have to beat the runes out and start again," he said. "The sickle isn't going to be much good for anything, unless you melt it down to sell."

"Yes, sir," I said.

"Overall, you've done reasonably well," Magister Tallyman added, raising his voice slightly. "Perhaps you would try to try something more complex?"

I nodded, although I had no idea when I was meant to be repairing the sickle. I'd have to scratch out the runes sooner rather than later anyway, unless I wanted them to start gathering magic. Magister Tallyman took the nine usable blades - the tenth was dumped in the recycling bin - and returned them to the box, then led us over to yet another workbench. This one was empty, save for a small collection of tools and a couple of textbooks.

"Pick something from this book and make it," he ordered. He pointed towards the giant storage cupboards. "You should be able to find everything you need in there."

I felt a thrill of anticipation as I went to check the stores. Here was a *true* challenge, something that would test me to the limits. *And* give me a chance to show off, just a little, to a teacher I respected. Dad had taught me to make sure I had everything before I began anyway, whatever the storekeeper said, so I opened the doors and checked the shelves. If anything, it was *bursting* with supplies. Large pieces of wrought iron, tiny spools of gold, silver and bronze thread, jars of tiny gemstones...it was like a dream. No one, not even my father, had so many supplies purely for his own use.

But Jude's probably wants to keep Magister Tallyman, I thought, as my eyes swept the shelves. *They'd do whatever it took to make him happy.*

I found myself smiling as I returned to the workbench and started flicking through my textbook. It listed a vast collection of Devices of Power, ranging from a far more precise magic-sensor to a focusing device and a magic-absorber. The focusing device - a wand, as the commoners call them - was useless for me. I had nothing to focus. But the absorber might be interesting...

...And the more advanced Devices actually reflected the magic back to their caster.

I made a mental list of everything I needed, then started to gather my supplies. Beside me, Akin had opened his book to show a focusing device. It was proof, I suppose, that he didn't lack magic himself. I sighed, knowing my work would take longer, then got started. It didn't matter. The chance to impress Magister Tallyman was worth missing lunch, if not dinner.

"I'll be in my office," Magister Tallyman said. "Call me when you're finished."

I was barely aware of him walking away as I bent over the workbench, carefully organising the tools and supplies before I went to work. Having so many tools was a luxury - I wasn't going to be fighting with my father's apprentices over who got to use what. I smiled down at the textbook, then started to work. It was complex, but I loved it. I lost track of everything, apart from the work in front of me. And slowly, the Device of Power started to take shape.

It didn't look like much, I had to admit. Two iron wands, tied together with gold and silver thread; five gemstones, three designed to focus the magic into the other two; a tiny handhold, barely large enough for my hand. I would have to make it larger, I thought, when I put the final piece into place. Mum had told me that I would have a growth spurt over the next couple of years and I would no longer be able to use the Device. It simply couldn't be scaled up for an adult. I looked closer, inspecting every last component. Devices of Power had been known to fail because a single element was out of place.

And we could mass-produce most of them, if they didn't keep breaking down, I thought, sardonically. I'd said as much to Dad, years ago. He'd told me that it never worked, no matter how much time and effort was invested into the program. The younger families kept trying, but they never recouped their investment. *There's still a place for forgers.*

My stomach growled. I looked up...and blinked. Akin was staring at me. He flushed bright red a second later and looked away, clearly embarrassed. The wand he'd produced was sitting on the workbench, ready for use. I looked up at the clock and started. It was four in the afternoon. Where had the time gone?

"You're good at this," Akin said. "Isabella said..."

That I was a zero, I thought, as his voice trailed off. *But there isn't any real magic involved in forging, and you know it.*

I pushed the thought out of my head. "I'll fetch Magister Tallyman," I said, instead. "You stay here."

Akin nodded, shortly. I turned and headed to Magister Tallyman's office, a tiny little room at the side of the workroom. Akin probably wouldn't tamper with my work, if only because Magister Tallyman might believe me instead of him. He wouldn't want to be kicked out any more than I did. I knocked at the open door, then peered inside. Magister Tallyman was sitting at a small wooden desk, playing with a Device. It looked like a tiny metal fan.

"Caitlyn," he said. "What do you make of this?"

I peered at the Device. "A fan," I said. "What *is* it?"

"Precisely," Magister Tallyman said. He held the Device up to me. I took it gingerly, stroking the metal with my fingers. "It is a fan. And it should work."

I studied it for a long moment. "Perhaps it needs a separate power source."

"Not according to the ancient texts," Magister Tallyman said. He took the Device back and rested it on the table. "I've done everything right, but it simply won't work for more than a few seconds. And then chunks of it just crumble."

I followed him out of the office. Something was nagging at my mind, but what?

Magister Tallyman took a moment to study Akin's work. "An impressive focus," he said, thoughtfully. "You've made focuses before?"

"I have, sir," Akin said. He seemed to have gotten over his early embarrassment. "This one is modified to allow a chain of incants to be triggered, one by one."

"You do have to program the incants first," Magister Tallyman mused. He pointed to a piece of wood. "Very well. Test it."

Akin glanced at me, then pointed the wand at the wood and spoke a single word. The wand spat a tiny fireball which punched through the wood and struck the stone walls. I half-expected Magister Tallyman to throw Akin out on the spot, but instead he just laughed. It dawned on me that he'd expected something like it.

"Not too bad," Magister Tallyman said. "Although I would be careful *which* spells you use in future. Focusing certain spells can be quite dangerous."

I nodded. Fireballs were easy - at least if you had the magic. Dad said they were boring, but practical. But focusing their heat into a smaller fireball...

"Caitlyn," Magister Tallyman said. "Let's see what *you* made."

I held up the Device. He studied it for a long moment, turning it over and over in his colossal hands. I thought he'd break it, but his touch was surprisingly gentle. And then he passed it back to me.

His voice was surprisingly warm. "Are you ready?" I held up the Device, quickly. "Let's see..."

He cast a spell. The Device jerked in my hands - and the gemstones started to glow - but nothing touched me. Magister Tallyman smiled, then cast another two spells in quick succession. The glow grew brighter, but nothing else happened. He looked puzzled, then cast a fourth spell. This time, there was a surge of heat that made me drop the Device on the floor. There was a brilliant flash of light as the gemstones shattered, releasing the stored magic.

"Get back," Magister Tallyman snapped.

I jumped back. Nothing happened, save for an eerie green glow that vanished a second later.

"Very good," Magister Tallyman said. "*Very* good."

He gave me a smile. "I shall expect great things from you, I think," he said. "And now--" he glanced at the clock "--I think you two had better go back to your dorms. I'll see you both in class."

"Yes, sir," Akin said. "And thank you."

I couldn't stop myself smiling broadly. "Thank you, sir," I said. "For everything."

And I was still grinning when I reached the dorm.

CHAPTER
TWENTY

Unfortunately, my happiness didn't last long.

The problem with getting into a rivalry with a magician, particularly when you don't have any magic of your own, is that it's hard to find newer and better ways to strike back. Isabella could - and did - cast spells on me at every opportunity, while I had to work hard to find tricks I could play on her. I don't know if she ever figured out how I made the itching charm work, but it didn't have any effect the second time I tried it. She - or Akin, perhaps - had deduced the truth and modified her protective wards.

And she was still treating Rose like dirt.

I didn't understand it. Rose had had almost no proper training at all, before she'd been sent to Jude's. Now, four weeks into the term, she was already casting spells that had taken Alana *months* to master. She still had a long way to go, but it was clear she had a remarkable talent *and* a great deal of natural power. And yet, Isabella was still looking down on her. Part of me was almost relieved. Isabella could have taught Rose a great deal, if she'd looked past Rose's origins to see her potential. She could have stolen Rose from me with ease.

"This simply doesn't make sense," Rose muttered, as we sat together in the library after lunch. It was the safest place. Several gangs of first and second-year students were playing a running game through the corridor and tossing spells in all directions. "Why *does* it matter if I stir clockwise, rather than anticlockwise?"

"Because you're shaping and channelling the magic," I told her. Rose *had* learned to cook, which gave her an advantage, but cooking and potion-brewing didn't have *that* much in common. A stew didn't care if you stirred clockwise or anticlockwise, yet it could make the difference between success and failure in brewing. "Don't try to rewrite the instruction book on short notice."

Rose scowled. "It still doesn't make sense."

"It does," I said. "You just have to track the progress of the magic through the brew."

I looked down at the open textbook, feeling a sudden wave of despondency. Rose and I had been lucky so far, but it wouldn't last. The more advanced potions, like the one Magistra Loanda had told us we were going to be brewing this afternoon, needed more than a simple stir. I had to guide the magic and I wasn't sure I could do that, not with a wooden spoon. It wouldn't be hard to make a Device to handle the magic, but that would probably cause the potion to explode. I just didn't understand it.

Maybe I can rewrite enough of the recipe to make it easier, I thought, sourly. I'd told Rose not to try, but I was desperate. *How do I avoid needing a second stir...?*

I flicked through the textbook, trying to recall everything my mother had told me. It wasn't *impossible* to switch out one set of potions ingredients for another, but each substitution would have side effects that would also have to be countered. The genius who'd produced a substitute for unicorn horn - one of the rarest and most expensive ingredients in the world - had crafted a cheaper potion that was also astonishingly complex. And the *reason* it was so complex was because a dozen different ingredients reacted badly with one another and had to be managed carefully.

Mum could have made her own, I thought. I worked my way through the list of approved substitutes, trying to parse out the consequences of using them. *But I couldn't have produced one without help...*

"Twenty minutes," Rose said. She glanced at the door. "Do you think the corridors are safe now?"

I shrugged. The upperclassmen would probably have broken the game up by now. "We can go in ten minutes," I said. It would take us that long to walk to potions class. "Just give me a few more minutes."

The textbook wasn't very helpful. Sure, there *were* substitute ingredients, but none of them were simple enough to cut the need for magic down to a single stir. Rose was going to have to stir my caldron at least twice during the lesson, each one running the risk of Magistra Loanda noticing and having kittens. One stir might not bother her *that* much, but if she never saw *me* stirring the caldron...

I sighed as I started to flip through the pages. There was no way to know what Magistra Haydon had told the other teachers - my last session with her had been strikingly unproductive - but I didn't dare show weakness in front of my fellow students. Isabella was just *looking* for proof that I didn't have magic. Coming to think of it, I didn't really want Magistra Loanda to be sure either. She might well use it against my mother at a later date.

If I mix that with that, I mused, *perhaps...*

It struck me like a thunderbolt. If I used something intensely magical - dragon scales, perhaps - I shouldn't need Rose to provide the magic. There *would* be a surge of magic...in fact, if I combined powdered dragon scales with a couple of other ingredients, I might be able to avoid the need to stir the caldron. I hastily grabbed for a piece of paper and started to scribble out the formula, trying to see why no one else had ever tried it. If it was *possible* to infuse magic without using *personal* magic, everyone would be using it. Mum would have shown me how to do it years ago.

But no matter how I worked the formula, I couldn't see any flaws.

It looked perfect. A surge of magic, followed by another...the potion shouldn't need any more. There didn't look to be any dangerous reactions either, as far as I could tell. I'd probably need to skim the scales out of the potion, but that wouldn't be difficult. Half the potions we brewed were skimmed afterwards. It *definitely* looked perfect.

And that worried me. I knew more than most of my peers about potions, but I was no Master Brewer. My mother and Magistra Loanda had both magic and years of experience. I knew brewers who were in their second century, men and women who had been brewing from the day they came into their magic. I couldn't be the first person to think of this, could I? There had to be a flaw I was missing, some reason why an infusion of magic was impossible. It was tempting to believe that the brewers hadn't *wanted* to tell everything, but still...

There are too many potions that can only be made by skilled brewers, I thought. *It would be cheaper if everyone could make them.*

I looked down at my paper for a long moment. It would be better to check with Mum before I did anything. I could write to her and ask. Perhaps she would tell me I was a genius - or perhaps she would point out the incredibly obvious flaw I'd missed. I folded up the paper and put it in my pocket as the ten-minute bell rang. We'd have to hurry or we'd be late for class.

"I don't think Magistra Loanda is going to like my homework," Rose confessed, as we sprinted through the door. "I could only find five legitimate uses for blood-based potions."

"There aren't any more," I said. Blood-based potions were borderline dark, as far as Magus Court was concerned. "I don't think they changed the law in the last couple of months."

We were running by the time we reached the potions classroom and popped inside, but we needn't have hurried. Magistra Loanda was berating Alana at great volume, demanding to know just *how* she could have messed up her homework. We slipped past her and took our seats, then settled back to enjoy the show. Alana couldn't go red in the face, but it was easy to tell she was humiliated. She'd never paid *that* much attention to potions and it was showing.

The door slammed closed as Magistra Loanda turned and stalked back to her desk. "We shall be brewing something more complicated today," she informed us. "Regeneration Potion. I have been informed that the infirmary is running low after the *last* set of potions disasters, so I have been asked to brew more."

She gave us all an unpleasant smile. "And I have decided that anyone who manages to brew it perfectly on their first try will have access to a potions laboratory."

I exchanged glances with Rose. If we could win, if one of us won, it would make our lives a great deal easier. Rose needed more practice brewing. If we had access to a lab, if we were allowed to work unsupervised... Magistra Loanda clearly believed we could be trusted, if we could make Regenerative Potion on the first try.

Magistra Loanda launched into a long and complicated lecture about the potion, forcing us to scramble to take notes. I'd taken the precaution of reviewing the potion ahead of time - it was another habit Mum had drilled into me - but Magistra Loanda still managed to say things I didn't know. I felt my wrist starting to ache within minutes. Magistra Loanda was clearly far too fond of the sound of her voice.

"Now," she said, nodding toward the blackboard. The recipe appeared in front of us. "As you will see, the potion requires you to add one of several possible ingredients just before it is completed. Alana...which one would you chose and why?"

I glanced back. My sister looked trapped.

"Elderflower Seeds," Alana managed, finally. "They are good for counteracting the effects of a number of curses."

"Interesting choice," Magistra Loanda said. "Would anyone care to comment?"

I hesitated, then raised my hand. "Yes, Caitlyn?"

"Elderflower Seeds have two problems," I said. "First, in order to be effective, they have to be harvested at precisely the right time. A day too late will render the seeds actively poisonous. Second, while they do counteract a number of curses, they *also* counteract protective magics. You might accidentally make the effects of the curses worse, even if you removed the curses themselves."

"Very good," Magistra Loanda said. She didn't sound pleased. "You actually gave some *thought* to the choice of ingredients."

Her eyes switched to Alana. "The easiest choice for ingredient is not always the best one, as I'm sure your mother taught you," she added. "For homework, I want you to revise all ten possible additions and determine their strengths and weaknesses."

I could feel Alana's glare boring into my back. Perhaps it had been a mistake to contradict her in front of the entire class. But it was the only way I could boost my marks.

Magistra Loanda peered down at me. "What would *you* use? And why?"

I took a moment to consider it. "I would use Dayflower Berries," I said, carefully. "They don't have such a strong effect, but they *do* help the body to regenerate without provoking a fight with any remaining curses. *And* you can harvest Dayflower Berries any time you like."

"A poor metaphor, but understandable," Magistra Loanda said. She looked around the classroom. "While the potion base is unchangeable, you do have some latitude in choosing the final ingredients. Just remember that you *must* make an accurate note of precisely *what* ingredient you added. Getting it wrong will not only cost you a detention. It may cost someone their life."

Rose nudged me. "Is she joking?"

I shrugged. Magistra Loanda probably *did* want to resupply the infirmary. But I was sure she'd check the potions carefully before sending them to the healers. It was quite possible to do everything right, but mess up the potion so it decayed rapidly or turned poisonous. Only a stable brew would suffice.

"Better be careful," I muttered. "Getting access to a potions lab would be *very* useful."

Magistra Loanda's eyes swept the room. "Start work," she commanded. "I expect you to be finished by the end of the period."

I glanced at the clock, then nodded. "I'll get the ingredients," I said. "You start boiling the water."

Rose smiled, rather wanly. I gave her a reassuring smile, then hurried back to the potions storeroom. The other students were struggling over jars and bottles of ingredients, forcing me to wait until Magistra Loanda arrived to restore order with a few well-chosen threats. I met Alana's eyes as I measured out the beetle legs and winced. My sister was furious. I half-expected to be hexed in the back as I walked to the desk, despite Magistra Loanda's flat ban on hexing within the classroom. Tomorrow - when we had Protective and Defensive Magic - was not going to be fun.

She could have studied, I thought, resentfully. *Mum would have been glad to teach her.*

I sat down next to Rose and sorted out the ingredients. Two caldrons were already bubbling, just waiting for us to start brewing. Rose took her share of the ingredients, then opened her textbook so we could read the recipe without having to look at the blackboard. Magistra Loanda was striding around, looking murderous. None of us wanted to meet her eye.

"That's the first set lined up," I said, shortly. Regenerative Potion needed a base, then additional ingredients. "Are you ready?"

Rose nodded. "Go."

I tipped the ingredients into the caldron. Rose glanced at Magistra Loanda - she was focused on Henrietta, who'd managed to blow up her potion twice in the last two days - and gave my potion a quick stir. The liquid shimmered, then turned brown. I checked my watch, silently marking the time as Rose stirred *her* potion. The liquid had to boil for precisely fourteen minutes before we could add the next set of ingredients.

There was a loud explosion behind me. I turned, just in time to see smoke rising from Isabella's caldron. Magistra Loanda stamped past me, her expression darkening rapidly. I couldn't help feeling sorry for Isabella, even though she was a bully. Magistra Loanda looked as though she wanted to strangle her.

"Detention," Magistra Loanda snarled. "What *were* you thinking?"

"I stirred twice," Isabella said, softly. "I didn't think I infused enough magic..."

"Well, you *obviously* overdid it," Magistra Loanda snapped. "You're lucky the wards absorbed the blast."

She examined the caldron, then snorted rudely. "Dispose of this...this *mess*, young lady, then start again," she ordered. "You *should* have just enough time to complete it before the bell rings. And you can report to me on Saturday for a couple of hours scrubbing caldrons. It might teach you to be more careful."

I couldn't help a flicker of vindictive pleasure as Magistra Loanda strode back to the front of the classroom, her eagle eyes peering from caldron to caldron. Isabella was meant to have netball practice on Saturday morning. I didn't *think* she could convince the team captain to reschedule. She might even lose her place on the team.

"We're coming up on the second stir," I muttered to Rose. "When I put the ingredients in, stir twice clockwise and once anticlockwise."

"Got it," Rose said. She glanced nervously at Magistra Loanda. I silently prayed for a distraction. Maybe if I walked around the desk, I could block her view. "Now?"

"Five seconds," I said. I didn't dare move too openly. "Two...one...now!"

Rose stirred the potion.

"Hey," Alana shouted. I jumped. "Don't touch my sister's potion!"

Magistra Loanda swung around, just in time to see Rose stirring the potion. I swallowed, hard. Alana had taken a *very* effective revenge. It wasn't easy to share the task of brewing a potion - indeed, it wasn't really practiced below fifth year. And that meant...

"Sneak," someone muttered.

Alana winked at me as Magistra Loanda stamped over to us. I glared back at her, feeling my heart sink. Alana knew, of course, what we'd been doing. I'd brewed more than one potion for her, back at the Hall. She'd just had to stir the mixture to turn it into magic. And while some people might think of her as a tattletale now, she'd still come out ahead.

"I trust," Magistra Loanda said, "that you have an explanation for this?"

I wanted to bluff, to try to claim that Rose needed the practice. I'd get detention for cheek, of course, but it would be worth it. I could endure a couple of hours scrubbing caldrons or cataloguing the store. And yet, the moment I met Magistra Loanda's eyes, the lie caught in my throat. There was no way I could lie to her. She'd know...

...And then I'd be in far worse trouble for lying to a teacher.

She held my eyes. "Rose, finish your potion," she ordered. She jabbed a finger at my bubbling caldron, now slowly turning green. "Caitlyn, did you make this potion?"

"I prepared the ingredients and put them into the water," I said. It was true. "I..."

"Stay behind after class," Magistra Loanda ordered, cutting me off. I wasn't sure *just* what she knew. "You can prepare the potion again, without anyone else around."

I swallowed as I heard someone titter behind me. Isabella, of course. Alana had shown her *precisely* what Rose and I had been doing. She'd probably wondered how I could work magic, but now...now the answer was right in front of her. Rose had done the magical part for me.

And when I can't brew the potion, I asked myself, *what will happen then?*

Rose glanced at me. "Caitlyn..."

"Silence," Magistra Loanda interrupted. Rose shut up, hastily. "Finish your work."

I shook my head. Rose couldn't help me now. No one could.

CHAPTER
TWENTY-ONE

The class filed out of the room silently as soon as the bell rang, leaving me alone with Magistra Loanda. Alana, the last to leave, shot me a nasty look and a wink before she hurried out. Rose hadn't even looked at me. And Isabella had followed her out, a wicked glint in her eye. I hoped that meant that Isabella was planning to trap Rose, rather than befriend her. She was sure, now, that I didn't have magic.

"Remain seated," Magistra Loanda ordered. "I have to check the other brews."

I closed my eyes, rubbing my forehead as I heard her moving from desk to desk. A couple of potions were marked as excellent, but the remainder were apparently not stable enough to meet Magistra Loanda's exacting standards. The Healers wouldn't be pleased, I thought, yet they'd be even *less* pleased if the potions didn't last. I rather suspected that Magistra Loanda would have to brew some more herself.

And she would be wise not to trust our work, I thought. *We're only students...*

"Brewing is more than just preparing the ingredients," Magistra Loanda said, drawing my attention back to her. I opened my eyes. She sat at her desk, her arms resting on the stone table. Her eyes were dark and cold and utterly merciless. "You need to learn to focus your magic to start the brewing cascade."

I nodded, not trusting myself to speak. Mum had said the same thing, time and time again. I *knew* that I needed magic to make the potion work, yet...yet I didn't *have* magic. No amount of stirring with a wooden spoon would be enough to start the cascade. It was futile. Utterly futile.

"Right now, all you are *really* doing with your magic is giving the brew a little push," Magistra Loanda added. "Learning to shape your magic is *necessary* before you start on the more advanced potions. You *must* master the skill before you reach the exams. They will be testing you on your ability to save a failing brew."

I just wished she'd shut up. My head was starting to pound. Maybe I should just get myself expelled, somehow. If they caught me in one of the male dorms they'd expel me, wouldn't they? Or perhaps if I hexed the netball players before they took to the field. Rose would be far better off without me...

Magistra Loanda slapped the table, right in front of me. I jumped. I'd been so lost in my thoughts that I'd tuned her out completely.

"Pay attention," she snapped. "I have to attend an urgent staff meeting. You will remain here and brew the potion, perfectly. And *after* you have brewed the potion, you will write three hundred lines. *I will listen to my teachers at all times.* Do you understand me?"

The Punishment Book suddenly felt heavier. "Yes," I said. "I understand."

"Good," Magistra Loanda snapped.

She rose and strode out the door, banging it closed behind her. I heard the telltale hiss of a locking spell and flinched. There was no way to escape. Maybe I could dismantle or discharge the spell, with the right tools...I shook my head. It was pointless. I was going to remain in the classroom until she returned, then get detention for not brewing the potion. If she didn't go straight to the Castellan and demand I be expelled...

I reached for the Punishment Book and froze as I touched a piece of paper. It was the formula I'd discovered earlier, the formula for releasing magical power. I hesitated, then pulled the paper out of my pocket and smoothed it out on the desk. The words I'd scribbled in a hurry seemed to mock me, yet...yet what if it worked? I caught my breath. What if it worked?

Glancing at the clock, I opened the textbook and hurriedly started adapting the formula for the brew. Everything seemed to make sense. The

Regeneration Potion wasn't *that* complex, compared to some of the brews my mother made regularly. But if I was wrong...I couldn't be the first person to think of it, could I?

I stood and hurried to the storerooms. Dragon scales were kept out of sight, unsurprisingly, but I knew where they were hidden. Magistra Loanda really *shouldn't* have made me list all the half-empty bottles and jars if she hadn't wanted me to learn my way around the storerooms. Oddly, the thought made me smile. She might have been trying to do me a backhanded favour. My mother's talent for brewing was well-known. And it wasn't uncommon for children to follow in their parent's footsteps.

There didn't seem to be a ward around the dragon scales - I tested with my sensor - but I still hesitated before reaching for the jar. My mother had booby-trapped *her* supplies, just to make sure we couldn't take them without permission. Nothing bit me as I touched the jar and removed it from the shelf...I puzzled over it for a long moment before deciding that too many upperclassmen needed access to the storerooms to make wards practical. It wasn't as if dragon scales were *rare*. The beasts shed their skins regularly.

I found the rest of the supplies, and carried them back into the classroom. I'd have to brew the formula in a separate caldron first, then start work on the potion itself. I glanced at the clock and then started to work, making sure to clean each of the red-gold scales individually before dropping it in the boiling water. In theory, the brew should start to glow of its own accord.

And I'll probably discover the flaw in my work, I thought. It defied belief that my mother hadn't stumbled across the formula. She had an instinct for potion combinations that I would never share. *It probably won't work.*

I prepared the rest of the ingredients anyway, then glanced at the brew. It was glowing with a faint pearly light that sent tingles down my spine. I felt a spark of excitement, even though I knew it was terribly dangerous. The magic reaction was uncontrolled. There was no way I could hope to direct it either, no matter what I did. All I could do was hope that my projections were correct.

And yet...it was the first time I'd made a potion that *glowed.*

I clamped down hard on my excitement as I began to brew the Regeneration Potion, then reached for a ladle and carefully splashed some of the formula into the brew. If it exploded, I was far too close...it didn't. Instead, it shimmered and turned green. I felt my heart stop, just for a second. I'd made it work! Somehow, I'd made it work! I sat down so hard I almost toppled over backwards. The rest of the potion might fail, but I'd already accomplished something great. I shouldn't have any trouble brewing potions that required only one surge of magic.

As long as I don't run out of dragon scales, I thought.

I shook my head. I'd clearly stumbled on *something*. Robin could get dragon scales for me, although I would probably have to give him most of my allowance to pay for them. Or I could ask my mother, when I went home. *She* would be utterly thrilled with my discovery...

Don't lose sight of what you're doing, I told myself, sternly. The Regenerative Potion needed a second infusion of magic. *You need to complete the potion before the teacher comes back.*

I kept a wary eye on my watch as the seconds ticked past. Part of me was *sure* that the glow would fade, but it didn't. The potion seemed stable. I waited, all too aware of my heart beating loudly in my chest, until it was time to add more formula to the brew. This time, it bubbled alarmingly for several minutes - I braced myself to dive under the table - before finally settling down into a shimmering blue colour. It was perfect. Or, at least, it *looked* perfect. I removed the flame from below the caldron and blew it out. In theory, the potion should cool rapidly...

There wasn't much of the formula left, I noted. There should be *just* enough for a single-stir potion, if my calculations were correct. I bottled up the remainder, stuck it in my pocket for later use, then sifted the potion before starting to clear up the mess. If I was lucky - if I was *very* lucky - Magistra Loanda wouldn't ask too many questions, once she saw the successful potion. I didn't want to share my secret with her until I'd told Mum and Dad.

But I will be telling Rose, I thought. Rose *had* to know. She had to be biting her fingernails right now, assuming she hadn't been frozen or turned into a frog. *She thinks I can't help but fail.*

I looked down at the shimmering blue liquid. Rose would have been right, too.

Sweat prickled on my brow. I wiped it away, unable to stop staring at the potion. Everyone talked about the day they first used magic, about how they never forgot the moment when they'd bent the universe to their will...I understood, all of a sudden, why so many people were boastful about their first magic. It had changed their lives. And I'd never felt that way because I'd never had magic.

I felt the tiny glass bottle in my pocket. I'd found a way to work magic, *true* magic...

And yet, I asked myself, *why did no one else think of it?*

The door clicked, then opened. I looked up. Magistra Loanda stood there, looking cross. I hoped she wasn't cross at me, although that was probably a false hope. She'd probably expected me to fail again.

"I brewed the potion," I said, as calmly as I could. "It's ready for you to test."

Magistra Loanda gave me a sharp look, then walked towards the desk. I tensed, despite myself. Who knew *what* she'd hoped would happen? A successful brew...or an embarrassment for my parents? Perhaps Magistra Loanda didn't know herself. Dad had often commented that the *really* smart people adapted to whatever happened. And a Master Brewer would be very smart indeed.

"It looks good," she said, as she took a ladle and dipped it into the caldron. "What did you add and why?"

"Terri's Flowers," I said. It had seemed the simplest way to brew the potion. "They make the potion a little more forgiving."

"There's no such thing as a *forgiving* potion," Magistra Loanda told me, stiffly. She tested the brew twice, dunking her wand into the liquid and stirring it, then nodded. "You appear to have made it work."

I looked down at the caldron. "Thank you."

"It is also the best brew I have seen for some time," Magistra Loanda added. I looked up, sharply. "It is stable - it won't decay in a hurry. It should react well to preservation spells, I think. I believe the Healers will be glad to have it."

I stared. "They'll take it?"

"They are permanently short of healing potions," Magistra Loanda informed me. "This brew is excellent and will be added to their supplies. Bottle it up, then label it properly. Make sure the label is *very* clear."

My hands were shaking as I rose to get some vials. I'd never expected it to be *that* good. But I *had* followed the instructions precisely *and* added the magic at the right time...I was going to have to work on my formula and find out a way to infuse the magic in a more focused manner. Maybe I could do the simpler potions now...the more complex potions were still beyond me.

I forced myself to focus as I poured the liquid into the vials. Each one would help save a life, if administered in time. I was tempted to try to pocket one, but I had a feeling that would be dangerous. Magistra Loanda was watching me like a hawk. I couldn't tell if she was pleased or upset by my success. If she knew I had no magic...

The sooner I talk to Dad, I thought, *the better.*

"Clean up the rest of the classroom," Magistra Loanda added, once the potion was bottled and sealed. "Make sure you dispose of everything properly, then stack up the dirty caldrons in the pile to be scrubbed."

I nodded and got to work. Maybe I could pile up *more* dirty caldrons in the washroom, where Isabella would be working on Saturday. It would be mean of me, particularly when *Alana* had caused the near-disaster...I sighed, torn between annoyance and gratitude. If she hadn't tattled on me, I wouldn't have risked using the formula without testing it. I'd have to find a way to thank her.

Magistra Loanda sat back at her desk and started going through the next pile of marking. I felt an odd moment of sympathy for her, even as she bent her head over a piece of paper and started to write on it with red ink. Some poor upperclassman was probably going to have to redo the essay in a hurry. I finished stacking up the caldrons, then wiped the desks clean. Whoever had potions tomorrow morning would have no reason to complain, I decided. And whoever had carved ANDI+DELLAH into the woodwork was in deep trouble, when Magistra Loanda caught them. I wondered, absently, which of them had dared vandalise the potions classroom. No Master Brewer would tolerate it for a moment.

"I've finished," I said, when I'd wiped the last table. "Is there anything else you want me to do?"

"You did the best potion," Magistra Loanda said, flatly. "I'm giving you access to Lab Thirteen and its attached storeroom. That's designed for first-years. Do *not* attempt to brew something that isn't in your textbook, even if your mother taught you how to brew it. If you need an ingredient that isn't in the storeroom, come and ask me. I'll expect a full explanation of *why* you want it. And keep a list of everything you use."

I nodded, feeling numb. I'd won. How could I have won?

"You may have *one* other person in the lab with you at any one time," Magistra Loanda continued. "Try to bring two people into the lab and the wards will bite you. I also expect you to follow the safety rules at all times. If you do *not* follow them, you will be denied further access to the lab."

She paused. "And if an upperclassman wants to use the lab, let them go first," she concluded, dryly. She scowled down at one of the papers. "Some of them have a *lot* of work to do."

I followed her gaze. There was more red ink than black on the page, half of the scribbled notes caustic comments about the writer's complete failure to realise that mixing a dozen highly-volatile ingredients together without careful control was asking for trouble. It concluded with an order to report to Magistra Loanda for detention on Friday evening, along with a promise of harder work in the future...

Magistra Loanda snorted. "I don't let others see *your* homework," she said, dryly. "I think you can change the lines I gave you. *I will not read private remarks to other students.*"

I groaned. "Yes, Magistra."

"Go now," Magistra Loanda said. "The lab will be open to you, outside normal timetables. I expect you to work harder in the future."

"Thank you," I said.

I turned and hurried through the door. It was nearly five, the dinner gongs already echoing through the school. I doubted I had time to go change before dinner, so I walked as quickly as I could towards the dining hall. I'd eat in my uniform, then shower after dinner.

"You smell," a third-year student said.

I ignored her as I pushed open the door to the dining hall. Isabella was standing by the table, talking to Akin and a boy I didn't recognise. There was a nasty red mark on her cheek. Two more boys were standing a little further away, both sporting bruises of their own. I wondered just what had happened to them, then decided it probably didn't matter. Isabella gave me a nasty smile as I walked over to the table. There was no sign of Rose.

"Well, little *zero*," Isabella said. "Did you get kicked out?"

I smiled back at her. "I have access to a potions lab," I said. I gave her a wink. "Would you like to study with me?"

Akin smiled. He hid it well, a second later, but I caught it. Isabella's mouth dropped open in shock.

"You...you won?"

"I won," I said. "Go check with Magistra Loanda if you don't believe me."

"I don't believe it," Isabella snarled. "It's a trick..."

"I told you she was good at forging," Akin put in.

"Believe what you like," I said, as the doors opened. "I'm going to have dinner, then get a shower."

"Your friend is back in the dorm," Isabella said. She rubbed her cheek, angrily. "I'm afraid we had to punish her."

I glared. "What did you *do* to her?"

"Nothing much," Isabella said. Her tone was so contemptuous that I wanted to hit her. Only the presence of several upperclassmen kept me from punching her smug face. "I'm sure she'll be okay in a few hours."

My stomach growled. I was turning around to go to the dorm when the door opened, revealing Rose and Sandy. Rose looked unhurt, but badly shaken. Beside her, Sandy looked furious.

"You're cleaning the washroom for the next two weeks," she told Isabella. "And don't even *think* of trying to get out of it."

Rose caught my eye. "What happened?"

"I'll tell you afterwards," I said. I wanted to know what had happened to her too. "Right now, we need to eat."

TWENTY-TWO

"She said you'd be kicked out in disgrace," Rose said, once we'd found a private room. "I thought...I thought you couldn't make potions."

I allowed myself to smile. "I found a new way to cheat," I said. I dug the tiny bottle out of my pocket and held it out to her. "This actually lets me infuse magic into the brew."

Rose took it. "Warm," she said, after a moment. "What *is* it?"

"Magic," I said. I winked. "I managed to make the perfect brew!"

"Well done," Rose said, seriously.

I met her eyes. "What happened to you?"

"Isabella started in on me as soon as I got back to the dorm," Rose said. "She said...she said you were a zero, that she'd take me in if I dumped you now. I slapped her, hard."

"Oh," I said. I had to smile. "What happened?"

"She stuck me to the ceiling," Rose admitted. "I didn't dare try to break the spell because I would have fallen to the ground. All I could do was stay there until Sandy got me down."

"Crap," I said. Alana had stuck *me* to the ceiling once. The ear-blasting Mum had given her had made sure she didn't do it again. "Did you tell Sandy what happened?"

"She already knew," Rose said. "Someone must have told her."

"Or she guessed," I said. I grinned at her. "Tomorrow, do you want to brew a potion with me?"

Rose smiled. "Of course!"

I felt my smile fade. "I just don't get it," I said. "Someone *should* have thought of this a long time before me."

"You *are* clever," Rose pointed out.

"Not *that* clever," I countered.

"You *also* have an incentive to look for other solutions," Rose added. "I mean...if you lost your leg, you'd want a peg-leg or wheelchair...you'd want your house redesigned to make it easier for you. But someone who had both legs wouldn't even *think* about it. He wouldn't know what you needed to make your life easier."

I frowned. It was a good explanation. I wanted to believe it. But Mum and her fellows had catalogued literally *thousands* of uses for each potion ingredient, even if they were seemingly useless or outdated. I'd watched her probing new herbs from all around the world, trying to determine what - if any - uses they had. Dragon scales were hardly *rare*. It was a great deal harder to get dragon's blood or dragon's bones.

Because dragons tend to dislike it when you try to bleed them, I thought. One of Dad's apprentices had gone off to bleed a dragon and had never returned. *And they're very resistant to normal magic.*

"I don't know," I said. I took back the bottle and rolled it in my fingers. It didn't feel warm to *me*. Perversely, that was a good sign. Rose could sense magic without a magic-sensor. "I think we're going to have to be more careful."

"Yeah," Rose said. "But how are we going to fool Magistra Solana or Magister Grayson?"

I shook my head. The mock-duels Magistra Solana made us fight always ended badly. I just couldn't cast a defensive spell to save my life. Maybe I could make a couple of protective amulets...they'd give me an advantage, once. But it wouldn't work twice.

And she might decide I was cheating, I thought. *She would be right.*

"We'd better get on with our homework," I said. We'd have to go to the library, but I didn't mind that. If nothing else, I needed to see if there were any books detailing the use of dragon-scale formula. "And I have lines to do."

Rose smiled as she stood. "You'll have to think of a cool name, you know."

I blinked. "What?"

"Your formula," she said. "If you were the first person to invent it, you should get to name it."

"True," I agreed. "Mum has a number of potions named after her..."

I considered it as we walked into the library and started hunting for useful books. Caitlyn's Boost? Cat's Claws? Caitlyn's Tears? A distressing number of healing potions were named after tears, for reasons I had never been able to understand. Maybe anyone who heard the name would think it was just another healing potion. It was certainly possible.

"Hey," Rose muttered. "What happened to them?"

I looked up. The two first-year boys I'd seen at dinner were walking past, their bruised faces clearly visible. It looked as though they'd been in a nasty fight. There was actually *blood* on their shirts. One of them snarled at me, but said nothing. Shouting or throwing hexes in the library would get them both kicked out within seconds. The librarian was already looking at them, her eyes dark and cold. If someone had been looking at me like that, *I* would have run for my life.

"I don't know," I muttered back. Football? Girls weren't allowed to play football, any more than the boys were allowed to play netball. "Or maybe..."

Akin entered the library, carrying a large pile of books in his arms. I waved to him as he handed the books to the librarian, beckoning him over. He gave me a tired-looking smile as he sat down at our table. Rose looked alarmed, just for a second. Akin *was* Isabella's brother, after all.

"Those two," I said, jabbing a finger towards the bruised boys. "What happened to them?"

"They claimed Scholar's Rights," Akin said. "And had a fight, right in the middle of the hall."

Rose looked at me. "Scholar's Rights?"

Akin answered. "It's when two people are so antagonistic that they just have to settle it by force," he said. "The loser has to bow to the winner."

"Sounds stupid," Rose said.

I shrugged. Duels between trained magicians weren't uncommon, particularly when most magicians were touchy about real or imagined slights, but Magus Court did everything in its considerable power to keep them from being fatal. Scholar's Rights sounded like a junior version, where the immature magician merely had to concede defeat. Dad had told me, if I recalled correctly, that the system saved trouble in the long run. But really, I had my doubts.

"Better that than hexing each other all night," Akin said. He gave me a tired smile. "I'll see you in a few days, right?"

He rose and strode off before I could answer. Rose kicked me under the table. "I think he likes you."

I gave her a sharp look. "His sister hates the ground I walk on."

"My sister hates her mother-in-law," Rose countered. "That doesn't stop her loving her husband."

I rolled my eyes and turned back to the pile of books. It was easy to lose myself in the tomes, ranging from dry textbooks discussing the different uses of a dead dragon to enthusiastic research papers by alchemists who thought they were on the verge of unlocking the secrets of the universe, but there was nothing about my formula. The closest thing I found was an assessment of how dragons could fly - they channelled the magic field, like bumblebees - that discussed the use of dragon scales. But the brewer didn't even touch on my formula. It was frustrating.

A hand touched my shoulder. "Bedtime," the librarian said. "Lights Out is in twenty minutes."

I glanced at Rose, horrified. We hurried back to the dorm, just in time to discover that Sandy was on the warpath against anyone who even looked at her funny. There was no time to shower, so we splashed water on our faces and climbed into bed. I half-expected Isabella to hex me in the night, but I was still human when I awoke. She had locked her drapes so tightly that Sandy had to open them by magic, just to get her up for breakfast.

"I think she's cross," Rose said.

We giggled together.

Classes went quicker than I'd dared hope, even though I wound up taking two pratfalls under Magistra Solana's gimlet eye and then getting marked down for not managing to cast spells in Charms. Magister Grayson told me off, but I barely heard a word he said. I was too busy thinking of how I was going to show off, after classes. If I actually *could* make a potion in front of Rose, I could teach her a great deal more...

And then I can show my mother, I thought, as classes ended for the day. *I'm sure she'd love to watch.*

"You're going to have half-marks in Charms," Rose predicted. "Is that enough to pass?"

"I don't know," I said, as we made our way to the potions classroom. I regularly scored high marks in my theoretical work, but my practicals were a joke. "I think I'd need at least a certain level before they allowed me to advance into second year."

The thought made me scowl. There were two sets of qualifying exams; the uppers and the lowers. I'd need at least a couple of lowers if I wanted to have a degree, let alone find work, although they really *had* to be in magical subjects. Maybe Rose and I could open a shop together. It wouldn't be *that* bad, would it?

I pushed the thought aside as I opened the door to Potions Lab Thirteen. It was a smaller version of the classroom, so dark and dingy that I wondered if Magistra Loanda was just trying to save on cleaning bills. My detention might have been much more useful if she'd set me to cleaning the lab instead. The lights came on a moment later, flickering madly for a long moment before settling down. I glanced up at the cobwebbed ceiling and sighed. She *was* breeding spiders. No other explanation made sense.

"We're going to have to do some cleaning," Rose said. She glanced at me. "Are you sure she didn't give you detention instead?"

"Yes," I said, rather crossly. How long had it *been* since someone had used the lab? "You go get some water and soap - I'll check the supplies?"

The supplies, at least, looked usable. Someone had wrapped a powerful preservation spell around the storage cabinet. Most people found such spells a little uncomfortable, but I barely even felt it. Maybe there were some advantages to my...*condition*...after all. Rose came back, carrying a bucket of steaming water and a jug of soap. I took one of the brushes she offered me and started to work. The nasty part of my mind insisted, as I scrubbed layer after layer of exploded potion off the workbench, that it would be easier to throw out the old workbench and bring in another.

"I meant to ask," Rose said. She was scrubbing the floor, vigorously. "How come you know how to wash and clean?"

I knew what she meant. "My parents used to punish us by making us help the maids," I said, after a moment. "We were not allowed to use magic - and we got in worse trouble if we tried to cheat. I picked up a few skills from them."

"You had servants," Rose said. "My mother had my sisters and I doing household chores from the moment we could walk. Dad took the boys out and put them to work in the fields, growing crops. We had to have dinner ready on the table when they came home."

I felt an odd stab of pain. Alana had said, more than once, that I would probably be sent to a workhouse, after Dad disowned me. I was a disgrace to the family...I hadn't believed her, not really, but there had been times when I'd feared the worst. Now...now, I'd made potions work. Perhaps I had a future after all.

"Isabella never had to work with the maids," I said, instead. Somehow, I wasn't surprised that she hadn't even known the basics. "No *wonder* she needs to be shown how to do everything."

We giggled together as we finished scrubbing the lab. The chamber looked much better, now the caked powders on the floor were gone. We checked the table one final time, then started digging out caldrons and potion supplies. Rose had a couple of potions she needed to practice, I knew. She'd been very lucky not to trigger an explosion two days ago.

I took the formula out of my pocket and placed it on the workbench. It looked still, yet I could see a faint glow surrounding the bottle. I smiled, then started to heat up the water. The glow seemed to get brighter, just for a second. I frowned, wondering if I was imagining it. If only I'd thought to bring the magic sensor...

"I'm going to brew a standard wakefulness potion," I told her. It was a very simple recipe, one almost every student knew how to brew. Dad hadn't allowed us to have any until we turned twelve, but I'd sneaked a taste years ago. It had been foul. I couldn't understand how the apprentices drank it by the tankard. "I was never able to get it to work."

"And you only need *one* stir to get it to work," Rose said. She eyed the formula doubtfully. "I thought the magic needed to be directed."

"It does," I said. *That* was going to be a problem later on. "But this potion is *very* forgiving. I shouldn't need to steer the magic too much."

I started to put the ingredients together, allowing the first batch to boil before adding the second. The boiling water turned dark brown, only a shade or two lighter than my skin. A faint smell started to rise, making my stomach heave. I knew the potion was effective, but I really couldn't understand how *anyone* could drink it. Mum had forced various potions down my throat over the years, including one that had made me throw up after I'd swallowed something dangerous...and all of them had tasted *much* better.

"It's nearly ready," I said. I checked the heat, out of habit. "But it has to rest before we add the magic."

Rose nodded. "You want to take a look at mine?"

I stepped over to peer into her caldron. The nutrient potion was bubbling nicely - it smelt much better than mine - and was clearly on the way to success. I couldn't help a flicker of envy, which I suppressed ruthlessly. Rose could do it easily, but I'd found a way to catch up...provided, of course, I could modulate and direct the magical surge. Perhaps if I experimented with runes...

"It looks good," I said. I gave her a reassuring look. "You'll master it soon."

"Isabella says I'll never be a great sorceress," Rose said. She looked downcast. "Is she right?"

"No," I said, firmly. I didn't understand why Rose doubted herself. "You have power and you have talent. You should be able to go far."

And if I can convince Dad to take you as an apprentice, I added silently, *hundreds of doors will be opened to you.*

The thought cost me a pang, but it wasn't as strong as I'd feared. I had those doors open for me simply because of my family name - assuming, of course, that I convinced people that I *did* have magic. There was no way I could join the upperclassmen, but I wouldn't be the first person to drop out and go on to a very successful career. Everyone expected *Alana* to be the heir, after all. No one would take a second look at Rose if she didn't have some very good connections.

"Stir it again," I said, as the liquid turned pink. Bella had thought it was funny, back when Mum had been teaching us, but I'd thought it was *too* pink. For once, Alana had agreed with me. "And then add the charmed salt."

Rose nodded and gave the potion a stir. It darkened, instantly. I tried not to be jealous as she added the salt, then took the potion off the heat. It would cool down and be bottled...she could offer it to the healers, if it passed Magistra Loanda's gimlet eye. But I'd made potions for the healers too...

I turned back to my potion and scowled. I was going to have to stir, but - at the same time - very carefully pour the formula into the liquid. Forgiving or not, it wasn't going to be easy.

"Take the formula," I said. I really needed three or four hands. There *were* spells for that, but they weren't particularly reliable. "When I give you the word, start pouring it down the spoon and into the liquid."

"You handle it," Rose said. She looked doubtful. "Magistra Loanda already caught me helping you once."

She smiled. "It's *your* potion."

I smiled back, then uncapped the tiny bottle. The formula felt warm against my palm, pregnant with possibility. Or perhaps I was imagining it. I'd never sensed anything from potions before...until now. I told myself that my life had definitely changed. I'd cracked a secret that would...maybe it wouldn't make me a magician, but it *would* make my life better.

"Here we go," I said. I held the bottle over the liquid, bracing myself. Part of me didn't want to find out what would happen...what if it had been sheer dumb luck? "Let's see how this goes."

I poured the clear liquid into the potion, stirring carefully. Rose leaned forward, her eyes narrowing as the potion began to bubble. I started. That wasn't meant to happen. It certainly shouldn't have happened...

"Get back," Rose snapped. I heard panic in her voice. "It's..."

There was a brilliant flash of blinding white light. And pain. I was burning...my entire body was on fire. Someone was screaming...

It took far too long, as I plunged into darkness, to realise that it was me.

CHAPTER

TWENTY-THREE

Pain. Pain everywhere.

Someone was talking, but who? I couldn't see...I could barely think. A haze had enveloped my thoughts, driving away the pain. There was a voice...someone I thought I knew. But my brain refused to work; my entire body was numb. Darkness rose up again and swallowed me, time and time again...

I jerked awake, my eyes snapping open. An old man was bending over me, pressing a silver wand gently against my forehead. I stared at him, utterly confused. Where *was* I? He stepped back and gave me a reassuring smile. I sat upright - my body felt weird, as if I was half-asleep - and looked around. The room was white, very white. Bella was sitting in the corner, staring anxiously at me. I looked back at the man and saw his white robes. He was a healer...

The potion, I thought. *Rose!*

My mouth was dry. I swallowed, hard. "Rose," I managed. My voice sounded raspy, even to me. "Where *is* she?"

"Alive," the healer said. "Lie back and relax."

I stared at him. He was an incredibly frail old man, his hair so white it almost glowed. I had the feeling that a gust of wind would be enough to blow him over. And yet, he was clearly still working. Jude's wouldn't want anyone but the most experienced and capable healers in its infirmary.

Bella rose. "Cat? What *happened*?"

"I..."

"That's enough, young lady," the healer said. "Your sister needs to rest."

I shook my head. Even *that* felt odd, as though my head had suddenly mushroomed into something twice its size. I didn't need to rest. I needed to find Rose and...and what? I wasn't even sure what had *happened*. The potion had exploded, right? My memories were a jumble, marred with pain...incredible pain. I hadn't been so badly hurt when I'd broken my leg as a little girl.

"Rose," I said, firmly. "Where *is* she?"

The healer tapped my forehead with his wand. The world went black.

It felt like bare seconds before I jerked awake again, even though I knew it had to have been hours. Sleep spells were dangerous, from what Dad said, if the victim didn't have at least five hours between being sent to sleep and being woken up. The room was dark, but I could hear two people talking. One of them, I thought, was the healer. The other...I didn't know him.

"She's proving oddly resistant to the sleep spells," the healer said. "They're falling apart quicker than they should."

The second voice sounded doubtful. "Does that mean she has a talent?"

"I don't know," the healer admitted. "Some of the healing spells didn't quite take either."

"She's been healed before," the second voice said.

"That was different," the healer told him. "I read her records. Her only serious injury was a broken leg, something that her parents could heal. This was extensive tissue damage. I need to reapply the spells every hour..."

I groaned as my head suddenly blossomed with pain. In my dazed state, I wasn't sure if I had a headache or if someone had kicked my skull. I heard footsteps, followed by another tap on the forehead. I tried to resist, but the sleep spell was too powerful. I fell back into darkness...

The next thing I knew, it was morning. And I felt much better.

"You've had something of a misfortune," the healer said. He bustled over to me, carrying a tray of food. My stomach rumbled as I saw the scrambled eggs on toast. "How are you feeling?"

I hesitated. Had he been talking last night? Or had I dreamed everything?

"Funny," I said, finally. "My body feels a little weird."

"I had to do a great deal of work to heal the damage," the healer told me. He passed me the tray of food. "Eat as much of this as you can. I'll be back in a moment."

I watched him go, then looked down at my hands. They looked... odd. My dark skin was paler in a dozen places, as if the healer had had to remove the skin and replace it. Maybe he had...I shuddered, almost pitching the tray onto the floor, as I remembered the brilliant explosion. I'd met Master Brewers who had scarred faces from their experiments...

My stomach grumbled, loudly. I reached for the toast and started to eat. It was good, good enough to make me finish the whole plate. The healer had probably mixed a dozen potions into the food, starting with something to give me a healthy appetite, but I found it hard to care. Mum had done something similar when we'd all caught the flu.

I looked into the corner. Bella had been there, hadn't she? I honestly wasn't sure what was real and what was not. My sister, coming to stay with me? It didn't seem too likely. But...what *had* been a dream? If the sleep spell had reacted badly to me, for some reason, hallucinations were the least I could expect.

The healer came back into the room, carrying a large glass of water. "Finished it? Good," he burbled. "Drink this."

"Thank you," I said, remembering my manners. The water tasted heavenly. "What did you put in it?"

"Merely something to help speed your healing," the healer said. "How do you feel now?"

I hesitated. "Still hungry," I said. "Is that normal?"

"I'll have more food sent up from the kitchens," the healer said. "Your body demands energy to heal, I'm afraid. Ask for food whenever you need it."

He looked me in the eye. "I'm afraid there are a few things we need to discuss, young lady."

I wanted to look away, but I didn't quite dare. "I know."

"Brace yourself," he ordered, as he pulled a small mirror out of his robes. "This isn't going to be pleasant."

He held the mirror up in front of me. My face looked...absurd, so absurd that it took me a moment to believe that it *was* my face. My skin was a patchwork of colour, from light to dark; my nose and jaw looked scarred...my eyes, at least, looked normal, but my eyelashes were gone. And my hair...

I reached up and touched my scalp. I'd never grown my hair very long, but now it was almost gone. Someone had clearly tried to do what they could, cutting away some of the surviving hair to give me an almost elfin look, yet...I swallowed hard. I didn't look like my father's daughter any longer.

"Your skin is currently healing, as I had to force-grow replacement tissue and then graft it onto your face," the healer said briskly. "I think your colour should be back to normal by the end of the week. Your scars will need a further operation to remove, unless you wish to keep them as a badge of honour. There's nothing particularly wrong with your hair, so you can either wait for it to regrow or take a potion to speed up the process. I advise you to wait at least a week, if you decide to take the potion. Right now, you have over thirteen different potions running through you."

I touched my jaw, gingerly. There was no pain, but it felt odd. A badge of honour...I shook my head, tiredly. More like a mark of shame.

"Bella," I said, suddenly. "She was here, wasn't she?"

"Your sisters were both here," the healer said. "You and your friend have been sleeping for the last three days."

I stared. "*Alana* was here?"

"Yes," the healer said. "I also briefed your parents on your condition. Your mother assisted in brewing some of the potions you needed."

"But they didn't come," I said. I sat back, feeling down. My parents had to be ashamed of me. And...I gritted my teeth. I didn't want to know, but I had to ask. "What happened to Rose?"

"She got caught by the blast," the healer said. "Thankfully, the healing spells worked better on her. I believe she should be back to normal by the end of the day."

I looked at him. "And her parents?"

"They haven't been informed," the healer said. "What could they do?"

Of course not, I thought. I felt a sudden flash of pure rage, mixed with sympathy. My parents were *important*. Rose's parents were commoners. *They don't need to be told their daughter has been injured.*

"Write to them," I snapped. "They have a right to know."

"I believe such matters are decided by the Castellan," the healer said. "And Rose herself will have a say, when she recovers. She may not wish to tell them."

He lowered his voice. "The bad news is that the Castellan wants to see you both," he added, darkly. "I have orders to inform him when you are ready to face him."

I swallowed. I really shouldn't have been surprised.

The healer helped me to stand, then insisted that I walk around the room several times before calling a nurse to assist me in the bathroom. It was embarrassing, but I had no choice. My entire body was covered with patchwork skin, its mere presence mocking me. What had I *done* to myself?

My blood ran cold. *What have I done to Rose?*

Someone - probably Sandy - had sent along a complete set of clothes. I dressed slowly, feeling dread deep in my chest. The Castellan was rarely involved in disciplinary matters, I'd been told. Normally, the upperclassman supervised the lowerclassmen. Only the worst offences, outside class, were handled by the staff. If he wanted to see us...I doubted it boded well.

Rose was waiting in the room when I came out, standing next to a seventh year girl with a grim face. Rose's hair was gone, save for a red fuzz covering her scalp. Her skin was pale, almost as pale as Isabella's. I looked closely and saw traces of the same patchwork grafting as there was on mine. Her grafts seemed to have settled better - or at least quicker. I suspected her magic must have helped the process along, but even so...she looked stunned, as if she couldn't quite process what had happened to her.

"I'm sorry," I said, quietly.

"Be quiet," the girl said. "I'm here to escort you to the Castellan."

I exchanged glances with Rose, then followed the older girl through the door and into the corridor. Bella was standing there, twisting her hands nervously. She opened her mouth to say something, but the older girl glared her into silence before she could say a word. I tried to shoot her a reassuring look, even as I glanced around for my parents...I would even have welcomed *Alana*. There was no sign of any of them.

It was the middle of the day, according to my watch, but there were still students moving through the corridors. I was grimly aware of them staring at us, their eyes following our procession towards the Castellan's office. If we'd been out for three days...I wondered, suddenly, just what rumour said about us. By now, the story might have turned into something so absurd that the truth was completely buried.

We stopped outside a large wooden door, which opened to reveal an office. A grim-faced woman sat at a wooden desk, eying us both with a stare that reminded me of Great Aunt Stregheria. There was a wooden bench pushed against the far wall and a Grandfather Clock in the corner, but otherwise the remainder of the office was bare. We were marched across to a second door, which opened as we approached. A gust of warm air struck me as we were motioned into the room.

The Castellan was seated behind his desk, reading something that looked like a medical report. He looked up at us as the door closed, then pointed to a spot in front of his desk. I walked over, clasping my hands behind my back to keep them from shaking. The Castellan returned his gaze to his report. I knew, from my father, that he was making us wait so we knew we were in trouble, but it struck me as absurd. We *knew* we were in trouble.

I forced myself to wait. Rose, beside me, fidgeted nervously. It felt like hours - or perhaps *days* - before the Castellan closed the report and looked up at us. There was no warmth at all in his cold eyes. He was angry, very angry. And it was hard to blame him.

"Magistra Loanda has examined the remains of Lab Thirteen," he said, without bothering to welcome us. "She informs me that you were experimenting with dragon scales. Is that correct?"

I nodded, wordlessly. There was no point in trying to deny it. A careful analysis of the remnants of the potion would turn up traces of dragon scales. Magistra Loanda wouldn't have had any trouble finding all the proof she needed. Even if she hadn't, her word would be enough. I had no doubt of it.

"Dragon scales," the Castellan repeated. His voice was still cold. "Dragon scales, which every fool knows are highly volatile. Dragon scales, which have to be treated with great care. Dragon scales, which are used in potions that explode if you look at them the wrong way."

His eyes bored into mine. "Tell me," he said. "What *were* you thinking?"

I tried to formulate a response that wouldn't get us in worse trouble, but nothing came to mind. I'd seen the formula work - I *had*! And yet...I didn't have any proof. Not until I could brew the formula again...

...But why had it exploded?

"You ignored every safety rule in the book," the Castellan continued. His gaze switched to Rose. "And it was only sheer dumb luck that you survived. You came *very* close to death."

He looked back at me. "What *were* you thinking?"

"It was my fault, sir," I said. "I thought I could..."

The Castellan cut me off. "Your father is a *very* well-respected magician, your mother a Master Brewer," he said. "Surely you *knew* the dangers?"

I swallowed, but said nothing. What *could* I say?

"You have wantonly defied safety rules intended to keep you *safe*," the Castellan said. "You are not trained magicians, pushing the limits to see what you can get away with. You are students who haven't even passed the first set of exams. What are you going to do next? If you'd tried this in a classroom, you could have killed the entire class!"

My legs wobbled. He was right. I didn't know precisely *what* had gone wrong, but *something* clearly had. And if I'd tried that in a classroom...

The Castellan cleared his throat. "I have decided that you both merit significant punishment," he said, his voice hardening. He met my eyes. "Caitlyn of House Aguirre, you will be suspended from Jude's for a period of one month. When you return, you will have to work hard to catch up with the rest of your class. Should you fail your exams, at the end of the year, you will not be permitted to retake them."

I felt cold. A month's suspension wasn't bad, but failing the exams...if I didn't get a degree of *some* kind I might as well slip into the countryside and live on a farm. There would be no hope of finding a *real* job. And if my parents were truly mad at me, they might not agree to front me the money for a shop...

...And yet, compared to what I'd feared, it was a surprisingly mild punishment.

The Castellan's eyes moved to Rose. "Rose of Erehwon, you will be unceremoniously expelled from this school and returned to your village. Your fees will not be returned. You will not have the opportunity to transfer your scholarship to other schools. I imagine you will have to spend the rest of your life paying off the debt."

Rose gasped. I stared. Rose was being expelled?

"You can't do that," I stammered. My voice sounded weak, even to myself. "You..."

"Both of you should be expelled," the Castellan said, flatly. "If I were you, young lady, I would count myself lucky that *I* had not been expelled."

You're not me, I thought. I felt a bitter flash of pure hatred. *You...*

I swallowed my words. Despite everything, I wasn't stupid enough to say it out loud. He hadn't just expelled Rose, he'd destroyed her life. There was no way she could pay off her debt. Her creditors would eventually come for her and her entire family. She'd be very lucky indeed if she *only* had to go into service with one of the Great Houses. Her talent would be wasted...

"It was my fault, sir," I pleaded. "Expel me instead."

"But she went along with you," the Castellan pointed out. "You are *both* being punished."

He pointed a finger at the door. "Wait outside," he ordered. "Your father will arrive soon to take you home."

Rose sounded stunned. "What about me?"

"The formal ceremony will be held tonight," the Castellan said. "After that, you will be sent home. Go."

I opened my mouth. "Sir, I..."

"Out," the Castellan ordered. "I will speak to you again after your suspension is over."

I felt magic pushing at me, shoving me towards the door. There was no point in trying to resist. And yet, I tried to struggle anyway. I wanted to shout and scream at him, but...but it was futile. Despair washed over me. I'd damaged my future in the explosion...

...And I had utterly destroyed *Rose's* only hope of a better life.

CHAPTER
TWENTY-FOUR

"Sit there," the secretary ordered. Her nose twisted, as though she had smelled something disgusting. "Be silent."

We sat on the hard wooden bench, staring down at the stone floor. I didn't want to look at Rose. I didn't want to see the accusation in her eyes when she looked at me. It had been *my* idea to experiment with the formula, it had been *my* decision to take the risk...I wanted to cry, to scream and shout until my cheeks were wet with tears. I'd ruined her life as surely as my lack of magic had ruined mine. It was all my fault.

And they're not going to expel me because of my family, I thought, savagely. *And yet, they're going to expel Rose.*

A dozen thoughts ran through my head, each one crazier than the last. I could get Dad to take Rose into service...she could learn from my parents, even as she worked for them. Or I could try to convince my parents to pay her debt before it was too late...it would be pocket change for my father. I wouldn't even complain if he took it out of my inheritance. Or I could beg for my inheritance ahead of time and try to open a shop, even though I was still legally a child. Or...we could run away, couldn't we? No one would care enough to hunt down Rose...

...But my family would look for *me*.

And Rose's family would have to pay her debts, I reminded myself. *Their creditors wouldn't stop demanding the money, even if Rose went missing...*

I looked up at her. She was trying not to cry, but her cheeks were stained with tears. I felt my heart break for her, even as I cursed myself.

I should have pushed her away. I should have told her to join Isabella or Alana...I should have let her hex me a hundred times, just so she could join the other girls. Better that than being expelled...

...But it was too late.

"I'm sorry," I said. "I'll get you out of this, somehow."

"Be silent," the secretary ordered.

I ignored her. "Rose, I'll think of something..."

The secretary muttered a spell. I froze. Rose froze too, utterly unable to move. Even the tears running down her bare cheeks were frozen. We could only look at each other, waiting helplessly for nemesis to arrive. My father was *not* going to be pleased. Maybe if I begged him to help Rose... would he listen?

I could hear the Grandfather Clock ticking, the sound echoing in the silent air. Seconds became minutes, steadily adding up...where *was* my father? If he'd been at home, he could be here by now. But if he'd been at Magus Court...it would take him considerably longer to disengage and race to the school. I wanted to think he was at home, waiting for news. Or perhaps pacing outside the school...

The spell broke. I sagged forward, crashing into Rose. She didn't move. Her limbs were still frozen. The secretary let out a gasp of shock, then cast the spell again. I felt a surge of pure rage as my limbs locked once again, but nothing happened. She could just keep casting and recasting the spell until my father arrived.

I tensed, inwardly, as the door opened. The secretary cleared her throat.

"Lord Aguirre," she said. "Your daughter is here."

"Open a private room for us," my father ordered. He sounded angry. I wished I could turn, just to see his face. "Have a maid bring two mugs of tea - and a large glass of juice. And then wait."

The secretary jumped up and hurried to obey. I felt a flicker of vindictive glee, mixed with dull resentment. Prune-faced toady though she was, she was still more important than I would ever be. I hoped my father kept her hopping for the next hour or two, steadily piling on more and more demands until she broke under the strain. She wouldn't want to bother her superior with anything trivial, yet eventually she would have to say no.

I felt myself lifted up by an unseen force and carried backwards, towards the door. My father was standing there, looking grim as he floated me down the corridor and into a smaller chamber. He lowered me to the floor and left me there, still frozen, as he cast a number of privacy spells, then jabbed a finger at me. The spell broke, sending me stumbling forward helplessly. He caught me before I could fall and hit the ground.

"Dad," I managed.

"Sit down," my father ordered.

He helped me to the nearest chair, then let go of me. I sagged into the comfortable seat as the maid entered, carrying a tea tray. Judging by her expression, the secretary must have told her to hurry. I knew the signs from home. Someone had added a plate of biscuits and hot chocolate buns, clearly trying to make my father feel welcome. My stomach rumbled, but I ignored it. I doubted I'd be eating chocolate any time soon. I'd be lucky if I wasn't disowned on the spot.

My father waited until the maid had left, then he sat down facing me. "Explain," he ordered, firmly. "Now."

I swallowed, trying to formulate an answer. My father had *never* been fooled when any of us had tried to lie to him. And yet...part of me didn't *want* to tell him. I told that part of me to shut up, loudly. The only hope of saving Rose from being expelled - or at least from being sold into slavery - lay with my father.

"I was carrying out an experiment," I said, carefully. "I..."

"They pulled a dozen fragments of dragon scales out of your skin," my father said. His voice was very calm, which worried me. *That* meant he had his temper under tight control. I would have preferred shouting. "What *sort* of experiment."

I looked back at him, trying to find the words. "I couldn't brew potions in class," I said, finally. "It didn't matter how carefully I followed the instructions. I just couldn't infuse magic into the brew. Rose had to stir the potions *for* me."

"I see," my father said. "And what does this have to do with dragon scales?"

"I worked out a formula for drawing magic out of dragon scales," I said, carefully. I reached for my pocket, then stopped as I realised it was empty. Of course...my old outfit had probably been destroyed. "I thought if I brewed the scales in water, with a handful of runes and other ingredients..."

"You would produce a burst of magic," my father finished. He looked resigned. "It's been tried."

My blood ran cold. "I didn't find any reference to it in the textbooks..."

"That's because anyone with a lick of sense would realise that the blast would be uncontrollable," my father finished. "It *has* been tried, time and time again. Every serious potioneer discovers it - rediscovers it - when they start trying to invent their own potions, but none of them have been able to get it to work. There's always an explosion."

His voice darkened. "It looks good, I know," he said. "But it never works."

I met his eyes. "Father," I said. "I got it to work."

My father's eyes went wide. "Cat...this isn't the time for jokes."

"I got it to work," I said. He could always tell when we were lying. Couldn't he tell when we were telling the truth? "Would you like me to swear an oath?"

He looked at me for a long moment. Oaths were sacred. No one with more than a gram or two of magic would take them lightly, although I really had no idea what would happen if *I* broke an oath. I didn't have any magic to bind my words. It wasn't something I would joke about, not with my father. Warlocks - oathbreakers - often wound up wishing they were dead.

"Explain," he ordered, finally.

I ran through the whole story, feeling my head start to pound as Dad questioned each and every detail. He *was* a skilled interrogator, as well as everything else. I told him about the formula, how I'd worked out the equations to guide the magic...I told him about Alana and how she'd betrayed me. And then I told him how, out of desperation, I'd put the formula together and splashed it into the potion. And it had worked.

"Magistra Loanda said it was the best in the class," I finished. "But I didn't use my own magic to make it."

My father looked doubtful. "Every potioneer who has tried something like that has *always* had the brew explode," he said. "What happened *next*?"

"I wanted to show off," I admitted. "I made a potion with Rose...one that should have worked. But when I inserted the formula, it..."

I shivered. The white light had been terrifying. And then...my memories were still jumbled.

"It exploded," I said, quietly.

"That's what should have happened, the first time you made it," my father said.

"That's not what the equations say," I countered. "*They* say it should work. And it did."

"For you," my father said.

He looked me in the eye. "Why didn't you tell Magistra Loanda?"

"I didn't know how she'd react," I admitted. "And I didn't want her to hurt Mum."

"They're not exactly enemies," my father told me. "More like friendly rivals."

He shrugged. "You really should have brought this to me. Or your mother."

I nodded. "I know."

"And you've been suspended," he added. "You'll have plenty of time to discuss it with us."

I swallowed, hard. "Dad, it was *my* idea. Rose shouldn't be expelled because of me."

He looked back at me, evenly. "That's not my decision."

"It could be," I said. "Dad, *please*..."

His eyes darkened, just for a second. "Do you have any idea how lucky you are?"

I flinched as he glared at me. "You could have been *killed*, Kitten," he said. "Your mother and I could have been burying you, right as we speak! And you could have been expelled too..."

His voice hardened. "If someone more important than a little commoner girl had been injured, Caitlyn," he added, "it would have been impossible *not* to expel you."

"It isn't *right*," I said. "Rose didn't do anything wrong."

I met his eyes, forcing myself to hold firm. "Please, Dad," I said. "I'll do whatever you want. I'll take whatever punishment you consider appropriate without a word of complaint. But *please*. Rose shouldn't be punished because of my mistakes."

My Dad looked back at me for a long moment. "I have spent the last thirty years building up a patronage network," he said. "Hundreds of magicians, from great to small, owe me favours I can call on at need. And you're asking me to use some of those favours to save your friend from her mistakes?"

"From *my* mistakes," I objected.

"She shouldn't have let you experiment," my father said, coolly.

"It was *my* fault," I said. "I...I took her under my wing. She has potential. I'll...I'll do the garden and sweep the halls and..."

Dad studied me for a long moment. "Rest assured, we will be discussing your punishment when you return home," he said. He picked up his tea and drank it slowly, giving me time to sweat. "And I will also discuss *her* punishment with the Castellan."

He rose. "There may be a price," he said. "And you will have to pay."

I nodded. "Anything."

"Don't say that, even in jest," Dad said, sharply. He headed towards the door. "Wait here."

He left, closing the door behind him. I found my hands were shaking. When had I found the nerve to stand up to my father like that? He could have disowned me...he probably *would* have disowned me, if someone *important* had gotten hurt. I forced my hands to still, then turned my attention to the chocolate buns. My stomach was growling loudly now, demanding that I eat. But the buns still tasted like ashes in my mouth. I tried to tell myself that it was going to be fine, but I didn't believe it. Dad didn't care *that* much about Rose, did he? She was nothing to him.

It was nearly an hour before the door opened again, revealing my father - and Rose. Rose looked torn between terror and relief, her eyes glancing from side to side as though she was waiting for the next blow to fall. Dad raised an eyebrow when he saw the empty plate, then called for food. It arrived five minutes later, fresh from the oven. Of course...it was Friday, when dinner was a less formal affair. I'd lost track of the days while I'd been unconscious.

"I discussed the matter with the Castellan," my father said, once Rose was tucking into a large chocolate bun. "It was not a very pleasant discussion."

He pointed a finger at me. "You now owe the Castellan a very large favour," he warned, darkly. "Do you understand?"

"Yes, Dad," I said. I took another bun. This time, it tasted heavenly. "What did he say?"

"I...*convinced*...him not to expel Rose or suspend you," Dad said, sipping his tea. "That's the good news. Like I said, it was not a very pleasant discussion. I had to threaten to call in several favours the Triad owes me before he agreed to unbend. But neither of you are expelled or suspended."

He paused. "I may have to call in additional favours with the other teachers," he added. "I doubt Magistra Loanda wants you back."

I looked at him. "Wouldn't she be fascinated?"

"Perhaps she'd think you merely had a stroke of dumb luck," my father countered. "It wouldn't be the *first* time something odd happened, something that couldn't be replicated under controlled conditions. There's a lot we *don't* know about magic, Kitten. We have a long way to go before we match the Ancients."

And we still don't know what destroyed their empire, I thought, numbly. *War...or Objects of Power?*

I looked at Rose, then back at my father. "And the *bad* news?"

"You will both be on punishment rotas for the next two weeks," Dad said. "He flatly refused to let you get away with it, although the injuries you suffered *were* a particularly unpleasant form of punishment. You'll be cleaning floors, washing laundry...every little chore that would normally be left to the maids. It will not be fun."

"Better than being expelled," I said.

Dad shrugged. "You'll be grounded for most of the holidays," he added. "What you did was incredibly dangerous. And Rose--" he looked at her "--will be coming home with us for the summer. There's work for her too."

I stared. "Dad..."

"I'll clear it with her family," Dad said. He gave me a sharp look, quelling the next set of objections. It wasn't uncommon for an aristocratic child to join another household for a few weeks, but Rose was a commoner. "You do understand *just* how lucky you were, don't you?"

"Yes, Dad," I said.

"Your mother will be writing to you soon," Dad added. "I expect she will want to...*discuss*...the matter with you."

I winced. Mum would be furious. I was surprised she hadn't accompanied Dad. But then, he hadn't expected to have to help Rose. They'd probably assumed I'd be marched home for a private scolding and a fortnight of chores.

"Don't cause any further trouble," Dad said. "Stick to jinxing your fellows and booing the netball teams when they lose. Slip a hex under someone's pillow or something along the same lines. *Don't* run the risk of getting expelled again."

I smiled, wanly. "I told Rose the truth..."

My father gave me a sharp look. "And yet, you managed to work some magic."

I looked back at him, wishing I knew what he was thinking. Did he think I'd unlocked some secret talent? Or did he think I'd somehow brought my magic out? Or...

The secretary froze me, I thought, suddenly. *But her spell didn't last.*

I corrected myself a moment later. *Her spell didn't last on me!*

My father sighed. "Do you remember what I said to Alana, during your tenth birthday party?"

I remembered. Alana had been a right brat. She'd thrown a tantrum in front of the guests - with magic - after discovering that my parents *hadn't* bought her the fancy wand she wanted. Dad had eventually told her to behave or the party would be unceremoniously cancelled.

"You told her to remember that magic brought responsibility," I recalled. The lecture had frightened *me* and I hadn't been the one in trouble. "And that she had to learn to do things for herself."

"Yes," my father said. "And you have to learn to do things for yourself too."

I stared down at the floor, feeling unpleasantly mutinous. I couldn't cast spells. I couldn't brew potions. And yet, I *had* managed to accomplish *some* things. If Dad was right...I had made the formula work, when countless more experienced magicians hadn't been able to produce more than an explosion. What did that say about me?

"Finish your tea, then go back to your dorm," Dad said. "And I suggest - very strongly - that you write to your mother this evening. She will need some reassurance."

He looked at Rose. "And you have to decide what you're going to tell your parents," he told her. "The truth would only upset them, I think."

Rose flushed. "Yes, My Lord."

CHAPTER
TWENTY-FIVE

"Well," Isabella said, as we stepped into the dorm. "Look at Scarface and her friend."

I scowled. I was too tired to argue with anyone. My body was insisting, loudly, that it needed food and sleep, perhaps not in that order. I didn't think Rose felt any better, but I didn't know. She hadn't said a word to me since we'd left the office and headed to the dorm.

"I was given lines for handing in my homework late," Isabella continued, sharply. "And do you know why? Because Magistra Loanda gave us all an extra essay on safety that we had to turn in on Thursday! It's *your* fault."

"Give it a rest, Isabella," Henrietta said, from her bedside. "We *all* got the essay. You just didn't do your homework because you had netball."

Isabella swung around to stare at Henrietta. I took advantage of the distraction to walk past her and sit on my bed. There were a handful of notes and cards piled on the sheets, including a surprisingly sweet card from Alana and Bella. I picked it up, feeling an odd flicker of affection for my sisters. Underneath it, there was another - unsigned - card. I turned it over and over, wondering just who had sent it. But there was nothing to point to the sender. I doubted there was any magical signature left, even if I'd been able to sense it. Whoever had sent the card wanted to remain unidentified.

I glanced at Rose, then looked back at the card. Rose looked...shattered. I wondered if she no longer wanted to be my friend. How could I blame her? I wanted to talk to her, but I didn't know what to say. She *had* to be mad at me. I'd nearly condemned her to death - or a fate worse than death. My folly...

...And yet, I'd made the formula work.

Isabella turned and marched towards my bed. "My wrists are aching," she said, holding them out for inspection. "What are you going to do about it, little *zero*?"

I tilted my head so she could see my jaw. "My jaw is itching," I said. The grafted skin felt papery as it melded into my flesh. "And I can't do anything about that either."

The dinner bell rang, a second later. I glanced at Rose and motioned for her to come with me. She nodded, but said nothing as we hurried down the stairs. Silence fell as we entered the dining hall. I forced myself to keep going as the students, even some of the teachers, stared at us. By now, rumour probably claimed we'd blown up the entire South Wing. It *had* been sealed off for the last four months.

Rose didn't say anything to me as we ate dinner, then returned to the dorm and climbed into bed. She just pulled the drapes around her bed before going to sleep. I felt my heart break a little more as I closed my own drapes. Rose had been my first real friend and she was rejecting me...and I couldn't even *blame* her! I felt my stomach heave as I lay down and gritted my teeth. The potions were working their way out of my body now. I was in for an uncomfortable night.

My dreams were so weird that I wondered if someone had hexed me while I slept. I was burning, yet I wasn't burning. I could move, yet I couldn't move. I was standing in quicksand, yet I wasn't sinking...I awoke, covered in sweat, at four in the morning. My brain refused to let me go back to sleep, so I opened a book and tried to read. Someone - and I suspected Magistra Loanda - had dumped a pair of volumes on particularly volatile potion combinations on my bedside cabinet. She'd probably been furious to discover that I hadn't been suspended after all...

My blood ran cold. What if I could no longer *forge*?

I'd done something reckless, if not stupid. *That* could not be denied. Magister Tallyman might think I shouldn't be allowed to work in his forge, certainly not without supervision. I felt tears prickling at my eyes as it sank in. I might have been banned from doing *anything* without supervision. Had I lost everything in one fell swoop?

Take your lumps, I told myself, sharply. *Rose could have been kicked out of the school because of you.*

It was a relief when it was finally time to get up and go to breakfast. The dining hall was completely empty when I entered, allowing me to sit down and eat in peace. Rose entered twenty minutes later, looking as though she hadn't had any sleep. I tried to signal that she should join me, but she sat at the other side of the room and munched her breakfast without saying a word. She probably hated me now. I wanted to lash out at her - I'd written my father a blank check - yet how could I blame her? Jude's was the best thing that had ever happened to her, and she'd nearly lost it because of me.

Sandy collared us both when we returned to the dorm. "Put these on," she said, shoving a pair of overalls at us. "You have work to do."

I winced. I'd hoped to speak to Magister Tallyman and discover if I was still allowed to forge. But Dad *had* said we would be punished. The overalls smelt unpleasant - I felt grimy after pulling them over my itchy skin - and looked worse. I glanced in the mirror and scowled. My face still looked like a patchwork doll. Rose, thankfully, looked almost back to normal.

"You're going to be servants for the rest of the day," Sandy informed us, as she led the way down the corridor. "You do what the janitor tells you, understand?"

"Yes," I said, tonelessly.

"And don't even *think* about trying to sneak off," Sandy added. "You *will* be caught and you *will* be punished."

I nodded as the janitor came into view. She was a tall woman, nearly as tall as my father, wearing a set of grimy overalls that revealed her muscular arms and legs. Her face was florid, set in an uncompromisingly pinched expression. I knew the type from experience. A female servant - almost a maid - but not a fainting flower. She would supervise the maids and work with the butler to run the household. Indeed, in some of the lesser houses, she would *be* the butler. And there was a wand dangling from her belt...

A magician, I thought. *And probably quite a formidable one.*

"I have brought them for you," Sandy said. "Please send them back to the dorms when you're done."

She shot us both a sharp look, then hurried away. I looked up at the janitor, feeling cold. I knew the type too well. They never let anyone get away with anything, even if the person they were supervising was the heir. Mum had hired one for four years - she'd been a governess - and even Alana had been terrified of her. I'd found it a relief when she finally moved on.

"There are brushes, buckets and sponges in the locker," the janitor said, coldly. "Take one of each, fill the buckets with warm water, then follow me."

We did as we were told. The janitor waited for us, then led the way down a hidden passageway and into a particularly muddy corridor. It took me a moment to realise that it led directly to the sports fields outside the school. The janitor barked harsh orders - we were to get down on our hands and knees and scrub the floor - and then left us to it with a parting threat. I thought she was bluffing - I didn't *think* she was allowed to slap us - but I didn't feel like testing it.

I looked at Rose as we began to work. "I'm sorry."

Rose said nothing. Instead, she turned away from me and continued to scrub the floor. I stared at her backside, torn between anger and bitter guilt. I'd helped her, hadn't I? But I'd hurt her too...I'd almost sooner have been hexed than endure her silent reproach. And yet...

"I don't know why it exploded," I said, addressing her back. I knew she could hear me. "It shouldn't have exploded..."

The equations said it shouldn't have exploded, my thoughts added. *But it did...*

My mind started to race as I scrubbed the floor. Dad had told me that figures never lied, unless someone was fiddling with them. He'd shown us all the household accounts, teaching us how a mistake - or deliberate malice - could alter the books. Someone taking money out - and not writing it down - could screw up the entire system. And yet...

I stopped, dead. Maybe it was something about *me* that had made the formula work.

"It worked once," I said, out loud. "Why didn't it work *twice*?"

I tossed the thought around and around. Dumb luck?

It didn't seem likely. Anyone could cast a spell without knowing what it actually did. I'd once tricked Alana into turning herself into a pig, just by giving her a spell I'd carefully rewritten to reverse the polarity of the magic flow. No, simple logic told me there had to be another answer. The equations insisted that the formula had to work for everyone - or someone more experienced than me would have found the flaw. And yet it didn't. I was the only person, as far as my Dad knew, who'd made it work.

Rose was there, my thoughts pointed out. *She was very close to the caldron...*

I stared at her. Everyone could sense magic, except me. There were people who never managed to cast a single spell, yet could sense magic. I was the sole exception, the sole person who never sensed magic. And I knew it all too well. My sisters didn't need to bother hiding their handiwork when they booby-trapped my chair. They knew I'd sit down without sensing anything amiss...

I don't have magic, I thought. *I don't have any magic.*

"I need to go to the library," I said, out loud. "I..."

Rose spun around and threw a hex. I was so surprised I couldn't even *move* before the magic struck me. My lips melted together. I couldn't speak. She glared at me as I stared back at her, shocked. I hadn't taught her *that* spell! It dawned on me, as she clenched her fists, that she must have looked it up in the library. She had to be doing *something* while I worked with Magister Tallyman and Akin.

"Shut up," Rose snapped. Her voice was breaking. "You...shut up!"

I would have made a sarcastic remark about not being able to talk anyway, but I couldn't speak. I wasn't sure I would have dared anyway. Rose...was shaking, her face darkening with rage. I'd often scored points off my sisters that ended with them throwing hexes, but this was different. Rose looked as if she was torn between crying and screaming at me.

"I was *expelled*," she shouted. "I was..."

She stared at me. "I could have lost *everything*! My *parents* could have lost everything! I could have been married off to some old geezer because my family needed to get rid of me before the creditors came calling! I could have lost everything..."

Her face purpled. "I could have lost everything and here you are, talking about going to the *library*!"

I tried to swallow. My mouth felt uncomfortable. I'd never liked the lip-sealing hex. One of my governesses had been fond of using it. Too fond, according to Mum. She'd literally tossed the governess out of the hall when she'd found out. And now, Rose had used it to silence me.

"Your father saved me," she added. "Who *is* he?"

One of the three most powerful magicians in the city, I thought. I couldn't say a word. Rose was talking to me now...but she hated me. *And yet, she still owed my father a favour.*

"You could have killed us both," Rose shouted. Tears were running down her cheeks. She raised her scarred hand, as if she were about to slap me or hex me, then dropped it back into her lap. "Or worse...you could have just taken a couple of weeks off, while I was sent home!"

All the fight seemed to go out of her as she sagged backwards. I crawled forward and put my arm around her as she cried, great heaving sobs that racked her body. She tensed, just for a second, then relaxed into my embrace. I couldn't help another stab of guilt that threatened to start me crying too. To Rose - to *everyone* - it had to look as though my father had saved me from punishment, while *she* had only been saved from a fate worse than death by an afterthought. She didn't know I'd begged my father to save her.

"I'm sorry," she said, desperately. "I'm so sorry."

She waved a hand at me. I felt my lips unseal.

"It was my fault," I said, softly. Rose had trusted me and I'd hurt her. Worse, I'd nearly *destroyed* her. If she wanted to hex me into next week... how could I blame her? "I'm sorry."

"*I'm* sorry," Rose said. She managed a weak smile. "Are we going to just keep apologising to each other?"

"It might not be a bad idea," I said. I managed to smile back. My lips still felt numb. "I had a thought."

Rose eyed me, nervously. "Does it involve sneaking up into the library?"

"Not yet," I said. The janitor would probably report us both if we sneaked away. I didn't feel like asking my Dad for a *second* favour. "But we do have to go up later tonight."

"If we can go," Rose pointed out. "We might have been banned from the library."

I swallowed, hard. The mere thought was a horror utterly beyond my imagination. How - precisely - were we to study without the library? It was impossible.

"I don't think so," I said. I rose and looked up and down the corridor. "I think we'd better finish here, then we can try and slip upstairs later."

"I suppose," Rose said. Her cheeks were still wet with tears. "Cat... please don't do that again."

"I won't," I promised.

I walked back to the bucket, picked up the wet sponge and turned back to her. And then I heard the spell, right behind me. There was no time to dodge. My ankles sprang together, sending me falling face-first to the floor. I heard a second spell, too late. I looked up to see Rose frozen in place.

"Well," Alana's voice said. "You're *finally* where you deserve to be. On the floor, washing up the dirt and grime."

She sounded angry. I wondered, absently, if Dad had said anything to her. It didn't seem likely. She'd probably only heard a few things from the school rumour mill, all hugely exaggerated. And yet, she'd sent the card... maybe *Bella* had sent the card. Or maybe she was back to normal, now she knew I'd recovered.

I tried to separate my ankles, but it was impossible. Magic held them together, magic I couldn't sense...I rolled over and glared at her, uncomfortably aware that my head was brushing against Rose's feet. She had to be trying to counter the spell, but it would be futile without being able to move her arms. No matter how talented she was, it would take time to learn to cast the spell without movement...

Alana glared down at me. "Everyone's mad at *me* because of you," she snarled. "What did you *do*?"

I gave her a smile I *knew* would irritate her. "Magic."

She lifted her hand into a casting pose, then stopped. "You can't do magic," she said, in a suspiciously calm tone. A thought crossed my head. Maybe, just maybe, I could trick her into doing something careless. "The potion exploded because you couldn't steer the magic..."

Her voice trailed off as it struck her. I'd never made a potion *explode* before. The best I'd done, without help, was a sludge that the gardeners had used to grow carrots in the vegetable beds. Only a magician could *start* the magical cascade, let alone control it. Alana...

...Had to be wondering if I really *was* a zero.

I pushed myself upwards, my hand raised in a casting pose. Alana cast the counterspell automatically, negating the magic. I threw myself aside, landing on one hand. Alana stared, then morphed into a frog. I'd tricked her into freeing Rose too.

"Hah," I said. Alana turned and started hopping down the corridor. "Bye-bye."

Rose, grinning from ear to ear, freed my ankles. I resisted the urge to chase Alana as I stood, rubbing my jaw. She deserved a good kick, but we'd already wasted far too much time. And besides, if she now believed I *did* have magic...

"She's going to be mad," Rose commented. "Will she go whining to your father, too?"

"I don't think so," I said. Alana *would* be furious when she figured out the truth, but it *had* been her own mistake. I'd spooked her. "I think she'll just set out to get revenge."

I picked up the sponge again and sighed. "Back to work," I added. It was frustrating, particularly since I had a *very* good idea, but we *were* being punished. "We'll go up to the library later."

Rose smiled at me. I couldn't help smiling back.

We were still friends.

TWENTY-SIX

As it happened, it was Monday evening before we managed to get into the library.

Sunday was practically identical to Saturday, except someone - I suspected Alana - had told the rest of the school what we were doing. Dozens of students, including Isabella and her cronies, made it their business to walk up and down the corridor in muddy shoes, forcing us to scrub the same places over and over again. Others hexed us from a distance or merely pointed and laughed at us doing the work of commoners. Rose learnt a couple of spells that should have sped up the cleaning, but the janitor caught her casting them and gave us an extra two days of detention. The only advantage to the whole affair was that it gave me time to think.

Monday wasn't much better. Protective and Defensive Magic was a disaster, of course, while in Potions Magistra Loanda hauled us to the front and gave us both a scathing lecture that nearly made me break down in tears. The rest of the class merely watched, not daring to either commiserate with us or laugh at us. I wasn't too surprised when she told me I'd need supervision from an upperclassman before I got to use the private labs again, not after what had happened. I *was* surprised she didn't bar me from using them altogether. By the time we finally managed to get into the library - after class, after dinner - we were both on edge.

"All right," Rose said, once we were in a private room. Thankfully, half the upperclassmen had netball practice. "What do you actually want to do?"

I reached for a sheet of paper and scribbled down a series of equations, working out the *precise* details of a spell. I'd been tempted to merely crib Anna's Amphibian, but that wouldn't have given me the test I needed. Rose watched me dubiously, her eyes clearly worried. She had good reason to remember the *last* experiment.

"This spell should work," I said, holding out the paper. "I want you to cast it on me."

Rose's eyes narrowed. "And what does it *do*?"

"I think it would work better if you didn't know," I told her. "I don't want your intentions bleeding into the spell."

"Then *no*," Rose said. She looked down at the paper, her eyes glazing over. "I can't even see what this spell *does*."

I stared at her in astonishment. "It's harmless," I said, although I knew that not everyone would agree. "All you have to do is cast it on me."

Rose passed the paper back to me. "What. Does. It. Do?"

We looked at each other for a long moment. "It should turn me into a frog for a precise period of time," I said, finally. I didn't want to go into more detail. "That's all it does."

"Really?" Rose asked, sardonically. "And you need a *new* spell to get turned into a frog?"

"Yes," I said. "This is one I devised personally."

I went on before she could say a word. "I've had a hunch," I added. "But if I tell you any more about it, your intentions might warp the spell."

Rose still looked doubtful, but she took the paper back. I didn't really blame her. One of the safety lectures we'd endured had been a warning about casting spells when we didn't actually know what they did. It wasn't unknown for magicians to accidentally cause all sorts of problems, just by casting the wrong spells. And Rose...well, she probably didn't trust me as much as she had, before I'd nearly killed her. It was hard to blame her for that too.

My heart twisted. Nothing was going to be the same again.

"Fine," Rose said. "And what do you want me to do while you're hopping around on the floor?"

"Nothing," I said, seriously. I nodded to the stack of books we'd borrowed for Theoretical Charms. "Read a book. Do your homework. Just wait."

Rose quirked an eyebrow. "And what if you get stuck as a frog?"

"It won't happen," I said. "There's nothing to keep the spell in place permanently. The worst that can happen is you having to turn me back before we go to the dorm."

I kept my doubts to myself. If I was right...the spell shouldn't last longer than an hour. But if I was wrong, I was dooming myself to three hours of utter boredom. I put my watch on the table, where I should be able to see it from the floor, then stood. Rose watched me as I moved to the centre of the room, her eyes still worried. I wished, not for the first time, that I could trust my sisters to help. Or someone else...

"Cast the spell," I said.

Rose reread the paper, then lifted her hand and cast the spell. The world spun around me, my eyesight blurring as my body twisted and changed. It felt different this time, even though I was used to being transfigured without warning. It didn't hurt, but it felt as though it *should* hurt. I'd been so intent on timing the spell - and boosting the magic as much as possible - that I hadn't worried about the sensation.

I looked up. Rose was peering down at me from a great height. My body twitched, as if it wanted to jump backwards. I still had nightmares, sometimes, about the day Alana had transfigured me for the first time. She hadn't hurt me - she wouldn't have hurt me, not when she thought I would develop magic soon - but the shock had been horrifying. I'd been shaking like a leaf when Dad removed the spell.

"Cat?" Rose asked. "Are you all right?"

I lifted a green hand and waved to her, then started to hop around the room. The frog body still felt twitchy...I wondered, absently, if I'd messed up the spell. It wasn't uncommon for someone to feel weird, after spending a long time in another form, but most spells had safeguards built in to prevent that from happening. Had I accidentally left them out? Or was it merely my imagination?

Rose took a final look at me, then sat down at the table and opened a book. I groaned inwardly as I looked at her, silently kicking myself for an obvious oversight. I should have asked her to read to me. I could have listened, even as I waited to see what happened. But it was too late now.

There was no way to signal anything more complex than a demand to be turned back. All I could do was wait.

I tested the concept in my mind, over and over again. Dad had always said I had magic, if only because I'd managed to break Great Aunt Stregheria's spell. I'd never believed him because I'd never been able to do it again. But what if there was something about me that had resisted the spell? Or broken it? Something about my nature that had actively negated the spell...?

The equations say the formula should work, I told myself. Time was passing slowly, so slowly. *But everyone thinks the equations are wrong, because it doesn't work. Except I did manage to get it to work...*

I'd been alone, the first time I brewed the formula. There hadn't been anyone else in the classroom. If someone had been standing right outside the door, they'd still been at least four metres from the caldron. But Rose had been right next to me when I'd brewed the *second* potion, the one that had violently exploded. She hadn't touched it, she hadn't done anything to interfere with the brewing...had it been her presence, her *mere* presence, that had caused the explosion?

Could it be, I asked myself, that the fault lay with *Rose*, not with me? And, by extension, with every other magician who had tried to brew the formula?

I *wanted* to believe it. But Dad had told me to be particularly careful when I *wanted* to believe something...

The world spun around me, violently. I screwed my eyes shut as my body changed. The sensation was worse, far worse. Being transfigured was normally uncomfortable, but this time it *hurt*. It felt as though my entire body had turned to water - or acid. Just for a moment, I thought Rose had liquefied me. And then I fell forward and hit the ground, my eyes jerking open. I was human again. And yet...

I sat upright, feeling the ghostly sensation fading away. It was almost a *phantom* sensation, as if it wasn't really there. I rubbed my hands together, puzzled. Something didn't feel quite right, but what? And yet, even *that* sensation faded as I stood.

"You broke the spell," Rose said. She was staring at me. "Cat...you *did* it!"

"Maybe," I said. I glanced at my watch. An hour. The spell had worn off in an hour. And it should have lasted longer. I'd feared Rose would *have* to turn me back when the library closed. "Rose...that spell should have lasted longer."

Her eyes narrowed, again. "How *much* longer?"

"At least four hours," I said. Rose didn't have the power to trap someone in another form for much longer than that, although it was just a matter of time. "I designed the spell to *last*."

Rose looked torn between pleasure and annoyance. I hadn't told her how long the spell was going to last, after all. She might have been condemned to sitting in the private room, reading, until we were kicked out of the library. I wouldn't have minded - I *loved* the library - but someone else might have a different opinion. Rose certainly would not have enjoyed waiting for me to turn back.

"I might have underpowered the spell," Rose mused. "Or..."

"The secretary didn't," I countered. Rose had remained frozen until my father had talked the Castellan into cancelling her expulsion. "She was astonished when I broke the spell."

I went on before she could say a word. "Isabella froze me on the very first day," I added, starting to pace around the room. "And *that* wore off too. So did the other spells she hurled at me. And so did your spell."

Rose met my eyes. "Is that normal?"

"No," I said. "If you cast a spell like that on someone who can't cancel it, the spell lasts until it runs out of magic or someone takes it off. The spell I gave you should have lasted for much longer than it actually did."

And Great Aunt Stregheria turned my sisters into little frogs for a whole week, I added, mentally. *But it didn't last on me.*

I felt as though I was on the cusp of a discovery. What was *different* about me? What was *special* about me? If I couldn't sense magic, let alone wield it...was it possible that magic couldn't touch me? But if *that* was true, it would be impossible to turn me into anything...and *that* was obviously untrue. And yet, the spells hadn't lasted...

My blood ran cold. The healer had said that some of the *healing* spells hadn't worked properly. I probed my memory, trying to remember *precisely* what he'd said. Some of his spells hadn't worked, but which ones?

Dad hadn't had any trouble mending my leg after I broke it...*that* was a simple spell, of course. Mending a broken leg was easy, unless there were real complications. No one had hexed the wound...

"The equations said the formula should work," I said, slowly. "It did, when I tried it. But everyone else who tried it got an explosion."

"So did you," Rose pointed out.

I rubbed my itching jaw. "You were with me," I countered. "You were standing right next to the caldron."

Rose glared. "I didn't make it explode!"

"Not deliberately," I said. "But I think your *presence* made it explode."

No one tried to make potions - no one *could* produce potions - without at least *some* magic. It was the only way to make the potion work. A person who tried without magic would get the same sort of useless sludge *I* got, when someone else didn't do the magic for me. But *that* meant that everyone who'd experimented with dragon scales had had magic. If Rose's mere presence could make the brew explode, and I knew she hadn't touched the caldron, what would happen if she actually *tried* to make the potion herself?

Bang, I thought.

"You're a strong magician," I said. "What if you were close enough to destabilise the brew?"

I sat down, facing her. "I have to try to brew it again. Alone."

Rose's mouth dropped open. "Are you *insane*?"

She leaned forward. "You got suspended - I got expelled," she snapped. "And we were *very* lucky to have both punishments cancelled. And now you want to go and *repeat* the same experiment that nearly got us killed?"

"Alone," I said. "If you're not with me..."

"You could get killed," Rose insisted. "Cat...are you *mad*?"

I looked down at the floor. I knew the risks. In truth, I'd known the dangers well before I'd come to Jude's. But I had to *know*. If there was an advantage to my condition, if there was something about it I could actually use...I had to *know*. It was worth any risk just to find out if my life had any value.

"I don't think so," I said. "I..."

"You're talking about doing something that could get you expelled," Rose said. "If it doesn't kill you! Why?"

I looked her in the eye. "I was told that I would have magic," I said. "Magic was my birthright. My father promised us that he'd teach us how to cast spells when we turned seven. Rose...we all longed for that day. We *wanted* to be great magicians. And there were three of us...we were triplets. Everyone *knew* we would be great.

"But I could never get the spells to work. Our triplet-triad never came into existence. Instead...Alana turned cruel, while Bella turned lazy. And everyone wondered what had happened to me. I heard people talking, when they thought I couldn't hear. They wondered if the blood was running thin. They asked if Dad had adopted a commoner girl because he wanted to fake a triad. They asked..."

I shook my head. "I don't fit into my family," I said. "And when Alana becomes the heir...the best I can hope for is being disowned."

Rose lifted her hand. "Do I have to slap you again? There's a world outside magic..."

"Not for me," I said. I suspected she wasn't bluffing. "I have to try. I have to *know*. Even if it comes at the risk of my life..."

"You're being an idiot," Rose told me. "And you can't get into a lab without supervision..."

"I know," I said. I'd have to get round that, somehow. I was pretty sure *Sandy* wouldn't agree to supervise. "I'll have to find someone to help..."

Robin might, I thought. *But what would he want in exchange?*

"I should report you," Rose said. Her lip was trembling. "Cat...I don't want you to die!"

"I don't want to die either," I said. "But if this can be used..."

I looked up at her. As far as I knew, I was unique. I was the sole person who couldn't sense magic, let alone use it. But that proved nothing. A zero like me, someone born out in the countryside, might never realise there was anything odd about him. He might think that he simply didn't have enough magic to cast a spell.

"I have to try," I said. Would she tattle? I didn't think so. And yet, if something went wrong...if someone found out she'd known what I'd intended to do...she'd be blamed. "Rose, I have to try."

"And let's just hope it doesn't kill you," Rose said.

The bell rang. I sighed, then picked up my books. I'd have to come back later and make a more comprehensive reading list, perhaps with some help from my mother. There *had* to be lists of dragon scale experiments, buried somewhere within the vast library. Or maybe I could wait until I got home. Dad's vast collection of books might hold the answer.

Except I've been promised a grounding, I thought, as we hurried back to the dorm. *Dad won't let me read his books.*

Isabella sneered at us, but said nothing. She was writing in her Punishment Book, clearly trying to catch up on her lines. I wondered who'd given them to her, but decided it didn't matter. We took a quick shower, then headed to bed. I wasn't too surprised when Isabella came over to me.

"You should do my lines," she hissed. "It's all *your* fault."

A madcap thought stuck me. Did I dare...?

Of course I did. "No," I said. I stuck out my tongue. "It's all *your* fault."

Isabella glanced around - there was no sign of Sandy, while Rose was still in the washroom - then jabbed a finger at me. I made no attempt to dodge as the spell struck me. My body twisted and shrank, the sensation sending unpleasant prickles down my spine. Whatever she'd turned me into, I could no longer move or speak. I wasn't even sure how I was still *seeing*. My eyesight was hazy.

"Hah," Isabella muttered.

She picked me up and dropped me on the bed, then pulled the drapes closed. I waited, sighing inwardly as the lights went out. There was no way to *know* how long Isabella had meant the spell to last...

...And yet it wore off, only forty minutes later.

I smiled. I didn't know what I was doing, but it was clear that I was doing *something*.

And perhaps there was something special about me after all.

CHAPTER
TWENTY-SEVEN

"And that...ah...concludes the lecture," Magister Von Rupert said. The class let out a sigh of relief, quietening quickly as Magister Grayson glared at us. "Does...ah...anyone have any questions?"

I rubbed the back of my neck, feeling sore. We'd just spent the last two hours listening to Magister Von Rupert explain the importance of a number of external factors to magic spells and diagrams. It was interesting, I had to admit, but my muscles were starting to cramp. The whole talk should probably have been classed as cruel and unusual punishment. On one hand, I wanted to listen; on the other, it was hard to concentrate. The warm air blowing through the classroom didn't help.

"Yes," Isabella said. "Why does a Casting Circle have to be drawn in Casting Chalk?"

"Because chalk can...ah...be removed," Magister Von Rupert informed her. "A simple sweep of your arm can wipe away the spell and defocus the magic. Resting the spell in something stronger will only make it harder to remove."

Isabella looked thoughtful. I wondered just what she had in mind. I'd learnt the uses of Casting Chalk from Dad, even though I couldn't use it to cast spells. What had *Isabella* learnt from her parents? Did she plan to try to cast a more permanent spell?

"For your homework, you will write an essay covering the uses of mud, wood and iron for runic magic," Magister Grayson said. "Pay special attention to the dangers. Dismissed."

The class didn't quite run for their lives, but it certainly looked as though they *wanted* to. I didn't blame them, even as I lingered behind. They were probably just as cramped as I was - and besides, half of them had netball practice. Rose remained behind, with me, as I headed up to the desk. Magister Von Rupert was clearing his papers, his bald dome glinting under the light. His partner eyed us both suspiciously.

"Magister," I said. "Can I ask a question?"

"Ah...yes, of course," Magister Von Rupert said. "About the homework?"

"No, sir," I said. "About magic."

I hesitated, then took the plunge. "What determines how long a spell remains in effect?"

"Ah...a *hard* question," Magister Von Rupert said. Beside him, Magister Grayson snorted rudely. "The simplest...ah, the simplest answer is that duration is a function of both complexity and power. The more complex the spell, the more power is required to hold it in place. Typically, a complex spell will last a shorter space of time than a simple spell."

He paused. "But...ah...there are other issues," he added. "The spell's target may be actively resisting the spell. Or the spell may be destabilised by an outside source. Both rogue flares of magic and...ah, focused wards have been known to cancel spells. I...ah...attended a party in my younger days when the hosts triggered a ward. Half the glamours suddenly failed, leaving a number of young guests unaccountably exposed."

I giggled. It wasn't considered *polite* to draw attention to a person's glamour - most magicians used them to make themselves look better - but who could have *avoided* noticing if all the glamours were cancelled at once?

"Ah...and even when there is no interference, the spell still degrades over time," he said, his face reddening slightly. "It is impossible to enchant someone for more than a week without some *very* careful preparation."

I frowned. I wasn't sure how to ask the next question. It would be far too revealing.

"If a spell kept wearing off ahead of time," I mused, "what would you think?"

"The spell...ah...might be underpowered," Magister Von Rupert said. "I recall a student who garbled his equations so badly that half his magic was wasted. Ah...the spell should have lasted for days, but it barely lasted an hour."

"It isn't easy to transfigure inanimate objects," Magister Grayson put in. "They tend to shift back at the worst possible moments."

"True," Magister Von Rupert agreed. "Ah...there was that girl who went to the ball."

Magister Grayson shot him a sharp look. I kept my expression blank. I'd heard the story - and a dozen variations. The poor girl had wanted to go to the ball, but she'd had nothing to wear. In desperation, she'd transfigured her sackcloth dress into a beautiful gown and gone to the ball. But the spells had worn off midway through the dancing...

One of my father's apprentices had had another version of the story. But Mum had shouted at her for telling it to us.

"Iron is a pain to work with," Magister Von Rupert said. "Ah...it simply *cannot* be held in its transfigured state for very long."

And iron is magically neutral, I thought. *Am I magically neutral too?*

"Thank you, sirs," I said. "It was very interesting."

Magister Grayson lifted his right eyebrow. "Can I ask why you wanted to know?"

I hesitated. "Some of my spells didn't last as long as they should," I said. His left eyebrow rose too. "I was wondering if there was a reason for it."

"I hope we were of some assistance," Magister Von Rupert said. "Ah... hand in your homework on Friday."

We left the classroom and headed down the corridor. Rose caught my arm just as we reached the stairs. "Are you sure you want to do this?"

"Yes," I said. "You go to the library. I'll meet you in the dining hall for dinner."

She paled. "Good luck," she whispered. "Be careful."

I nodded, then turned and hurried down to the upperclassmen common room. A grim-faced fifth-year stood on guard outside, glaring at everyone who walked past. Younger students had a habit of trying to sneak into the common room, even though getting caught meant writing lines until their wrists threatened to fall off. It was just another long-standing tradition so old that no one remembered when it had actually started - or why.

He scowled at me. "What do you want?"

"I want to speak to Robin Brandon," I said. "Please, will you ask him to come out?"

His scowl deepened. "No," he grunted. I didn't *think* he recognised me, even though I suspected I was one of the few firsties almost everyone knew. My face had nearly healed by now, but the rumours would take longer to fade. "Go away."

I felt a hot flash of anger. "I am Caitlyn Aguirre," I said. "I am the daughter of Lord Joaquin Aguirre, who is Master of Apprentice Brian Brandon. Fetch his brother at once."

He stared at me in honest surprise. I groaned, inwardly. I was probably going to get a million lines - or worse. But instead, he merely motioned for me to wait as he stepped into the common room. Two minutes later, he emerged with Robin who gave me a surprised look. I'd visited once before, when I'd picked up the supplies he'd found for me, but we hadn't arranged another meeting.

"Hamish looked peeved," he said, when we were halfway down the corridor. "What did you tell him?"

"I had an Alana moment," I said. It was easy to imagine my sister ordering upperclassmen around. I didn't *think* she'd get away with it, but she might. Dad had always told us that you could get away with anything if you had the nerve. "I'm surprised he didn't give me lines."

Robin shrugged. "What can I do for you?"

"I need a supervisor for the potions lab," I said. "Will you help me?"

He caught my shoulder and swung me around to face him. "Are you *mad*?"

"No," I said. I pushed his hand away, annoyed. "I need an upperclassman to help me..."

"You nearly manage to get yourself killed," Robin said. "And you want to go back into the potions lab? And you want *me* to help?"

"There's no danger," I insisted.

Robin glared. "Rumour has it that you and your commoner friend were killed and they had to resurrect you," he said. "No danger?"

I glared back. "Rumour *also* says that we blew up the South Wing," I snapped. "And *that* happened long before we came to the school."

"You *were* badly injured," Robin said. He made a show of peering at my face. "I can still see the scars."

I put rigid controls on my temper. "Please."

"No," Robin said. "Do you think I would threaten my future for you?" He turned to go. "Wait," I said. He stopped. "Name your price."

Robin turned back to me. "Name my price?"

I nodded. I didn't have anyone else to ask. Sandy was the only other upperclassman I knew, and *she* wouldn't help me. I didn't think she would do anything more than her duties demanded, particularly after I'd gotten her in trouble once already. Coming to think of it, *someone* had probably told her off *after* Rose and I had nearly been killed. The staff seemed more interested in looking for scapegoats than anything else.

"Yes," I said. "What do you want?"

Robin studied me for a long moment. I could practically see the wheels turning inside his head. I couldn't give him enough money to make the risk worthwhile, but there were other options. On one hand, it was vanishingly unlikely I would ever be in a position to *really* help him; on the other hand, a favour from me might be worth its weight in basilisk skin or dragon's blood. If I *had* developed magic - and I *had* made a potion explode - I might just wind up in a position to be useful...

...And a young magician, climbing up the ladder, needed all the help he could get.

"A favour," he said. "One day, I'll ask you for a favour. And you will give it to me."

"Saving only the honour of my family and my power," I said. It wasn't exactly a blank cheque, but it was alarmingly close to it. The ties of honour and obligation that bound the city together would keep him from demanding too high a price - I hoped - yet any reasonable price might be terrifyingly high. "Do we have a deal?"

Robin held out a hand. "Of course."

I looked up at him. "But you have to do as I say."

"As long as you are careful," Robin said. He was still holding out a hand. "Deal?"

I shook his hand. I didn't know if any promise *I* made would be bound by magic, but I certainly intended to keep my word. Besides, there was no point in taking chances. He gave me a final look, an odd glimmer of triumph in his eyes, then led the way down to the potions labs. I expected him to go into Lab Thirteen, but instead he took me to Lab Seven.

"This is the one we upperclassmen get to use," he said. He waved a hand at me. I went deaf, just long enough for him to say a number of words. "They'd do something unspeakable to me if you heard the passwords to lock the doors and unlock the stores."

I scowled at him. I was so *sick* of people treating me like an object.

Robin smirked. "Where would you like me to sit?"

I surveyed the room, silently measuring distances. Lab Seven was large enough to pass for a classroom. If Robin sat by the door, he would be over four metres from the workbench. I wasn't sure what was on the other side of the far wall, but I didn't think anyone apart from me would be closer than four metres. That should be enough, I hoped. It was a guess, an *educated* guess. I just hoped I'd guessed right.

"Sit by the door," I ordered. "Do *not* come any closer."

Robin's eyes narrowed. "What are you doing?"

"Wait and see," I said.

I stepped into the storeroom before he could answer. I'd been worried that Magistra Loanda would have confiscated the dragon scales, but there was a large jar of them on the topmost shelf. I dragged a ladder over and scrambled up to get them, then collected the rest of the ingredients and a couple of caldrons. Piling them up on the workbench, I lit the flame under the caldrons and settled back to wait for them to boil.

And if this goes wrong, I thought...

I felt cold. Rose had sensed something wrong, a moment before the explosion. If Robin was too far away to sense the surge in magic, I wouldn't have any warning before the blast. And while Rose wouldn't be blamed for *this* experiment, *Robin* certainly would be. It was possible he might be expelled, although they couldn't strip his academic qualifications. He shouldn't have any trouble finding a job.

I'm being selfish, I thought. I felt a pang of bitter guilt. *But I have to know.*

The formula seemed to sparkle with potential as I brewed it, then moved to the second caldron and started brewing the potion. I'd deliberately picked the simplest recipe I knew, one nearly everyone mastered on their first attempt. I didn't know if it *would* minimise the explosion - if there *was* an explosion - but it was worth a try.

"It looks like a very simple brew," Robin called. "Care to enlighten me?"

"Not yet," I called back. "Are you sitting comfortably?"

"I haven't sat so comfortably in...oh, the last thirty minutes," Robin said. "I was flirting with Dana when you summoned me."

"Sorry," I said, unapologetically. The liquid was starting to bubble. I hoped that was a good sign. "I would have tried to call you earlier, but I was busy."

"Cleaning corridors," Robin said. He snickered. "The Castellan *must* be really mad at you."

"He was," I confirmed. "And we have to keep cleaning corridors for the next few months."

"Look on the bright side," Robin advised. "Magister Grayson once threatened to give me so many detentions that my grandchildren would still be serving them."

I snorted, rudely. "I don't think he could actually do that."

"I'm sure he'd have a lot of fun trying," Robin said, gloomily. "The old bat has always disliked me, ever since I set that firework off in his class. I thought he was going to strangle me on the spot."

"He's a genius," I protested.

"He's also a very strict teacher," Robin said.

I looked down at the potion, then checked my watch. It needed to boil for five minutes, unstirred. I wondered, as I counted the seconds, if that was deliberate. Mum had worked with potions for so long that she had to keep herself from infusing magic into the brew while stirring. In hindsight, perhaps that was why she'd let me help her so often.

"I just wish I wasn't so bad at the practicals," I said, finally. "The theory is great - the practicals are awful."

"Everyone else thinks it's the other way round," Robin pointed out. "I bet you're the only person in the school that thinks theory is more fun than practical."

I didn't bother to dispute it as the last of the seconds ticked away. It was time.

"Stay there," I warned, as I splashed a little of the formula into the caldron. "Don't come any closer."

"I hope you know what you're doing," Robin said.

I ignored him as I stirred the liquid. The colour changed from brown to green, a pearly light that seemed to float *above* the potion. I felt my heart jump in my chest. It had worked. It had *worked*! I'd made it work...

Carefully, very carefully, I took the caldron off the heat, then bottled up the rest of the formula. Rose had been able to handle the bottle safely, although I wasn't sure what would happen if she touched the liquid with her bare hands. The bottles were crafted to *prevent* outside influence from harming their contents. I'd have to think - carefully - about how to use it in class. Rose sat too close to me...

And how close, I asked myself, *is too close?*

A dozen ideas ran through my mind. I could experiment - I could do a dozen experiments, with a little effort. And then...I pocketed the formula, thinking hard. What made me special? What made the formula work - for me - when it didn't for everyone else? How did my lack of magic allow me to use the formula...?

"Make sure you clean up the mess," Robin warned. "It's almost dinnertime."

I put the bottles and jars away, then washed up every last trace of my work. The wards would probably record that *Robin* had entered the lab, ensuring that he would be blamed for any mess. I grinned at him as he showed me out, then surprised myself by giving him a hug.

"Thank you," I said. "I...thank you!"

Robin nodded. He looked relieved. "Just remember you owe me a favour," he said, firmly. "And I *will* call on it one day."

"I know," I said. I didn't blame him for being relieved. No matter what I'd said, he would have been in deep trouble if there had been an explosion. "And I will repay it."

I would have to pay, I knew. Magic or not, I'd given my word and I intended to keep it. I hoped he wouldn't want something too onerous. It would be dishonourable to ask for something I couldn't reasonably give him. And even if I was wrong...

The bottle felt warm, in my pocket. Robin didn't know it, but he'd helped me prove my theory. I could make the formula! It hadn't been dumb luck. And now I knew I could do something, I could figure out how to use it.

And something was nagging at the back of my mind. Something important.

But what?

CHAPTER

TWENTY-EIGHT

Rose hadn't been quite sure what to make of it, when I went back to the library - after hiding the remains of the formula in my trunk - and told her everything. On one hand, the formula worked as long as no *active* magician came close; on the other hand, it wasn't as if we could use the formula in class. If Rose's mere presence at the table could cause an explosion, I hated to think what would happen with nineteen student magicians and a full-fledged Master Brewer. There was no way I could risk using the formula. I wasn't even sure what would happen if I carried it into the room.

"At least you know it works," Rose said. She gave me a worried look. "What will Robin want from you?"

I shrugged. "Nothing in a hurry," I said. "He'll wait until the favour is worth calling in."

Rose didn't look reassured. "What if he asks you to give him an apprenticeship?"

I shook my head. "He wouldn't want one with me," I said. "I could urge my father to take him on, but there would be no guarantee my father would agree. Robin will wait until I have something I can reasonably give him, something he actually wants."

"I hope you're right," Rose said. "What happens if you say no?"

"I don't know," I admitted. "I don't have any magic."

We went for dinner, then straight to bed. I slept well that night, ignoring Isabella's snide remarks and getting up early enough to read before classes. It felt like a good omen, but it wasn't. Potions class was a disaster, a disaster made worse by my success the previous evening. And even History was surprisingly dull for me, even though Rose seemed surprisingly fascinated. I was relieved beyond measure when we finally lined up to go into Forgery. Maybe, just maybe, I could lose myself in a few hours of craftsmanship.

"So tell me," Magister Tallyman said, once we were in his classroom and the doors were firmly shut. "What is *this*?"

He held up a sword in a scabbard. I stared at it, feeling a wave of genuine admiration for the long-dead artisan. A green gemstone had been placed in the pommel of the sword; five more ran down the scabbard, with a sixth clearly missing. The scabbard itself was silver, decorated with gold thread. Magister Tallyman drew the sword in one smooth motion and held it up, allowing the blade to catch the light. Someone had carved runes into the sword, each one a different shape. It was truly magnificent.

"An Object of Power," Isabella guessed. She was sitting next to Akin, her face pinched. I didn't know what was bothering her and I didn't really care. Maybe she'd expected a more catty response to her spiteful comments. "And one that's now useless, or you wouldn't be showing it to us."

Akin elbowed her, hard. Magister Tallyman gave him a sharp look, then nodded.

"Correct," he said. "According to legend, this sword was made for one of the ruling families of the empire. The sword blade would glow like the sun, cutting through everything it touched, while the scabbard protected its wearer against all curses and even sped up his healing. If this was in working order, it would be literally priceless.

"As it is--" he held up the scabbard to reveal the missing gem "--someone decided that an emerald would be better used elsewhere and accidentally rendered the sword useless."

I frowned as he put the sword and scabbard down on the table. Why would anyone destroy such a priceless artefact? It was literally irreplaceable, utterly impossible to repair. My father would expend most of his fortune to buy a working model, if one was on the market. The bidding war would probably bankrupt half the kingdom, if not the city. And yet, it looked so *easy* to repair. A replacement gemstone...

"We know how they did it," Magister Tallyman continued. He dropped a book - a copy of a copy - on the table. "The techniques are well understood. And yet, we cannot produce a sword that lasts longer than a few months. The complexities of the magic used to produce them are beyond us. They should not be, but they are."

He strode around the room. "And there are other sets of instructions in here, ranging from protective charms to weapons," he added. "Half of them cannot be duplicated at all - and half of them simply don't work for very long. A basic protective charm amulet needs to be constantly renewed if it is to hold out, even without a real challenge. Something more complex--" he nodded towards an evil-looking manikin in the far corner "--simply won't last very long at all."

I glanced at Rose. She looked tired, dark circles clearly visible around her eyes. It had been a long day.

"The runic diagrams that you are going to use to make the swords are very simple," Magister Tallyman informed us. He waved a hand at the blackboard, causing the runes to appear in front of us. "You will note that the *first* rune corresponds to sharpness, the second to solidity, the third to weight...put together, working in unison, they ensure that the sword will cut through almost anything - easily. It is important, vitally important, that you line them up and link them properly. The results of making a mistake will be shattering, literally."

I nodded. Runic magic was simple, as long as everything was perfect. A mistake, even a tiny misalignment, could be disastrous. Getting one rune wrong was irritating enough, but getting it wrong when all three runes were linked together would ruin the entire network. It was why Magister Von Rupert and his partner drilled us so extensively. A mistake in the wrong place could lead to outright disaster.

"Check and recheck everything," Magister Tallyman continued. "Do *not* attempt to insert the silver - or the gold - before you are *sure* that everything is perfect. If you make a serious mistake that cannot be corrected, put your work in the bin and start again. There are no prizes for something that is *almost* perfect. I've known bladesmen who lost limbs - or worse - because they didn't take care of their runes."

Sir Griffons keeps complaining about it, I thought. *His swords keep breaking in combat.*

I kept my expression blank. Dad had said - when he thought we couldn't hear - that Sir Griffons didn't bother to take care of his swords. He didn't seem to understand that there was no such thing as a sigil that kept the other three runes intact, not if he wanted to take advantage of their magic. Or that carving his name on the sword would speed up the runic decay. I supposed it didn't matter *that* much, really, as long as the kingdom didn't go to war. A bunch of burly knights crashing around on the jousting field - and losing, because their swords and armour didn't last - wasn't that much of a problem. Very few people were actually killed...

Of course not, I thought. *The protective spells see to that.*

Rose nudged me. Magister Tallyman was still speaking.

"We'll be spending the afternoon working on swords," Magister Tallyman said. "Follow the instructions precisely. I want you to see what you make of the instructions. My assistants--" he looked at Akin and me "--will provide advice, if you need it."

I would have preferred to craft my own sword, or work on a Device of Power, but I didn't really have a choice. Magister Tallyman hadn't banned me from the workroom - with or without supervision - and I really didn't want to annoy him. Rose hurried to a workbench to collect her supplies while I reread the instructions. They didn't look to have changed since the last edition of the book, the one I'd used back home. Forge the sword out of iron, carve a number of runes into the blade and it would last for a few weeks. An experienced forger might *just* be able to make one that would last a year.

Akin and I moved from table to table, watching as the swords were carefully hammered into shape. Thankfully, most blacksmiths preferred to use a proper forge rather than use magic to melt the iron and mould it into shape. Rose was doing well, for someone who had never worked with metal less than two months ago, but Isabella was having problems. I dreaded trying to help her and was silently relieved when Akin moved in to assist.

"You can try a sword later," Magister Tallyman told us. "I'm going to need some complex help on Saturday."

I swallowed. "I have detention."

Magister Tallyman looked displeased, although not with me. "I shall discuss the matter with the Castellan," he said. "I require assistants to help with my project."

I groaned, inwardly, as he headed off to assist one of the boys. The Castellan would *not* be pleased, I was sure. Nor would the janitor. Maybe they'd just give me double detention on Sunday. Or maybe Magister Tallyman would be told to forget having me as an assistant. His work was important, but so was school discipline.

The hour passed slowly, very slowly. None of the swords looked very good. A couple of the boys started a mock swordfight, only to have their blades shatter on impact. Magister Tallyman gave them both a sharp lecture, then assigned detention. I did my best to ignore the racket, instead thumbing through the textbook while Rose cleaned up her work. There were a *lot* of Objects of Power listed, magical tools we'd long since forgotten how to make. One of them even promised to store magic and release it on command. I could use it...

"You will all be making more swords as we proceed through the next four years," Magister Tallyman informed us, when class finally came to an end. "By then--" he shot a nasty look at the two swordsmen "--I expect you to actually know what you're doing. There are skills that you need to master before you can go to join the upperclassmen."

Rose caught my arm. "Are you going to the library?"

"I want to use the workroom," I said. It felt like I was abandoning her, but I needed some devices for my experiments. "Is that okay?"

"Just make sure you don't do anything stupid," Rose said. She looked downcast. I couldn't help another stab of guilt. "I'll be in the library."

I nodded, then turned to study the sword. The pommel felt cold to the touch, while the handle felt oddly uneven. I'd expected it to feel like the family sword, but *that* felt perfect when I drew it from the stone. The blade itself looked...*saggy*, although I wasn't quite sure where I got that impression. I touched it and frowned. It didn't *feel* very solid. I couldn't help feeling that a single hard poke would be enough to shatter it.

The magic must have held it together, I thought. *But the magic was broken the moment the gemstone was removed.*

I picked up the scabbard, quietly admiring the workmanship. The artisan who'd created it had worked a miracle. I could trace out the lines of gold thread linking the embedded runes together, a piece of work far in advance of anything I could do. The magic detector and deflector was simplicity itself, compared to this. And yet, some *idiot* had ruined it by removing the sixth gemstone. It was no longer anything but a fancy piece of metalwork, barely suitable for someone's wall.

Magister Tallyman cleared his throat. I looked up and jumped. The entire class had slipped out while I'd been studying the sword. I was alone.

"It is a remarkable object," Magister Tallyman said. "But I cannot duplicate it."

I felt a stab of sympathy. I knew what it was like to struggle with an apparently unsolvable mystery. Even now, even after I'd worked out one advantage I could glean from my condition, I still was no closer to understanding it. I knew I was missing something, but what?

"It's beautiful," I said. "What *happened* to it?"

Magister Tallyman shrugged. "There are a dozen different stories, five of which defy belief," he said, quietly. "The remaining seven contradict each other in several places. There is no way to tell, now, which one is actually *true*."

"Or if any of them are actually true," I said. If I'd damaged an irreplaceable sword beyond repair, I wouldn't want to admit to it either. "Do you have a hunch?"

"One of the stories claims that the owner's brother stole a gemstone and replaced it with another," Magister Tallyman said. He stroked his chin thoughtfully. "Apparently, he didn't realise that a replacement would never fit into the runic network. Or maybe he just didn't care. When the owner took it out to do battle..."

"He was killed," I finished.

Magister Tallyman nodded. "I have to close the classroom," he said. "Take the sword to the workroom and leave it in the office. Stay and do something yourself, if you want."

"Yes, sir," I said.

I put the sword back in the scabbard, carefully. *Very* carefully. The family sword had felt *light*, moving easily in my hand as though it were made of paper. But the dead Object of Power was so heavy that I had to struggle to lift it. *None* of the runes were working any longer, not even the ones that should have made it easier to carry. And while the scabbard *looked* intact, it felt oddly rusty to my bare fingers. I was honestly reluctant to try to carry the sword anywhere.

The corridor was deserted as I made my way into the private work-room. I'd half-expected Akin to be already there, but he was gone. The room was empty. I carried the sword over to the office and placed it on the table, then returned to the main room. There was nearly two hours until dinner. I could make quite a few Devices of Power in that time.

I reached for one of the textbooks and frowned as it fell open at a marked page. The tiny fan was spread out in front of me, every last component clearly marked. It shouldn't be difficult to make, I realised. A couple of pieces of metal, battered into shape to make blades; a spring, a rod, a handful of runes and a gemstone to focus the magic...and yet, a forger as experienced as Magister Tallyman couldn't make it work. It *should* work. I *knew* it should work. And yet, the best anyone had been able to produce was a machine that ripped itself apart within seconds...

Just like no one ever managed to get the formula to work, I thought. *It should have worked, but it didn't work...until I tried it.*

I stared at the pages, barely seeing them. I'd made a Device of Power to give Isabella an itch, hadn't I? It shouldn't have lasted long before it crumbled into rust. I *knew* it shouldn't have lasted. And yet, it *had* lasted. It hadn't started to crumble until I'd deliberately scored out the runes. How long would it have lasted, I asked myself, if I *hadn't* destroyed it?

The thought was tantalising. *Forever?*

I blinked, hard. The diagram was open in front of me, demanding attention. I hesitated, then started to hunt for the components. I had to know, even if it meant giving up the chance to make a few more devices. Pieces of metal, rods of iron, a runic sheet...I placed them on the desk and went to work. It was easy enough to assemble, as long as I was careful. The sheer *ease* of putting the device together, once you knew what you were doing, must have driven Magister Tallyman and his fellows insane.

It was nearly an hour before the fan was sitting in front of me, complete in every detail save for one. The gemstone rested in my hand, waiting to be inserted. I swallowed hard, wondering if I dared. If I was wrong...no one would know, save for me. I'd be a freak of nature, a rare throwback to the days before magic...days that were so legendary that no one believed they truly existed. The fates had given humans magic the day they allowed us to walk on the earth.

My hand was shaking as I reached forward and put the gemstone in place. The runes were already there, angled towards the stone. It wasn't a potion. It didn't need a surge of magic to kick it off. All it needed was a gentle touch...

I reached forward and pushed the fan. It spun to life. I stared as a gust of cool air washed across my face, sending cold shivers down my spine. It wouldn't last. It couldn't last...

It lasted. It shouldn't have lasted, but it lasted.

I forced myself to look at my watch, then back at the fan. All the textbooks agreed that the fans, when produced by the greatest forgers in the world, only lasted ten minutes. And that was the best anyone had done, without adapting the fan into a Device of Power. Ten minutes...I watched and waited. Twenty minutes went past, mind-numbingly slowly. The fan continued to spin. It didn't look as though it was on the verge of shattering. The first traces of rust should have appeared, but there were none. It was just humming steadily, blowing cold air across the room.

I started to giggle, despite myself. I'd done something no one had done for a thousand years, something everyone had *wanted* to do for almost as long.

I'd made an Object of Power.

CHAPTER
TWENTY-NINE

I don't know just how long I sat there, staring at the fan.

I knew, now, just what had been missing from the ancient textbooks. I knew what they'd considered so obvious they'd never bothered to write it down. A person with magic, real magic, could *never* produce a *real* Object of Power. Their magic made it impossible for the runes to settle, just as Rose's presence had caused the formula to destabilise and explode. It was different - it *had* to be different - once the magic was settled, but until then...

I looked up at the unkempt stack of textbooks, some copied from books that dated all the way back to the Thousand-Year Empire. One looked as if it had been thrown across the room in frustration. A hundred books, crammed with instructions that no one could follow...no one, but me. I started to giggle again, despite myself. I'd hoped for power. I'd clung to the hope as I grew older, even as my powers stubbornly refused to manifest. But now I'd found something I'd never expected. I couldn't *wait* to tell Dad.

The door rattled. I panicked. I wanted to show Magister Tallyman what I'd done, but at the same time I was also worried about his reaction. And my father's...surely, *he* should be the first to know. My hand jabbed out, sending the fan falling to the ground. It shattered, the blades and runic sheets crumbling into dust a second later. The magic must have destabilised the moment the runes were bent out of shape. I bent down to sweep it up as the door opened, trying to stay out of sight. I needed to compose my face.

"Caitlyn," Akin said. "I heard a crash. Are you all right?"

I rose, fighting down the urge to laugh. If Akin knew what I'd done...

I pushed the thought aside, savagely. Akin could *not* know.

"I thought I'd try to make a fan," I said. The best lies always have an element of truth in them. "But it ran for five minutes and then fell off the table."

"I couldn't get it to work either," Akin told me. He didn't *sound* as though he was trying to torment me. "I only managed to get it working for a minute before it collapsed into dust."

I nodded, absently. I loathed Isabella, but I couldn't deny she was a powerful magician. And her brother was very talented too. Forgers had had it wrong for centuries. The stronger the magician, the *less* capable they were of forging. It turned everything we knew about magic on its head. And yet...the more I looked at it, the more I thought it all fitted together. We *were* taught to balance our intrinsic magic with runes and sigils to make it work. If intrinsic magic was one end of the spectrum, what was at the other?

Objects of Power, I thought. I *was* a zero. It just wasn't a bad thing to be. *I may be useless in one area, but I'm unbeatable in another.*

Akin gave me a wink, then hurried past me to his workbench. He was putting together a complex device I didn't recognise, one I thought he'd invented himself. Unless, of course, he'd copied the designs from a book belonging to his father. House Rubén would have its own collection of ancient texts, of course. Even now, with the printing press churning out thousands of copies, there were still hundreds of ancient books that were almost completely unique. My father certainly had plenty himself.

I looked back at the bookshelves. I could start working my way through them, one by one. I could construct a dozen Objects of Power, a hundred...it wouldn't be hard, once I mastered the skills. *Some* of them would be beyond me at first, just as there were Devices of Power I couldn't make, but I would learn. Others...might need two or three zeroes. As far as I knew, I was unique. Some Objects of Power would probably be forever out of reach.

But there will be others, I thought. The dinner bell rang. *And I can find them.*

I hurried to the storerooms and hunted around, looking for a bag of pre-prepared opals. They were used to sense raw magic, once coated in potion. They glowed when a magician touched them, but they'd never reacted to me. I had a theory about that, now. Magic itself didn't remain on me. I took the bag, dumped it into an insulated box and found a few other items before hurrying back into the workroom. Akin was bent over his table, looking as though he intended to skip dinner. I checked my table, making sure there was nothing in view, then headed for the door. If Akin wanted to stay behind - and get into trouble for missing dinner - that was his problem, not mine.

Rose met me in the dining hall, looking pale. "A couple of upperclassmen kicked me out of the library," she said. "I didn't move fast enough to suit them, so they gave me lines."

I scowled as we opened the door and hurried into the room. "I'm sorry," I said. There was nothing I could do about it, not now. "But I do have something to tell you."

We ate dinner quickly, then carried the box of opals to the library. The upperclassmen were gone, thankfully. I found a couple of books I'd wanted and carried them into the private room, then waved to Rose to shut the door. She did so, looking puzzled. I hadn't dared tell her what I'd done in the dining hall. There'd been too many listening ears. Part of me thought I shouldn't tell *anyone*, but I wanted to tell *someone*. It was too good to keep to myself.

I sat down. "Rose," I said. "Guess what I did?"

She shot me a sardonic look. "Magic?"

"Sort of," I said. Her eyes went wide. "I made an Object of Power."

Alana - or Isabella - would have understood the implications at once. They'd been raised in houses where Devices of Power were common. Rose took a few seconds longer. She'd only heard about Objects and Devices of Power when she'd come to school.

Her mouth dropped open. "You're sure?"

"Yeah," I said. I couldn't keep myself from grinning. "I made something no one has been able to make for a thousand years!"

Rose frowned. "You're sure it would have lasted?"

"Yes," I said. The fan wouldn't have lasted more than five minutes, if it hadn't been a *genuine* Object of Power. "It was perfect."

"Was?"

"I had to break it," I said. "Rose...do you know what this means?"

Rose paled. "Do *you*?"

I blinked. "I'm not useless," I said. "I can do...well, I can't do *magic*, but I can make Objects of Power."

"Cat," Rose said. "Are you...are you sure you should tell *anyone*? Anyone else, I mean?"

"I have to," I said, astonished. I'd expected her to be pleased for me, not...not worried. "My parents have to know."

I smiled, again. My parents were going to be delighted. And relieved, although they'd never admit to it. I wasn't a weak link after all.

My smile grew wider. *And paying off that favour will be easy*, my thoughts told me. *Where else could Robin get an Object of Power?*

Rose pointed a finger at me. "I can still hex you," she said. "That's true for anyone else, isn't it?"

I nodded, slowly.

"So you tell the world what you can do," Rose said. She looked worried. "You're suddenly the most important person in the world. What happens next?"

"I..."

I stared at her. "What do you mean?"

Rose met my eyes. "A couple of years ago, a farmer died suddenly," he said. "He didn't have any sons, so he left his farm to his daughter. The only problem with that is that daughters aren't allowed to inherit land."

I blinked. I'd never heard *that* before. "Why not?"

"Sons inherit the land, daughters marry and move away," Rose said. She shrugged. "She didn't have any close male relatives either. Her father's brother had died years ago, while her mother's brothers lived far away. Everyone said her father was selfish for not marrying again. Not having a son...it raised questions about who would inherit.

"So the village council met and decided, after careful consideration, that they would arrange her marriage to a younger son, who would take the farm. No one cared what *she* thought about it. They just married her off."

I blanched. Alana had often taunted me with the prospect of being married off to a commoner. And yet, there had never been any suggestion that my sisters and I couldn't inherit, even though we were girls. I - and everyone else - expected Alana to be declared the heir when she came of age. She had magic and talent and determination. And yet...

The thought was sickening. "That's monstrous!"

"It was necessary," Rose said. "*Someone* had to take the farm - and her - in hand."

She looked down at her pale fingers. "Cat...she was married off because whoever married her got the farm," she said. "What's going to happen to you when the world finds out what you can do?"

"I'm too young to get married," I said. Alana and Bella had talked about fairytale weddings, but none of us were likely to tie the knot for *years*. "I..."

My voice trailed off. Rose was right. I *was* vulnerable. Sure, I couldn't be turned into something permanently, but I *could* be overpowered and tied up. Alana and Bella knew a dozen cantrips that would help them escape, if they were captured...I knew them too, yet I couldn't make them work. Dad had warned me, more than once, not to discuss my lack of power with anyone. My family was powerful - and my parents would protect me - but that might not be enough to keep me safe. I was the weak link...

I laughed, bitterly. I was *still* the weak link.

"Dad still has to know," I said. If nothing else, I had to reassure him that I *was* useful. "I won't tell anyone else."

"Good," Rose said. "You can write to him, can't you?"

I frowned. Yes, I could...but could I ask him to come? I'd need a very good excuse...parents weren't normally allowed to enter the school unless their children were in deep trouble. Maybe I could do something that would get me expelled...no, that would mean I had an expulsion on my record. Perhaps that wouldn't matter, now, but I knew my mother would hate it. None of *her* family had ever been expelled.

"It might have to wait until the winter hols," I said, finally. Winter *was* coming. We *were* allowed to go home for the solstice, if we wished. "Will you...will you come home with me?"

Rose frowned. "Do you think your parents would want me?"

"I think so," I said. I smiled. "And I would like you to come too."

I opened the box, revealing the opals. "I want to try something," I said. "Can you stand at the far side of the room?"

Rose nodded. "Is this something else you want me to do blind?"

"Not really," I said. "It shouldn't matter if you know or not."

I waited for her to reach the end of the room, then held up the first opal. It was dark in my hand. I couldn't help the stab of bitter regret and shame, even though I knew it wasn't a bad thing any longer. Perhaps Mum and Dad had always known I hadn't had magic. The opals reacted to anyone above a certain level, even if they couldn't cast spells to save their life.

"This is an opal," I said. I held up the gem. "When properly prepared, it glows in the presence of magic. It is sometimes used to trigger embedded spells aimed at powerful magicians because it is very hard to prevent the opal from reacting to magic."

I shrugged, feeling another flicker of regret. There was a part of the family gardens that was illuminated with opals. My sisters and I used to walk down the path at night, but the opals had never reacted to *me*. The glow faded as soon as Alana and Bella hurried ahead, leaving me behind. I'd held the opals in my hand, willing them to react. But they'd done nothing.

And Dad said it was because I hadn't developed magic yet, I recalled.

"Here," I said. I passed her the opal. "Hold it up."

Rose did. It glowed, of course.

"It's warm," she said. She was smiling, an open honest smile. I felt a rush of affection that surprised me. "I can *feel* it."

"Yep," I said. I took another opal and placed it by her foot. It glowed. "How close do they have to be to react to you?"

I put the next opal down, a metre from her. It remained dark. I studied it for a long moment, then placed the *fourth* opal in the middle, between the second and third opals. It glowed, but very faintly. A fifth opal, sixty centimetres from Rose, didn't light up either. She'd been closer than that to the exploding caldron, hadn't she?

"You have a magic aura surrounding you," I mused. "Roughly half a metre, centred on your feet."

I put two more opals down, trying to get a more precise reading. They glowed, suggesting that the aura was a perfect sphere. But what *was* I reading? Rose's magic? Or the magic surrounding her? No one really understood what magic *was*, even though it was the cornerstone of our society. Opals didn't react to ambient magic...

Rose lay down. The field seemed to expand...no, it had merely moved. I walked around her, moving the opals. The field was a perfect oval, extending roughly fifty-two centimetres from her bare skin. I wondered, suddenly, if it was stronger for an older and wiser magician - or weaker for a child. I'd have to do some more experiments...

"I think I understand what happened," I said. "Your aura came into contact with the potion, while I was inserting the formula. It caused the explosion."

"I didn't mean to," Rose said, nervously.

"I know," I told her. "A normal potion wouldn't have such a reaction."

And yet, my thoughts reminded me, *potions explode all the time.*

I put that aside for later contemplation and started to lay more opals on the ground. They lit up when they were within Rose's aura, but went dark as soon as she moved away. I motioned for her to stay still, and laid a chain of opals that ran to the far side of the room. It looked messy, when I'd finished, but the ones closest to her were still glowing. I stood at the other side and winked at her.

"Freeze me for a couple of minutes," I said. I tilted my head so I could see my feet - and the opals surrounding them. "And then undo the spell."

Rose lifted her hand and cast the spell. The opals lit up - a line of glowing gemstones - as the spell lanced from her fingertips and struck me. I froze. The opals at my feet kept glowing, but the ones further away - a bare ten centimetres away - went dark. I'd tracked the spell as it crossed the gulf between us, the spell holding me in place...

Wonderful, I thought, tiredly. *I've invented a whole new magic sensor.*

But it was more than that, I knew. I'd actually devised a way to track magic. There was nothing about auras in any book I'd read, nothing that suggested magic...that magic behaved the way I'd seen it behave. Had the ancients forgotten to write that down, too? Or had the post-empire magicians simply never thought to question it? Or...

The gems around my feet glowed brighter for a second, then went dark. I lurched forward, catching myself before I could fall to the ground. The opals were dark. Only the ones near Rose were glowing...

I looked back at the textbooks. All of a sudden, another piece of the puzzle fell into place.

"Everyone has magic," I said. It was official dogma. Even people who couldn't do more than sense magic *had* magic. "So what happens when they get turned into frogs or statues or...or whatever?"

"They get trapped," Rose said. She paused. "Or...do they trap *themselves*?"

I smiled. "You turned me into a frog, using a spell that should have lasted for several hours," I said. The words came tumbling out of my mouth. "And it didn't. What if...what if the spell starts drawing from the target when it runs out of magic? I mean...magic from the original caster? It starts feeding on the target's aura and uses that power to keep the spell in place."

Rose frowned. "Wouldn't that drain the target's magic?"

"Maybe," I said. "But the drain might not be significant. The spell wouldn't last long enough for the target to notice. But when the spell is cast on me..."

"It wears off when the original charge is expended," Rose finished. She shook her head. "But no one ever thought to write this down?"

I grinned. "They must have thought it was obvious," I said. Much of *our* magic had been inherited from the empire, rather than developed from scratch. Obviously pieces were missing. "And in hindsight, they might well have been right."

"Oh," Rose said.

I grinned as I opened the box. "I know I have to keep this to myself," I said. "But I think I can have some fun, don't you?"

Rose looked doubtful. "Be careful," she said. She didn't sound happy. "You really don't want to be exposed until you have a plan. Or your father has a plan."

She looked at me, biting her lip. "You've changed everything," she added. "What happens now?"

CHAPTER
THIRTY

Rose was right, of course. I really *shouldn't* do anything to attract attention to myself, at least not until winter hols. I could go home - with Rose - and confess everything to my father, who would be delighted to discover that his daughter was far from useless. He'd help me to test my abilities, then give me everything I needed to make Objects of Power. The thought of the expression on Alana's face, when she learned the truth, made me smile. Her weak sister might be far more important than she was.

And yet, I couldn't resist the urge to experiment further.

I'd been weak - I'd been unimportant - and I hated it. I'd hated knowing I was constantly at someone else's mercy, I'd hated being shunned and ignored because I didn't have magic...I wanted, desperately, to show them just what I could do. And I could! I didn't need to make a flying machine or something impossibly complex to show off. Now that I knew what the ancients had left out of their textbooks, I could understand them. It was suddenly very hard not to spend every last hour in the workshop, grinding out all sorts of protective amulets and other surprises.

The real problem was keeping everything from Magister Tallyman - and Akin. Magister Tallyman would notice, sooner or later, that I was raiding his storerooms every day for my private projects. And he would want to know what I was doing. And so would Akin, if he realised that I was hiding something. His mere presence was a threat, just because of his aura. I'd given him a runic sheet to hold, just for a second or two, then tried to insert it into an Object of Power. It had crumbled to dust within minutes.

If he touches something I make before it's ready, I thought, *he'll ruin it.*

It was frustrating. The textbooks in front of me contained instructions for making everything from potion stirrers to magic reflectors, but I couldn't use half of them. Some could be made to work for a few minutes - I'd watched Akin try to build a spell-trap that had lasted for nearly ten minutes before shattering - yet others were completely useless, unless I was the maker. The *sole* maker. Akin couldn't even pass me the raw materials without ruining it.

There must have been other zeroes in the empire, I thought, as I carried my work back to the dorm and hid it in my trunk. *They could forge in teams.*

"I didn't know you wore earrings," Rose said, taking one of the trinkets I offered her. "Have you changed your mind?"

"Mum said we had to wait until we were sixteen to get our ears pierced," I said. Mum had gone mental when Bella had come home, after spending the night with a friend, with two golden earrings on each ear. She'd torn out the earrings, mended the piercings, and grounded Bella for a month. "These are ear clasps, technically."

Rose frowned. "What do they do?"

I smiled. I'd found the instructions in one of the older books. Someone - one of Magister Tallyman's predecessors, probably - had added a set of notes, stating that the tiny earrings had proven impossible to adapt into Devices of Power. Given what I now knew, it was obvious that no magician could forge them without focusing their minds - and auras - on their work. And the earrings were too small to do anything but fail at once.

"They break down magical structures," I said. I'd heard that the queen had a set of similar earrings, but no one else. "If someone casts a spell on you, they will speed up its collapse."

Rose glanced at me. "Are you sure?"

"I think so," I said. We really needed a third person to help, just so I could see what happened when Rose wore the earrings, but I had no idea who to trust. "The only way to find out is to try it."

"Right," Rose said. "And what happens if I get turned into a frog?"

"They should still work," I said, after a moment. There were still a lot of unanswered questions. For starters, what happened to my clothes and anything I was carrying while I was transfigured? Coming to think of it, what happened to my mass? I wasn't particularly fat...but I was *much* bigger than the average frog. "Or they may block the spell altogether?"

I tapped the pair I wore on my ears, then held out a small ring. A simple blue gem, wrapped in gold and silver. "This is something a little different," I said. "I want you to wear this and cast a spell."

Rose took it and slipped it on her finger. "What sort of spell?"

"Freeze me," I said.

I braced myself. Rose cast the spell. The gemstone glowed, but nothing happened. And then she swore and yanked off the ring. It landed on the floor and bounced.

"Hot," she yelled. There was a nasty mark on her finger. "Was that meant to happen?"

"I'm not sure," I admitted. I picked up the ring and slipped it on my finger. The gemstone was still glowing, but it was cool to the touch. "Can you try with another ring?"

Rose eyed me suspiciously, but nodded. "Which spell?"

"A blocking spell," I said. "I've had an idea."

The bell rang before I could finish outlining what I had in mind. Rose cast the spell for me - this time, the ring didn't get so warm - and then followed me back to bed. Isabella and her cronies were sitting on their bed, looking smug. They'd been playing netball, I guessed. I wondered if they'd won.

"We'll be having the first proper game this Saturday," Isabella called. For once, she sounded almost friendly. I was suspicious at once. "You two are coming, aren't you?"

I glanced at Rose. "We're still scrubbing floors."

"I can get you out of that," Sandy said. I jumped. I hadn't heard her come up behind me. "I think the two of you should both go to the game. Show some support."

But I don't want to show some support, I thought. *And I have homework to do...*

I caught a glimpse of Sandy's face and knew that arguing was pointless. "Fine," I groaned, sourly. "We'll go."

"Show a little more enthusiasm too," Sandy advised, dryly. "You have to support your friends."

I bit down the rather sarcastic response that came to mind. Mum, who really should have known better, had kept insisting that Alana and Bella's friends were mine too...at least until the tenth birthday party. Sandy should know that we *weren't* Isabella's friends. She'd seen us fighting often enough. And yet...

"It's good for the dorm," Sandy said, quietly. I blinked in surprise. She couldn't read my thoughts, could she? I didn't know any magicians who could do *that*. But then, I'd always suspected my *mother* could read my mind. She was certainly very good at spotting us trying to lie. "And it will keep you two out of mischief."

I sighed as I went to bed. I *definitely* wasn't enthusiastic about wasting an evening watching Isabella and her friends playing netball. Either Isabella would win, which would make her (more) insufferable, or she'd lose and take it out on me. Sandy knew that Rose and I would have preferred to spend time in the library...

She's just trying to help, I thought, charitably. *But she's not really helping.*

I wasn't enthusiastic about the following day, either. I managed to wake up late, which meant I had to snatch breakfast in a tearing hurry. One of the upperclassmen took objection to my table manners and gave me lines, which left me smarting with helpless fury. And then we had to attend Protective and Defensive Magic, in which Magistra Solana lectured us for what felt like hours. My head was pounding like a drum when she finally reached the interesting bit.

"In order to recognise the existence of dark magic - as opposed to merely defensive magic - we have to appreciate the existence of *intent*," Magistra Solana told us. "Indeed, you have to determine the *intent* before you start accusing magicians of meddling in the dark arts. How might you determine intent?"

Her gaze swept the room. "Adamson?"

"By truth spells," Adamson said. He was a brown-skinned boy, handsome in a bland sort of way. I knew him, vaguely. His mother had courted scandal by marrying a sailor from the other side of the world. "You *ask* the caster what he had in mind."

"That assumes, of course, that you have the caster," Magistra Solana pointed out. She looked from face to face. "Henrietta?"

"You consider the methods," Henrietta said, carefully.

Magistra Solana didn't look pleased. She tilted back her head until she was looking down her nose at Henrietta. "Elaborate."

I rubbed my aching forehead as Henrietta went on. "A spell designed to cause pain *might* be used for torture," she said. She shot an assessing look at me. "But it might also be used for testing a person's nerves after they were regenerated. Objectively, the patient might be in terrible pain either way; subjectively, the intent would be quite different."

She paused. "And the simplest way to determine what the *intent* actually was lies in the method used," she added. "Did the caster merely poke the nerves - or did he hurt the patient as much as possible? If the latter, we can reasonably conclude he was practicing the dark arts."

"An interesting observation," Magistra Solana said. Her voice sharpened as she caught sight of me. "Cat. Are you trying to catch up on your sleep in my class?"

I was tired and headachy, but I still knew the right answer. "No, Magistra."

"Glad to hear it," Magistra Solana said. "Perhaps *you* can tell the class how to identify the victim of a dark arts spell?"

"Spells cast by dark magicians are often imprecise," I said. "They want - they *need* - dark emotions to power their spells. This drains their control, ensuring that they inflict additional damage on their targets. It isn't enough to kill. They must hurt their victim too. Their feelings taint their magic, and are often clearly detectable by investigators."

Alana glanced at me, nastily. She knew I was going by theory - and theory alone.

"Very good," Magistra Solana said. Her voice hardened. "And how would this let you determine intent?"

"There would be too much damage," I said. "The spell could not be cast with an *innocent* explanation."

Magistra Solana eyed me for a long moment. "It is my observation that most people are perfectly capable of deluding themselves about their intentions," she said, turning back to the class. "One does not *have* to be mad to walk into the dark arts. The path to utter darkness is paved with selflessness just as often as selfishness. To believe that your cause is just, to believe that what you are doing is right...it can be just as corrupting as the belief that you are *entitled* to whatever you take."

She paused. "But once you step over that line," she added melodramatically, "you can never step back."

There was a long pause. "For homework, I want you to research the life of Sir Travis Mortimer. Did he fall into the darkness, or was he pushed? Pick a side and argue it - remember, you have to knock down opposing arguments as well as put forward your own."

I heard a couple of gasps from the rear of the room. Sir Travis Mortimer was either a hero or a villain, depending on who you asked. A light wizard, or a dark magician. The saviour of the kingdom, or a vile traitor...I'd read about him in school. Half the books had insisted he was the greatest man ever to live, while the other half had accused him of all sorts of crimes, including some that had only been considered theoretically possible and a few more he'd invented specifically. Writing about him would be fun, but which angle should I take?

"That concludes the lecture," Magistra Solana said. Half the class breathed a sigh of relief, which the teacher pretended to ignore. I probably wasn't the only one feeling headachy. It was only mid-morning, but it felt like afternoon. "We will now continue with our practical tests."

I groaned inwardly, even though I had the earrings and both rings on my fingers. I *hated* Magistra Solana's practical tests. They were really nothing more complex than shooting hexes at each other, but I couldn't cast spells...

"Akin and Adamson," Magistra Solana said, once we had moved into the next classroom. "Why don't you take the lead?"

Adamson looked pleased as he headed to the duelling circles Magistra Solana had drawn out on the floor. The combatants weren't allowed to get close to one another, but *he* didn't care. Akin didn't seem quite so happy, although I knew he was a powerful magician. I suspected Isabella bossed him around a lot. Magistra Solana counted to three as soon as the two boys were facing each other, then told them to start. Adamson had his first hex on the way a second before she finished the order.

I watched, as dispassionately as I could, as they exchanged spells. Adamson was powerful, tossing off spells in rapid succession; Akin was blocking or dodging, rather than throwing back anything of his own. And yet, I couldn't help noticing that Adamson hadn't come *close* to scoring a hit. Each of his spells was either blocked or absorbed by the wards. He was draining himself at terrifying speed...

Akin smirked, then cast a single spell of his own. Adamson, caught by surprise, tried to raise his defences, but it was too late. He shrank rapidly, letting out a strangled cry as his arms and legs sprouted fur. A second later, a small dog was sitting in the middle of the duelling circle, barking loudly. Magistra Solana counted to ten, giving Adamson a chance to break the spell, then declared Akin the winner. He cancelled his spell as he strode back to the wall. I couldn't help noticing the look he shot at Isabella.

He's not as pushy as his sister, I thought. *But he may be a more competent magician.*

"Very good," Magistra Solana said. She gave Adamson a few more words of advice, then glanced from face to face. "Rose...why don't you and Zeya show us how it's done?"

Rose shot me a worried look, then stepped into the circle. She'd learned magic terrifyingly quickly, but Zeya had been honing her powers since her seventh birthday. I honestly wasn't sure why Zeya and her sister were so attached to Isabella. Perhaps their family had a secret alliance with House Rubén. I made a mental note to ask my father. It was certainly worth checking at some point.

I watched as they traded spells, silently rooting for Rose. But Zeya's greater experience in both casting and blocking gave her an advantage. I looked away as Rose blocked one hex, only to have another sneak through her protections. She yelped and clutched her eyes. A second later, she was frozen in place.

"Zeya," Magistra Solana snapped. "What have I told you about blinding hexes?"

"Sorry," Zeya said, unconvincingly.

"Detention, this evening," Magistra Solana said. She undid the hexes with a wave of her hand. "And you will write me five hundred lines for Friday. *I will not blind my opponents in class.*"

I gave Rose a tight hug. I hadn't experienced the blinding hex very often - my father had flatly banned my sisters from using it, except in direct self-defence - but I *hated* it. Being blind, utterly unable to see...it was a nightmare. I was more scared of it, really, than I was of being turned into a slug. I couldn't help myself.

"Caitlyn," Magistra Solana said. "Perhaps you and Alana could have a try."

I sighed as I stepped into the duelling circle. Behind me, I heard sniggers. It had always been disastrous before - all I could do was dodge - but this time...maybe things would be different. Sadly, I couldn't leave the circle and punch her before it was too late.

"Go," Magistra Solana ordered.

Alana took her time, waggling her fingers at me before throwing the first hex. I dodged it, keeping my eyes open for the second. She *enjoyed* watching me jump and dive, knowing my luck would run out eventually. But this time...

I triggered the ring. Rose's protection spell, the one I'd stored in the gemstone, shimmered to life. The second hex splintered, then vanished. I heard someone clapping behind me, but I didn't dare turn my head to see who it was. Rose, perhaps. She was the only one who knew what I'd done.

Alana's eyes went wide. She'd just seen me use magic.

I winked at her. She recovered and shot a freeze spell at me. I couldn't dodge in time.

"Hah," she said.

"One," Magistra Solana said. "Two. Three..."

I braced myself. If I was right, the spell shouldn't last more than a few seconds. And then...

The spell came apart. I waved my hand and triggered the second ring, grunting in pain as it flared with heat. Alana had no time to react before a freeze spell struck her. She was trapped.

"One," Magistra Solana said, again. "Two..."

She reached ten. Alana didn't move.

"Well done, Caitlyn," Magistra Solana said. There was a smattering of applause. I turned to see Isabella staring at me, dumbfounded. "That was a very effective spell. I'm glad to see you're finally applying yourself."

"Thank you, Magistra," I said. "I was lucky."

"It was a very well timed spell," Magistra Solana said. She unfroze Alana with a gesture. "Full marks."

I smiled, pleased. But I wondered, deep inside, just how long I could keep up the pretence.

CHAPTER
THIRTY-ONE

"Is there any way we can get out of going to netball?"

I shrugged as Rose and I made our way down to potions. My bag felt heavy. I'd crafted a couple of new Objects of Power, then charged them up with Rose's help. But there was nothing - short of getting another set of detentions - that would save us from having to watch Isabella and her friends running around on the field. And I didn't *want* another set of detentions. I was already in quite enough trouble.

"I don't think so," I said, tiredly. "We could bring books, couldn't we?"

"I think they want us to watch," Rose said. She smirked. "She might lose."

I shrugged. Isabella had been eying me oddly all day. She thought I was a zero...and yet, she'd seen me use magic. But...I wondered, suddenly, if she'd noticed I was wearing jewellery. It wasn't uncommon among young girls - Alana wore enough gold necklaces to keep a commoner family fed for life - but I hadn't made a habit of wearing anything. It got in my way when I was forging.

And besides, I thought, *it's easy to hex someone's jewels.*

Magistra Loanda watched from her desk as we filed into her classroom, her face set in a dark frown that made me wonder just *what* had happened in the previous class. The air smelt faintly of smoke and one of the desks was missing. I spotted it a moment later, placed against the far wall. The entire wooden top, hardened to resist even the most unpleasant accidents, was charred and broken. I hoped that whoever had been sitting behind it had been quick enough to get out of the way before the explosion.

The door slammed closed. Magistra Loanda rose and paced around the desk.

"I should not have to tell you," she said, "to be *very* careful when you bottle ingredients for later use. One particularly careless student was stupid enough to put Manticore Eyes in a bottle marked Gorgon Eyes. The resulting explosion was spectacular--" she waved a hand towards the ruined desk "--and put seven of your fellow students, all fifth-years, in the infirmary. Two of them may have been crippled for life."

I shivered. Beside me, Rose looked pale.

"As yet, I have been unable to identify the idiotic student responsible," Magistra Loanda continued, after a chilling moment. I felt, more than heard, a feeling of guilt running through the room. "Everyone above third year is a potential suspect. They may be unaware, themselves, of just what they did. They may *never* know, they may never even *suspect*, that they are responsible for injuring seven other students. But I warn you, here and now, that if I catch any of you mislabelling ingredients or returning them to the wrong bottles, it will be the last time you ever set foot in a potions lab."

She looked around the class, her eyes lingering on me long enough to send icy shivers down my spine. "I will do everything in my power to have you expelled," she added. "And I will report you to the Potioneers Guild. You will be blacklisted. No one will take you on, neither as a student nor an apprentice. Do *not* try me on this."

I swallowed, hard. If some of the victims were to be crippled for life... some of the potion's more dangerous ingredients must have been embedded in their bodies. They'd be enduring surges of raw power that would react badly to healing spells, preventing the healers from removing them. And that meant...

The opposite of my problem, I thought. *I have too little magic and they have too much.*

Rose nudged me. "What does that mean?"

Magistra Loanda had *very* sharp ears. "It means, young lady, that anyone who gets blacklisted will never be able to work with potions, ever again," she said. "And it will ruin them for life."

I kept my face impassive. Magistra Loanda was right. The Potioneers Guild could and would blacklist someone for extreme carelessness. It was vaguely possible that the careless idiot in question would find a teacher who was willing to defy the guild, but he'd never be able to get any qualifications anyone would recognise. His best bet would be to leave the kingdom altogether, yet any nearby country would certainly check with *our* guild before offering him training. They wouldn't want him either.

"You will all have an extension on your last piece of homework," Magistra Loanda concluded. "This week, you will *all* write an essay on the importance of labelling your potions and their ingredients correctly."

She launched into a lecture, marching back and forth as she spoke. We scrambled for our notebooks, and started to take notes as she talked about more advanced potions that demanded careful handling. This one, apparently, was really *two* potions blended together, requiring no less than *three* infusions of magic. I breathed a sigh of relief that I'd been careful enough to prepare *three* stirrers, then hurriedly scribbled down the next set of detailed notes. Magistra Loanda was on the warpath, and no one wanted to catch her ire.

At least they can't blame this on me, I thought, as the lecture finally came to an end. *It wasn't my fault.*

"You will all have a bottle of quelling solution beside you," Magistra Loanda stated, pointing to the storeroom. "If there is even a *hint* of an explosion, you will dump the solution into the liquid and throw it away."

I nodded. It was wasteful, but I understood. Magistra Loanda didn't want another explosion.

"This is going to be tricky," Rose said, as we started to sort out the caldrons. "Timing isn't going to be easy."

"Start preparing both sets of ingredients first, then start brewing the first potion," I said. The first potion needed an extra ten minutes before it reached the boil. "They have to start the cascade within two minutes of each other or we'll have to throw them out and start again."

I pulled the wooden runic sheet out of my bag and placed it on the table, gemstone face-up, then went to get the ingredients. This time, there was no pushing and shoving. Magistra Loanda had scared us all into mute obedience. I found the containers we needed, carefully measured out enough for each of us, then checked the ingredients carefully. Everything *looked* to be in order.

When I got back to the table, Magistra Loanda was studying the runic sheet.

"What is this?"

"An experiment," I said. "It was something I devised in Forging to detect if the potion is about to explode. The surge of magic will cause the gemstone to glow, giving me a few extra seconds to jump under the table."

Magistra Loanda eyed me, suspiciously. "A skilled brewer would be able to sense the flare of magic."

"Yes," I said. Thankfully, I'd anticipated the question. "However, this rune is considerably more sensitive than the average magician. It will give us a few seconds of extra warning."

Her expression darkened. "I trust you are not planning to blow up the caldron just to see if it works," she said. "I would be *most* displeased."

"No, Magistra," I said. "If nothing goes wrong, it should be fine."

She put the rune back down and headed off, moving from table to table. I breathed a sigh of relief, then started to sort out the ingredients. I hadn't lied to her, but I'd known she might want me to remove it. Potions tended to react badly to unexpected surges of magic and a rune, even an uncharged rune, could be dangerous. Clearly, she either thought it was worth trying or she believed it was harmless.

And it is far more sensitive than I claimed, I thought. *If, of course, the books were correct.*

"Remember to clean the nettle leaves individually," I said to Rose. No one liked doing it, even with gloves, but unclean leaves could cause problems. "They have to go in one by one."

"Good thing she didn't look at the stirrers," Rose told me. She reached for the bottle of dried fish eggs and started to spoon them into her caldron. "What would you have said *then*?"

I shrugged. Making one's own tools was a time-honoured tradition, although - much to the annoyance of my father - it was slowly going out of fashion. One got *better* results from tools one made, he insisted. Magistra Loanda had no legitimate grounds to forbid me from carving my own and bringing them into class, but she *could* make a fuss on the grounds that everything had to be standardised. She was, after all, the school's Master Brewer.

No one would accept that argument in Shallot, I thought, as I sliced the onions. *But we're not in Shallot.*

Alana, behind me, let out a disgusted sound. I guessed she'd found the beetles she was supposed to dissect. I didn't like it either, even when the beetles had been killed peacefully rather than smashed with a hammer, but it had to be done. Some of the boys chuckled, only to quiet down rapidly as Magistra Loanda's gaze moved across them. *They* thought it was gross, not disgusting.

I smiled. I'd put beetle eggs in Alana's bed, once. The scream had made the lecture I'd got from Mum worthwhile.

"I think that's everything ready," I said, rereading the instructions one final time. It felt as though I was checking them again and again, but it was better to make *entirely* sure that I knew what I was doing. "Good luck."

I dropped the ingredients into the water, one by one. The liquid slowly started to turn apple-green, souring to light brown as I added more caterpillar legs. Rose looked to take it in her stride, but I could hear a couple of girls muttering their disgust. I rolled my eyes, wondering precisely which magician had thought that dissecting a beetle would lead to new and interesting potions. I'd wanted to be a researcher, once upon a time. *That* hope had died with my dreams of magic.

But now you can do something new, I told myself, firmly. *Or something very old.*

The second potion was less complex, but more fiddly. I counted the seconds as I added the ingredients, one by one. I'd watched my mother brew the potion years ago and *she'd* said it was very unforgiving. A loud hiss from behind me, followed by a small explosion, told me that *someone* hadn't been as careful. Isabella's voice muttered a couple of nasty curses, followed by a grunt of pain. I guessed the hot water had splashed on her.

"Detention, young lady," Magistra Loanda said. "And you *should* just have enough time to start again."

I felt a flicker of sympathy, which I rapidly suppressed as two more potions exploded in quick succession. Bella was whimpering...I turned and cursed under my breath as I saw greenish warts popping into existence on her dark face. She'd been unlucky - the nettle juice had mingled with the beetles before they'd exploded. Magistra Loanda checked on her, then ordered her to go to the healers. I hoped, as I turned back to my brew, that she'd be all right.

"Nearly time to stir," Rose whispered. "Do you want me to...?"

I shook my head, shortly. Magistra Loanda was keeping an eye on us, even though we hadn't caused any explosions. I didn't really blame her. The explosion we *had* caused had been far worse. And besides, I had to know if the stirrers *worked*. I took the first one out of my bag, followed by the other two. Hopefully, Magistra Loanda wouldn't look *too* closely. She might ask, quite reasonably, why I'd brought *three* stirrers...

The final seconds ticked down as I brandished the stirrer. If this worked, everything would be fine; if it failed, there was about to be another explosion. I took a nervous look at the rune, then dipped the stirrer into the caldron as soon as the last second ticked away. It should work, I told myself. I'd made it perfectly, then given it to Rose to charge. But my inability to sense magic made it impossible for me to be *sure*. The rune would react to a major surge...

I sucked in my breath as the liquid changed colour. It had worked. Carefully, very carefully, I put the first stirrer down and picked up the second. It seemed to hum in my fingers as I lowered it into the second caldron and stirred, muttering a mnemonic just loudly enough to be heard. My mother had taught me the words, years ago. They were useful things to remember.

"Not bad," Magistra Loanda said. Again, I'd missed her sneaking up on us. This time, I didn't jump. "Add the first caldron to the second in five minutes."

I nodded, silently hoping she'd go away before I used the third stirrer. Most of her students would use a simple charm to clean the spoon after each use, but that wasn't a real option for me. I had carved cleaning runes into the spoon, of course, yet they took hours to work properly. The textbooks hadn't suggested any way to speed up the process and I wasn't prepared to risk ruining the magic completely. I'd need to do some experiments when I was well away from school.

Magistra Loanda watched me like a hawk. I gritted my teeth, then picked up the third stirrer as I poured the first potion into the second. It bubbled, alarmingly, but soothed itself as I gently stirred, counting every clockwise stir. Five stirs later, I lifted the stirrer out and watched as the liquid bubbled and went smooth.

"Very well done," Magistra Loanda said. She held a hand over the potion for a long moment. "Take it off the heat, then bottle and label it. *No one* will leave this classroom until I have checked every bottle."

I heard some mutters behind me, which tapered off as Magistra Loanda glared. It was easy to be annoyed - it was nearly dinner time - but I understood, all too well. Seven students had been injured on her watch, two critically. Their families would demand answers, if the healers couldn't fix the damage. Magistra Loanda might wind up facing an inquest, even if she wasn't hauled up in front of Magus Court. I couldn't help feeling a flicker of sympathy.

The idiot who mixed up the eyes will get away with it, I thought. *And her teacher will be the one to face the court.*

I felt my head starting to pound again as Magistra Loanda inspected the bottles, then nodded and moved on to Rose. Isabella was working frantically over her caldron, trying desperately to stir it into submission... it started to smoke, a faint wisp of blue smoke...

"Get back," Magistra Loanda snapped. "Now!"

The caldron exploded in a flash of light. I threw up a hand to cover my face, then relaxed as the wards caught the blast. Isabella fell over backwards and landed hard - the room snickered - but she was otherwise unhurt. Magistra Loanda yanked her to her feet, marched her to the front of the room and delivered a scathing lecture that had the rest of us torn between the urge to hide and the suicidal desire to laugh. Beside her, Zeya looked pale. She'd been right next to a blinding explosion.

"You *cannot* force a potion to speed up," Magistra Loanda thundered. "How many times do I have to tell you? You *cannot* force a potion to speed up!"

She jabbed a finger at me. "Caitlyn has power and talent and knowledge," she added. "You merely have power. You are pushing your magic too hard, disrupting the cascade reaction that makes the potion work. Why are you not learning from the others in the class?"

Isabella clenched her fists, but made no answer. I didn't blame her. I'd have been silent too.

"This is not a place to be careless," Magistra Loanda snapped. She sounded as if she was on the verge of losing control altogether. She'd been in a foul mood all day and now she'd found a target. "Carelessness will get you killed - or worse! Be careful!"

She controlled herself with a visible effort. "You will have detention with me every night for a week," she said. "And you will write out a thousand lines. *I will not try to push my potions too hard.* And you will not! Do you understand me?"

Isabella looked pale. But, as Magistra Loanda turned away, she glared at me.

"Hand in your potions," Magistra Loanda ordered. "Put them on my desk. I'll inspect them tonight. And if any of you have made a mistake, rest assured you will be hearing about it on Friday."

I glanced at my bottle. I hoped I *hadn't* made any mistakes. I doubted I'd survive.

"Isabella, remain behind," Magistra Loanda said. "The rest of you, dismissed."

Isabella shot me another nasty look as I rose and hurried for the door, following the others. No one wanted to stay near Magistra Loanda, not when she was in such a vile state. I couldn't help feeling genuinely sorry for Isabella...

Sure, my thoughts mocked. *And how are you going to feel after she takes this out on you?*

A fifth-year - I didn't know him - was leaning against the wall when I came out of the classroom. He straightened the moment he saw me.

"Caitlyn?"

I nodded. I was surprised he was admitting to knowing who I was. My identity wasn't actually a secret, but I'd learnt that most upperclassmen pretended not to know anything about the lowerclassmen. They were bugs running around their feet, as far as the upperclassmen were concerned.

"Magistra Haydon wishes to speak with you," he said. "Come with me."

"Fine," I said. I glanced at Rose. I'd made a mistake. I should have anticipated Magistra Haydon demanding a chat. "See you in the library?"

"Sure," Rose said. "Or dinner, if it takes that long."

I groaned.

CHAPTER
THIRTY-TWO

"It's been a while since we spoke," Magistra Haydon said. She sipped a cup of tea. Mine sat on the table beside me, untouched. "I have missed our conversations."

I tried to lift one eyebrow, like my father. It didn't quite work.

"Talking to students is *always* interesting," Magistra Haydon assured me. "And you are quite an interesting case."

She took another sip. The tea was meant to be relaxing, but I was on edge. Magistra Haydon wanted to talk to me *now*. Not after the potions accident...*now*, after I'd apparently used magic in class. Twice, in fact, if you counted potions...or would that really be four times?

"You've used magic," she said. "Do you know that?"

"Yes," I said. It was hard to keep the irritation out of my voice. I wasn't a girl of *eight*. My parents might remember me as a little girl, but Magistra Haydon had never laid eyes on me before I entered Jude's. "I know what I did."

"Of course you do," Magistra Haydon said. "Are you finally starting to understand your magic?"

I eyed her for a long moment. The question was normal, yet...there was nothing normal about me. It could be an innocent question or it could be a verbal trap. My father often used them on the apprentices, forcing them to reconsider everything they thought they knew. I'd never been able to keep up with his reasoning for very long.

"Yes," I said, finally. I picked up my cup and lifted it to my lips, but didn't take a sip. "Can I ask a question?"

"Of course," Magistra Haydon said. "This *is* a school. We are here to educate."

"Healers take oaths of confidentiality," I said, challengingly. "What oaths have *you* taken?"

Her expression seemed to freeze, just for a second. I would have missed it, if I hadn't been watching for a reaction. Oaths weren't exactly a taboo subject, but most magicians got a little edgy when discussing them. The prospect of something that might do real damage to their magic - or kill them - was terrifying.

"I am bound by the standard conventions," she said, finally. She schooled her expression into a blandness that would have impressed my mother. "Does that answer your question?"

"No," I said. "Because I don't know what the standard conventions *are*."

Magistra Haydon looked displeased. "It's complicated," she said. I had the feeling she hadn't wanted to discuss it. "As a general rule, I am not allowed to disclose information relating to your case without your permission. However, as you are a minor, I *am* allowed to discuss matters with your parents. *And*, as you are a student at this school, I am required to report anything that might pose a genuine threat to either the staff or the other students."

I frowned. "I thought Healers were much more limited."

"Minor children are in no position to appreciate their situation," Magistra Haydon told me, primly. I had the feeling that was an unsubtle jab at me. "If you were twenty-one, where you would be deemed an adult, I could not share anything concerning you without your permission. I would, however, urge you to grant me that permission if you were in trouble."

She leaned forward. "Imagine you were married," she added. "And then you were badly injured, so badly injured that you needed treatment urgently. Would you want me to ask your husband for permission, as we could not proceed *without* permission, or leave you to die?"

I considered it. "I can't imagine being married," I said, after a moment. "But if I was...it would depend, wouldn't it?"

"Yes," Magistra Haydon said. "A number of Healers have campaigned against the oaths, believing them to be too restrictive. Magus Court, however, has been resistant to the suggestion of *any* changes."

She leaned forward. "How did you discover your magic?"

I hesitated. In truth, I wasn't sure how to answer. Magistra Haydon would share whatever I told her with my parents...and with the school, if she believed I posed a threat. And she might, given that I was working with Objects of Power. She wouldn't have to be *right* to talk to the Castellan. She'd merely have to *believe* she was right.

"In class," I said, finally. "Some things just started working."

She eyed me for a long moment. I didn't think there were any truth spells in the room - and the earring I wore should protect me from them, if there were - but she was probably almost as good as my father at sniffing out lies. I'd certainly given her plenty of incentive to think I'd lied to her. Did she think I'd finally managed to glean a spark of magic? Or did she think I was tricking the teachers somehow?

"That's...ah, very interesting," she said, finally. "Do you know why?"

"No," I said.

"You have managed to brew several potions, successfully," Magistra Haydon said. Her voice was very composed. "*And* you used hexes in defensive class..."

"I did," I said.

"On your sister," Magistra Haydon said. "How do you feel about your sister?"

I shrugged. It wasn't a question I wanted to answer.

"Bottling it up doesn't help," Magistra Haydon said. "How do you feel about your sister?"

"I don't know," I said. It wasn't entirely untruthful. "My feelings are mixed."

Magistra Haydon gave me what I suspected *she* thought was meant to be an encouraging smile. "Can you describe them?"

I shifted, uncomfortably. I'd been raised not to admit weakness - and feelings could be a weakness. I wouldn't have broken down in front of

Rose if I hadn't been struggling with wave after wave of emotion. And I *really* wasn't sure I wanted to give Magistra Haydon more ammunition. Whatever I told her would be passed on to my parents.

"The bonds of family are unbreakable," Magistra Haydon said, after a long moment. She sounded mildly surprised. I realised, after a moment, that there probably *was* a spell in the air, one tuned to encourage me to talk. "Our brothers and sisters can be our best friends and worst enemies, at the same time. I love my brother, but there were plenty of times I resented him too."

"You could never get away from him," I said.

"No," Magistra Haydon agreed. "Do you feel the same way too?"

I scowled. It was clear she expected an answer.

"My sister hated me from the moment she discovered I didn't have any powers," I said, finally. It was hard to keep the bitterness out of my voice. "She mocked and scorned me - she hexed me - because I was *weak*. Because others would think *she* was weak. She treated me like...like a freak, because I *was* a freak. And I could never get away from her.

"I wanted to love her," I added, after a moment. My heart ached, painfully. That was truer than I cared to admit. "And I wanted her to love me. But instead..."

I shook my head. Everything had changed, yet nothing had changed. I was *still* a freak, even though I could make Objects of Power. Alana would *still* resent me. I would steal the limelight from her as soon as Dad found out the truth. His third daughter had no magic, but that didn't make her unimportant.

"But now your magic is finally starting to surface," Magistra Haydon said. "Do you think your relationship will change?"

"Probably," I said, sourly. "She won't be able to hex me whenever she's in a bad mood."

She smiled, humourlessly. "And how do you feel about that?"

"Good," I said.

Magistra Haydon met my eyes. "You spent a large part of your life feeling powerless," she said, gently. "How did you feel about *that*?"

"I hated it," I said, honestly.

"And now you have power," Magistra Haydon said. "It isn't uncommon, you know, for children like your friend Rose to go home and start casting nasty spells on their former tormentors. There was a case, a few years ago, of a young boy who murdered his older brother and five other villagers. I don't think he meant to do it, but he was so lost in his rage that he fell to the darkness. He became a dark wizard."

I swallowed. "What happened to him?"

Magistra Haydon shrugged. "Look up the details, if you like," she said. "The point, Caitlyn, is that he embraced the emotions that drove him towards the darkness. His desire for revenge broke him."

I met her eyes. "And if they bullied him," I asked, "was it wrong of him to want revenge?"

She looked back at me. "At what point does revenge for bullying turn into even *nastier* bullying?"

"I'm not going to kill my sister," I said, irritated. "Can I go now?"

"You will face temptations over the next few years," Magistra Haydon said. Her voice was still even. "I want you to understand the problems you may encounter."

"Thank you," I lied.

She gave me a lazy wave. "You may go," she said. "But I think we will be having another discussion soon enough."

Only if I can't get out of it, I thought, as I rose. I had no idea just how much Magistra Haydon knew, or what she would do if she *did* know. *I won't be coming back willingly.*

And yet...I turned the thought over and over in my head as I walked down the stairs. What would happen to me if I saved a dark spell in a gemstone, then cast it? Would I be risking the same kind of mental problems that had killed many a dark wizard? Or would I have an immunity to the curse? I wouldn't be casting the spell myself, would I? But how would I *get* such a spell? Rose would refuse to cast it for me...

A shiver ran down my spine as I considered the implications. Dark wizards went mad. I knew that - everyone knew that. No dark wizard had ever been able to do more than cause a lot of damage before his inevitable death. But what if they didn't? What if I could design an Object of Power that kept the madness in check? Or even one that allowed them to cast the spells without the raw emotions? It was a terrifying thought.

I met Rose in the library, still contemplating the problem. We worked our way through the homework essays until dinnertime, then slipped back to the library to finish our work. I'd hoped for more time to research, but it was clear that the homework came first. I made a mental list of things to study as I finished my essay, and checked Rose's for spelling and grammar errors. She'd gotten much better over the last few months, but I knew a particularly sharp teacher might deduct marks for basic mistakes.

Precision is important, my mother had said. She'd drummed reading and writing into us with terrifying zeal. *A mistake now means a disaster later.*

The bell rang. "It should be fine," I assured Rose. "Magistra Loanda isn't planning to skin us alive."

Rose looked doubtful. "Are you sure?"

I had to smile as we left the library and hurried back to the dorm. The corridors were surprisingly empty, something that puzzled me. I didn't *think* anything important was happening...but then, Magistra Loanda might have given *everyone* the same homework and the same almost-impossible deadline. The library had been unusually crowded. We certainly hadn't been able to get a private study room.

"Ah," Isabella said, as we walked into the dorm. "*There* you are."

I tensed. She looked furious. Two angry red blushes could be seen on her cheek.

"You're a..."

"That will do," Sandy said, from her bed. "Or do you want me to change my mind?"

Isabella shot me a final venomous glower, then raised her voice. "Everyone over here," she called. "Now!"

I rolled my eyes. Her cronies hurried over at once, but the others - the ones who were more inclined to assert their independence - moved slowly. A couple of them glanced at me, as if they expected me to do something. My family and Isabella's were rivals, after all. They would have gathered around me, in the finest traditions, if it wasn't clear that my magical skills were far inferior to Isabella's. Alana probably had her whole dorm bowing and scraping to her every day. *My* dorm mates were much less impressed.

And they probably want to play me against Isabella, I thought, sourly. It was supposed to be good practice for later life, when graduated magicians sought patronage, but I'd always thought it was silly. *Except they know I can't offer protection.*

"You will all be attending the netball game on Saturday evening," Isabella said. It wasn't a question. Sandy had made it clear that attendance was compulsory. "Afterwards, we are going to have a feast."

I looked up, surprised. My mother had talked about midnight feasts - and about how they were an old school tradition - but I'd always assumed they didn't start until after we moved up to second year. There *was* an older student in the dorm who was meant to be keeping us in line, wasn't there? I glanced at Sandy and saw, to my surprise, that she was smiling. I wasn't the only one looking at her.

"I will be turning a blind eye, as long as you behave yourselves," Sandy said. "You do *not* want the staff bursting into the dorm in the middle of the night, demanding to know what the noise is. You'll be scrubbing floors for weeks."

Her voice hardened. "More to the point," she added, "you do not want *me* to be scrubbing floors for weeks."

Henrietta coughed. "They make upperclassmen scrub floors?"

"Yes," Sandy said. "And if you get me in trouble, I'll make your life not worth living."

She glanced from face to face. "I'll be just down the corridor," she added. "If I can hear you, I'll be back early."

Isabella smiled. "This leaves us with an obvious problem," she said. "Who's going to get the food?"

I nodded in agreement. Mum had admitted that *her* midnight feasts had always started with raids on the kitchen storerooms. Bread and jam, biscuits and cakes...it was an old tradition - and a good one too, if you didn't get caught. If you got caught...

"It was your idea," Rose said. "You should get the food."

"Oh, no," Isabella said. "Tradition demands we pick a victim...sorry, a fetcher - at random."

She reached into her pocket and produced a set of cards. "Ten cards," she told us. "The person who draws the ace gets to sneak down after Lights Out and break into the storerooms."

Her smile widened. "I have been told it's easy."

"If you're good at charms," Sandy added. She gave us all a wry smile. "But if you get caught, something dark and gruesome will happen to you."

"Like cleaning floors," Zeya said. She smirked at me. "Or washing the netball court."

"Yeah," Isabella said, evilly. She held up the cards, allowing us to see that she was being honest. "Are you ready?"

I glanced at Rose, who looked resigned. I understood. There was no way to avoid the midnight feast, even if we didn't get lumbered with the job of collecting the food. And trying would just make us outcasts. We'd won a little respect over the last few weeks. I didn't want to lose it.

Isabella fanned out the cards. "Take one," she ordered. "And don't look until *everyone* has a card."

"Don't offer one to me," Sandy said. "There are limits."

I took a card. Isabella smirked, just for a second. I *knew*, even before turning the card over, that it was the ace. A spell? I didn't *think* she could enchant a card while I was wearing the earring. Maybe it had been good old-fashioned sleight of hand. I'd had an uncle who had been a poor magician, but he'd loved playing mundane tricks with cards and tools. He'd always been able to trick me, even without magic.

"Turn your cards over," Isabella said.

I did. The ace stared up at me. I wasn't surprised at all.

"It looks like it will be you," Isabella said. She couldn't keep the gloating out of her voice. "Remember, you have to bring back enough food for everyone or you'll have to go back down."

I glared at her. Sneaking into the kitchens would be tricky, even for an upperclassman. For me? It would be almost impossible. And yet...the kitchens couldn't be *that* heavily warded, could they? The tradition wouldn't have continued if it had been *impossible* to steal from the kitchens.

I wanted to back out. But I knew that would get me nowhere.

"Fine," I growled. "I'll get you your food."

"Good on you," Isabella said. "And we'll all give you a round of applause."

"And now you'll all get into bed," Sandy said, before I could think of a crushing response. "I don't *think* you want to be late for class tomorrow."

Rose touched my hand as the small gathering broke up. "I'll come with you?"

"You might have to," I said. I'd sneaked into Alana's room more than once, but the kitchens were likely to be a great deal more heavily protected. "I'll see what I can do."

I groaned as I climbed into bed. Old tradition or not, it was silly. Surely it would be better to sleep through the night. I had to be up early on Sunday, even if they didn't. But I was committed. I'd been committed from the moment I'd taken the card. Isabella hadn't used magic to trick me into taking the ace...

...And if I backed out now, I - not her - would take the blame.

THIRTY-THREE

"This isn't going to be easy," Rose said. "Is it?"

I shrugged. I'd had a brainwave and checked the library for the original kitchen plans - we weren't meant to enter the kitchens without permission - but they'd turned out to be surprisingly detailed. I wasn't sure if the Castellan had left them in the library to see who would be smart enough to check, or if it was just a careless oversight, yet they were enough to put me off trying to sneak through the door. Scrying wards, freeze spells, transfiguration traps...some of my father's private rooms were less heavily-protected than Jude's kitchens.

But then, my father's rooms are inside the hall, I thought. *He doesn't need to render them absolutely secure.*

"No," I muttered. "It isn't."

The earrings would give me some protection, I was sure. And I could take a sensor or two along and evade some of the nastier traps. But I'd have to find a way to break through some of the more comprehensive protections, including the one on the storeroom itself. And all my planning would be rendered moot if the defences had been changed at any point in the last ten years. The plans didn't look to have been updated since then.

"You don't have to come with me," I said. "I can go on my own."

"And then you'd have to make two trips," Rose pointed out. "Better I come with you, I think."

I shrugged. "I'd be glad of it," I admitted. "But we could get in trouble again."

The door opened before Rose could answer. I looked up and blinked in surprise when I saw Bella. I'd never seen *her* in the library before. Alana had been in at least twice a week, looking up new and nastier hexes in the stacks, but Bella...I'd barely seen her anywhere, outside classes. I'd never really cared, either. Bella hadn't gone out of her way to be friendly.

"Cat," she said. "Can we talk? Privately?"

"Rose is my friend," I said, stiffly. "Whatever you want to say to me can be said in front of her."

Bella jabbed a finger at Rose. She lifted her hand to cast the counterspell, too late. Her body turned grey, then froze. I shuddered - I hated being turned to stone - then glared at Bella. My sister looked wholly unapologetic.

"This is family business," she said, closing the door. "Outsiders are not allowed to hear."

I debated, briefly, pointing out that Rose could still hear. Bella's spell was nowhere near as powerful as a gorgon's curse. Even then, Rose would be able to hear until her mind dissolved into nothingness. But there was no way to know what Bella would do if she realised she'd made a mistake. Better to leave her thinking Rose was deaf as well as stone.

"Fine," I said. I'd have to apologise to Rose later. "Just make sure you turn her back before you go."

Bella gave me an odd look, then sat down. "I need your help," she said. "Please."

I met her eyes, torn between the urge to stand up to her and the grim understanding that Bella was still far more powerful than I.

"You turned my friend into stone," I said. "And you want me to help you?"

"*Please*," Bella said. She reached into her pocket and pulled out her Punishment Book. "I'm in danger of failing my classes."

I took the book and skimmed through it. There were over a dozen entries, all but one lines assigned for not completing homework on time. Magistra Loanda, Magistra Solana...even Magister Von Rupert. I found it hard to imagine the even-tempered man handing out lines like candy, but it was clear even *he* had run out of patience. Bella was on the verge of spending all of her free time writing lines.

"Maybe you should have worked harder," I said. Oddly, not having any inherent magic had given me a far greater insight into the theory. Bella - and Alana - had neglected their theory for practicals. "You wasted the last four years."

The look Bella gave me should, by rights, have killed me on the spot. There were spells that could do just that.

"I thought I didn't need to study," she said, finally. "I thought...I thought..."

"You were lazy," I said. "Alana did more studying than you."

Bella lifted her hand. "You..."

"Careful, now," I mocked. "I'm not going to be helping you if I'm spending the next few hours hopping around croaking loudly."

My sister lowered her hand. "Help me, please."

I smirked. I was probably enjoying the moment more than I should. "What's it worth?"

Bella looked at me for a long moment. "What do you want?"

"Right now, I want you to undo the spell on Rose," I said. "And then I want you to assist us with a little project. And *then* I want your word you won't tell anyone until I do."

Bella hesitated. Thinking wasn't her strong suit, but I could practically see the wheels grinding in her head. Giving her word...no one would ever trust her again if she broke it, even if it wasn't a magically-binding oath. Helping me...it would annoy Alana, but Alana wouldn't help her unless she was paid through the nose. And going home to tell our parents that she'd failed all her exams...she couldn't do *that*. Mum would be disappointed and Dad would be furious. I wouldn't be the only daughter grounded for life - or at least for the summer hols.

"Very well," she said, finally. She rested her hand on Rose's forehead. It started to lighten as the spell unravelled. "What do you want me to do?"

"Go fetch your homework assignments," I said. "I need to talk to Rose."

Bella nodded and hurried off, just as Rose returned to normal. "That was unpleasant," she said. "My body felt *wrong*."

"It's not a pleasant spell," I agreed. I had no doubt that Bella was going to pay for that. "Are you all right?"

"Well enough," Rose said. She looked down at her pale fingers as if she'd never seen them before. "Are you going to help her?"

"If she helps us," I said. The door opened, again. "I think she will."

Bella dropped a stack of paper onto the table. "This is all of them," she said. "I..."

My mouth dropped open. "Are these..."

I had to swallow and start again. "Are these from the very *start* of term?"

"Yeah," Bella said. "I couldn't complete more than a couple before I ran out of time."

"Ouch," I said. "What were you *doing* when you weren't in class?"

Bella didn't answer. I reached for the papers and started to thumb through them. Bella and I didn't share *every* class, but it was clear that the magisters used the same lesson plans. Most of her homework was identical to mine. The only real exceptions were a pair of punishment exercises, both from Magister Grayson. I wondered, absently, just what Bella had done to annoy him. He thought I wasn't applying myself...perhaps he thought Bella wasn't applying herself either.

"Right," I said. "I can give you copies of some of my essays, but you'll have to rewrite them or someone will smell a rat. Think you can handle it?"

"Of course," Bella said.

"They'll know you stole them if you don't," I warned her. "And you'll be in *deep* trouble."

I met her eyes. "But you'll have to do more practical work too," I added. "The less you understand, the less you'll be able to do later on."

"It's not fair," Bella said.

I felt a hot flash of irritation. Bella had magic. Bella had magic and an easy life. How *dare* she moan and whine? It was *Rose* who had cause to whine, if anyone had. *She'd* grown up on a farm. It had been sheer luck her talent had been noticed...and sheer luck she hadn't been expelled, after the potions disaster. Even my life was easy, compared to hers...

"Tough," I said. "Do you *want* to go home and tell Dad you failed?"

Bella couldn't physically pale, but her hands shook. "No," she said. "He'll kill me."

"He'll probably hire someone to tutor you over the holidays," I countered. Bella would probably consider that a fate worse than death. "And I don't *think* it'll be the sort of person who is willing to let you slide. Dad will choose some really grim old master who thinks that anyone who doesn't get straight A's is lazy."

I grinned at her. "Are you ready to help us?"

"Yes," Bella said. "What do you want me to do?"

"Do as I say," I said. "Stand at one end of room and wait."

Rose took the other side of the room and watched as I scattered opals around the floor, carefully measuring and noting the distances between them. My sister was standing five metres from Rose...I placed an opal every twenty centimetres, noting which ones lit up and which stayed dim. Bella's magical field was actually *smaller* than Rose's, stretching out a bare forty centimetres from her toes. Did that mean that Rose had more raw power, I wondered, or less control? Bella *had* been studying magic - or at least she'd had the *opportunity* to study magic - since her seventh birthday.

Or maybe I'm completely wrong, I mused, as I wrote down my notes. *There may be aspects to this I don't know.*

"All right," I said. "Bella, I want you to stay precisely where you are. Rose, freeze her."

Bella's mouth opened, then froze as Rose's spell struck her. I resisted the urge to laugh at her expression, frozen in time, as I glanced at the opals. They were glowing brighter and brighter, although it didn't *look* as though the aura had grown any bigger. I reached out carefully to touch Bella's arm, but felt nothing. The opals didn't react to my presence.

"Sorry, Bella," I said, a little too cheerfully. "But you're going to stay that way for a while."

Rose caught my eye. I strolled over to stand next to her.

"She's going to be mad," she whispered. Rose, at least, remembered that being frozen didn't make someone deaf. "Are you sure you *want* to leave her like that?"

I shrugged. Bella couldn't do *much* to me, not if she wanted my help. Besides, anything she *did* do - I knew now - wouldn't last. Unless she wanted to actually *punch* me...

It was nearly an hour before the opals dimmed. "I think your power wore off," I mused, thoughtfully. "Release her."

Rose waved her hand. Bella started forward, stumbling. I braced myself to dodge if she hurled a spell, but instead she merely glowered at me.

"What was *that* for?"

"Testing the length of a spell," I said.

Bella screwed up her face as if she were trying to think. It looked painful. "But...but your friend..."

"Rose," I prompted.

"But Rose undid the spell," Bella said. "You don't *know* how long it will last."

"I suppose not," I mused. I didn't really want to tell Bella everything. I'd proven my theory to my own satisfaction. "Still..."

"I don't understand," Bella added. Her voice turned calculating. "You could have cast the spell yourself."

I groaned, inwardly. Bella was lazy. She wasn't stupid. She'd seen me cast spells...or *thought* she'd seen me cast spells. Why would I *need* Rose to cast the spells?

"Rose needs the practice," I said, blandly. "Let's see what else we can do."

Rose and Bella obligingly threw spells at each other for the next hour as I tried to figure out a way to measure their power. Freezing someone in place took less power - the original power seemed to last longer - than turning someone into a toad. There was more power involved, I reasoned. The drain had to be a great deal higher without runes or spell geometrics to hold it in place. But the spells still wore off surprisingly quickly.

I glanced at Bella. "When someone turns you into something, and you stay that way until the spell wears off...do you feel *tired*?"

"Only once," Bella said. I knew what she was going to say before she said it. "When that *hag* turned us into frogs."

I blanched. Great Aunt Stregheria's spell hadn't unravelled. It had merely run out of power.

"I was eating for *hours* afterwards," Bella added. "I was so hungry."

"She's horrible," I agreed. She'd known the spell wouldn't last...she *must* have known. And yet, she'd left my sisters that way for days. No *wonder* Dad had been furious. I dreaded to imagine just how long the spell would have lasted if she'd cast it on an adult! "I don't want to see her again."

"She'll probably be back, sooner or later," Bella predicted, glumly.

I shrugged. "The opals react to magic," I said. "But they can't tell the difference between different casters."

"You need to be able to read someone else's spells," Bella said. "Dad can do it."

"Of course." I smiled. "But I don't know how to do it."

The bell rang before Bella could answer. "I'd better get back to the dorm," she said, picking up her homework. "I'll see you here tomorrow evening?"

"Yeah," I said. "I'll bring my old essays."

Rose was quiet as we made our way back to the dorm. I glanced at her, then started to think about some of my other ideas. A number of books talked about infusing potion magic into Objects of Power, but - again - the technique had been lost centuries ago. I thought I understood how it had been done, now. Once again, outside magic - active magic - would destabilise the potion and cause an explosion.

And even if there isn't an explosion, I thought, *it would render the Object of Power useless.*

I found myself considering a handful of ideas. I'd had an uncle who'd had a mental problem, one that had forced him to take a specific potion every week. My mother hadn't talked about him much. I'd only heard about him from Great Aunt Stregheria, who'd flung his existence in my mother's face over dinner. Apparently, the side-effects of the potion had eventually addled his mind and killed him. But what if he'd been able to wear something - a bracelet, perhaps - that had all the magic and none of the side-effects? Or...

"Your sister is nice when she isn't being stuck-up," Rose said, suddenly. "Does she like you now?"

"I doubt it," I said. I didn't want to believe otherwise. It would just hurt, all the more, when I found out I was wrong. "She just wants someone to do her homework for her."

Rose snorted. "Has she tried it before?"

"Back home," I said. I smiled at the memory. Bella might have gotten away with it if she'd merely copied my work, but she'd taken the sheet with my name at the top. Dad had been laughing too hard to think of a proper punishment. "Dad wasn't fooled."

"I bet he wasn't," Rose said. "He struck me as a very smart man."

I sighed as we walked into the dorm. I loved my father, but growing up in his shadow...none of us could *really* live up to him. How could we?

"Caitlyn," Sandy said. "Come here. I want a word with you."

I blinked. What had I done?

There was no help for it. I walked over to Sandy's bed. She was sitting in a comfortable armchair, reading a fifth-year textbook on advanced magical theory. I'd tried looking through one a week or so ago, but I hadn't been able to make heads or tails of it. It would be several years before I was ready to comprehend it, if I lasted that long. Dad might pull me out of school altogether once he learnt what I could do.

"Caitlyn," Sandy said. She moved her hand in a complicated pattern, setting up a privacy ward. "You *are* going to fetch food, aren't you?"

I scowled. "Do I have a choice?"

Sandy gave me a sweet smile that didn't fool me for a moment. "It's important to engage with your dorm mates," she said. "I understand that you have not had an easy time of it, but..."

My temper flared. "It strikes me that it must be easier to say those things if you haven't lived it," I snapped. "I'm an outcast here!"

"You're developing your magic," Sandy said. "You're already well ahead of most of your classmates in theoretical studies."

I snorted. I could draw out perfect spell diagrams, if I wanted, and plot out enough runes to cast a really complex spell for an encore. That wouldn't stop a ten-year-old from turning me into a frog, if she'd been taught to wield magic. And yet...my fingers touched the earring, gently. That wasn't true any longer, was it?

"Learning to spend time with people you don't like is an important part of life," Sandy told me. I was surprised she didn't give me lines for cheek. "I expect you to cheer loudly whenever someone scores a goal."

I met her eyes. "Why?"

Sandy opened her mouth, but I spoke over her. "Raven Dorm does not have a netball team," I said. "The only thing special about *this* team..."

"...Is that one of your dorm mates is *on* the team," Sandy said. "And you will show support for her."

I scowled. "Oh I will, will I?"

"Yes, you will," Sandy said. She crossed her arms under her breasts. "I'm not asking you to *like* Isabella. Nor am I asking her to like you. But I *am* asking you to support her, just as I would ask her to support you."

"We would both be happier," I said, "if we were on opposite sides of the school."

"You'll meet plenty of people you don't like as you grow older," Sandy said. "Like I said, dealing with them is an important part of life."

Dad had said the same thing, I recalled. But had he really spent his schooldays with Carioca Rubén?

Probably, I thought, as I headed for bed. *And they still hate each other.*

CHAPTER
THIRTY-FOUR

S aturday came too soon.

It wasn't something I'd expected to feel, not really. Rose and I had charged enough stirrers - and gemstones - for me to fake my way through Friday's lessons, while spending half my time trying to determine who now had access to Lab Thirteen. I had experiments I wanted to try, but I doubted Robin would agree to supervise me a second time. And Saturday morning, spent in the workroom, would have been fun, if I hadn't needed to make a great many magical tools in a hurry. I was surprised, really, that Akin asked no questions. He had to know I was working on my own projects too.

I ate my evening dinner with Rose, feeling like I'd been condemned. Sandy hadn't spoken to me since Thursday night, but Ayesha and Zeya stayed close to us, chatting happily about famous netball players throughout the ages. I found it hard to believe that anyone really *cared* about netball players, yet it was easier just to let them blather on. At least *football* players were assured of good careers, if they managed to get into one of the international teams. And they'd be safer, too, than jousters in tournaments. I wanted to sneak off to the library, but I had a feeling it would be futile. Sandy would have no trouble finding me.

"Waste of an evening," I muttered to Rose, as we trailed Ayesha and Zeya down to the courtyard. "We could be learning new spells."

Rose shrugged. "It might be fun."

The netball court was larger than I had expected, based on my mother's descriptions. A large field, surrounded by powerful wards; a dozen rows of seats, only around a third filled...it was mainly girls, I noted. There were only a handful of boys, sitting at the back and trying not to be noticed. They didn't seem very interested - one was even reading a book. I guessed they'd come to support their girlfriends.

"Have a seat," Zeya said, as the players loped into the court. I couldn't help rolling my eyes when I saw them. The shirts and shorts they wore would have been considered indecent anywhere outside the school. "That's Isabella in the green, just in case you don't recognise her."

I rolled my eyes. Isabella might have her long hair tied into a bun, but she was still recognisable. She was easily the youngest player in the court. I found myself torn between admiring her nerve - some of the red players looked tough - and hoping she'd be knocked out of the match. Perhaps, if she fell flat on her face, she'd be kicked out of the greens.

The sports mistress blew a whistle. She looked tougher than anyone else on the field, wearing a white shirt covered in black runes. They would need to be re-stitched regularly, but as long as she was wearing the shirt it would be difficult for anyone to hex her. I found it hard to believe that anyone would have the nerve, yet accidents *did* happen. Dad had joked about tournaments that had ended with the referee being *accidentally* turned into something unpleasant.

Rose leaned forward, then winked at me. "Which side are we meant to be cheering for again?"

"The ones in green," Zeya said.

"The ones in red," Rose said. "Got you."

"No, the ones in *green*," Zeya said.

"The reds?" I asked. "I thought we were meant to be cheering for the greens."

"No, the greens," Zeya insisted.

"You said *red*," I said. "We heard you, didn't we?"

"Yep," Rose agreed. "You want us cheering for the reds."

Luckily for Zeya's sanity, the sports mistress blew her whistle again and terminated the discussion. We sat back and watched as the ball was hurled into the court, some of the bigger girls darting forward to snatch it while the smaller girls hung back. The victor spun around and passed the ball to another player, who lost it to a *third* player. A second later, someone hexed that player in the back, but the ball flew onwards just in time. Isabella caught it and tossed it onwards.

Rose glanced at me. "How does this *work*?"

I shrugged. I'd never bothered to look up the rules. Zeya, luckily, was happy to explain.

"The aim is to score a goal by getting the ball through the hoops," she said. One of the players threw the ball, bouncing it off the wards and missing the goal by a bare centimetre or two. "However, none of them can actually *hold* the ball for longer than ten seconds. Anyone who does gets shocked badly. The moment you have the ball, you either have to shoot for the goal or pass it to another player."

I glanced at her. "And the hexes?"

"You're not allowed to turn someone into a frog or anything else that might get squashed," Zeya said. "Other than that...anything goes."

"Ouch," Rose muttered.

I nodded in agreement. The older students were exchanging hexes at a terrifying rate. Most of them were skilled enough to break spells, even without moving their arms. I saw a dozen students get hexed, free themselves and then get hexed again. Isabella caught the ball and dribbled it down the court, only to be caught by a leg-binding hex and fall flat on her face. I couldn't help feeling a flicker of sympathy for her as her older teammates grabbed the ball and ran on with it, leaving her to free herself. But I had to admit that she was brave enough to pick herself up and keep going.

A loud gong echoed though the room. "Goal," the sports mistress bellowed. "One-nil!"

Rose was grinning with excitement when the game finally came to an end. I had to admit I had found it exciting too, although I knew I couldn't play. The players had hexed each other so badly that nine girls had lined up in front of the sports mistress, waiting for her to remove the hexes. One of them had somehow wound up with her hand melted into her skull...I would have laughed, if I hadn't known it was deadly dangerous. She could have been seriously hurt.

And Isabella...? She was grinning from ear to ear as she waved at us.

"That was fun," Rose admitted. "Cat?"

I shrugged. "I can't afford to waste *all* my time on sports," I said. It was true, but part of me would have loved to be down on the courtyard. Isabella was being congratulated by several of the other players. Students who would normally have disdained to learn a firstie's name were treating her like a queen. "But maybe we'll come again."

"You had your chance to try out," Zeya said. "You can try again next year."

Rose smiled. "You *could.*"

I shook my head. I had a feeling jewellery wasn't allowed in the court. None of the other players had been wearing anything, not even a watch. And without my earrings - and anything else I could design - I would be vulnerable. My sisters had taught me how to dodge hexes, but a single hit would be enough to bring me down. I certainly couldn't break the spell without help.

"You go, if you want," I said. Would I have to go watch? Probably... friends did that for friends, didn't they? "I can come watch."

Her smile widened as Zeya led us down to the court. Isabella was standing there, drinking from a bottle of water and grinning widely. Her face was streaked with sweat. I hoped she was going to take a shower before the feast...the thought reminded me of what we had to do, after Lights Out.

"Thank you for watching," she said. For once, she sounded polite. "What did you think?"

"You did very well," I said. Her eyes opened wide in surprise. "I was expecting you to be booted out in the first five minutes."

She shrugged. "It's all a matter of learning to dodge," she said. Her eyes hardened. "And mastering the spells needed to counter the hexes."

I groaned, inwardly. It was easy to read the hidden message. She *still* suspected I couldn't do magic.

"We'll see you upstairs," Zeya said. "Come quickly."

I would have enjoyed the next couple of hours if I hadn't been fretting about sneaking down to the kitchens. Sandy turned a blind eye to us sitting in the middle of the room and playing a modified - and incredibly complicated - version of snakes and ladders. Henrietta had invented the rules, apparently. Midway through, we started arguing over other improvements that could be added to the game. It rapidly started to look *far* too complex for me.

"Well," Isabella said, finally. She held out a piece of paper. "Here's the shopping list. Good luck."

I glanced at the clock. It was midnight. Everyone should be fast asleep, save for whoever had night duty in the gatehouse. Unless, of course, someone *else* was planning to raid the kitchens. Perhaps the red team was having its own midnight feast. Or...

Rose nodded to me. "Let's go."

I pocketed the list, then led the way to the door. Isabella waved, cheerfully, as we opened it and peered outside. It was dark, save for a single light at the far end of the corridor. We slipped outside, closing the door behind us, then stopped. I dug into my pouch and produced two pairs of modified spectacles. Night-vision spells were complicated, but I didn't need them to see in the dark. All I needed was a few hours in a workshop.

"It looks odd," Rose whispered.

I slipped my own spectacles over my nose, then nodded in agreement. The school looked...*fuzzy*, as if the corridors were illuminated by an eerie grey light. I had a feeling that the protective wards were interfering, very slightly, with the spell. Rose looked weird in the semi-darkness too, her body illuminated by eldritch light. I dug through my pocket and found the other charms, then passed two of them to her. Her form blurred a little more, even though I *knew* she was there. It wasn't an invisibility cloak - I doubted I could make one of those without a great deal more practice - but it should hide her from a casual glance. Mine did the same, with a couple of minor modifications. Someone would have to be *looking* for us if they wanted to see us.

Which might happen, if we do something to draw their attention, I thought. *We have to be careful.*

I gave her a reassuring smile, then pulled my magic sensor out of my pocket and led the way down the corridor. Going the long way around would add some time to our journey, but it would limit the number of places that could be effectively warded. Rose carried her own sensor, checking the side-corridors. There might be *something* just waiting for us in the shadows.

The stairs looked downright *creepy* as we inched down the main stairwell towards the lower levels. Giant stone statues took on thoroughly unpleasant forms, all teeth and claws, as we passed. I felt a nasty sensation at the back of my neck - a sense that we were being watched - but there was no one there when I turned to look. The air was cold and utterly silent. My heart beat so loudly I was surprised I hadn't woken half the school. We reached the hallway and stopped, alarmed. I could hear a faint sound, echoing down the corridor. Someone was coming our way.

I caught Rose's hand and pulled her into the shadows as the patroller came into view. It was hard to be sure, in the half-light, but I thought it was an upperclassman, not a teacher. Sandy *had* warned me that the upperclassmen patrolled the school, after all. If we were caught out of bed at this hour, lines would be the least we could expect. I felt Rose's hand shaking in mind as the upperclassman passed by, his gaze sweeping over us without seeing a thing. The shadows moved so often at Jude's that most students were trained to ignore them. He probably thought we were more of the same.

Rose sagged against me, just for a second, as the upperclassman vanished up the stairs and into the distance. I squeezed her hand, then led the way down to the kitchens. The main doors were locked and heavily warded, according to the plans, but the rear door wasn't so heavily defended. Unless, of course, the wards had been updated in the last decade. It was what *I* would have done.

I dug into my pocket for the dispeller, then held the sensor against the door. It vibrated over the lock, warning me that someone had placed a hex there. I checked the rest of the door, just to be sure there wasn't an additional surprise - Alana had made a habit of hiding one hex under a second - and then pressed the dispeller against the lock. The gemstones glowed, brightly, as the hex collapsed.

"Stay back," I warned, as I reached for the next tool. "If this goes wrong, go straight back to the dorm."

I pushed the unlocker against the lock. It clicked open. Carefully, very carefully, I twisted the knob and opened the door, holding the sensor out ahead of me. Nothing moved, deep within the kitchen. I peered into the darkness, catching sight of dark and cold fireplaces, caldrons, roasting pits and other pieces of equipment. The staff would be down in a few hours to light everything, I knew. By the time the students stumbled into the dining room, everything would be ready for them. I nodded to Rose, then headed into the room.

A voice echoed through the air. "Stop," it said. It was so odd, so *creepy*, that I thought I'd imagined it. "Relax. Wait to be collected."

I blinked. Maybe it *was* just my imagination. But the sensor twitched in my hand...

Something clattered to the ground. I jumped, then spun around. Rose had dropped her sensor and was just standing there, her eyes vacant. I stared. What...I swore under my breath as I remembered the voice. A subtle hex, one designed to capture anyone who sneaked into the kitchens and hold them until they were found. Useless against me, but very effective against anyone with a wisp of magic. And Rose had no experience in resisting *any* such spells...

I caught her arm and shook her. She jumped, glancing around in shock. "What...?"

"They would have caught you," I said, grimly. She stared at me in horror, only dimly aware of what had happened. The hex was so subtle that its victims rarely realised they'd been caught. If I hadn't caught her...

I gritted my teeth. There was no time for her to catch up. "You'd still have been standing there when the staff came down in the morning."

"Oh," Rose said. Her voice sounded very small. "I...I didn't even know it was there."

"Neither did I," I said. My lack of magic had saved us both. Alana would be furious, when she heard. I hoped I'd have the chance to tell her. "We have to move."

I pulled her onwards, into the storeroom. There was a second hex on the door and a third on the knob itself. I dispelled them both, then opened the door. The pantry was huge, crammed with everything from preserved biscuits to cured meat. I glanced down at the list, then started to take what Isabella wanted. Biscuits and cakes, bread and jam...it was going to be a big feast, if we managed to carry everything upstairs. I didn't know if the bags were big enough.

Rose caught my arm. "Shouldn't we be taking stuff from the back?"

I shook my head. Tradition, according to my mother, dictated that no one would make a fuss, *if* we weren't caught in the act. The staff would know that someone had broken into the kitchen - there was no way we could keep them from noticing the missing hexes - but we wouldn't get in trouble. Coming to think of it, could they pick either Rose or I out as possible suspects? We hadn't used inherent magic to break into the pantry...

"It should be fine," I said. I hoped I was right. The staff might make an exception for a couple of students they considered troublemakers. "As long as we don't get caught..."

I glanced around the pantry as we finished dumping food into the bags. There was nothing else we wanted, as far as I could tell. I picked up one of the bags and grunted under the weight. The bag was surprisingly heavy...I wished, suddenly, that I'd thought to show Rose how to lighten things. The charms weren't *that* complicated. Rose didn't seem to have any trouble with hers, but then she *was* surprisingly muscular. Being on a farm had given her more strength than anything I'd done.

"Come on," I hissed. "We need to move."

I held the sensor in one hand as we sneaked back towards the door. Dad had taught me a *little* about traps - and about how setting one to catch the thieves on the way out was surprisingly effective. It was when most thieves relaxed, he'd said. They got careless. But there was nothing. We slipped out of the door, closing it behind us. I motioned for her to stay very still and listen, but we heard nothing. The entire school was silent.

And then I heard a voice snapping out a spell.

I froze. I couldn't move a muscle. I couldn't see Rose, but I knew she was frozen too...

We were trapped.

THIRTY-FIVE

"S he was right," a male voice said. "Someone *did* try a kitchen raid." *Isabella*, I thought. *She wanted us to get caught.*

I would have shook with pure rage, if I'd been able to move a single muscle. Isabella had set us up. She'd tricked me into taking the card, then tipped off the upperclassmen to the raid. No doubt they'd expected to find us trapped in the kitchen...I pushed the thought aside. We were trapped. The spell wouldn't last as long as our captor clearly expected - at least, it wouldn't hold *me* indefinitely - but what then? I doubted I could free Rose and then escape before we were caught again.

The upperclassman came into view, his face oddly wrapped in shadow. A concealment charm, I guessed, probably not too different to the one we'd used on the way down to the kitchen. Dad had told me that magicians preferred to use concealment rather than invisibility, knowing that the human mind preferred to accept a simple explanation for any flickers at the corner of one's eye rather than look for an invisible target. But no charm would hide us, now the upperclassman knew to look. I stared at him as he cast a simple light spell, waving a beam of light over our faces. I couldn't even *blink*!

His face grew clear. He was tall, but completely unfamiliar. A pale face, just starting to show signs of stubble; muscular arms...a faint smile curling around his lips. The seven bands around his upper arm told me he was a seventh year, someone trusted enough to patrol the corridors after dark. I had half-hoped we'd been caught by someone who might want an apprenticeship - or something - from my father, but I had no way to know if we had any room to bargain at all. I wasn't sure *what* would happen to anyone caught raiding the kitchen - apart from writing lines until our wrists dropped off - yet I doubted it would be fun.

The upperclassman reached out with his wand and tapped me on the forehead. A faint tingle ran through my body. My head moved, but everything below the neckline remained frozen...I would have been impressed, if it wasn't confirmation we were trapped. He tapped Rose too, then looked down at me. I couldn't help wondering if he *recognised* me. Most upperclassmen pretended not to know *anything* about the lowerclassmen, but my sisters and I were *very* well known. Rose, of course, was a complete stranger.

"Well," he said. His voice would have been pleasant, if he hadn't been sneering. "What do I have here?"

I briefly considered claiming to be Isabella. But I didn't think it would fool anyone.

"We got out of the kitchen," I said, instead. "That means you *have* to let us go."

"Actually, you have to get back to the dorms, young lady," he said. "I'm afraid I caught you red-handed."

He cocked his head. "Although I *am* impressed you managed to get in and out of the kitchen," he added. "Are you *really* first years?"

"No," I said. "We're actually seventh years in disguise."

"Then you'd be sneaking over the walls instead of into the kitchen," he said, dryly. He smiled. It utterly transformed his features. "Besides, you're just a *little* bit short to be seventh years."

He smirked. "So...what should I do with you?"

I thought fast. "Give us a slap on the wrist and then let us go?"

"Now," he said. "What would the Castellan say if I did?"

"He'd say you were upholding an old school tradition," I told him. "Particularly as *someone* thought it would be fun to tip you off."

He smiled. "I'm afraid that's part of the game too, little firstie," he said. "What *else* can you offer me?"

I groaned, inwardly. There was nothing. I wasn't going to write another blank cheque, certainly not for *this*. The punishment we would face if we were marched in front of the Castellan - or whichever staff member was on duty - would be unpleasant, but survivable. I could put up with another few weeks of scrubbing floors, if necessary. It would give me plenty of time to plot revenge. Isabella wouldn't know what had hit her by the time I was finished.

Rose cleared her throat. "You can take half our bags," she said. "How about that?"

The upperclassman smirked. "You're trying to bribe me?"

I blinked. Trying to bribe him with our ill-gotten gains had honestly never occurred to me.

"Yes," Rose said. Her voice was very even. "We've got biscuits and bread and cakes and plenty of other nice things. You could take half of them and have a feast of your own."

"Yeah," I said. "You could have a last feast before you graduate."

The upperclassman snorted. "And what's to stop me from simply taking your bribe and turning you in anyway?"

"You would have to explain what happened to the food," I pointed out. I would never be the chess grandmaster my father was, but I *did* know how to spot the weakness in someone's position. "Even if we didn't rat you out, the kitchen staff would notice the missing food and demand answers. Sneaking into the kitchen might be traditional, but what about taking the food from younger students?"

He studied me for a long moment. "You have nerve, for a firstie," he said. He took my bag and opened it. "And you were greedy too. Planning to feed the entire dorm, were you?"

I nodded, curtly.

"I'll leave you with a packet of biscuits," he said. He took Rose's bag and dumped most of my food into it, then slung it over his shoulder. "The spell will wear off soon and you can go back to your dorms. Just pray no one else comes along before it does. And congratulations on getting in and out of the kitchen. Very few firsties could have managed that."

I glared at his retreating back as he walked into the kitchen, closing the wooden door behind him. Isabella...Isabella was going to *pay*. Rose was sniffling quietly, clearly upset about being caught again. I wanted to hug her - or at least to take her hand - but I still couldn't move. It was nearly ten minutes before the spell broke, allowing me to free Rose too. No doubt our captor had intended for us to be caught again. There was no point in trying to sneak back into the kitchens, so I grabbed my bag and led the way back up the stairs. If we were lucky, we could sneak back to the dorms without being caught again.

"I'm sorry," Rose whispered, as we crept down an empty corridor. "I didn't think he'd take it all."

"We'd have lost it anyway," I whispered back. I glanced into my bag. True to his word, the upperclassman had left us with a packet of flavourless oatmeal biscuits. They were normally eaten with cheese, but we didn't have any. "Why did you think of trying to bribe him?"

"He sounded like a taxman," Rose said. "The swine will happily claim that you have nothing, if you bribe them. If you don't, they tell the king you live in a castle and that you swim in gold coins."

"That sounds uncomfortable," I said. I couldn't imagine anyone actually *believing* that, although I doubted King Rufus would bother to leave his comfortable palace just to check on a peasant hovel. Dad had told me, more than once, that it was dangerous to rely completely on one's servants. They eventually - inevitably - tried to take advantage. "Do you *really* swim in gold coins?"

Rose elbowed me. "What do you think?"

I shrugged. I'd read a story, once, about a greedy governor from the empire who'd been killed by having molten gold poured down his throat. And another, an even *less* pleasant fellow, who'd been turned into a golden statue and melted down. There had even been a story about a king who had gained the power to turn anything he touched into gold, but that had ended badly. Dad had told us the story as a warning against using magic to solve everything. In my case, the warning hadn't been necessary.

Although it might be now, I thought, as we stopped just outside the dorm to remove our spectacles. *I may not have magic, but I have power.*

I pushed the door open, bracing myself for a fight. Isabella and the others were sitting in a circle in the middle of the dorm, playing a game that involved passing a hexed ball around as fast as possible. Sandy was sitting on her bed, keeping her back turned. I figured she wanted to be able to deny everything, if we got caught. And we *had* been caught.

Isabella looked up. I saw her eyes widen in surprise.

"You told them we were coming," I snapped, as I yanked the biscuits out of the bag. "We were caught as we left the kitchen!"

"I did not," Isabella said, hotly. She rose to her feet. I couldn't help noticing that she had changed into black pyjamas, with her family's crest clearly visible. "You tripped an alarm and got caught!"

"We did not," I snapped. I threw the biscuits at her, angrily. She jumped aside a moment before they could hit her. "They *knew* we were coming!"

"Well, *I* didn't tell them," Isabella snapped back.

"Maybe someone else was planning to raid the kitchen," Zeya put in, her eyes flickering between Isabella and me. "You just got caught up in someone else's trap!"

I glared at her. "And what are the odds of someone else going to raid the kitchen at the exact same time as us?"

"Better than you'd think," Sandy said. I glanced at her. She still had her back to us. "You cannot hold a midnight feast when you have classes tomorrow. A feast, therefore, has to be held on either Friday or Saturday night. There's a good chance that *someone* else might have decided to have a feast of their own..."

"And that someone might have decided to tip off the upperclassmen?" I countered. "She made sure *I* would go and she made sure *we* would be caught!"

Sandy said nothing. I glowered at Isabella. The students *most* likely to tip off the upperclassmen were the firsties, the ones least integrated into the school. A sneak wouldn't have a very happy time of it, if he or she was caught. And Isabella might assume she could ride out any problems. She was *still* her father's probable heir.

"We had enough food to last for a week," I snapped. It was a slight exaggeration, but pardonable. "We could have sneaked it all up here if they hadn't been waiting for us."

Isabella glared back. "And how do we know you even made it into the kitchens?" She countered. "You could have brought those biscuits from home!"

I clenched my fists. "Do you really think I would have brought *those* biscuits from home?"

"We have the bags," Rose offered, gently. "*They* came from the kitchen."

"That's not proof of anything," Isabella sneered. She leaned forward. "I think you just lurked around outside, then came up with this story to justify your failure. Who caught you, anyway?"

"I don't know," I said. "It isn't as if he bothered to make formal introductions!"

Isabella snorted. "You should know everyone in the upper years," she jeered. "But then, your father never bothered to teach you, did he?"

I glowered. My father *hadn't* taught me. And I didn't *think* he'd taught Alana or Bella either. I knew most of the important lords and ladies, the heads of the greater families and the masters of the guilds, but not the students. Had Isabella been forced to memorise them all? I could believe it. A show of knowing who she was talking to - and proving that person had been noticed - could move mountains. Dad had always taught us to take an interest in the servants, even though they *were* servants...

And if Isabella had to memorise everyone who might be important, I thought with an odd flicker of sympathy, *no wonder she's in such a cranky mood all the time.*

"I know everyone who's important," I said, dismissing the thought. Right now, I had no room for sympathy. "And somehow, my father forgot to mention you."

Isabella reddened. "No one bothered to mention you either," she snapped. "I suppose a mere *zero* isn't worth mentioning."

"I've done magic," I said, sharply. "And..."

"It's a trick of some kind," Isabella said. "If you had magic, if your parents had three children who were strongly magical, they'd never let anyone forget it."

"Like your parents talk about you and your brother?" I asked. She was right, so I chose to ignore her. "It must be hard having to be constantly told you're the great hope of your generation."

Isabella took a moment to calm herself. "I didn't sneak on you," she hissed. "And you are a liar for even suggesting it."

She lifted her hand. "Recant."

I met her eyes. "Or what?"

"Or you'll be a toad for the next *year*," she said, icily. "Recant."

I shrugged, mockingly. It was an empty threat. There was no way she could *keep* me as a toad for more than an hour, not unless she'd somehow mastered *very* advanced charms and spell formations over the last few months. Even if she had, she would have to turn me back on Monday or explain to the teachers why I was missing class. I didn't think she'd *enjoy* scrubbing floors for a week...

"We were caught because someone tipped off the upperclassmen," I said. I touched the rings on my fingers, bracing myself. "And that person had to be you."

I jumped to one side as a nasty-looking hex flashed over my head, expending itself uselessly against the far wall. Isabella swung around, turning her hand to follow me; I triggered one of the rings, shooting a hex back at her. She deflected it with a wave of her hand - I would have been impressed, if she hadn't been fighting me - and shot another hex at me. I triggered a second ring and deflected the hex, feeling odd tingles running down my fingers. Clearly, I hadn't quite mastered the art of forging the rings...

"See?" I said. I threw a second hex at her. "I *do* have magic."

Isabella deflected the hex, straight into Sandy's back. It fizzled out against a protective ward, multicoloured sparks flying in all directions. We both jumped in shock, then tried to look innocent as Sandy spun around. *That* hadn't been meant to happen. The look on her face promised that we were *both* in deep trouble.

"Enough," she said. She made a show of glancing at her silver watch. "You *do* know what time it is, don't you?"

"Midnight," Isabella said.

I resisted the urge to shoot her a rude gesture. Sandy was clearly on the warpath.

"Close enough," Sandy said. She gestured. The packet of biscuits lifted up from the floor and shot into her hand. "Taken from the kitchen, I see."

Isabella snorted. "How do you know?"

"Jude's has its own bakery," Sandy said. She held it up so we could see the label. "Every day, they produce thousands of biscuits for the staff to dunk in their tea. You can't buy these outside for love or money."

She gave me a thin smile. "How *did* you get past the hexes?"

"I grew up sneaking around the hall," I said. It was true, although much of my knowledge had been hard-won. Dad didn't bait the interior hexes with anything lethal, but being caught had still been unpleasant. "The kitchen wasn't *that* heavily defended."

"Very well done," Sandy said. She glanced at Isabella. "I trust you accept, now, that they actually *did* get into the kitchens?"

Isabella turned red, again. "Yes," she said, slowly. "But I *didn't* tell on them?"

Sandy studied her for a long moment, then clapped her hands. "I want everyone in bed, now," she said, raising her voice. "It's been an adventure, I am sure, but all good things must come to an end."

She caught my eye, then nodded to Rose. "And you two did very well," she added, quietly. "I tried to sneak into the kitchens myself at your age."

Rose smiled, weakly. "What happened?"

"I got through the door, then ran straight into a hypnotic hex," Sandy admitted. She looked embarrassed. "They had me clucking like a chicken for days, every time someone mentioned the word. Do you know how many ways you can work the word *chicken* into a conversation?"

I flushed. Alana had been *particularly* fond of the hypnotic hex. Thankfully, none of her commands had lasted very long, but they'd still been embarrassing. It was funny how I'd never *noticed* I was acting like a dog, even when everything I said came out as a barking sound. Someone had had to *tell* me I was running around on all fours before I'd managed to stop myself.

"And *then* I was scrubbing floors afterwards," Sandy added. "I'd say the two of you got off pretty lightly."

"Thank you," I said. She was right. I *knew* she was right. But being betrayed still stung. I had never even *considered* that Isabella would rat us out. I'd assumed she had just hoped we'd either be caught naturally or ensnared by one of the nastier hexes. But betrayal...

I glowered at Isabella as she climbed into her bed, using a spell to pull the drapes into position. She'd betrayed us. I was sure she'd betrayed us. And I was going to find a way to make her pay. And yet...

We *had* sneaked in and out of the kitchen, hadn't we? That was something to be proud of.

And on that thought, I climbed into bed and fell asleep.

THIRTY-SIX

I was surprised, waking up the following morning, to discover that I was still human. I had honestly expected Isabella to try to hex me in my sleep, although I had scattered a few surprises around my bed and drapes to make that difficult. But Rose and I *were* still meant to be scrubbing floors for the entire day, so perhaps Isabella had decided it wasn't worth risking the wrath of the janitor.

Indeed, I barely *saw* Isabella for the entire day. She was at lunch, but then she vanished again until dinner, looking so tired that she didn't even bother to make snide remarks about how dirty and smelly we were after scrubbing the toilets. I suspected she was up to something, but what? Alana, sitting on the far side of the dining hall, eyed me curiously, yet said nothing. She had to know that Bella and I had reached *some* kind of agreement.

I was expecting trouble when I went back to the dorm, tired and sore and filthy, but nothing materialised. The water didn't turn to ice when I showered - a trick Alana had mastered as a child and used ruthlessly - nor did I stumble over a hex on my bed. Isabella looked too tired to say any-thing as she went to bed, somewhat to my surprise. What was *she* doing? I slept lightly, half-expecting to hear her sneaking through the drapes. But the night was still and quiet and eventually I dozed off.

"We have double charms," Rose told me, the following morning. "And most of it is theoretical."

I allowed myself a sigh of relief. My charm marks had improved over the last two weeks, but I knew they wouldn't get much better. I *was* good - *great*, even - at theoretical work, yet practical spells continued to defeat me. My best spell formulations failed when I tried to cast them, even when I had a charged ring. It was difficult - perhaps impossible - to charge a ring and then use it to cast a diagrammed spell. Some of the old forgers must have done it - there were Objects of Power that cast remarkable spells - but I had yet to master the techniques. I suspected there were more details that had been lost, over the years.

"Ah...we move now to dedicated spell fragments," Magister Von Rupert informed us. "I...ah...trust that you have each cast various hexes on each other?"

He plunged on without waiting for an answer. "Each magician has his own unique signature," he continued. "A spell cast without careful preparation can be traced back to the caster, without delay. Resonance spells can be used to locate the caster - if the forensic sorcerer is incapable of recognising the caster directly. This is often true of potions too, although rarely so of potions that...ah...require two brewers. Ah...

"You may be wondering about the importance of such signatures. In truth, such signatures often tell the inspectors more about the caster than may be supposed."

He launched into a long lecture about different styles of training and how they affected the casters. I listened with interest, noting how a Jude's graduate could almost always be identified from his spells - and how a magician who'd been given private tutoring could be detected, simply by the more focused signature. It wasn't something I'd ever considered, even though I'd loved reading the Inspector Sherringford, Detective Sorcerer books as a child. But then, Inspector Sherringford had been long on drama and short on realism. He'd always wound up exchanging spells with the murderer, normally after a dramatic parlour scene...

I frowned as a thought struck me. If Rose cast a spell for me - and the spell was stored in a ring for later use - which of us had actually cast the spell? Me...or Rose? And if the latter, could someone determine that Rose had cast the spell for me? A thought struck me and I smiled. If I could trap some of Isabella's magic, I could get *her* blamed for something. It wouldn't be nice, but it would give her a taste of her own medicine.

She deserves it, I thought. *She betrayed us.*

"Magical signatures have a tendency to fade," Von Rupert said. "Ah... it normally takes between an hour to a day for the signature to fade completely. At that point, it is still...ah...possible to determine that magic was used, but...ah...impossible to identify the caster. And magic itself can fade back into the background..."

He paused. "Homework for the week involves studying the use and abuse of magical signatures," he concluded. "I want you to pay specific attention to how signatures can be used outside the criminal investigation sphere."

I heard several students groan. I didn't really blame them, even though Magister Grayson was giving them nasty looks. Criminal investigation was interesting, if nothing else. I'd once dreamed of being an inspector myself. But instead...the class was dismissed, leaving Rose and I behind. I wanted to ask the magisters a couple of questions.

"Ah...yes?" Von Rupert asked, as we approached his desk. "You...ah... you have a question?"

"Yes," I said. "What would happen if something caused the signatures to *mingle*?"

"It would depend," Von Rupert said, after a moment. "Ah...magic spell structures do break up over time. If there were two or more signatures, they might blur together and render themselves useless, if...ah...someone wanted to tell who had cast the spell. Or a skilled sorcerer might be able to separate the two. Ah...that would be easier if the two magicians came from different schools."

Rose leaned forward. "Because they would have traces of *all* the teachers in their magic?"

"They would be taught to cast their spells a certain way," Grayson said. He sounded oddly distracted by a greater thought. "Your practical casting comes from me *and* Magistra Solana, so you would have elements of both of us in your style. You also gained elements from Magistra Loanda, as she drilled potions into your head. Someone who only learnt from me would essentially copy my style."

I nodded. "What if someone copied my spell?"

Von Rupert looked up. "Ah...I beg your pardon?"

"If I wrote out a spell and someone from another school cast it," I said, "would I get the blame?"

"Probably not," Grayson said. He gave me a sharp look, as if he was wondering precisely *why* I was asking. "The spell might be yours, and it would be obvious that you were taught here, but the actual *style* would be different."

"I see, I think," I said. "And what if someone used someone else's magic?"

"There...ah...have been cases where a person was mind-controlled into casting spells," Von Rupert said. "I...ah...I believe that Magus Court was able to identify the casters and free them from their enslavement. They were not held responsible for their actions."

"But what if someone used a wand I charged?" I asked. "Or..."

Magister Grayson gave me a sharp look. "Is there a *reason* for these questions?"

I thought fast. "There was a story," I said. "*Inspector Sherringford and the Golden Ear of Zangaria*. The culprit *borrowed* magic from a friend to cast his spells."

"Ah," Von Rupert said.

Grayson snorted. "And, in the *real* world, *borrowing* magic is not possible," he said. "I believe that several of the more...unpleasant dark wizards have tried to steal magic from their captors, but the results have always been limited. It has simply proven impossible to deny a person access to their magic permanently. Warding the prisons is a complex, constantly ongoing task."

But I did manage to borrow Rose's spells, I thought.

"I suggest you hurry onwards to your next class," Grayson added, coldly. "Unless you *want* some extra homework...?"

We grabbed our bags and fled out of the door, heading for the dining hall. I heard them muttering together as we left, probably wondering just why we'd been asking such odd questions. I didn't know if they'd believed my story or not. There were just too many tales of magic - and magicians - that were clearly made up, when the reader knew a little about magic.

Stealing a person's magic was impossible. If it *was* possible, I had no doubt my parents would have found someone like Rose and forced them to give me their powers. Dad wouldn't have hesitated for a moment.

But I have power of my own, I thought. I couldn't *wait* to tell him. *And that will change everything.*

"I never read those books," Rose said, wistfully. "Are they any good?"

"They're fun," I told her. I stopped as a thought struck me. "And there's a couple of really mushy romances you should read too. They're sickeningly sweet, but they do tell you a *lot* about life in the big city."

Rose didn't look convinced. "What happens?"

I shrugged. "Boy meets girl. Girl likes boy, but mother-in-law wants girl to marry someone else. Boy elopes with girl. Mother-in-law declares war on boy's family. Lots of people get injured or killed because of this pointless feud. Father realises that mother-in-law is a shrew and kicks her out into the street, then blesses the match. Boy and girl live happily ever after."

"I'm sure it's a great story," Rose said, sardonically.

"It was turned into a great play," I said. "The mother-in-law is normally played by a man in drag, for comic relief. And they throw pies instead of hexes..."

I shook my head as we entered the dining hall. "There's two or three like it, but with all the roles switched around," I added. "They may be boring and soppy, yet they do tell you a lot about High Society."

Rose glanced at me. "Do you ever wish you'd been born somewhere else?"

"I don't know," I admitted. I had wished that, years ago. Growing up on a farm...I would never have known what I'd missed. "My parents are great, but they put a lot of expectations on me. Even now..."

We ate lunch together, then headed down to Forging and joined the line waiting outside the classroom. Isabella was leaning against the wall, chatting quietly to Akin. I couldn't help noticing that her cronies were keeping their distance, something that meant...what? Akin didn't seem to *have* many cronies, at least as far as I could tell. But then, the boys would probably be more careful about showing their allegiances too openly. Swearing blood brotherhood at their ages would bring their families down on them like the wrath of an angry god.

"Welcome, welcome," Magister Tallyman told us. He hurried us into the classroom and pointed at the workbenches. "I trust that you all read the chapters I specified?"

I nodded, hastily. The chapter had been nothing new to me, but I'd reviewed it anyway and then broken it down for Rose. Interlocking runes and sigils had always been interesting, even before I'd uncovered my true talents. These days, I had a whole new reason to study. I might have access to thousands of books - all useless to anyone else - but I figured I might be able to craft Objects of Power I'd designed myself. We knew a great deal more about certain runes and their interactions than the ancients had ever done.

"I want you to start carving out a basic runic diagram," Magister Tallyman said. He pointed a finger at the blackboard. A series of runes appeared in front of us, all carefully angled away from each other. "Plot out their interactions, then check with me or my assistants before you actually start carving. You do *not* want to waste the iron sheets."

Rose nudged me. "I thought we had a vast supply?"

"We do," I whispered back. "But we won't after we graduate."

I looked around the room as Magister Tallyman continued to lecture us. The forges alone were worth hundreds of crowns, perhaps thousands. I'd looked it up after my fight with Rose. And the steady inflow of raw materials; wood, metal, gemstones...I dreaded to imagine how much *they* cost. A lot could be recycled, I knew, if melted down carefully, but there would still be a great deal of waste. I couldn't help wondering if even my father could afford such a vast expenditure indefinitely.

And what will happen, I asked myself, *when Dad finds out what I can do?*

I had to smile at the thought. There was literally no one on the entire planet who could make Objects of Power, except me. I glanced up at the textbooks, the completely useless textbooks...I could use them, if I had the time and raw materials. Even a simple unbreakable sword would be worth ten times its weight in just about anything. And I could turn out everything from protective ankhs to magic-dampening fields and solid wards. We could make a fortune.

Another fortune, I thought.

"You may begin," Magister Tallyman said. "My assistants and I will move from bench to bench."

He nodded at me, then at Akin. I grinned and headed over to the next bench, where Zeya was already drawing out a runic diagram. It was a neat piece of work, I had to admit, although it was very simple. It was clear she didn't want to waste time carving out something that would fail if she made a tiny mistake. I could see several ways to fix any problems, but she might feel differently.

"Very good," I said, seriously. "Just be careful what you use to carve it out."

Isabella gave me a nasty look as I stepped towards her. She glanced around for someone else, but Magister Tallyman was inspecting Rose's work and Akin was drawing out an improvement for one of the boys. I was tempted to just walk past her, but I doubted Magister Tallyman would approve. He'd made it clear that we were to put aside all feuds in his classroom while we were his assistants.

"Go away," Isabella hissed. She held up one finger, threatening me. "Go."

"I have to check your work," I said. Her face darkened, angrily. Clearly, putting it *that* way had been a mistake. "It has to be done before you start carving."

"Fine," Isabella growled. She jabbed a finger at me, just to watch me flinch. "But don't you *dare* tell me it's wrong."

I eyed her as I took the paper. "What got into your breakfast this morning?"

Isabella shook her head, angrily. "Check it, then go."

I sighed, but did as she said. The runes were very well drawn - it was clear she intended to use the runic diagram to protect something - but they were out of alignment. The magic would fizzle, when the runes were carved into metal. I doubted they would last for more than a few seconds, even if I'd carved them. Isabella lacked my talent...

The nasty part of my mind was tempted to let her waste her time, but I knew Magister Tallyman would not be pleased. I had a two-star award. There was no way I wouldn't notice that something was wrong. This wasn't a subtle mistake. If anything, she'd drawn it out too blatantly.

"You need to adjust the runes," I said, reaching for a pencil. "If you draw them out..."

"They're *fine*," Isabella insisted. "You don't have to change them!"

"Yes, I do," I said. I knew she didn't like me, but...*really*. "If you try to draw these out on a sword, the best you can hope for is slow rusting..."

"Akin," Isabella snapped. Her brother looked up. "Come check these, *please*."

Akin came over, looking wary. I wondered, just for a second, what their relationship was actually *like*. Everything I'd heard told me they were close, but I hadn't seen them talking very often. My sisters and I were hardly friendly. And yet...it wasn't as if they could share a room. Maybe their parents hoped they'd build different networks of friends and supporters that could be merged together...

"You need to realign these four, at the very least," he said. "The runes won't hold together for long."

"Not more than an hour," I added.

Isabella gave me a murderous look. "You utter..."

She waved a hand in front of my face. I felt my body go limp, my head falling forward until I was looking at the ground. I knew I should be panicking - the spell *had* to be powerful, if it had overwhelmed my protections - but I felt nothing. It was almost as if I was looking at my body from outside...

She's put you in a trance, my thoughts warned. It was hard, so hard, to realise there was a problem, let alone drag up the determination to fight. *You have to resist.*

"Don't," Akin snapped. "Isabella..."

He snapped his fingers in front of my eyes. I jerked back to awareness as Magister Tallyman stormed over. "Isabella," he said, sharply. "What do you *think* you are doing?"

Isabella's mouth opened. "I..."

She turned and started towards the door. She got about a metre before her feet were suddenly frozen to the floor.

"I do not allow students to hex each other in my classes," Magister Tallyman said. His voice was very cold. "And I *particularly* do not allow hexes that could cause real harm."

I gritted my teeth. She'd hypnotised me. I felt a surge of pure anger, mixed with bitter shame. She could have made me say or do or believe anything...it wouldn't have lasted, but it wouldn't have mattered. A few minutes under her spell would be more than long enough to wreck my life.

"Get back to work," Magister Tallyman ordered. He took Isabella by the arm and marched her out of the classroom. "I'll be back soon."

CHAPTER

THIRTY-SEVEN

"What's wrong with her?" I asked Akin, as soon as the class came to an end. "Why...?"

"Our father doesn't think she can serve as his successor," Akin said. He shook his head in annoyance. "He wanted two or more sons, not a daughter."

I glanced at him, surprised. "Isabella isn't going to be his heir?"

"She *wants* to be," Akin told me. "And she has the talent to be his heir. But father...isn't too keen on the idea of her taking his place."

I wasn't sure I believed him. Magical talent was magical talent, no matter who held it. And as much as I detested her, I had to admit that Isabella had plenty of talent. She wasn't *that* far behind me in theoretical work, while she had a colossal advantage in practical work. Apart from forging, I supposed. I was well ahead of her there.

"Father didn't want her to learn anything outside charms," Akin added. "She wasn't permitted to learn potions or forgery..."

"Oh," I said. I believed *that*, although it was odd. Isabella *should* have been taught the basics, if nothing else. "And now she hates me because she's having to catch up?"

"Probably," Akin said. He shrugged, expressively. "I've given up trying to understand my sister. She is a very complicated person."

I rolled my eyes. Isabella hadn't come back to the classroom with Magister Tallyman, which meant...what? A week of detentions and scrubbing floors...or something more serious? I didn't *think* she would be expelled, but she might just be hauled in front of the Castellan and given an ear-roasting. Her father would not be pleased...

Just for a moment, I felt another flicker of sympathy. My father had been disappointed in me too, although he'd hid it well. But then, he'd always *believed* I had powers, even if they stubbornly refused to manifest. I knew he'd be delighted when I finally told him the truth, when we went home for the hols. Isabella's father, on the other hand, was upset because Isabella hadn't been born a boy. I didn't know what she could do about that.

It was odd, I had to admit. Magic played no favourites. Women and men competed for the same posts, for the same training...I didn't know any spells or rituals that could only be carried out by men or women. Maybe there had been, once upon a time, but they'd only lasted until the spells were written to allow more people to cast them. Isabella would make a *good* heir, once she learned more magic. Her father shouldn't dismiss her so quickly.

"I hope she isn't too awkward tonight," Akin added. He gave me a sidelong glance. "She really doesn't like you."

I sighed. If I'd had magic...

"She and I are the highest-ranking girls in the dorm," I said, instead. If I'd had magic, I would have had my own circle of cronies...whether I liked it or not. Isabella and I could have spent the rest of our lives distributing patronage...and keeping people on tenterhooks with the promise of *more* patronage. "She sees me as her competition."

Akin smirked. "Poor you."

I eyed him. He was nice enough, I supposed, but he *was* a Rubén. It was something I ought to remember more. Just because he wasn't fool enough to get kicked out of Magister Tallyman's class didn't change the fact he was a Rubén, one of my family's rivals. I liked him more than I should. Dad would not be pleased, when he found out. And what would Akin do when he found out about me?

"Yeah," I agreed. I gathered my bag and headed for the door. "Poor me."

There was no sign of Isabella when Rose and I went to the library, or when we went to the dining hall for dinner. I couldn't help wondering if she'd been sent home, although I had to admit that was unlikely. Isabella *was* a Rubén too. The Castellan would need a *very* solid reason to send her home and hexing another student, even me, wouldn't be good enough. It certainly wouldn't convince Isabella's parents.

Of course not, I thought, sourly. *They'd have to expel the entire school if hexing another student was considered a suitable offense.*

It wasn't until we returned to the dorm that I saw her, sitting on her bed. She looked upset, her face pale and wan. It struck me, suddenly, that she might have been kicked off the netball team. Even if it hadn't been part of her punishment, being given several weekend detentions would be enough to keep her from practice. And then she'd be dumped from the team...

She looked up at me, her face twisting with hatred. I winced inwardly, fighting down the urge to run. I'd charged the rings again - Rose had helped - and I had a couple new trinkets on me, but I knew I was still no match for her. If she wanted to fight...I'd have to get close and then hit her before she could react. And yet...she could have protected herself against physical force, if she'd thought of it.

My heart sank. There was no sign of Sandy.

Isabella rose. "I'm off the team," she said, flatly. I would have been sympathetic, really I would, if she hadn't been readying a spell. "It's *your* fault."

I stared at her in genuine shock. "How is it *my* fault? You ensorcelled me!"

"You lied about me," Isabella snapped. "You told everyone I ratted you out!"

"You did," I snapped back.

"I didn't," Isabella said. "Do you want a Blood Oath?"

That brought me up short. No one, absolutely no one, joked about Blood Oaths. A person who broke a Blood Oath died. It was forbidden to demand one from anyone, under any circumstances. Isabella wouldn't even *dream* of offering one, unless she was innocent. I stared at her... *was* she innocent? Or was she gambling that I wouldn't be able to accept the oath? A Blood Oath needed a *very* powerful magician to serve as its warder.

My thoughts raced. Was she gambling? Or...the upperclassman had never actually *named* Isabella, had he? I'd thought nothing of it at the time, but now...? What if someone *else* had tipped him off? Sandy? One of Isabella's cronies? Or someone who hoped that Isabella would get the blame....

For that matter, I conceded silently, *we could have been caught up in someone else's trap.*

Rose stepped to one side. "If not you," she asked, "then who?"

"Be quiet, *commoner,*" Zeya snarled from her bed. I felt Rose flinch. "This is between Isabella and Caitlyn."

"It's a good question," I said, evenly. "If not you, then who?"

"I don't know," Isabella snapped. "All I know is that it wasn't *me!*"

She took a step forward. "And then you have the nerve to tell me my runes are out of shape!"

"They were," I said. I wasn't sure what kept me standing in front of her. Part of me just wanted to turn and run. "Even your *brother* agreed that they weren't right."

Isabella's expression twisted. I saw a complex surge of emotions cross her face, too many to follow. I wondered, suddenly, just what she thought of her brother. She had to be jealous of him, just as I was jealous of Alana and Bella. And yet, she had the opportunity to prove herself better than him. House Rubén needed the strongest and most capable magician in command. Only a complete idiot would refuse to name the *better* sibling his heir.

"Akin has been spending too much time with you," she growled. "Why?"

I couldn't resist. "Perhaps he enjoys my company?"

She purpled. "Just because you share a talent for forging? Just how far do you think you'll get without magic?"

I snickered, helplessly. If only she knew...

"I still don't think you have magic," Isabella said. She met my eyes, challengingly. "You didn't wear any jewellery when I first saw you, not even a family ring. And now you have rings on all of your fingers and a pair of earrings."

Her voice became calculating. "And Akin said you were spending a lot of time in the workroom," she added. "What were you making, I wonder?"

I tensed. In truth, I was surprised it had taken so long for *someone* to notice. I was sure my sisters had *definitely* noticed, although neither of them had said anything. Isabella was clearly more perceptive than I'd realised. She was definitely, alarmingly close to the truth.

"Would I be at this school," I asked finally, "if I didn't have magic?"

"Perhaps," Isabella said. "I've never actually *seen* you use magic without your rings."

She smiled. "Take them off and turn me into a cat?"

I glared at her. There was no way I could and she knew it. Even if I palmed a ring, I couldn't change the spell. She'd suspect *something* if I turned her into a frog instead. It was time to go on the offensive.

"Tell me something," I said. "Are you *really* so desperate to prove that I don't have magic?"

She blinked, but I went on before she could say a word. "What would it prove about you," I asked, "if I *didn't* have magic? That you could snap your fingers and turn me into a three-headed horned toad whenever the whim struck you? Would that make you a great magician, or just a bully who likes kicking babies down the stairs? Do you really think that would impress your father?"

Isabella went white. "What do you know about my father?"

She clenched her fists. "Why did Akin tell you that?"

"I don't know," I said. I probably shouldn't have mentioned it at all, but I wanted to twist the knife. And I probably shouldn't push her any further, yet I couldn't stop myself. "Perhaps he prefers my company to yours..."

Isabella slapped me, hard. I twisted my head, a moment before she struck me. Something dug into my skin, pieces falling to the ground...I realised, as I staggered to the side, that she'd smashed the earring. My head was spinning in pain...it was the second time I'd been slapped, but it hurt worse. Far worse...

I heard Isabella chanting a spell, but I was too dazed to move. All I could do was throw up my arms, uselessly. The world spun around me, growing larger and larger...no, I was shrinking. Rose said something behind me, her voice cutting off mid-word...I hoped she was fine, even though I knew she wasn't. Zeya or her sister could easily have zapped her while she was trying to help me.

The world stopped spinning. I looked up. Isabella towered over me, her face twisted with rage and hatred. And, perhaps, a touch of self-loathing. She lifted her foot and brought it down hard. I scurried back, dimly aware that I'd been turned into a mouse. Isabella shouted something, deafeningly loud to the tiny creature's ears, then kicked out again. A hex struck the floor a second later, the blast so close that the shockwave picked me up and tossed me across the room. I landed against something soft - a bed - and fell to the ground. A great pair of feet stamped towards me. I ran to the wall, then stopped dead. There was nowhere to run...

Isabella raised her foot again, then froze. Her entire body locked solid, then plummeted forward. I squeaked in horror and ran between her legs, just as she hit the ground. It felt like an earthquake. And then an invisible force caught me, yanking me up into the air. My entire body was spinning, but I managed to get a glimpse of Sandy standing there. She looked furious. I wondered, as my spinning slowly came to an end, just how much trouble *she* was in. Rose had nearly been expelled, I had endless detentions and Isabella...

...Isabella had just been kicked off the netball team.

Sandy dropped me to the ground. "Turn back," she ordered, as she strode over to Isabella and released the spell. "Now."

I twitched. I *couldn't* release the spell. And I didn't know how long I'd have to wait until it broke. It wouldn't happen quickly enough to suit her.

"She can't," Isabella said. "She's a *zero*. No magic!"

"Be silent," Sandy ordered. She snapped her fingers in my direction. "Get up!"

I allowed myself a moment of relief as the spell unravelled. My entire body felt battered, as if I'd been pummelled from head to toe. I picked myself up carefully, catching sight of Rose behind me. Someone had frozen her...Zeya? Or Sandy? I tried to shoot her a reassuring look, but it was hard to fake it. Sandy looked murderous.

"Tell me," Sandy said. "What *were* you trying to do? Kill her?"

Isabella glared at her. "Did you hear what she said?"

Sandy looked back at her, her gaze cold. "Do you think it matters? What do you think would have happened, if you'd stamped on her? You would have crushed her!"

"It doesn't matter," Isabella snapped. Her voice rose. "She's a *zero!*"

"And you're on the verge of being expelled," Sandy said. "Do I have to watch you all every second of every day? Do I have to tie you to your beds and stun you to sleep? Do I...?"

"No," Isabella said. She darted a finger at me. Expecting a hex, I jumped aside. "I claim Scholar's Rights!"

Sandy took a step backwards in astonishment. "A honour duel? You would challenge Caitlyn to a honour duel?"

My head spun. A honour duel? Was she mad?

"Yes," Isabella said. Her voice was almost hysterical. "She *lied* about me. She...she...she...tricked me. She..."

"You're a firstie," Sandy said, coldly. "First years are not supposed to engage in any form of duelling."

"That's a tradition," Isabella said. She sounded very sure of herself. "It isn't actually a rule."

She lowered her voice. "I looked it up. A first year student can issue the challenge, if she feels she has cause. And you have to honour it."

I swallowed, hard. I hadn't bothered to look up the rules, but I suspected Isabella was right. Once the challenge was out in the open, it could not be denied. No one, not even a teacher, could deny her the right to demand the duel. And that meant...

"If you won, you would have the right to insist that Caitlyn left the dorm," Sandy said, coolly. I couldn't tell what she was thinking. "But if you *lost*, Caitlyn would have the right to insist that *you* left. Do you really want to take the risk?"

"I will not lose," Isabella said.

Sandy studied her for a long moment. "And you *really* want to explain the duel to your family?"

"They will understand," Isabella said. She eyed me. "Do you accept my challenge?"

I forced myself to think. Sandy would have told Isabella that she couldn't do it...if, of course, she *couldn't* do it.

"I don't know the rules," I said, playing for time. I knew the *adult* rules, but I couldn't imagine schoolchildren being encouraged to exchange death-spells. "How does it work?"

"It's very simple," Sandy said. "The two of you go into a warded circle and fight, exchanging spells until one of you can no longer continue. At that point, the winner gets to gloat a lot while the loser is put back together by the upperclassmen."

I paled. "Don't worry," she added, encouragingly. "The worst that could happen is that one of you has to go sleep somewhere else."

"I hear the janitorial staff have spare beds," Isabella put in, nastily. "Soaking wet, shared with frogs and their spawn..."

"Shut up," Sandy said.

I looked at her. "Are there any other rules?"

"Neither of you are allowed to do anything that might kill the other," Sandy said. I couldn't help feeling relieved, although I knew that accidents happened. "You can bring a wand if you like--" Isabella snorted "--but not a dagger or any other form of charmed blade."

She cleared her throat. "The challenge has been issued. Do you wish to accept or decline?"

Common sense told me I should decline. I *wasn't* a match for Isabella, even if I brought a dozen charged rings to the circle. And I *might* have been wrong when I'd accused her of betraying us. And yet, if I *did* decline, what would happen? I'd have to leave the dorm...I'd have to leave *Rose*. I couldn't leave her alone, not when the entire dorm would be against her.

And I didn't want to back down, not now. I'd come so far...

"I can take anything I like into the circle," I said, "as long as it won't actually *kill*?"

"Correct," Sandy said. "Do you accept?"

Isabella smirked at me. And I knew I was going to accept. Perhaps it was stupid, perhaps it was dangerous, but I was going to accept.

"Yes," I said, flatly.

"Very well," Sandy said. "I will make the arrangements for the duel. Until then, I expect the pair of you to behave yourselves. No arguing, no fighting, no hexing...I'll hex the person responsible into next week. Do you understand me?"

"Yes, Sandy," Isabella said, sweetly.

She shot me a look full of pure malice, combined with something I didn't care to interpret. I looked back at her, as steadily as I could. She thought I was a zero. She was right...

But that didn't mean I was powerless. Or helpless.

And Isabella, I promised myself silently, was in for a very nasty surprise.

THIRTY-EIGHT

The first thing I did on Tuesday, as soon as we had finished breakfast, was to go to the library and look up the rules for myself. Sandy might have gotten something wrong, after all. But the rules were almost exactly as she'd said. One student could issue a challenge to another and expect to have it honoured. There were a handful of rules surrounding the challenge and the honour duel itself, but nothing I could use against her. She'd issued the challenge and, in theory, we were equally matched.

Except she doesn't believe we are matched, I thought, sourly. Her obsession with proving I couldn't do magic was growing alarming. I couldn't help wondering if I should have been paying more attention to dorm politics. The McDonalds were firmly on Isabella's side, but what about the others? *Are they using me as an excuse not to side with her?*

Rose caught my eye. "Your sisters are coming over," she warned. "Look busy."

I looked up. Alana was striding towards me purposefully, Bella looking nervous as she brought up the rear. They'd probably heard already. The challenge had been issued last night, giving plenty of time for the story to spread around the school. My dorm mates had probably told everyone at breakfast. I braced myself, unsure what to expect. Alana had to be worried about the prospect of me losing. Someone would probably wind up using my defeat against her.

"Cat," Alana said. She shot Rose a sharp look. "We have to talk to you."

Rose shrugged. "I'll go find a couple more books," she said, as she stood. "Good luck."

"See if you can find a book on duelling tactics," I said. "And perhaps something on barely-legal hexes."

Alana's eyes flickered as she sat down. "Cat...are you mad?"

"I think that's the nicest thing you've said to me for the past five years," I said. It wasn't wise to bait her, but I *was* in a bad mood. Besides, classes started in twenty minutes. She didn't have time to do anything to me. "Are you well?"

"My ears must be playing tricks on me," Alana said. She made a show of rubbing them. "I have been informed by my spies that you accepted a formal challenge last night."

"Your spies are quite right," I said, dryly. Alana probably didn't *have* any spies, although I wouldn't put bribing one of my dorm mates past her. *Someone* had to keep an eye on Isabella for the family and *I* wasn't doing it. "Isabella challenged me to a honour duel."

Alana met my eyes. "I ask again," she said. "Are you mad?"

She went on before I could think of a response. "Maybe you have magic now, I don't know," she said. "But Isabella has been using magic since her seventh birthday. You don't stand a chance!"

"Perhaps," I said. I looked back at her for a long moment. "Are you worried about me or worried because you might be embarrassed by my fall?"

Alana twitched. "The family honour is at stake," she said, stiffly. "You *cannot* lose the duel."

"But you might," Bella put in. "And what happens then?"

"I get kicked out of the dorm," I said. I held up the rulebook. "I'll be forced to pack my stuff and find somewhere else to sleep."

"Which will be bad," Alana pointed out. "All your friends will be somewhere else."

I snorted. Apart from Rose, I didn't *have* any friends. But Alana *did* have a point. The girls in the other dorms would have already made friends by the time I arrived. Patronage networks would already be well-established. I would be lucky if I managed to find a place for myself.

Everyone would be resorted at the start of next year, of course, but even then...I would be lucky if I found a friend or two in another dorm.

"I don't have anything to lose," I said, instead. "You never know. I might wind up in your dorm."

Alana gave me a nasty look. I rather suspected that she'd make my life hell, if I *did* wind up sharing a dorm with her. It wouldn't take *her* long to notice that there was something wrong with my - presumed - magic. I was surprised she hadn't already commented on my new jewellery. *She* knew I hadn't been in the habit of wearing anything at home.

"Fine," she growled. "Do you want us to help you practice?"

"No, thank you," I said. "I can handle it."

Alana shook her head. "How long has it been since you started actually *using* magic?" She asked. "Three weeks? Four? You don't stand a chance against her. And what will happen to the family *then*?"

I laughed. "I'm sure the family is going to be ruined by two twelve-year-old girls exchanging hexes for an hour," I said, sarcastically. "Do you *really* think Isabella and I can do *real* damage?"

"It might," Alana said. "If you are exposed as a weak link..."

"I have time to learn," I said, trying not to show how much that comment *hurt*. "Alana..."

"I don't want to see you hurt," Bella put in. "Cat...we *do* care about you."

I glared at her. "Who was it who thought it would be a funny idea to hex my birthday presents? Who was it who decided it would be amusing if I couldn't move a muscle on our tenth birthday? Who was it who openly said I'd be kicked out of the family simply for not having magic? Who was it..."

"That was then," Bella said.

"You have magic now," Alana added. "I..."

I cut her off. "Would it have made a difference," I said, "If I *had* had magic back then?"

Alana opened her mouth, then closed it again. I knew the answer. If I'd had magic, *real* magic, things would have been different. I would have been able to trade hex for hex, rather than relying on trickery and dumb luck to keep myself afloat. They'd treated me poorly because I didn't have magic, but that didn't make me any less of a person. And I found it hard to care what they wanted, now. They didn't deserve anything from me.

"You know plenty of spells," Alana said, finally. "But you don't know how to cast them effectively. She'll wipe the floor with you."

"And I'm sure you will enjoy watching," I snarled. The bell rang. "You can tell everyone your old story about the foster child. I'm sure they'll believe you."

I rose and stalked away from the table. Rose joined me as I walked through the door, expecting a hex to strike me in the back at any moment. But nothing happened as I walked down to class, save for a handful of eyes following me. Everyone seemed to be staring, even upperclassmen. Word of the duel had clearly spread from one end of the school to the other.

Rose caught my arm. "What did they want?"

"Nothing important," I said. I forced myself to calm down as we joined the line outside Practical Charms. "They just wanted to make sure I didn't lose."

"That's not a bad thing," Rose said. "Is it?"

I sighed. If my sisters had cared about me - me *personally* - I wouldn't have minded. It would have been *nice* to feel that someone was looking out for me. But I knew they didn't really care about anything, but their reputations. If Alana was right and Isabella *did* wipe the floor with me, their reputations were going to suffer too. Alana might be challenged herself by an emboldened enemy...

Which will give that enemy a very nasty surprise, I thought. Alana had been practicing since her seventh birthday. Her remarks about Isabella applied just as much to her. *I'm sure she'll give anyone who tries to hurt her a bloody nose.*

Classes were as boring as I'd expected, although Magister Grayson seemed to have trouble keeping his eyes off me and Magistra Solana insisted on running through the basic principles of a honour duel, before subverting them ruthlessly by telling us just how many ways there were to cheat. Isabella said nothing - tradition demanded that she didn't even acknowledge my presence until Saturday, when the duel would be held - but her cronies kept glancing at me and sniggering. I think they expected her to wipe the floor with me too. They'd have kept their options open if there was the slightest doubt.

It was almost a relief when classes came to an end and I could make my way down to the workroom. Akin was already there, fiddling with something that looked like a clockwork monstrosity. I made sure he kept his distance as I set up my supplies, including the sole bottle of my formula. If I survived the duel, I told myself, I really *would* have to think of a proper name. I couldn't be the *only* person who could use it safely, could I?

Probably not, I told myself, as I started to put together a dozen Objects of Power. *But finding another genuine zero might be tricky.*

I would have enjoyed myself, if it wasn't so serious. Watching a protective ring take shape - I planned to wear it on my toe, hidden under my sock - was fascinating. So too was the brew that took a potion's magic and infused it into a gemstone. It wouldn't be *quite* as effective as a *real* potion - I had the odd feeling that some of the magic was leaking - but it would suffice for the duel. A cluster of interlocking rings - some worn around my neck, others on my wrist - would give me an unexpected advantage. And the wands...

If this works, I thought grimly, *there will be no going back.*

I'd considered simply getting Rose to help me charge up a dozen rings. But that wouldn't be enough, not against Isabella. She already knew there was *something* odd about my jewellery, even if she didn't know precisely *what*. The ancient textbooks open in front of me provided other options, some of which could pass for Devices of Power as long as no one looked at them too closely. Isabella hadn't objected to me taking Devices of Power into the ring. I rather assumed that meant she'd been taught how to handle them.

And if my work survives the coming duel, I reminded myself, *someone will insist on taking a very close look at them.*

The thought was enough to make me shiver. I'd planned to tell my father the truth, over the winter hols. Now...now, he was going to find out after the duel. I had no idea how he'd react, when he found out about the challenge...let alone the Objects of Power. Would he want me to back down, to grovel rather than risk revealing the truth? Or would he expect me to uphold the family's honour? I had no way to know.

"Caitlyn," Akin called. He was bending over his workbench, putting together a focusing device. It looked remarkably fragile - a set of carved lenses, held together by silver wire - but I knew that was an illusion. Done properly, the device would remain intact until the stress crumbled it into dust. "Can I have a word?"

I strode over to his workbench. I *really* didn't want him taking a close look at some of *my* work. Akin was knowledgeable as well as smart. He might figure out, ahead of time, that there was definitely something odd about my devices. Some of them - the rings, in particular - had lasted much longer than they should.

"I suppose," I said. I looked down at his focusing device for a long moment. "That's for her, isn't it?"

"Yes," Akin said. He didn't look particularly embarrassed. I wasn't sure why that bothered me. "She wanted a few Devices of Power of her own."

I scowled. "Doesn't that bother her?"

Akin looked up at me, one elegant eyebrow rising. "Doesn't it bother you?"

I shrugged, conceding the point. "What are you making her?"

He smiled. "What are you making for yourself?"

"Nothing I care to talk about," I said. Akin was good, but he couldn't match me. And he'd given me an idea. I had three days to add a few other tricks to my list. "You should be teaching her how to make them for herself."

"I believe she is currently training with her friends," Akin said. His smile grew wider. "Or playing games. It's hard to tell the difference sometimes."

I nodded. Dad had taught all three of us some games that were meant to help us develop our magic, although they'd been useless for me. I'd always wound up frozen, waiting helplessly for the spell to wear off or someone to release me. In hindsight...I wished, suddenly, that Dad had known the truth. But so much knowledge had been lost with the Thousand-Year Empire that Dad had no way to know what he was missing.

He didn't even think there was something odd about the way I threw off spells, I thought, tiredly. *That* was going to change, whatever else happened. *He just thought my magic was repressed.*

"I'm sure it will be a spectacular duel," I said, crossly. "Are your friends already laying bets?"

"Of course," Akin said. "The odds are currently five-to-one in Isabella's favour, although quite a few people are betting on you. Do you want to place a bet?"

I shook my head. My parents had warned us against gambling. Maybe it started out harmless, Dad had said, but it could easily grow into an addiction. He'd known people who had gambled away their entire lives, just because they were convinced their luck would change tomorrow. And they'd almost always been wrong. It was a mistake, he'd warned, to gamble when you couldn't afford to lose.

And I don't have anything to gamble with, I thought. *Unless I ask for an advance on my allowance...*

I glanced at him. "Are you betting?"

"That would be unfair," Akin said. "And I think the odds are a great deal more even than Isabella thinks. Is that not correct?"

"Of course," I said. "I may have only recently started using magic, but I have been making up for lost time."

"So I hear," Akin said. He shrugged. "You *do* know that Isabella won't be holding back?"

"I know," I said. I shivered, feeling cold. I'd been convinced, last night, that she intended to kill me. Sandy might well have saved my life. "I won't be holding back either."

Akin smiled as he slotted the lenses into place. "I trust you'll understand if I don't wish you luck," he said. "Isabella and I do have to share a house, you know."

"I understand," I said.

The thought made me smile. I'd never been to Rubén Hall, but I doubted it was much smaller than Aguirre Hall. Akin and Isabella could avoid each other for the entire winter holiday, if they wished. They probably had their own dining rooms. Why not? Alana and Bella had asked for their own, years ago. Mum had said no, but I had a suspicion she might change her mind as her daughters grew older. All three of us were meant to be developing our own network of friends and clients over the next few years.

I met his eyes. "What's she like? As a sister, I mean?"

Akin shrugged. "Driven," he said. "I told you about my father, didn't I? Isabella spent most of the last five years in the library, trying to master as many spells as possible to prove herself worthy. I generally find it easier to nod and then let her get on with it while I concentrate on my own studies. Dad...was not too pleased when I insisted on taking the one-star exam."

"But he let you continue," I said.

"Yeah," Akin agreed. "I took the two-star the following year."

I frowned. Carioca Rubén *should* have been delighted that his son was learning to forge Devices of Power. If nothing else, he and his successors wouldn't be dependent on outside forgers who didn't have blood ties to the family. But if he felt that Akin *had* to be his successor, he might have had other ideas. Studying for the two-star would have consumed much of Akin's time for the entire year.

"She's vindictive," Akin added. "She never forgets a slight. She's been known to drive servants out of the family, simply because she dislikes them. She once destroyed my favourite toy because we'd had a fight. I sometimes think she'll eventually challenge our father for control over the family. *That* will be something to watch, from a very safe distance."

"Ouch," I said. I couldn't imagine *Alana* challenging my father. It would end badly. But then, Alana had no reason to doubt that she was the heir. She could be patient. Isabella didn't have that luxury. "Are you going to let her?"

"I don't want to lead the family," Akin said, bluntly. "Isabella...is the one who takes after our father. No *wonder* they don't get along."

"I suppose," I said. What would happen, I wondered, to Isabella if she issued the challenge...and lost? Her father wouldn't be particularly forgiving. A challenge burned bridges, no matter the outcome. "Do you have more in common with your mother?"

"I'm not sure, really," Akin said. He sounded oddly dismissive. I was surprised. No one would ever dismiss *my* mother. "Mother...is a society wife. She's not interested in anything *magic*."

I blinked. "Why not?"

Akin held up a carving blade. "Power comes in many forms," he said. I blinked. Was there a hidden message in his words? "You should know that. Don't you?"

And he smiled.

CHAPTER
THIRTY-NINE

I couldn't help feeling nervous when I stepped into the Great Hall on Saturday, even though I'd had a week to prepare my defences. The crowd of students - lowerclassmen and upperclassmen - parted as I walked through them, followed by Rose and Henrietta. I was wearing enough jewellery to make me rattle, a handful of earrings jangling together as I headed toward the centre of the giant room. A low rustle ran through the room as they saw the spectacles on my nose and the devices on my belt. I tensed, despite myself. There didn't seem to be a teacher in sight.

"Stop," Sandy ordered, shortly. She sounded as tense as I felt. My heart was thumping like a drum. "Wait there."

I looked around the room. Someone had drawn out a giant warding circle on the floor, surrounded by a handful of glowing runes. Our spells would be trapped inside the circle, if they'd done their work properly. We could step out of the circle at any moment, but that would be counted as a forfeit. The rules *also* stated that shoving someone out of the circle was a perfectly legitimate way to win.

Isabella was standing on the far side of the room, flanked by Zeya and Ayesha McDonald. She wore the same school uniform as myself, but she'd added a belt lined with three wands and two Devices of Power, one of which I didn't recognise. Akin had made it for her, I assumed. I'd tried to sneak a peek into his private storeroom, but he'd warded it against all intrusion. Luckily, the hex had worn off before anyone had come to investigate.

Isabella looked confident, yet I thought I knew her well enough to tell that she was nervous. I knew she had far more to lose than I.

And our family will really not be weakened if I lose, I thought, dryly. *This duel is nothing more than hurt feelings run amuck.*

I met Isabella's eyes for a second, then looked away. Alana and Bella were standing in the middle of the room, their faces expressionless. Robin stood next to a couple of other upperclassmen, exchanging bets. I wondered, absently, if he was betting on me or Isabella, although I suspected I'd probably never know. He wasn't the only one placing bets, either. I could see several older students doing the same thing. Maybe, in hindsight, I should have put a bet on myself. The odds were strongly against me.

Sandy cleared her throat. "Be silent," she said. The whisper of conversation faded into the background as we all stared at her. "Isabella of Raven Dorm has claimed Scholar's Rights against Caitlyn of Raven Dorm."

There was a long pause. My heart was beating so loudly I was surprised no one else could hear it.

"By tradition, the winner may ask the loser to leave the dorm," Sandy added, her voice calm and composed. She glanced at me, then at Isabella. "There will be no other consequences for losing. Is that understood?"

I nodded. I was too nervous to speak. Isabella nodded, too.

"Very good," Sandy said. "Isabella of Raven Dorm. Do you still wish to claim Scholar's Rights?"

"I do," Isabella said.

Sandy looked displeased. I couldn't help feeling sorry for her. She wouldn't face any punishment - not officially - for allowing Isabella and I to duel, but unofficially...the whole affair would look very bad on her record. Caught between two powerful families, she'd let the whole affair spin out of control. In hindsight, perhaps she should have clamped down harder on us. But she didn't want to turn our families into *enemies*.

Too late for that now, I thought, as Sandy turned to face me. *No one is going to be very pleased with her.*

"Caitlyn of Raven Dorm," Sandy said. "Do you wish to accept the challenge?"

I hesitated. Would it really be that bad if I conceded? I could go to another dorm...but I didn't want to run. No one would respect me if I just surrendered. And besides, I didn't want to leave Rose alone in Raven Dorm. She'd be outnumbered eight to one. Isabella wouldn't show Rose any mercy for not bowing the knee to Isabella when Rose had had the chance.

"I do," I said.

My voice sounded weak, even to me. This could go horrendously wrong. I didn't *think* I could be killed, or even seriously injured, but I *could* be humiliated. If I was wrong, if I'd made a mistake...I swallowed, hard. It had to be done. I wasn't going to allow Isabella to intimidate me into submission.

But perhaps you should, a little voice whispered at the back of my head. *She is far more powerful than you.*

I told that voice to shut up. My sisters had been far more powerful than me from the moment we'd turned seven, but I'd never let them crush my soul. I'd fought back, using trickery and knowledge to even the balance. And yet...I knew, all too well, that eventually I would have lost. Permanently.

And yet, I now know what I can do, I told myself. *I am not weak or powerless.*

"Then enter the circle," Sandy ordered.

My legs felt like they were made of lead. I had to force myself to walk forward and cross the circle. The runes seemed to brighten as I passed, sealing us inside. Most magicians would be a little uncomfortable inside the circle, according to the books. Isabella certainly looked jumpy as she crossed the line. Maybe that was an advantage, I told myself. Or maybe it was something that didn't matter. Jumpy or not, Isabella was still a formidable opponent.

I braced myself as the upperclassmen walked around the circle, checking and rechecking the wards. Judging by the runes, it looked as though the circle would absorb any stray magic rather than reflecting it back at us. That was a good thing, I supposed. Neither of us would be able to bounce a spell off the wards and into the other's back. Isabella met my eyes, just for a second, as the runes grew even brighter. I could make out the disdain on her face.

Zero, she mouthed.

I glared at her, but my planned insult was cut off by Sandy.

"You both know the rules," she said, sternly. She'd gone through them with us the previous evening. "The duel will start when I blow the whistle and end when one of you is unable to continue. If either of you want to quit, you can just step out of the circle. Do you understand?"

I nodded. After a moment, Isabella nodded too.

"Good," Sandy said. She lifted the whistle to her lips. "Good luck."

She blew the whistle. Isabella held up her hand and cast a hypnotic spell. I rolled my eyes at her as the crowd started to laugh. The spell wouldn't have caught even a weak magician for long. One of my earrings grew warm as she pushed more and more magic into the spell, but it had no effect on me. I lifted my hand and mimed casting a spell, then released one of the spells I'd stored in the rings. Isabella darted to one side, tossing back a trio of spells of her own. I dodged two of them and caught the third with a deflection spell.

Isabella eyed me darkly, then hurled a nastier-looking spell at me. It struck me...and shimmered out of existence. I felt the world spin, just for a second, before everything snapped back to normal. She'd tried to turn me into something, only to have the spell break down too quickly to do anything. I saw her eyes go wide - for a moment, I thought I saw fear - as she cast five more hexes in quick succession. Two were absorbed by my defences, while the remaining three missed.

I smirked. "Give up?"

Isabella snapped out three more spells as I drew a wand from my belt. I was very proud of it, even though using the device in public was a risk. Her first spell impacted on the wood and faded away, a faint tingle passing over my fingers as the last of the magic shimmered out of existence. I battered away her next spell too, taking a step towards her. Isabella moved back, then stopped herself before she could accidentally back over the line. I groaned, inwardly. It would have been a great deal easier if Isabella had managed to forfeit the duel.

Her hand dropped to her belt. She drew a wand and pointed it at me. I braced myself, knowing that the wand would focus her power. It might - *might* - be enough to let her win, if she struck me with concentrated magic. I stepped to one side as she cast the spell, then threw back another stored spell. Isabella deflected it, her own spell slashing into the ground in front of me. I grinned as I waved my wand, tauntingly.

I realised my mistake a second later as the floor below me shifted and melted, trapping my feet. Isabella laughed, then launched a series of spells at me. I ducked and dodged as best as I could, but I knew it was only a matter of time before I was caught. Two of my earrings were already burning hot, the pain making it hard to concentrate. I unleashed two more of my own spells in quick succession, then hastily scrambled out of my shoes. Laughter echoed from behind me as I jumped backward, leaving my shoes stuck in the floor. Someone was going to have a very hard time getting them out afterwards.

Isabella cast another spell, then another. My earrings grew even hotter. I gasped in pain, then hastily pulled the overheating ones off before they actually started to burn my skin. I heard her snicker, an instant before the next spell struck me. My entire body locked solid, unable to move. With two of the earrings missing, my defences were weakened...

"She can't move," Isabella called. "I..."

The spell broke. I saw her eyes widen with astonishment as I launched two more stored spells at her, making her leap aside. The crowd cheered, some of them calling my name while others booed Isabella. I wondered, suddenly, just how popular Isabella actually *was* outside the dorm. Perhaps it was her father they were booing.

Her eyes hardened as she yanked one of the odder-looking devices off her belt and pointed it at me. I saw it light up, a second before an overpowered spell blasted over my head and slammed against the wards. Someone shouted in disbelief. I allowed myself a smile - Akin *had* done a good job - as I pulled the dispeller from my belt, catching and dispelling the second spell before it could do any harm. Isabella recoiled as I plunged forward, holding the dispeller out ahead of me. Her protections started to collapse, but she managed to force me back just in time.

I grabbed one of my more interesting creations and held it up, just as Isabella blasted me with a third spell. A beam of light struck me...and froze. The device vibrated in my hand, violently. I realised, in a moment of brilliant amusement and relief, just what she was trying to do. Shatter spells were designed to break Devices of Power - they were the standard defence against people armed with magical weapons - but they were useless against *Objects* of Power. I heard people gasping behind me as my device remorselessly *failed* to shatter into debris. Brilliant magic cascaded around me, never touching my skin.

And then it flickered, suddenly. Isabella stared at me, real fear written all over her face. I'd done the impossible. Everyone had *seen* me do the impossible. She'd planned to use the shatter spells as her ace in the hole - the harmonics they created should have destroyed my devices - but instead, they'd survived. And what did that say about me?

I held the device up, reaching for a second device with my other hand. Isabella merely stared, her face glistening with sweat. She'd probably pushed herself to the limit casting that spell. And yet, I'd survived it. I could practically *see* her trying to decide what to do...if she should try to find a way to continue the fight or if she should take a step or two backwards and concede. And yet, if she conceded, she'd never hear the end of it. She'd made her bed, and now she had to sleep in it.

Silence fell as we studied each other for a long chilling moment. Isabella moved first, casting a series of brilliant spells towards me. I dodged or deflected them, silently complementing her on her chosen tactic. With half of my earrings gone, a couple of direct hits might be enough to take me out long enough for her to win. I gritted my teeth, then threw the second device towards her. It lit up so brightly that I heard her cry out in agony - my spectacles darkened automatically - before she managed to hit it with a blasting hex. The device exploded, brilliantly.

Quick thinking, I conceded, ruefully. *Too quick.*

Isabella let out a snarl and hefted her focusing device. I pulled my last Object of Power off my belt and held it up, just in time to catch the spell she hurled at me. This time, the magic was redirected right back at her, the spell reshaped into something different. Her Device of Power shivered in her hands, then shattered, pieces flying in all directions. Isabella screamed in agony. I saw blood dripping from the cuts on her hands and splashing on the floor. If she chose to concede now...

She didn't. Somehow, she drew her final wand and launched a spell at me. I adjusted the Object of Power, caught the spell and threw it back. Isabella threw up her bleeding arms, an instant before she shrank with terrifying speed. A moment later, there was a slug on the floor where she'd been standing. I blinked in astonishment. I really *hadn't* expected it to work *that* well.

Silence fell. I was aware, suddenly *very* aware, of hundreds of eyes watching me. I'd bent - if not broken - an unspoken rule. Turning someone into a frog or a mouse or something that could *signal* was one thing, but turning someone into something that couldn't...it was a duel, but still. I had a feeling I'd be made to pay for that, sooner or later...

I caught my breath. Sandy started to count, loudly. Isabella hadn't broken the spell. Perhaps she *couldn't* break the spell. And if she stayed that way for another twenty seconds, I'd win.

"Twenty," Sandy said. Others were starting to chant along with her, their voices shaking the hall. "Twenty-one...Twenty-two..."

My heart pounded. Either I won or...

"Thirty," Sandy said. The crowd went wild, screaming and shouting in delight. I wondered how long that would last when everyone who'd bet against me worked out how much they had to pay. "I declare Caitlyn the *winner!*"

I sagged, feeling sweat pouring down my back. I'd won, barely.

"Undo the spell," Sandy ordered.

I reached for the dispeller and pressed it against Isabella's quivering form. There was a flash of light and she returned to normal, lying on the floor and looking stunned. Sandy helped her to her feet, taking the opportunity to give her a brief examination. It didn't look as though she was physically hurt, but she was clearly shocked. I almost felt sorry for her.

"Well, Isabella," Sandy said. "Do you have any words for Caitlyn?"

Isabella looked at me. I saw a confusing mixture of emotions cross her face before she shook her head, once. She knew what I'd done, she knew what I'd made. There was no way the secret could be kept any longer, not now.

"Very well done, Caitlyn," Sandy said. "Do you wish to order Isabella out of the dorm?"

I hesitated. Part of me *wanted* to put the boot in. Isabella wouldn't have hesitated to kick *me* out, if she'd won. And yet...it would be cruel. Or would it be crueller to let her *stay* in the dorm, with everyone *very* aware she was only allowed to stay on sufferance? I honestly didn't know.

"Leave Rose and me in peace," I said, as Rose ran up to me. Alana and Bella were right behind her. "And you can stay."

Isabella nodded, wordlessly.

Rose gave me a tight hug. Alana looked at me as if she'd never quite seen me before, as if she thought someone else was impersonating her sister. I wondered if *she* realised what I'd done. There had been so much light - and raw magic - that it was possible that she hadn't realised, not really. But Isabella definitely knew. Akin...had he suspected my true nature? I had to speak to my father as quickly as possible.

The crowd parted as the Castellan strode forward, followed by Magister Tallyman. I blinked in surprise. I hadn't realised that he'd be monitoring the duel...although, in hindsight, that had been a little naïve of me. The teachers would have wanted to make sure the duel didn't get out of hand.

Or any more out of hand, I thought, darkly.

Magister Tallyman took the device I was holding and inspected it, briefly. "Young lady," he said, sharply. "I think you owe us an explanation."

I sighed. There was no way I could fool *him* into thinking it was an ordinary Device of Power. He knew too much to be fooled. It was time to face the music.

Again.

CHAPTER
FORTY

The Castellan's office looked a *little* more welcoming this time, I decided, as I leaned against my father and sipped a cup of tea. Magister Tallyman and Magistra Haydon sat beside us, while the Castellan himself occupied the seat behind the desk. My surviving Objects of Power rested in front of us, one of them partly dismantled. It hadn't taken Magister Tallyman long to deduce the truth, and insist on summoning my father. I really didn't blame him.

"Caitlyn," the Castellan said. I put my tea aside and sat up. "Perhaps you could tell us *exactly* what happened?"

"And why," Magistra Haydon put in.

I took a breath, then launched into a full explanation. The potions formula - and the explosion, the explosion that shouldn't have happened. The experiments - and how no spell had clung to me for very long. The fan I'd made - and the Objects of Power. The gemstones and rings and everything else I'd put together, then used in the duel.

"Objects of Power," my father breathed. "You *made* them."

Magister Tallyman leaned forward. "*How?*"

"I'm a zero," I said, simply. "I don't have *any* magic of my own, not even a *hint* of magical sensitivity. But that means that I don't have any magic to disrupt the Objects of Power as they're put together. And *that* means that their magical fields are not disrupted right from the start."

"I see, I think," Magister Tallyman said. "But why didn't they write this *down?*"

"They may have thought it was obvious," I said. I'd guessed as much, back when I'd worked out the truth. "And the term *zero* has changed its meaning over the last few centuries. Back then, it referred to...well, to someone like me. Now, it means anyone with low magical potential. But someone with low potential still couldn't produce Objects of Power."

"Clever," Magister Tallyman said. "Why didn't you tell me?"

I hesitated, choosing my words carefully. "I wanted to tell my family first," I said, finally. "And then events got a little out of control."

"A *little*," the Castellan repeated. "You've had a very eventful year, Caitlyn."

He looked at my father. "How do you intend to proceed?"

"I will have to give it some thought," Dad said. "Obviously, it's now clear that Caitlyn will *never* be able to pass most of the traditional classes. But her true talents need to be developed too. It may be better for her to be trained somewhere else."

"There are few places safer than Jude's," Magister Tallyman said. "You *do* understand the implications, sir?"

My father nodded, stiffly. "I am aware of the potential dangers," he said. "However, allowing Caitlyn to remain at Jude's brings its own dangers. Exploding potions may be the least of them."

"We *can* alter our classes for her," Magister Tallyman said.

"At some cost," the Castellan countered. He looked at Dad. "The decision must be yours, sir."

"And hers," Dad said. He smiled at me. "With your permission, I would like to speak to my daughter before we come to any final agreement."

"Of course," the Castellan said. He met my eyes. "I don't think I have to tell you, young lady, that you were very lucky."

I nodded, eyes downcast.

"Try not to get into another duel," the Castellan added. "It would be most awkward."

My father rose. I followed him through the door, past the grim-faced secretary and down the corridor. Isabella was standing at the bottom, talking to a pale-skinned man with a nasty scar on his face. Her father, I guessed. He gave *my* father a sharp look, which became calculating when he looked at me. I wondered just what Isabella - and Akin - had told him over the last hour or so. He knew what I was...

I half-expected my father to challenge him, right there and then. Instead, the two men merely glowered at one another before heading onwards. Isabella glanced at me, her face pale. I wondered just what her father had said to her, while I was explaining what I'd discovered. I didn't think her father would be pleased she'd fought the duel and lost. Despite myself, I felt sorry for her. Her father was clearly a very unpleasant man.

"You shouldn't have fought that duel," my father said, once we were in a private room. "It could have ended very badly."

"I couldn't back down," I said, stiffly.

"You really should have contacted me at once," Dad added. "Your gift...Caitlyn, your gift is unique. Do you know that?"

"I don't think so," I said. "My gift might not be noticeable if I'd been born to a commoner family."

"Perhaps," my father agreed, after a moment. "We will certainly be looking for other true zeroes."

He sat down, heavily. "Right now, you're probably the single most important person in the kingdom," he added. "Even the king himself may be less important. Your gift will allow us to produce dozens - perhaps hundreds - of Objects of Power. There will be trouble when the story leaks - and it will."

I swallowed. "Dad..."

"I should take you home right now," Dad added. He looked concerned. "Jude's is supposed to be politically neutral, Cat, but...but someone might decide it's worth running the risk of starting a war just to get at you. You are important, and you are vulnerable."

"I know," I admitted. "I wish..."

"I know you wanted to fight," Dad said. "And I am proud of you."

I smiled. I'd wanted to hear those words for a very long time.

"I suspect you were meant to craft weapons for your sisters," Dad added, after a moment of thought. "The triplet triad would have worked, if we'd understood your true nature from the start. Alana and Bella could have wielded Objects of Power you created. Now..."

He sighed. "I understand that you have been getting along better with your sisters?"

"Just a little," I said. It would be hard for Alana to claim I was useless after I'd beaten Isabella, even if I *still* didn't have any magic. "Dad...it isn't easy for me to trust them."

Dad looked regretful. "I know," he said. "I'm sorry, Cat. I have failed you."

"At least you taught me what I needed to know," I said. "And...things will be different now, won't they?"

"Yes," Dad said.

He met my eyes. "Do you want to stay at Jude's?"

I looked back at him. "Is it not the safest place?"

"It depends," Dad said. "On one hand, the school is heavily defended; on the other, a student could hurt or kill you without being stopped until it was too late. And while I doubt someone would try to take you from the school, they might well try to have you killed. Your mere existence upends the balance of power between the king and his rivals.

"And yet, keeping you at the hall will cause its own problems," he added. "There will be no major incidents if you are kidnapped there."

He sighed. "What do you want to do?"

I honestly didn't know. Jude's had been a very mixed experience for me. I'd found a good friend in Rose and discovered my talents, but...but I'd also faced attack from other students *and* now everyone knew what I was. I wanted to keep working with Magister Tallyman - and potions, now they knew what I could do - yet I didn't want them to make too many accommodations for me.

And yet, if I left, Rose would be alone. Dad wouldn't even *consider* taking her as an apprentice until she graduated.

"They'll have to make some allowances for me," I mused. "Won't they?"

"We can work out the details," my father said. "You probably won't be able to graduate - not in most of your classes - but I don't think that matters. You can set your own price for Objects of Power."

I smiled. Repaying my debts to Robin would be easy.

"But there is another point," my father added. "You've made an enemy of Isabella Rubén and...and *that* will cause you problems."

"I know," I said.

"And you've been working with her brother," Dad said. "What do you think of him?"

"I think he's a nicer person than his sister," I said, after a moment. "He isn't a bad guy."

"He's a Rubén," Dad warned. "And *cannot* be trusted completely."

He paused. "Do you remember what I told you, back when I picked you up from school?"

I nodded, slowly. "That Carioca Rubén is trying to take our place in Magus Court."

"Yes," Dad said. "But now - as long as we have you - our position is secure. He may do something drastic when it sinks in."

"But not at Jude's," I said. "Right?"

"Perhaps," Dad said. He held up a hand. "Never underestimate what a desperate man will do. Your mere existence shatters all of his dreams."

I groaned. I didn't want to think about it. I'd been raised in a magical family, but I'd never expected to inherit anything beyond the name. In hindsight, it had given me a freedom that I'd never really appreciated. But now...now I wished I knew more. It would have prepared me...

My heart sank. On one hand, I was *important* now. It was what I'd wanted. No one could deny that, not now. But, on the other hand, I was still vulnerable. *Very* vulnerable. I'd traded one kind of prison for another. Dad had good reason to want to keep me under firm control. So did anyone else who understood what I could do.

"I'm going to take you home for the weekend," Dad said. "Under the circumstances, the Castellan can hardly deny me *that*. Your friend Rose can come too. But...after that, you'll have to make a choice. And whatever you choose, you will be stuck with it."

I nodded, stiffly. Did I *want* to stay at Jude's? In truth, I didn't know.

Rose needs me, I thought. It was an answer, of sorts. *And I can try to mend fences with Alana and Bella.*

"I'll stay," I said, finally.

"Very good," Dad said. He didn't look pleased or unhappy. It was hard to tell what he was thinking. "Cat..."

He paused. "I wish I'd known more, right from the start," he added. "I know you didn't have an easy time of it at home...and I even encouraged it, in the hopes it would bring out your magic. I didn't want to consider the possibility that you wouldn't have magic. It certainly never occurred to me that that might prove an advantage."

I swallowed. My father had always struck me as infallible. He'd always been a reassuring presence in my life - in *our* lives. Strict, but fair; authoritative, but reasonable. Even when he'd insisted that I had magic, that I *had* to have magic, he'd had a reason for it. Now, his quiet admission that he'd been wrong *hurt*. I would have traded almost anything if it meant I would never to have to hear him say those words.

"I understand, Father," I said. "All is forgiven."

"I doubt I can ever forgive myself," my father said. He rose, holding out a hand. "I am proud of you, Cat. *Very* proud."

I took his hand. "Shall we go?"

My father smiled. "Why not?"

The End

AFTERWORD

You may be interested to know some of the story behind this novel (and possible trilogy, if sales hold up.)

Back in late 2014, I had a brilliant idea for *Schooled In Magic*. It would, I reasoned, allow me to avoid one of my pet hates - ancient artefacts of power that are superior to anything in the modern world - by giving said artefacts a very good reason to exist. There was just one minor problem...I couldn't fit the story into *Schooled In Magic*. By then, I was writing *Love's Labour's Won*...Book VI of the series. It couldn't be changed enough to work without either rewriting the series (which was obviously impossible) or a great deal of reworking (which would cost me the original concept.) And so I put the idea aside for later consideration.

A couple of years later, I went through my list of ideas and dragged this concept back out into the light. I wanted to expand my reader base *and* explore some ideas that couldn't be included in *Schooled In Magic*. Once separated from SIM, the idea expanded rapidly into a complete backstory - some of which is mentioned here, some of which will be explored in the next two books - and a universe of its own. Eventually, I had to write it.

I've always been fascinated by how societies change, for better or worse, when new ideas and concepts are introduced...or lost. What would happen, I asked myself, if magic was effectively as universal as music? There would still be great magicians, as there are great musicians, but there wouldn't be such a tight barrier between the magical world and the muggles. Most people would know - and use - a few simple spells, even if they don't understand how they work. What sort of world would this create?

And what would happen if someone couldn't use magic at all?

Cat was an odd character to write, for many reasons. She's four years younger than Emily was, when she started her adventures. She combines the knowledge of her family with a painful teenage insecurity, something made worse by the grim awareness that she's powerless, that she's effectively a squib. The limits to her knowledge - like most young teens, she has no idea of the limits of her knowledge - actually weaken her. She thinks that magic is the be-all and end-all of life and spends most of her time trying to study it, to grasp it for herself, but she doesn't have the perspective to realise that there is a life outside of magic or the experience to realise that magic doesn't quite work right around her.

And, despite her disability (and it is a disability), Cat manages to keep going.

It probably will surprise a few of my readers to know that I went to boarding school - and I hated it. 'Boarding School Syndrome' is a real thing. And yet, it is difficult to explain this to adults. Most of the people I know didn't live away from their homes until they turned eighteen, when they were (slightly) more mature. They went to university or joined the military or something along those lines.

For children, it's a different story. Going to boarding school is like going to prison, only with worse food. (The scandal about lobster takeaways in UK prisons broke while I was at school.) There is simply no way to get away from your fellow inmates - sorry, pupils. You are forced to be with them 24/5. (We got to go home on the weekends.) There is no escape, ever. The teachers do as little as possible, leaving the weaker boys at the mercy of the strong.

Some students do well in such an environment. Those who *are* strong either gain friends easily or, at the very least, are relatively safe. Others do not. People like me are isolated, bullied and sometimes driven to suicide.

Cat, in many ways, has it far worse - she's seemingly powerless, a weakling trapped in a world of superpowered kids.

And yet, she keeps going. I find that admirable.

I hope you enjoyed this book. If you did, please leave a review. And if you want a sequel, please let me know.

Christopher Nuttall
Edinburgh, 2017

If you enjoyed *The Zero Blessing*, you might like...

INSTRUMENT OF PEACE
Rebecca Hall

Raised in the world-leading Academy of magic rather than by his absentee parents, Mitch has come to see it as his home. He's spent more time with his friends than his family and the opinion of his maths teacher matters far more than that of his parents.

His peaceful world is shattered when a devastating earthquake strikes and almost claims his little brother's life. This earthquake is no natural phenomenon, it's a result of the ongoing war between Heaven and Hell. To protect the Academy, one of the teachers makes an ill-advised contract with a fallen angel, unwittingly bringing The Twisted Curse down on staff and students alike.

NEW GIRL

M itch gaped at the new girl. It had been two years since a student last transferred into the Academy and Nikola had at least had the decency to come from the Munich Academy of Magic; Hayley had come from Auckland Girls' Grammar. Who cared if she was a genius at maths? Mitch and his team would have won the interschool competitions if it weren't for her. Not that that mattered at the world's premier school of magic.

Mitch knew most of the school, he knew many of his year mates better than he knew his own family, he'd certainly spent more time with them, and all of them had been enrolled since birth. Many of them came from families that had attended the Academy for generations; Mitch himself was eleventh generation. All of them were gifted magicians. Hayley was just a gifted wet blanket; Mitch didn't recall ever seeing her with any friends.

How long? he scribbled in the margins of his book, tilting it so that his best friend, Bates, could read.

One week max, Bates wrote back, his tidy hand highlighting just how messy Mitch's was. Mitch looked at where Hayley stood awkwardly at the front of the classroom. The inter-school competitions were largely pointless, their teachers had some bullshit reason about learning to interact with non-magicians but the accelerated curriculum taught at the Academy meant that they outstripped their opponents by miles. They were rarely willing to make friends after that. Mitch was willing to concede that Hayley was indeed a genius at maths but she'd never be able to catch up in everything else. It was only a matter of time before their teachers realised that and sent her to study at another of the magic schools. He thought the closest was in South Africa.

Hayley turned away from Mr McCalis, flipping long black hair over her shoulder. Mitch had overheard some of her classmates calling her Angel Girl. With that curling black hair and darkly tanned skin she didn't look much like the traditional image of an angel but what little he'd seen of her suggested that she was cold, remote and flawless.

She looks nervous. Bates wrote.

She should be. Mitch scrawled back. It wasn't just academics she'd be behind in, even Mitch's baby brother would be better at magic than she was. They'd grind her into the dust by the end of the day, the first magic class of the term was always dangerous and for once Mitch was looking forward to it.

"Why don't you introduce yourself Miss Lake," Mr McCalis said, signing off on the last of the paperwork she'd given him, "and then we can get started."

"Hi," she plastered a smile across her face, "my name is Hayley. Doctor Dalman offered me a place at your school last year and I'm excited to be here." She almost sounded sincere. At least she wasn't saying 'it's nice to meet you, let's all be friends'. Nikola had been here for two years and he hadn't made any with the possible exception of the infirmary staff. Mitch had never met anyone so sickly.

"Thank you Miss Lake," Mr McCalis said, "please take a seat." He walked around the classroom distributing worksheets and there was a collective groan as they recognised the questions from last year's exam, the hard ones that had been at the end, though Mitch noted that he'd changed the numbers in case anyone had thought to memorise the answers. "I'm not going to let you lollygag around just because it's the first day of a new year," Mr McCalis said. Anything you don't finish now you can complete as homework." There was another groan; they'd had better things to do over the summer break than revise maths. Mitch had spent most of the holidays at the beach with his new surfboard. A glance at the front of the room showed Hayley already hard at work, no doubt the final questions would trip her up.

"Earth to Mitch," Bates said, prodding his arm when he failed to respond, "not all of us are maths geniuses you know."

"Genii," Mitch retorted. He set his work out clearly, even though he could do it in his head, so that Bates could see what he was doing. Mitch glanced around the room, running a hand though sandy blond hair; everyone else was still working or having whispered conversations that were probably not about whatever question they were on. Hayley had finished and was standing by Mr McCalis' desk as he marked her work. Mitch scowled and began the final set of problems, his work bordering on illegibility.

"It's not a competition Mitch," Bates said, "slow down, I can't follow what you're doing." Mitch kept working; of course it was a competition, he'd been first in maths for years and he wasn't going to let Hayley take that away from him. He scribbled out the final answer and handed his work to Mr McCalis.

"I should make you rewrite this," Mr McCalis said. Mitch stared at the desk where Hayley's work was neatly laid out, every question correct. "But you may go," Mr McCalis said, ticking the final answer, "Miss Lake could use a tour of the school."

Mitch scowled, that wasn't what he'd had in mind. He glanced at where Hayley was seated, did his best to ignore the sniggers around him and waited impatiently while she put away her book, a year nine text on magical theory.

"Where are we going first?" Hayley asked once they'd stepped outside.

Mitch shrugged and ran through his friends' timetables in his head. Perhaps he did have to show her around but he didn't have to be seen doing it.

"The zoo," he finally decided. It would be empty at this time of year. Theory always came before practice and the animals were brought into the habitats as they were needed for Cryptozoology instead of being kept at the Academy. It was probably a logistical nightmare. The gardens and greenhouse for Cryptobotany were next, again empty.

"Do you want to see the lake next?" Mitch asked, shoving his hands into his pockets.

"I can see it just fine from here," she said fiddling with something hidden under her sleeve. Mitch sighed and led the way towards the Alchemy workshops. Hayley didn't seem to be impressed by the view of

Mount Ruapehu or Lake Moawhango or even the old buildings. Mitch had been told that they were amongst the oldest in the country and the then-principal had ensured that the army base would be built nearby. Nothing discouraged the curious like live weapons testing.

"You know we're not allowed jewellery right?" Mitch said. She was still fiddling with whatever it was in her sleeve and the brief flash of gold almost blinded him. He'd never been sure why jewellery was forbidden, one of the first things they learnt was that anyone who needed magical nick-knacks and toys would never be more than a second rate hack.

"You mean this?" She pulled out a long golden feather tipped with a white eye.

"What is that?" Mitch asked, "some kind of mutant peacock feather?" He'd never heard of gold peacocks before and he was reasonably sure that real animals didn't have 'shiny' versions like Pokémon did. Hayley shrugged.

They passed the Alchemy workshops and Mitch turned them towards the mundane classrooms, pointing out the blocks where their lessons on Teratology, Ancient Languages and Xenobiology would be held.

"Did you have to do languages at your school?" Mitch asked.

"They insisted, I spent the last two years learning French."

"They give us a new one every year," Mitch said. He probably half remembered more French than she did. Their teachers were very big on the linguistic underpinnings allowing him to pick up the sentence structure of most languages easily even if he was lousy at the vocabulary.

"So do you remember me, Angel Girl?" he asked. The library was next and while Mitch supposed he could explain the shelving system used for the magical texts he didn't really want to go indoors.

"Surfer boy was it? Or skater boy? After a while all of the sore losers start to blend together." Mitch scowled, after a summer spent surfing he could hardly complain about that one, he certainly looked the part, but he wouldn't be caught dead on a skateboard with his jeans hanging around his knees. He would never understand normal kids.

"I guess I deserved that, Hayley," he said realising that she might actually be fun to torment. Nikola had ignored their efforts to tease them and it had quickly become boring.

"It's Mitchell isn't it?"

"Yeah." Technically it was Bartholomew but he would go by that when Hell froze over and his classmates would laugh themselves sick if he started to go by his middle name, Harry. They'd provided him with a complete set of the Harry Potter books when they discovered it and followed it up with the Dresden Files a few years later. And as for the family tradition of naming your first son after your father? It would be a cold day in Hell before he named any child of his Archibald.

"What do you want Mitchell?" she asked, "You're not showing me around out of the kindness of your heart." She slipped the feather back up her sleeve, twisting it around her arm. Mitch would have suspected magnets if it had been sturdy enough to support them.

"I'm just trying to be friendly since it's your first day and all," Mitch said, forcing himself to meet her pale blue eyes. He thought they'd been a shade darker before but it was probably just a trick of the light.

"Friendly?"

"I never said I was good at it," Mitch mumbled, "but surely we can manage a friendly conversation."

"I'd settle for intelligent," Hayley replied.

"Yeah, sure, I can do that," Mitch said, realising as he did so that he sounded like a complete idiot. Hayley's tiny smile said that she agreed. "Err..." how did one go about talking to people they didn't know. He'd spent the last ten years with the same 32 people – 33 now, he corrected himself, and his year was one of the larger ones. He found it easier to talk to them than he did his own family; with the exception of Nikola of course, he'd prefer another awkward family dinner to that.

"It's a nice day," he managed. Dear god, did he really just say that? Maybe he should just give up on intelligent conversation. Hayley certainly didn't seem inclined to help him.

"It was." How was he supposed to respond to that? Point out the perfectly clear blue sky or the fact that Ruapehu had stopped spewing smoke into the air. Or possibly just take the not so subtle hint that he should get lost. The bell would be ringing for second period soon and they'd seen everything interesting.

"The Academy is very exclusive you know," he said, "some of the others aren't going to be happy about you getting in." Why the Hell was he warning her? He was one of them and he'd just committed social suicide. Well, maybe not, it seemed unlikely that Hayley would ever be close enough to their classmates to tell them about it.

Hayley shrugged, "I'm used to it. Anything else?"

"Umm," he racked his brain, trying to remember what else normal kids did that was different here. "No cellphones," he said at last, "magic interferes with wireless." TV and radio had never really caught on in the magical world and even DVD remotes were completely useless. God help them all the day someone invented wireless electricity.

"Internet?"

"Only in the library," Mitch said with a shrug. He'd never had much use for it.

"I've got Alchemy next," Hayley said a second before the bell rang. It sounded like a cross between a fire alarm and a dentist's drill and Mitch was certain that it was higher pitched than last year.

"That way," he pointed and happily set off in the opposite direction until he remembered that his next class was Xenobiology. He'd always hated biology, he doubted its magical cousin would be any better.

***

Mitch didn't see Hayley again until lunch time, surprising given the size of their classes. She was sitting alone in a corner of the dining hall, the rest of the students having made it clear that she wasn't welcome. No one talked to her. He was beginning to think that Bates' estimate of a week was overly generous, the teachers would see that she wasn't fitting in and send her somewhere else. Mitch snorted; if they were going to do that they would have sent Nikola away years ago. Mitch couldn't see him anywhere, he was probably sick again, neatly ruining any chance of Hayley making a friend.

"Do you want in?" Mindy asked as he slid into his place between her and Bates. They glared at him but shuffled aside, no one wanted to spend lunch watching them make out and this was the only reliable way of stopping them.

"In?"

"How long before the new girl calls it quits?"

"Most of the good ones are already taken," Bates said, "but there are still a few slots left."

Hah, it hadn't occurred to him that Hayley might leave. He wondered if they would let her. There were plenty of magic users out there who never attended school but most of them were losers with no real power and questionable ancestry. Hayley never would have been admitted if she lacked raw power.

Mitch scanned the list of names and dates and whistled softly to himself; Bates had half the Academy listed here. Adnan already had a red mark by his name, he had lost when Angel Girl stuck around after second period. No one expected her to last till the end of February.

He glanced up at where she was sitting, eating with one hand and leafing through a book with another. It must have been a damn good book, most visitors gawked at the ancient oak beams supporting the ceiling or the stained glass windows before feigning nonchalance. Maybe she just didn't appreciate the architecture.

"Put me down for the end of the term," Mitch said, he was pretty sure she could stick it out a month and once she did they wouldn't want to transfer her until the Easter break. He'd already seen enough to suspect that she'd hold out until graduation but he could just imagine what Bates would say to that.

"You sure?" Bates asked with a raised eyebrow.

"Yeah."

"You're insane," Bates said, "just look at her."

A couple of girls were walking past her table. Gwen 'slipped' on the hardwood floor and her glass of orange juice went flying as her companion helped her regain her balance. The juice splattered across Hayley's shirt, staining the previously white cloth a sticky yellow. It shouldn't have, Hayley had slid out of the way but the juice had followed her with the tenacity of a homing pigeon. Mitch quickly scanned the room and Bates did the same, technically they were allowed to use magic out of class but that probably didn't extend to ballistic juice attacks.

"Oh, I'm so sorry," Gwen said, "I can't believe I did that, I'm not normally such a klutz."

Neither could Mitch but Gwen was a much better actor than he was and she managed to sound sincere. Angel Girl brushed them off and left, taking her half eaten lunch with her as the room filled with sniggers and whispered conversation.

"Are you sure you want the whole term?" Bates asked, watching her leave. Not that there was much to watch, Angel Girl really couldn't afford to miss meals. Gwen on the other hand...

"I'll give you till the end of the day to change your mind," Bates said, completely derailing his train of thought, "assuming she lasts that long of course."

"I'm sure," he replied, returning his attention to his food. "What do you have after lunch?"

"Teratology."

"I had that this morning," Mindy said, "it's basically social studies with monsters and we aren't even getting to the monsters till next term. The teacher's a real bore as well."

Mindy proved to be right on both counts. Once Dr Henly had finished reading out the class roll, first and last names, he informed them that they would spend the term tracing their genealogy back ten generations, including illegitimate lines, and then pick an angle of the family history on which to write an extensive report. At least the report wasn't due until the last day of term, but Mitch thought the entire thing sounded unbelievably tedious. Who wanted to write a report on ten generations of Archibald and Bartholomew Mitchells?

At least the legitimate lines would be easy enough, the Academy library maintained extensive records on past students and notable wizards, but he preferred not to think about illegitimate lines and what his parents and grandparents may have got up to before he was born or they were married. Hayley raised a hand.

"Is there a problem Miss Lake?" Dr Henly asked.

"I'm adopted sir."

"Well then this is an excellent opportunity to learn a little more about your birth family," Dr Henly replied. Adoptions were common enough in the magical world. The life of a trained magician tended to be short and exciting or long and boring and many of their fellow students had been raised by their grandparents or aunts and uncles.

"No one knows who my birth parents are," Hayley said.

"Adoption records can be unsealed," Dr Henly said, "I believe you'll be able to look up the proper procedures in the library."

Hayley flushed, her eyes seeming to pale. "I was abandoned, no one knows who my parents are," she repeated. Mitch and Bates exchanged glances; that was unusual though it did explain how she'd gone unnoticed for so long.

"Well, I expect a thorough investigation will turn up something," Dr Henly replied, rubbing his hands together and turning his attention to the rest of the class. He clearly didn't want to deal with any more awkwardness. "I suggest you get moving. I very much doubt you will find the information you need in here."

Chairs scraped across the floor as everyone repacked their bags and headed for the library. Forewarned by Mindy, Mitch and Bates hadn't bothered to get anything out and were the first to leave.

"What do you think?" Bates asked once the door closed behind them, "she could be from one of the old families."

Mitch shrugged, he actually felt a little bad for her. At least he had ten generations of family to research, no matter how boring and inglorious they proved to be.

"You have to realise that she'll never make the whole term now," Bates added, "as soon as this gets out everyone will make her life a living Hell, remember some of the things we used to do to Nikola?"

Mitch grunted; he'd never done anything to Nikola but he hadn't wanted to risk becoming a social pariah by befriending him either.

"Yeah, and look where that got us," Mitch said aloud. Nikola had ignored them right up until the day he thrashed Richard, a monster of a guy who was easily twice his size. Everyone had left Nikola alone after that but he had a hard time imagining Hayley breaking anyone's nose. He threw his weight against one of the library's heavy double doors and shoved it open, wondering for the hundredth time when the Academy was going to replace them. They were ancient and badly balanced and more than one

specting student had been bowled over by them. While most of the
.ademy's fixtures were updated and well maintained, the library doors
were a torture instrument in disguise.

Bates followed him in and they trooped up to the third floor where
the Academy's historical records were kept, trying to find their families
before anyone else arrived. He found the M's and leaned on the railing
to watch as the final members of their class trailed in and headed up the
stairs. Hayley started tapping away at one of the computers instead, waiting for the sluggish network to log her in. Supposedly the Academy had
the most up to date equipment but that couldn't make up for the fact that
they were in the middle of nowhere and none of their teachers actually
knew how to maintain the technology.

"Seriously Mitch?" Bates asked, following his gaze, "you keep this up
I'm going to start thinking you like her. Is that why you bet on her lasting
the term? I was stuck with her in Xenobiology and she's cold enough to
make interstellar space look warm."

"Of course not," Mitch protested, swallowing uneasily. His first
Xenobiology lesson had been alright but it was only a matter of time
before they got to the blood and squishy things. "I'm just trying to work
out the best way to win everyone's money." He turned away and opened
the book at random.

Bates laughed. "You won't get very far with that." He pointed to the open
page and Mitch scowled; 'Mara Malik 1500-1567 AD' the heading read.

"Neither will you," Mitch retorted returning to the table where he'd
left his bag and flipping to the right page.

He had just finished documenting the short and surprisingly
uneventful life of his great grandfather, Archibald Mitchell the no-one-
could-be-bothered-counting-any-more, when the fire alarm went off.
He exchanged puzzled looks with Bates; drills were never held this early
in the year and it was usually a couple of weeks before anyone started
experimenting with Pyromancy. They hadn't even had their first magic
classes yet. The rest of the class looked just as puzzled.

The alarm kept ringing, loudly and annoyingly. Bates shrugged
and in contravention of every fire-drill they had ever had they started
shoving their notes into their bags. They left the books on the table; it was

them, he muttered a quick spell under his breath and set off at a run, following his blood ties to Cullum.

The ancient building had not stood up to the quake well. There was dust and broken glass everywhere. Holes gaped in the ceiling where the panelling had fallen down and water seeped out of the bathrooms. The lights flickered fitfully and made it seem like a scene from one of those horror movies Mindy liked so much. Mitch ran past it all, swearing every time he tripped or caught his clothing on something. He found a door that hung crazily, one of the hinges having pulled away from the wall. For once he was glad of his speciality in self-manipulation, it gave him the strength he needed to rip the door aside. He wished he'd thought of that sooner, maybe if he had he wouldn't have grazed palms, a skinned knee and an ankle that refused to take his weight.

He hesitated but his brother was definitely down there. Mitch just couldn't work out why; there was nothing in the basement but darkness and storerooms. And dust, he coughed as his irrational speed down the stairs added clouds of the stuff to what was already falling from the ceiling. It wasn't enough to slow him but the dark was. It was years since he had last come down here on a dare and almost got lost, there was no telling what it was like now.

He choked out another spell and his hand started to glow softly. He could just imagine the lecture his teachers would give him if they heard his improvised incantation. They had been taught how to make light with a second's concentration but all he could concentrate on now was his brother. He didn't even care about the inevitable teasing he would get for having a hand that glowed in the dark. He held his hand up like a torch and resumed running, it wasn't far now, Cullum was just ahead.

A door stood open to his left, faint light spilling out of it and Mitch felt a second of relief, his brother was through there. He braced himself on the door-frame and stared into the room panting. He threw up a hand to shield his eyes as a torch swung around to point at him, almost blindingly bright after the gloom of the corridors and his luminescent hand.

"I need the torch Abby," said a soft voice.

"Someone's here to rescue us," Abby said as the torch swung away. Mitch blinked and lowered his hand, desperately scanning the room for his brother and all too aware that Cullum should have said something by now. Other than Abby's high piping voice and the occasional pain filled whimper it was silent, almost eerily so after the cacophony outside.

"I told you someone would come," the voice replied, it was maddeningly familiar but Mitch's eyes still hadn't adjusted to the gloom and he couldn't place it. He longed to rub the dust and flashing afterimages from his eyes but he knew that that would be the opposite of helpful.

Finally his vision cleared and he was able to confirm his worst fears. The room was small and narrow, occupied by a huddle of kids his brother's age but no Cullum. There was a gaping hole in the ceiling and a pile of rubble where the rest of the room should be. The blood tie pointed directly to the pile of rubble. Mitch gulped, the blood tie just told him where his brother was not if he was alive and Mitch couldn't imagine anyone being alive under that.

Two boys and a girl that he vaguely recognised stared at him through fear-widened eyes while the torch-wielding Abby kept its narrow beam fixed on a whimpering boy who was cradling a broken arm. Mitch felt his stomach lurch, there was a piece of bone sticking out of the boy's arm. If that had been him he would have been screaming in agony, or unconscious; the latter he hoped. He looked away before the sight could make him throw up but not before he saw Hayley crouched at the boy's side, doing her best to fix his arm in place with strips torn from her cardi. He swallowed again, the Academy gave them all regular first aid training but he had always known that he'd never actually be able to use any of it. Mindy had laughed at him for that, she was good with blood and with her affinity for necromancy she would make a great evil scientist one day.

"What are you doing here?" he asked, carefully not looking at the boy with the broken arm. He couldn't understand how Abby was managing to hold that torch so steady.

"Trying to get them out," Hayley replied. "How is that?"

"It still hurts," said the boy.

"I know."

Mitch heard movement and forced himself to look in their direction, Hayley was helping the boy to his feet. It didn't look so bad now but there was still far more blood and bone on display than he was capable of handling.

"That's Mitchell," Hayley said, ushering the rest of the children to their feet. "He's going to help everyone get out aren't you Mitchell?"

"Yeah, sure," it wasn't as if he could do anything else and their teachers knew better than to rush into a collapsing building during an earthquake.

"Take his hand Adam, that way you won't get lost or separated." Adam shuffled over and silently took his hand. Mitch couldn't imagine Cullum doing that, you didn't hold your brother's hand when you were twelve years old. Of course Cullum had never had a piece of bone sticking out of his arm.

"Give me the torch Abby, I'll follow you out." Abby handed over the torch and came to stand by Adam, the other children crowding around.

"Mitchell...Mitchell," Hayley repeated when he failed to respond. He shook his head slightly, trying to think or at the very least focus on something that wasn't the pile of rubble that had buried his brother. "You need to lead the way out," Hayley instructed. Mitch nodded, even covered in dust from head to foot she looked good, her eyes, so pale they were almost white, shining in the gloom. It seemed almost perverse that he should be so aware of her now when Cullum...

Her eyes widened, "RUN!"

Mitch jerked into motion, tugging Adam along behind him as another quake struck. He half ran down the corridor, doing his best to ignore Adam's cries of pain and his own injured ankle. They would all hurt a lot more if the ceiling came down on them. Thankfully he didn't trip on the heaving floor though he had to catch himself more than once as he almost fell. He could hear the children and Hayley panting along behind him, guided only by the light of his glowing hand. Maybe she really did deserve that name, Angel Girl, he couldn't imagine anyone else coming down here for a bunch of children they didn't know. If it weren't for Cullum... he pushed that thought away and pounded up the stairs. He would have taken them three at a time if he could have but Adam had a death grip on his hand.

They made it to the top of the stairs and staggered along the corridor, keeping one eye on the ceiling and the other on the still shaking floor. Surely it would stop soon. A chunk of ceiling fell and he stopped so suddenly that Adam crashed into him with a cry of pain but it was better than being squashed like...no, he needed to keep moving. He edged around the rubble and resumed his staggering run, not noticing when the shaking ceased, not stopping until they were clear of the building and had been engulfed by familiar faces.

It was only then that he realised Hayley wasn't behind them.

CULLUM

M itch watched as the Academy's medical staff bustled about. One of them had fed Adam some sort of Alchemical concoction that had numbed his arm, before they straightened out the bone and gave him something else to help it set. It would still be tender for a few days, and Adam had been fitted with a proper sling, but he no longer had a broken arm. There wasn't even a cut where the bone had pierced the skin. They'd bandaged Mitch's ankle as well and ordered him not to run into any more collapsing buildings. As if he would, he'd only done that to find Cullum.

Someone incredibly brave and stupid and much more successful than he was, had retrieved half the infirmary storeroom and the large marquee that was serving as a makeshift hospital. There were surprisingly few patients. He hadn't even had to wait to get treatment for the ankle he'd twisted running through a collapsing building like an idiot. Bates and Mindy were here somewhere, they'd given Mindy something to calm her down after he'd told her what he'd found underground. Mitch just felt numb. His baby brother was dead. They hadn't even been that close but now he was dead and somehow that changed everything.

The parts of the sky that weren't blocked off by the marquee were clear and blue and perfect. They were a lie. The world wasn't perfect, it was dirty and chaotic and perfection was nothing more than a deceitful dream. He shivered as he felt an aura of incredible power flare nearby. He ignored it, all the magic in the world couldn't bring Cullum back. A second later the power vanished and he heard someone throwing up.

"How are you feeling Mitchell?" asked the doctor. "Staring at the ceiling is not a response Mitchell."

Mitch turned his head to the side and saw that the cot next to his had been filled by Nikola, his golden hair darkened by sweat and his usually-pale face flushed. The doctor was putting a needle in his arm but he still managed to keep one eye on Mitch.

"My brother is dead, how do you think I feel?" Mitch asked, wishing the doctor would just go away. Surely he had other patients to tend to. Nikola laughed, or perhaps he was coughing. He retched into the bucket the doctor gave him and shook his head when he was offered a glass of water.

"If you'd drink something I wouldn't have to stick needles in your arm," the doctor said as Nikola tried to make himself comfortable despite the drip.

"I've thrown up five times in the last hour, if I drink something it will come up again in the next quake which is entirely too close for my liking."

"You know when the quakes are going to strike?" Mitch said, finding the energy to sit up. If he could sense the quakes coming then he could have saved Cullum.

"No, I just..." he flinched and lay there panting. "Are you sure you have everything you need?" he asked.

"If we need anything else we'll get it the old fashioned way," the doctor replied, "you're in no shape to be doing any more magic."

"I'm fine."

"Most people's definition of fine does not include nausea, a severe headache and a slight fever." Nikola was definitely laughing this time. Mitch couldn't remember ever hearing Nikola laugh before. He had always seemed so utterly miserable, now he sounded on the edge of hysteria. Maybe the two of them had traded places.

"You sound like my cousin," Nikola explained.

"And do you listen to your cousin?"

"Of course I do, he'd tie me to the bed if I didn't," the laughter in his voice died as did his fleeting smile.

"Get some rest or I will follow his lead." The doctor rose to his feet and left.

"You've never mentioned a cousin before," Mitch said. In fact Nikola had never mentioned any kind of family before. Nikola studied him with over bright grey eyes.

"Stars curse you," he finally spat, "I'm not going to be your distraction."

Mitch slumped back onto the cot. A distraction. A distraction would be nice right now. Maybe he could get Nikola to talk about something else, though he suspected Nikola had exhausted his allotment of words for the day.

"What kind of magic do you use?" he asked.

"Which part of I'm not going to be your distraction did you not understand?" Nikola replied, "I don't..." he retched, bringing up bile and not much else.

"Brace yourselves," a magically amplified voice roared just as the fourth quake struck. Mitch was almost thrown from the cot as the first wave of the quake rushed through the ground and for a second he thought the marquee was going to come down on top of them. Magic coiled around him, rapidly expanding to encompass the entire tent. Cots stopped bouncing up and down, jars stopped shaking and the marquee stopped rattling on its poles. The ground still heaved violently but somehow the marquee and everything it sheltered was protected.

Mitch stared at the source of the magic; he had known Nikola was powerful, it was the only way he could have transferred to the Academy, but he had never expected this. The ground stopped shaking and the magic vanished as quickly as it came. The doctor rushed over almost as quickly and inspected Nikola.

"Are you going to rest or do I need to find one of those suppressants you just saved for us?" he asked.

Nikola shuddered and pressed himself into the cot, his face turning a waxy grey, "I'd settle for a blanket." Mitch had never taken a magical suppressant but evidently Nikola had.

"I'd prefer to give you a sedative, you need to rest before you make yourself really sick."

"Give me the blanket and I'll let you," Nikola said. He was shivering though it had to be almost thirty degrees. The doctor waved one of the nurses over and a minute later she returned with a blanket and a needle. There were some things that science did better than Alchemy. Nikola curled up under the blanket and was soon asleep.

"What kind of magic does he have?" Mitch asked, genuinely curious now.

The doctor shrugged, "No one's entirely sure, I had no idea he could do that."

"Belle!" Mindy's ear-splitting shriek ripped through the air. Mitch and the doctor both flinched, Nikola didn't even twitch; apparently the doctor had wanted to make sure he stayed asleep.

Mitch looked at Mindy who was sprinting towards the end of the tent where Belle and Cullum had just been escorted in by Mr McCalis. Mitch lurched to his feet, almost nosediving before the doctor steadied him, and dashed towards his brother, ignoring the pain in his ankle. Belle clutched a torch in one hand and Cullum in the other. Mitch enveloped Cullum in a bear hug that his brother didn't return while Mindy inundated her sister with questions.

"We're trying to bring Miss Band out now," Mr McCalis told the doctor, "Miss Lamdon says that her leg was trapped beneath some rubble."

The doctor nodded and ordered one of the nurses to prepare while the other succeeded in freeing Belle from Mindy's grip and examined her.

Mitch released his brother and took a step back. Under the dust coating him Cullum was dead white and Mitch had never seen anyone's eyes so wide. It wasn't like Cullum to be so quiet either and he wouldn't stop shaking.

"Cal? Cullum, it's alright now, you're safe."

Cullum didn't respond.

"Let's get him onto a bed," the doctor said. Cullum still didn't react so Mitch was forced to take him by the hand and half drag him down to his cot. A few years ago he would have been able to pick Cullum up, but Cullum wasn't seven any more so he had to make do with a painfully slow zombie shuffle.

"He isn't seriously injured," the doctor said at last.

"But he hasn't said anything," Mitch said.

"He's probably in shock," the doctor said, "the best thing for him now is rest." He produced another needle. Surely that would elicit a reaction; Cullum had screamed the house down last time someone tried to inject him with something. It didn't. Cullum just sat there staring at nothing as the doctor cleaned a patch of arm and plunged the needle in. A minute later, Cullum was asleep.

***

It was dark when they were finally allowed inside. They had spent almost eight hours under the blazing sun without any sunscreen. Something that no one realised until they got inside and saw their burnt faces. There had only been one more big quake and as soon as the Academy's resident earth wizard, Mr Crane, had assured them it was safe to so do they started checking the buildings.

The infirmary was the first to be cleared and reopened. They'd let Mitch help carry Cullum up to it but refused to let him stay and he'd been forced to sulk back to the field and join Mindy, who was also sulking after being abandoned by Belle in favour of Hayley. It was Hayley who had found her and Cullum trapped in the back of the room after the third quake. They hadn't been buried after all, just cut off.

Angel Girl had sent Belle and Cullum out and stayed with Miss Band until the teachers had rescued them, bringing Miss Band to the marquee just as the final quake struck. They had almost been buried when the marquee collapsed on top of them and it seemed like everything that could break or fall over did so. Mitch had concentrated on keeping Cullum in his cot and wondered if the doctor regretted his decision to sedate Nikola. One of the teachers had caught the marquee and held it up until all the lines and pegs could be properly set once more.

"I see the quake didn't do much damage," Bates said, eyeing the clothing scattered across Mitch's bedroom floor.

"Guess I got lucky," Mitch replied. He'd had to close a couple of drawers and pick up the desk chair but so far nothing seemed to be broken or any messier than it had been when he left that morning. Mitch had mastered the art of unpacking but putting things away had always eluded him; why waste time shoving things into drawers when there was a perfectly good floordrobe to use?

"Want to play cards?"

"Sure," Mitch said, picking his way across the room and following Bates next door to his far tidier room. Bates had even made the bed, which Mitch promptly ruined by sitting on it. Bates rummaged through a desk drawer, he hadn't time to straighten everything, and pulled out a pack of cards. There was a knock at the door followed by Mindy letting herself in. Mitch shuffled across the bed so she could join them.

"What do you want to play?" Bates asked.

"Threes," Mitch said.

"Presidents," Mindy said at the same time.

"Presidents it is then," Bates said, beginning to deal.

"I thought you said you would never let a girl come between us," Mitch said.

"That was five years ago, I was ten," Bates said, dealing the last of the cards.

"What kind of excuse is that?" Mitch said, inspecting his hand. If he didn't know better he'd think Bates had rigged the deck, his cards were terrible.

"You're just jealous because Sam dumped you over the summer," Bates retorted.

"It was mutual."

His friends laughed and they started to play.

"I thought you'd be with Belle," Mitch said, handing his best cards over to Mindy as he had lost the first round.

"I thought you'd be with Cullum," she replied. Mitch flinched, he had thought his days of babysitting Cullum were up but he hadn't enjoyed thinking his brother was dead. It was almost enough to make him envy Bates; his best friend didn't have any siblings. The teachers had given permission for the children with older siblings to stay together that night. The primary dormitories and classrooms had both been declared unsafe and for now the entire school was staying on the secondary campus, the children sleeping in the gym and auditorium. Bates reached over and squeezed Mindy's knee gently.

"Sorry," she said, "Belle wanted to stay with Hayley and no one could be bothered arguing. She can be someone else's problem for the night."

"Think there'll be any big aftershocks?" Bates asked. There had been little tremors throughout the afternoon but there hadn't been any more big quakes.

"I hope not," Mitch said, trying to get out of his room in an earthquake would not be fun. Maybe he should shove everything into the drawers after all.

"I overheard Mr Crane talking," Mindy said, "he doesn't think they'll be any big ones but they were saying something about keeping an eye on Ruapehu." Great, that was just what they needed, an active volcano.

Made in the USA
Lexington, KY
14 March 2018